SHADOWS IN THE DARK

A CHARLIE MACCREADY MYSTERY

SHADOWS IN THE DARK

A CHARLIE MACCREADY MYSTERY

James M. McCracken

Copyright © 2020 James M. McCracken

JK Press

2nd Edition

ISBN-13: 978-17359233-0-7

All rights reserved. No part of this book may be reproduced or transmitted in any form or by any means, electronic or mechanical, including photocopying, recording, or by any information storage and retrieval system, without permission in writing from the copyright owner.

This is a work of fiction. Names, characters, places and incidents are either the product of the author's imagination or are used fictitiously, and any resemblance to any actual persons, living or dead, events, or locales is entirely coincidental.

CONTENTS

1	THE ANNOUNCEMENT	1
2	SHADOWS IN THE NIGHT	19
3	SUMMER	22
4	THE MISSING NOVICE	27
5	HOWARD'S SECRET PLACE	31
6	IT WAS A DREAM	48
7	FATHER ICHABOD	50
8	THE NEW DEAN	68
9	THE SHADOW	76
10	THE PHOTOGRAPH	84
11	BROKEN POTS	97
12	THE RETAKE	111
13	SISTER MARGARET MARY	115
14	DOUBTS	130
15	THE FRESHMEN	133
16	CURFEW	146
17	A DAY IN THE LIFE OF A FRESHMAN	151
18	THE TRAP	165
19	ALL HALLOW'S EVE	172
20	ALL SAINTS' DAY	188
21	UNMASKED	204
23	TIME IS RUNNING OUT	221
24	CHRISTMAS	233
25	CHARLIE'S PLAN	242
26	WORKCREW	263
27	ABSOLUTION	274
28	GOOD BYE	282

DEDICATION

To my grandmother,
Edythe Evelyn Mace,
For all of her love, understanding and support.

ACKNOWLEDGMENTS

With sincere appreciation to Dennis Blakesley, Michael Anne Maslow, Christopher Martin, Quintin Maurer, Patrick Huff, Eric Meese, Kailie Stover, Piper Stover, Pam Bainbridge-Cowan and Doug Helbling for their continued encouragement and support.

THE ANNOUNCEMENT

Quietly, Charlie MacCready looked around the refectory on the first floor in the east wing of St. Michael's Abbey and Home for Boys. It was hard to believe that just ten short months ago he was happily living with his grandmother on Tam O'Shanter Drive.

Thoughts about the day he was sent away by his mother's older brother, his Uncle Chester, filled his mind. Uncle Chester was an intimidating man, standing over six feet tall with big, broad shoulders. His dark hair and even darker eyes reflected his cold heart.

In contrast, Charlie's grandmother Ophelia was a small, five-foot-tall woman, Charlie's height. Her gentle features reflected her warm, kind heart. Her long white hair was always pinned up in a tight bun. She smelled of rose petals and ivory soap, a scent that was comforting to Charlie. She always wore a colorful bib-apron with pockets over her knee-length house dress. In fact, on the day he was sent away, she pulled from her apron pocket an old, tarnished brass key. She pressed it tightly into his hand and whispered a warning, "Whatever you do, do not let this out of your sight. Do not tell anyone where it came from and do not give it to anyone, no matter who may ask. It is very important."

Charlie felt the key that hung from a chain around his neck beneath his surplice and black cassock, the school uniform at Saint Michael's. He also felt the small golden locket that hung from the same gold chain. In it was a tiny photograph of his parents, Patrick and Faith MacCready.

Charlie had no memory of his parents. He was only two years old when they dropped him off at his grandparents' house in the middle of the night. They promised to return for him, but never did. Over the years, his Uncle Chester and Aunt Bernice came to the conclusion that their sister and brother-in-law were dead. A conclusion shared by neither his grandmother nor himself.

No, my parents are alive and one day they will come for me, just as they promised, Charlie thought, and tightened his grip on the back of his chair.

He looked at the table in front of him and then around the room. He had become accustomed to the tall, dull white walls of the refectory. If it were not for the gold ornate frames on the paintings of deceased Abbots that lined the west wall, and the dark navy-blue velvet curtain that hung behind the head table on the south wall, the refectory would feel sterile. Charlie did not mind that the windows on the east wall were curtainless. When he was standing, he could see the green fir trees of the forest outside. Four long wooden tables stretched from the front of the refectory to the back. The tables that were full at breakfast were nearly empty. Charlie was able to see just how many residents there were.

The student body of Saint Michael's was made up of students, those boys curious about becoming priests, and residents. The residents were boys for whom Saint Michael's was the only thing keeping them from the state juvenile home and boys who are orphans. Charlie was listed as a resident, a title he hated because in his mind, he was neither a delinquent nor an orphan.

Charlie looked at the head table on the raised platform at

the front of the refectory. The prefects, as the dorm overseers were called, and the Abbot of Saint Michael's Abbey stood in their places and looked out at the boys.

Father Vicar, the tall, gaunt priest at the far, right end of the long table, was prefect for the notorious Saint Peter dorm. It was common knowledge, among the boys anyway, that the bullies, who lived and thrived in that dorm did so under Father Vicar's approving eye. Charlie knew firsthand just how true that was, and shuddered at the memory of being dunked, head first, in the toilet by the worst of them.

Next to Father Vicar stood Brother Conrad. Though just as slim as Father Vicar, he did not have the sinister look. His brown eyes were gentle and his smile was warm and kind. He oversaw one of the smaller dorms, Saint Thomas the Doubter, and was known among the boys for being very protective of his boys. It was also said that he wished he could move his dorm anywhere but where it was, across the hall from Saint Peter; but that was impossible.

At the opposite end of the head table stood Brother Owen, the prefect of Saint Sebastian dorm, across the hall from Saint Nicholas, Charlie's dorm. Brother Owen was the quietest of the four, and barely opened his mouth when he spoke. Some of the boys from his dorm said it was because he had worn braces for years as a teenager, and was a habit he had not broken.

Next was Brother Simon, the prefect of Saint Nicholas dorm. He could have been a twin of Father Vicar, or so Charlie thought when he first met them both. Brother Simon had that "more-sinister-than-holy" look. However, since that night in the attic, Charlie came to realize that beneath his gruff image Brother Simon had a soft heart. They would forever share a special bond and an understanding. Charlie would always be grateful to Brother Simon, too, for telling him about his father, Patrick MacCready. As it were, Patrick had been a resident, an orphan, at the Abbey years ago. He was a member of Saint Peter dorm but had become friends with the young Brother Simon, a member of Saint Nicholas. Charlie had yet another reason to be grateful to Brother Simon. Charlie knew, earlier that day, that it was Brother Simon who had secretly left a photograph of young Patrick on his bed in Saint Nicholas dorm. Charlie smiled to himself as he thought about the photograph he had tucked safely away in his closet before coming to dinner.

Seated between Brother Simon and Brother Conrad, at the center of the head table, was the head of Saint Michael's Abbey, Father Abbot Ambrose. From the first day Charlie met him, he liked the Abbot. Finding out that the tall, thin monk with white hair and a long, white beard was actually his great-uncle, his grandmother's brother, was a pleasant surprise, though still a shock.

After the prayer, the boys took their seats. Dinner was then served. The refectory filled with the aroma of beef stew and freshly baked dinner rolls. Charlie poured himself a glass of cold milk and sat quietly, looking around.

"What's the matter? Don't you want your dinner?" Gustav Kugele asked, leaning over his plate.

Charlie looked across the table and smiled at the portly, round-faced boy. Gus's sandy blonde hair, which looked as though someone put a bowl on his head and cut around it, was mussed. His coal-black, beady eyes twinkled as he looked at Charlie's dinner.

Charlie looked down at his plate. He was not really hungry, even though the beef stew did look inviting. He looked back at Gus.

"No, guess not," he answered. "You want mine?"

"Sure." Gus beamed.

Charlie looked up to be sure no one from the head table was watching, then slid his plate across the table to Gus. Gus quickly scraped the stew onto his plate and slid the empty plate back.

"Thanks, Charlie," Gus said, sticking his fork into a large chunk of potato. He quickly stuffed the whole piece into his mouth.

"Good thing Rick wasn't here to see that," Howard said

dryly, as he watched them. Howard Miller was Charlie's best friend. The two met the day Charlie arrived at Saint Michael's. As bunkmates, they shared a cubicle, an eight-foot by eight-foot square space separated by a wood panel partition, in the corner of Saint Nicholas dorm. Even though they were opposites in appearance, the two were constantly mistaken for the other by some of the older monks. Howard was tall, thin and had short, curly, very dark and very thick hair. He also wore black, thick-rimmed glasses on his beak-like nose. Whereas, Charlie was just as thin but a bit shorter and had thick, wavy, reddish-brown hair freckles on his nose, and ears that seemed to stick out just a bit too far.

"Speaking of Rick." Charlie glanced at his bare wrist as though seeing a watch. "His plane should be taking off right about now, don't you think?"

"Wow," Gus breathed, stew gravy smeared on his face around his lips. "He gets to fly in a plane, that's so cool."

"So what," Howard sneered and rolled his eyes.

"Well, have you ever been in an airplane?" Charlie asked, looking at Howard.

"Once, when I was still with my dad." Howard nodded as he remembered. A tear came into his eyes. It seemed the older he grew, the more he missed his father. Or perhaps it was because Charlie's unwavering hope that his parents would return for him made Howard secretly wish his father would realize he'd made a mistake and come back for him. He fought hard to keep the others from noticing. "Ah." He shrugged. "Who cares? I hope he has a rotten time at Disney World. Hope that big mouse bites him."

Charlie smiled knowingly. In just the short ten months they had known each other, Charlie had become very good at reading Howard. He knew that Howard's jealous act was just a cover, but it was best not to pursue that conversation. Besides, for as long as Charlie had known the two of them, Howard and Rick had always had a love-hate friendship. It seemed that no matter how much they tried to be friends, they were always rubbing each other the wrong way.

"So, what do you think the big announcement's gonna be?" Charlie changed the subject.

Howard sat back in his chair and looked around the refectory. His thick, black rimmed glasses slid down his nose. He pushed them back up without thinking.

"I guess it has to be something really big for Abbot Ambrose to cancel this year's baseball games," he said, and scratched his head. "I don't think they've ever canceled the games before."

"Well, the suspense is killing me," Charlie sighed.

Gus looked up from his plate. Gravy dripped down his chin and his cheeks bulged as he chewed. "Who died?" he mumbled.

"No one died," Howard sighed in his usual disgusted tone. He really did like Gus, even though it seemed he had no patience for him. "Wipe your chin before it drips onto your surplice. The Brothers in the laundry are getting tired of getting the stains out of your robes."

Gus quickly wiped his chin with his napkin.

"I don't know why we have to wear these stupid things." Gus sighed as he inspected the red, loose fitting, bellowing-sleeved, waist length shirt called a surplice that he wore over his floor-length black cassock.

"You're fine," Charlie assured him. "Howard was just teasing you."

"No, I wasn't," Howard spoke up with a tone that said he was a bit annoyed by not being taken seriously. "I talked to the Brothers in the laundry this morning before Mass. They were soaking a red surplice that was caked in mud. It had Gus's name on the inside tag."

"It isn't mine!" Gus protested. "I didn't send any of my clothes to the laundry. They're still upstairs in my locker and I'm not missing any either. I'll show you after dinner if you don't believe me. It has to be someone else's."

Howard looked confused. "Are you sure?" he asked. "If it isn't yours, then whose is it?"

"I don't know." Gus shrugged. "But I'm telling you it isn't mine," he added in a more confident note.

"Well, we'll just have to take a look then," Howard nodded, with an accusing tone in his voice. It was obvious to Charlie that Howard still did not believe Gus.

"You're both missing a major point here," Charlie said.

Howard looked at Charlie and wrinkled his brow. "What point?" he asked.

"The point is how and where would someone get covered in mud?" Charlie answered, glancing back and forth at the both of them. "It hasn't rained in weeks."

"There's always mud in the Abbey's pig barns," Gus said dismissively.

"Pig barns?" Charlie cocked his head curiously. He had not heard of the Abbey having pig barns.

"Ah-ha!" Howard lunged at Gus with an I-told-you-so laugh. "For someone who claims the surplice isn't his, you sure know where the mud is."

"Oh, everyone knows about the pig barns," Gus scoffed. "That doesn't prove a thing."

"I didn't know," Charlie admitted. "Why hasn't anyone told me about them?"

"The Abbey owns lots of property. There're a lot of places not everyone knows about, and places that are off limits." Howard shrugged.

"There are?" Charlie said. "Like where?"

Howard looked at Charlie, at the familiar glimmer in his brown eyes. A sinking feeling filled the pit of his stomach.

"No!" he said sternly. "This is *not* another mystery to solve," he growled and shook his head. "I've had enough."

Suddenly, the familiar clap of the wooden block against the head table silenced the room. All heads turned, and all eyes were on the Abbot, who stood up.

Abbot Ambrose smiled and his blue eyes twinkled as he looked over his spectacles at the faces of the boys in front of him. Slowly, he walked around to the front of the table where he leaned back against its heavy wooden top.

"What's with all the sullen faces?" he frowned at them. "It's not that bad," he smiled warmly. "As you have all heard by now, I have called off this summer's baseball games for two reasons," he began softly. "The first reason is, with the graduation of our senior class, and with all of the students going home for the summer, we no longer have enough boys to qualify for our team."

None of the boys made a sound as they all listened intently. Even Dougary Duggan, the dark-haired boy who was the winner of last year's most valuable player award and the ringleader of the hoodlums of Saint Peter dorm, was silent. Charlie looked at the other five boys of Saint Peter dorm seated at their table against the west wall, near the hall doors. They were all dressed in their dark purple surplices over their black cassocks. It was the uniform for the boys of Saint Peter dorm, which made it easy to identify them and, more importantly, to avoid them. That was the real reason behind the different colored surplices, Charlie believed, to identify to what dorm and prefect they belonged; red for the boys from Saint Nicholas dorm, blue for Saint Sebastian, yellow for Saint Thomas and purple for Saint Peter.

"The other reason why I have called off the summer games," Abbot Ambrose continued, "is that I have appointed Prior Emmanuel to head up the Abbey's new project. It will involve the majority of our Brothers for the better part of the summer and coming year. We are going to begin building a new residence hall and school for all of you, on the side of the hill to the west of the front grounds, between the Abbey and the parking lot. This old building is getting a bit too cramped. The new building is going to be one story with two daylight basements. The basement will have a new recreation room with a small kitchen and a supply room. The sub-basement will house classrooms and offices for the teaching staff. The main floor will be divided into four dormitories, a chapel, a common room for you to read and study in and a large auditorium."

"Wow!" Howard breathed and nudged Charlie.

Charlie looked around the refectory at all of the shocked and excited faces. He even felt excited by the thought of a new building.

"Beginning this week, trucks will be delivering the building materials and machinery. Since some of the equipment will need to be stored on the athletic field behind the Abbey, we are going to open up the front grounds to you boys. However, I would appreciate your full cooperation in staying away from the restricted work areas. And I warn you, behave yourselves. Any reports of unruly conduct will be dealt with swiftly and severely."

Abbot Ambrose paused and his smile faltered slightly. Charlie could have sworn he saw a tear in his great uncle's eyes for a moment.

"With this new project, there are going to be some other changes in the Abbey." Abbot Ambrose paused and took off his glasses, wiped them clean and put them back on the end of his nose. "In recent months, matters of the Abbey have increased, and therefore I will be assigning a new Dean of Men to take over my duties here with you."

A collective gasp rose from the boys. They looked at each other with stunned faces and then back at the Abbot, the man they had come to love like a father.

"I know this comes as quite a shock," he said in his usual gentle tone. "If there were any other way—" He shook his head. "But I assure you, I will always be available to you boys. For the next year, while the new Dean is getting used to his new duties, I will remain as head of the prefects. I am keeping my office on the main floor here, and you are always welcome to drop by at any time. We will be converting two of the visiting rooms into offices for Prior Emmanuel and the new Dean. I know they would welcome your visits too.

"And, one last announcement. I am also pleased to inform all of you that Brother Simon has graciously agreed to stay on in the position of Prefect to Saint Nicholas dormitory for the coming year." Abbot Ambrose smiled and led everyone in congratulatory applause as he nodded at Brother Simon. However, for the majority of Saint Nicholas dorm's residents, their applause was a bit less enthusiastic as they realized Brother Simon's strict, militaristic rule was not over. Charlie grinned and applauded happily, much to Howard's surprise.

"Now, do you have any questions?" Abbot Ambrose asked, immediately looking at Rick Walter's empty chair. He smiled. Rick Walters had gone home for the summer. Rick was always good for at least two or three questions. Abbot Ambrose looked around the room. There were no raised hands. He looked back at the boys of Saint Nicholas dorm.

"Howard," he said. "I can tell you have a question."

Howard jumped at the sound of his name. It was true, he did have a question but he was still playing back the Abbot's words about Brother Simon in his head. Slowly he stood up.

"Ah, have you decided on who the new Dean is, yet?" he asked a bit awkwardly.

"No," Abbot Ambrose admitted. "I intend on making that decision very soon."

A hand at Saint Peter table popped up.

"Yes?" Abbot Ambrose nodded to it.

"You said the front grounds will be opened to us, but does that mean we have to wear these things all of the time?" a brown-haired boy asked as he tugged at his surplice.

Abbot Ambrose raised an eyebrow. "If you mean by 'those things' your cassock and surplice, the answer is yes," Abbot Ambrose said plainly. "When you boys are on the front grounds, just as it is every Sunday, you are to be dressed in your uniforms and you are to conduct yourselves accordingly. Remember your actions are being observed by the outside world, and what you do reflects on our Abbey."

A groan rose from Saint Peter table and from the boy who asked the question. Slowly he sank back into his chair.

"Oh, there is one more thing." Abbot Ambrose stopped and turned back around. "Tomorrow Father Vicar will post on the bulletin board in the common area of the fourth floor, the courses that we will be offering this summer. You may feel free to sign up for whichever course you choose, but please take special note of the age requirements on a couple of them."

The meal concluded with the usual prayer and the boys silently filed out of the refectory. Charlie looked at Abbot Ambrose as he passed by the head table on his way into the hallway. He wanted to have a word with him, but the Abbot appeared to be in a deep conversation with Brother Owen and Father Vicar.

"Cra-"

"Howard!" Charlie snapped, interrupting him and giving him a stern look as they entered the hallway.

Howard scowled at Charlie. He breathed a sigh as the three started up the stairs to their fourth-floor dormitory. "I can't believe it. Brother Simon is our permanent prefect."

"I'm doomed," Gus groaned. He held his stomach as though he were going to be ill. "I'll never make it. Brother Simon hates me."

"Oh, he's not such a bad guy," Charlie defended his new friend. "He's only strict because he actually cares about all of us. He doesn't want us to show any weakness because the other boys will use it against us. He's really thinking about us."

"Yeah, right," Howard scoffed. "What a bunch of b. s. Hey," Howard smiled fiendishly as a thought occurred to him. "B. S. Brother Simon. From here on out, that's what I'm going to call him."

Gus let out a chuckle. "Me too," he laughed.

Charlie frowned disapprovingly at them both but especially at Howard. Neither Howard nor Gus knew the truth about Brother Simon and his motives, so they would never understand.

"Well, I'm more concerned about who the new Dean is going to be," Charlie said as they passed through the heavy fire doors at the east end of the fourth-floor students' wing. "He could be even worse than Brother Simon."

Gus froze and his eyes widened in fear. "You don't think.

. . ?"

"Oh, no one could be worse than ol' B. S.." Howard turned and looked at Charlie curiously. "What's the matter with you?"

"I just think that maybe sometimes we're a bit too hard on Brother Simon," Charlie answered.

"Brother Simon, Brother Simon, Brother Simon!" Howard snapped and looked at Charlie. "What's with you all of the sudden? Why are you defending him? Is there something you aren't telling us?" he asked while studying Charlie's eyes.

Charlie felt his palms begin to sweat. He did not like being put on the spot, and looked nervously at Gus, then back at his best friend.

"No," he answered flatly. "It's just that he did save my life." Charlie answered. "And I think he's also the one who gave me that photograph of my dad."

Howard continued to stare at Charlie's eyes, then slowly nodded. "I see," he said, but his tone said he still was not sure that Charlie was telling him all he knew. "So, one act of kindness and the guy's suddenly a saint?" he asked.

"Oh, never mind." Charlie shook his head, frustrated with the entire conversation. He turned around and started toward their dormitory. He glanced to his left at the large painting of Saint Peter beside the dormitory doors. A chill made Charlie suddenly shiver as he remembered the warning that Austin Fuller, a member of Dougary's gang, gave him. "Be careful around Dougary this summer. He's really mad at you because his father was committed to the loony bin. He's out for revenge."

Charlie looked to his right at the painting of Saint Thomas the Doubter. His thoughts slowly returned to the conversation of the moment.

"I'm telling you, it was not mine," Gus said sharply.

"Well, we'll see soon enough," Howard answered smugly.

The three passed through an arched doorway and into the common room. To their left was a row of white porcelain sinks beneath a long mirror. The swinging doors to the restrooms and showers were on either end of the row. Across from the sinks, to their right, a small half-wall separated off the common area. Boys had already filled the four tables beneath the tall windows and busied themselves with their games of checkers and chess. A handful of the more studious boys made themselves comfortable on the sofas and big overstuffed chairs with their library books.

"A little too boring for me," Howard said, with a shake of his head. "Come on Gus," he prodded as Gus slowed his pace. "You're so sure it's not yours, so hurry up."

"I'm telling you I'm not missing any," Gus said and pulled an apple from beneath his robes and took a messy bite.

As they passed through another archway and neared their dorm, Charlie glanced at the door to Brother Simon's room. The glow from the evening sunlight made it hard to tell if the room was occupied. "You guys go on ahead. I want to talk to Brother Simon," he informed them.

Howard and Gus gave him a disgusted look and then proceeded on to their dorm.

Charlie knocked lightly on the oak door with a large opaque window. The shiny brass nameplate under it bore Brother Simon's name. Charlie was not nervous about talking with Brother Simon, at least not as much as he used to be. The two shared a special bond since that night in the attic when Brother Simon saved him from being dropped out the window.

"Ave!" came the gravelly voice on the other side of the door.

Charlie opened the door. The room had not changed much from when Father Emmanuel was the prefect. Books lined the many shelves on the wall behind the large, oak desk. However, they were now void of any plants or photographs. The two chairs still sat under the large window that overlooked the front grounds. A cardboard box sat in the chair nearest the bookcase. Brother Simon was busy unpacking, placing his books on the shelves. He turned around as Charlie walked into the room.

"I thought you might be stopping by," he said in his usual

distant voice and resumed organizing his shelf.

"So, you're staying?" Charlie asked.

"I know you heard the announcement," Brother Simon replied dryly. "It is a waste of words restating the obvious. What can I do for you?"

Charlie looked around the room. "Nothing. I just wanted to thank you for the photograph."

"Photograph?" Brother Simon paused and muttered thoughtfully to himself. "I don't know what you are talking about." He slid another book into place on the shelf.

"The one of my father," Charlie started to explain but then stopped.

"I know of no such thing." Brother Simon turned around and gave Charlie a stern look.

Charlie stiffened as though hit by a sudden gust of cold air. Brother Simon smiled slightly. "But I'm happy you have one. He was a good kid, a good friend," he said taking the last of the books from the box.

"Can I ask you a question?"

"You just did," Brother Simon pointed out. "And it is, *may* I ask you a question?"

"Oh." Charlie said and lowered his head. He pushed back the all-too-familiar feelings of nervousness and silently reminded himself that underneath his harsh exterior, Brother Simon was really his friend. "What made you change your mind? I mean, about being our prefect?"

Brother Simon froze. He let the books in his hand fall back into the box. He turned around and looked at Charlie.

"Is it because of what happened that night?" Charlie added quickly while he studied Brother Simon's cold, dark eyes.

Brother Simon thought for a moment. His mind flashed with the images of the attic. He debated about whether or not to answer Charlie or simply order him from the room. He clenched his teeth. He hated feeling cornered. In fact, he hated feeling anything at all.

"Yes, Master MacCready, it is," he finally spoke in a softer tone than his normal cold, stern voice. He looked at Charlie with the same tender look in his eyes that he had that night in the attic, after Charlie was safe. "You see, you made me realize that I haven't put that night all those years ago behind me. Facing my past has made me want to move on with my life. When Father Abbot asked me to stay on as prefect, I thought maybe this would be a good way to do just that. So, I accepted. I'm not doing this because of you, but at the same time, because of you, I am."

Charlie felt a tear start to well up in his eyes and a lump tighten in his throat. He fought it down. He knew that Brother Simon would not approve.

"Oh, but don't misunderstand," Brother Simon continued with a slightly colder tone. "I still don't like children." He paused for a moment and looked at Charlie. "But, you remind me so much of your father. It's like having my old friend back again."

Charlie smiled. He could not believe what he was hearing and seeing. This was the side of Brother Simon that no one ever saw; a side he kept hidden from everyone.

Brother Simon nodded knowingly at Charlie.

"Well, Master MacCready, I have a lot of work to do. We shall talk again."

"Okay." Charlie's nodded. "I'll get out of your way." He headed for the door.

"Charlie," Brother Simon halted him.

Charlie turned around. There was that odd look in Brother Simon's dark eyes again, a look of concern and caring.

"With all of the construction work going on, there will be a lot of strangers about. Promise me you'll be careful. Hold onto that key. Don't let it out of your sight. It is very important," he warned. "There are people who will stop at nothing to get it."

Charlie's back stiffened as a feeling like a rush of ice water swept over him. He felt his chest, for the key that hung beneath his robes. Feelings of panic and curiosity rose up inside his head and left him confused. He took a step back into the room.

"You know about my key?"

"I saw it the day I picked you up at your grandmother's and when you were pulled back into the attic, it fell from beneath your pajama top." Brother Simon nodded. "Your father had a key just like that as I recall."

"He did?" Charlie gasped. He could not believe his ears. "What's it for?"

"I can't tell you that, I'm sorry," Brother Simon sighed. "I gave my word. Just, be careful. Promise me?"

Charlie's mind exploded with questions. Who did he promise? Why? How did he know?

"I promise." He nodded at Brother Simon.

"And one more thing," Brother Simon's voice changed back to his familiar cold tone. "If you tell anyone of our conversation, I will deny it."

Charlie nodded and left the room.

Charlie was deep in thought as he walked back to his dorm. He did not even glance at the large life-size painting of Saint Nicholas that hung between the prefect's door and the double doors to his dorm. In a daze, he opened the doors to Saint Nicholas dorm and entered. He could still hear Brother Simon's voice echoing in his ears. "Your father had a key just like that as I recall." Could it be the same key? he wondered. Why did Brother Simon get to know what the key was for, and, like his grandmother, why would he not tell?

Charlie looked around the familiar dormitory. Along three of the walls were twin beds of various styles, all donated by the churchgoing townspeople. Beside each bed was a nightstand. Some matched the headboards of the beds but most did not. Large wooden panel partitions were placed between every other bed, forming two beds into what the monks called a cubicle. In the center of the dorm was a sitting area. Two overstuffed, green and gold plaid chairs sat opposite a matching sofa on a braided rug. An old trunk with a glass top served as a coffee table but more often as a footrest in the center. Two tall floor lamps stood at either end of the sofa like silent sentries keeping watch.

Mechanically, Charlie headed for his bed in the corner cubicle, the cubicle he shared with Howard.

"Hi, Charlie," Howard greeted.

"Hey," Charlie answered distractedly and sat down on his bed.

Howard swung his legs around and sat up on his bed opposite Charlie. He could tell Charlie was thinking about something. He cocked his head slightly, "What's the matter?"

Charlie looked at Howard. "Ah, nothing really," he answered. "Brother Simon just told me some stuff and I don't know what to think about it."

"Like what?" Howard pressed.

Charlie looked around the room to be sure the other boys were not around. Then carefully he pulled the brass key out from beneath his robes and stared at it.

"He said my father had a key just like this one," Charlie whispered. "He said that there are people who would try to get it. He also knows what it is for but he won't tell me. He said he gave his word."

"And your grandmother won't tell you either," Howard added as he looked at the key.

"Yeah," Charlie agreed and put the key back under his robes.

"Well, I wouldn't worry too much about it." Howard tried to sound reassuring. "No one's going to want an old key like that, and even if they did, they won't be able to get at it here."

"Get at what?" Gus asked as he stood at the foot of Howard's bed.

Howard and Charlie both jumped. They did not hear Gus walk up.

"Nothing!"

Gus recoiled at the sharpness of Howard's tone. "My foot!" he snapped back. "You guys are up to something. What is it?"

"Really, Gus," Charlie spoke in a kinder tone. "It's nothing. I just had a conversation with Brother Simon and that's all. Hey, what did you find out about the surplice? Were any of yours missing?"

A smug look came over Howard's face as he looked at Gus. "Yes, Gus, tell Charlie about your surplices."

Gus glared at Howard slightly before looking back at Charlie.

"I am missing one," he admitted. "But honestly, I don't know how it could've happened."

"But who'd want to take your surplice?" Charlie shook his head.

"Who would want to steal your mail?" Howard added in a somewhat condescending tone. "And who always wants to make trouble for us?"

"Dougary!" Gus said through clenched teeth.

"Bingo! Give the fat boy a prize." Howard clapped his hands and laughed. Gus glared at him harder.

"Howard!" Charlie snapped.

"Oh, you know what I meant." Howard brushed them both off. "Dougary, Larry, Travis and Austin," he added and looked directly at Charlie. "All of them have been out to get us."

Charlie did not say a word, although he had his doubts about Austin. Before he had gone home for the summer, Austin warned him that Dougary and the others were out to do him serious harm. If he were as rotten as the rest of them, he would not have warned him, but Howard would never believe that.

"We'll just have to watch them closer," Charlie said.

SHADOWS IN THE NIGHT

The glow of the summer moon shone through the window across Charlie while he lay sleeping, and onto the cold grey floor. Charlie tossed and turned in his bed. Tiny beads of sweat dotted his forehead. He let out a soft whimper as he grimaced.

"No," he murmured.

Charlie ran deeper and deeper into the dark forest. Small, brittle twigs snapped under his bare feet, but Charlie did not feel a thing. The forest became darker and darker until only a few thin slivers of moonlight were able to pierce the branches of the tall trees. He stopped. He was alone. Lost. He looked all around.

"Char-lie," a strange yet familiar, deep voice called from the darkness.

Charlie spun around.

"Char-lie," a woman's voice called in the distance from the other direction.

Charlie spun around again. Frantically he searched the darkness. Suddenly there was a movement; a shadow disappeared behind a tree.

"Dad? Mom?" he called and stepped forward as tears clouded his eyes.

"Char-lie!" the voices called out in unison, but came from

opposite directions.

Charlie spun around. Through his tears he could see a dark shadow standing beside a tree.

"Char-lie," the voice called again.

Charlie ran toward the shadow. It disappeared. He spun around, frantically searching the darkness.

"Char-lie," the woman's voice called.

"Mom, where are you? I can't see you," Charlie cried, blinded by the tears that streamed down his cheeks.

Charlie turned around and around, wiping the tears from his eyes. Suddenly he saw a shadow of a man. The shadow reached out its arms to him.

"Dad?" he cried and tried to see through the blur of his tears as he hurried toward it.

Suddenly Charlie froze. Fiery, red eyes glowed from the darkened face. He could feel its hot breath against his face as its powerful hands gripped his arms, lifting him off the ground. The shadow drew him closer. Charlie closed his eyes and turned his face away from the menacing shadow. He struggled and struggled to scream but could not.

He opened his eyes. A paralyzing fear rushed over him like a warm ocean wave. He looked up from his bed at a black, shadowy figure that was bent over him. He watched silently as a thin, bony hand with long fingers and fingernails like an eagle's talons pulled on the thin gold chain that was beneath his pajama top. Charlie felt the key raise from off his chest.

"No!" he screamed and sat straight up in his bed. He grabbed the key, still under his pajamas and scrambled to the corner of his bed. He searched the darkness but the shadow was gone.

Howard woke with a start and sat up.

"Charlie?" he said in a sleepy, half-awake tone. He grabbed his glasses from his nightstand and slipped them on. He looked around the dark dormitory and then over at Charlie.

Charlie did not answer.

Howard climbed out of his bed and went to his friend. He

sat down on the edge of Charlie's bed and looked into Charlie's eyes that were wide with fear. He noticed Charlie's hands trembling as he clutched the key beneath his pajamas.

"Charlie." Howard reached out and touched Charlie's hands.

Charlie pulled away sharply, then looked at Howard for the first time.

"What is it? What's the matter?" Howard asked and looked around.

"S-s-someone w-w-was h-h-here," Charlie's voice quivered.

Howard looked around the room.

"There's no one here," he said, turning back to Charlie. "It must've been a bad dream."

"No!" Charlie snapped. "Th-th-there was s-s-someone. I-I-I saw him. He-he-he wanted th-th-the key."

Howard sighed and relaxed. For a moment, Charlie was beginning to scare him, too. "You just had a bad dream. That's all," he said in a soft, reassuring voice. "Remember we talked before lights out about your key and B. S.? You just had a dream. It's okay."

Charlie looked at his best friend. For the first time he began to wonder if it was just a dream; but it felt so real.

"A dream," he repeated out loud as his pulse slowed to normal and his fears eased.

"Yes, a dream," Howard echoed and smiled. "Now, try to relax and go back to sleep." He yawned and stretched. "I'm so tired."

Howard returned to his bed and slipped under the warm covers. He stirred for a moment and then was fast asleep again.

Charlie slowly inched his way back under his covers. "A dream," he repeated quietly as he lay back down. He closed his eyes. "A dream," he yawned.

Just as he was drifting off to sleep the sound of the dormitory doors closing touched his ears. "A dream."

SUMMER

The sun was bright in the summer sky. The air was thick with the smell of diesel exhaust and dust. Charlie, Howard and Gus sat on the bleachers that were moved next to the back of the Abbey building in order to make room for the construction trucks and machinery. All morning they watched as truck after truck pulling trailers of various sizes chugged up the narrow service road and unloaded their cargo on the baseball field. Howard groaned every time one of the heavy machines tore up the green grass of the outfield.

Charlie watched, but his mind kept going back to his dream from the night before. He could not shake the shadowy image from his thoughts. It was all too real.

Howard noticed Charlie was not acting like his usual self. At breakfast Charlie barely ate a thing. He seemed quieter and more distant.

"You're still thinking about that dream, aren't you?" Howard asked.

Charlie looked at him. "Yeah." He nodded. "It's just that I heard their voices."

"Whose voices?" Gus asked.

"My mom's and dad's, I think," Charlie answered. "They

were calling me but I couldn't see them. Then that shadow appeared, and I thought it was my dad, but it wasn't." Charlie shivered.

"It's okay," Howard said, putting his arm around Charlie's shoulders. "We all have dreams about our parents. Isn't that right, Gus?"

Gus thought for a moment. "I don't—" He looked at Howard's intense stare. "Yeah, we all do." He nodded and agreed unconvincingly.

"Don't let it bother you," Howard tried to reassure Charlie. "Try to think about something else."

"Like what?"

"Like this," Howard said and held out his open palms toward the field.

"Isn't this exciting?" Gus said with a big smile. "It's almost like Christmas."

Howard gave Gus a puzzled look. "You're truly nuts."

Charlie bit his tongue to keep from laughing. He liked Gus a lot and did not want to hurt his feelings, but Howard did have a point. Sure, the building project was exciting, but in no way did it compare to Christmas.

"No, I'm not!" Gus snapped back. "I just meant that all of this stuff is going to make us a new home. What a neat present." It was obvious he was annoyed with Howard.

Howard rolled his eyes and continued watching as a flatbed truck tore another chunk up of the outfield as it came to a stop across. "Well, I've had enough of this," he said, and stood up. "Let's go see if Father Vicar put up the course lists. This year I want to sign up for something fun before those creeps in Saint Peter dorm take all the good classes."

"Don't hold your breath." Gus shook his head. "I'm sure Father Vicar's shown the lists to those goons already."

"Yeah." Howard shrugged and started off the bleachers.

Charlie and Gus jumped to their feet. Since this was his first summer at Saint Michael's, Charlie wanted to be sure he could get into a class with Howard and Gus. It did not matter to him which class they ended up in, as long as they were together. The three hurried up the three flights of stairs and started down the hall toward the common room.

Just as they were passing by Saint Peter dorm the doors swung open. Dougary, the dark-haired, athletic troublemaker, strutted into the hall. For Dougary, Saint Michael's was the only thing keeping him from the state juvenile home. Close behind him, as usual, was Larry Hertz, who resembled a tall, menacing bulldog, and Travis Bleckinger, a short, stocky boy with blonde hair that was course like straw.

"So where're you girls going in such a hurry?" Dougary jeered.

Howard clenched his teeth. He did not say a word. He was determined to get to the bulletin board before Dougary. Charlie was relieved Howard did not stop to argue with Dougary. The last thing he wanted to do was fight with the likes of him. Charlie grabbed Gus's arm and hurried after Howard.

"Oh!" Howard groaned as he looked at the lists of courses. "I don't believe this!"

"What?" Charlie asked while he looked over Howard's shoulder.

"They've done it to me again," Howard said, clearly disgusted. "All of the good classes have been taken."

Charlie stared at the lists with a bit of confusion. It was true. Most of the courses were already filled, but none of them looked any better or any worse than the few that were left. "It's okay, Howard, there're some classes left with enough openings for the three of us."

"Where?" Gus asked as he tried to see over their shoulders.

"There is candle making and weaving," Charlie read out loud. "Hey, only one person has signed up for pottery." Charlie sounded excited as he looked at Howard for his response.

Howard could not hide his disappointment as he read the course sheet. "Do you know why no one has signed up for pottery?"

Charlie shook his head.

"It's because it's the most boring class there is next to weaving. Candle making is only slightly better because you get to play with fire," Howard answered, in his usual cynical way.

"Well, I want to sign up for pottery," Gus spoke up.

"Of course you do," Howard retorted. "You get to play with more mud. Honestly!" He shook his head and folded his arms over his thin chest.

"Howard!" Charlie snapped. He was beginning to grow annoyed with Howard's attitude. "Be nice," he pleaded through clenched teeth.

Howard frowned at Charlie.

"I agree with Gus." Charlie nodded as he took the pen from the paper cup that was tacked to the bulletin board beside the lists. "I think pottery sounds like it could be fun. Besides with the three of us in it, how could it not be?" He signed his name to the list and then turned to Howard. He held out the pen to Howard. "Come on, we have to sign up for *something*."

Howard stared at the pen as he thought to himself.

Charlie could see the disappointment in Howard's eyes at not being able to sign up for the class he really wanted. "At least we'll be together," he repeated. "That's the important thing, isn't it?"

"Oh, all right." Howard caved in and took the pen. "Who's teaching the course?" he asked as he signed his name under Charlie's.

"A Father Ichabod," Charlie read.

"Oh no," Howard groaned again and handed the pen to Gus.

Charlie gave Gus a confused look.

"What's the matter with Father Ichabod?" Gus asked before Charlie had a chance. He quickly scribbled his name on the list and dropped the pen back into the paper cup.

"For starters, he's old and creepy and smells like an ashtray." Howard wrinkled up his nose.

"That's not a very nice thing to say," Charlie spoke up in the absent monk's defense.

"Oh, that was being nice," Howard said but still sounded disgusted.

"Howard, there's nothing we can do about it," Charlie reminded him. "There aren't that many choices left."

Howard took a deep breath. "I know," he sighed. "What's done is done."

The three turned around, only to come face to face with Dougary and his thugs. They were standing right behind them the whole time, and heard every word. Dougary grinned his usual sinister grin that instantly made the hair on the back of Howard's neck stand up.

"Oh what's the matter? Poor Howie didn't get his first choice?" Dougary said with a mock pout.

"Out of our way, dog breath!" Howard sneered back, and pushed his way through them. Charlie and Gus quickly followed without a word.

Just before turning into their dorm, Charlie glanced back at Dougary and his goons. They were standing at the bulletin board, looking at the courses, and whispering to each other. Charlie turned around and entered Saint Nicholas dorm.

THE MISSING NOVICE

The gentle summer breeze felt cool against Charlie's warm face. He pulled at the collar of his black cassock, releasing some of the heat from under his robes. He wished Abbot Ambrose would have removed the requirement of wearing their uniforms whenever they were on the front lawn.

Slowly, he took in a deep breath. The air smelled clean with the scent of freshly cut grass. Charlie watched the novice monk and Brother Tobias pushing the riding lawnmower into the garage. He wondered if it had broken down or just ran out of gas. After all, the front lawn was quite large.

The moment of quiet was shattered as the wood chipper started up. Charlie turned his attention back to watching the monks feed the loose branches they gathered from the toppled trees into the wide end of the chipper. As the branches disappeared, small chips began to shoot out the chimney at the other end, filling the bed of the waiting pick-up.

Charlie did not intend on staying out too long, but time had a way of slipping by; suddenly it was time to head back inside to meet up with Howard before dinner.

Quickly Charlie made his way around the small fish ponds that dotted the great lawn. Around each pond was a carefully maintained flower bed filled with colorful flowers, some of which Charlie had never seen before. Pink dogwood trees and bigger maple trees around the ponds provided shade and a haven from the heat of the summer sun, while neatly pruned fir trees standing here and there provided green all year round.

As Charlie neared one of the ponds, he noticed a small gathering of boys from Saint Sebastian and Saint Thomas dorms lounging on the ground beneath one of the maple trees. They appeared to be listening to one of the novices who was seated on the stone bench in front of them. Charlie slowed his pace, walking closer to hear what was going on. He recognized the young novice. It was Dominic, the one who had served lunch to him and his grandmother a few weeks ago.

"It was on an evening just like this," Dominic said in a hushed, eerie whisper. "The wind gently blew through the trees and rustled the branches. The moon was bright in the sky. The Abbot called the novices together in the Abbey church. He had a job for them to do. It seemed that one of the older Brothers had passed away in the orchard shed the day before while resting in his chair. His body was not discovered until the next morning. I don't need to tell you, but after sitting for so long in the chair, rigor mortis had set in, his muscles had tightened so the Brothers had to tie the body down in his coffin to keep him from sitting back up." Dominic looked around at all of their young faces as he told them the story. Their wide-eyed expressions let him know they were hanging on his every word. He smiled, seemingly satisfied with himself.

"The Abbey had the custom of not burying their dead for three days and three nights. Something to do with Jesus' being resurrected on the third day, I imagine. Anyway, they would keep the coffin open in the small cemetery chapel, and post a guard outside. It just so happened that the novices were to be the guards.

"The first night passed and nothing happened. The second night passed and still nothing. On the third night, it was the youngest novice's turn to be on guard. It was dark. Clouds covered the night sky. Everything seemed to be going along as the previous two nights. Then suddenly, at midnight, he heard a noise. He quickly looked around in the darkness to see if someone was hiding behind the bushes around the chapel. Just as he returned to his post, he heard a thud inside the chapel. Slowly he opened the chapel doors. The hinges creaked, which made the hair on the back of the young novice's neck stand up.

"The candles were still burning at the head of the coffin and flickered in the night air. From the doorway, he could see the ropes that held the body down had come undone. Slowly he walked into the chapel to take a closer look. The body was still and lifeless. Slowly he reached out his hands to retie the rope. All at once the body lunged forward," Dominic lunged at the boys. They all jumped and some of the younger boys yelled. Dominic smiled seemingly pleased by their reaction. "When the body sat up, the air pushed out of its lungs causing a deep groan.

"The novice let out a scream so loud it could be heard from the Abbey clear down to the town. Immediately, the Brother came running. When they reached the chapel, the novice was gone. They never heard from him again." Dominic paused and studied the shocked faces of the young boys in front of him.

"Some say, the novice is still alive and doing well on the east coast somewhere. Others say he's locked up in the state mental hospital," he mused with a slight shrug of his shoulders. Then his expression turned serious. "But I think he's still out there, lurking around in the Abbey's forest somewhere." He ducked his head fearfully. "In fact, he could be watching us right now," he breathed slowly turning to look at the trees behind the boys. His eyes widened. "Look out! Behind that tree!" he shouted and pointed at Charlie. The boys jumped. The younger ones screamed and grabbed for the older ones for protection.

"Oh, hi." Dominic greeted Charlie with a smile.

"Hi, Dominic." Charlie nodded, not really buying into his story even though he jumped too.

Dominic smiled. He looked at the other boys. "Well, I guess you should all run along. We can tell more stories later."

"Night, Dominic," the boys each said as they all stood up and dusted off their cassocks and surplices.

Dominic watched as they all headed off toward the Abbey, then he turned back to Charlie. His smiled faded as he looked into Charlie's disapproving eyes.

"It's just a story, Charlie," he said and stood up.

"Do you really think it's wise to be telling them stuff like that?" Charlie asked.

"Well, they're the ones who started it." Dominic shifted the blame. "Besides, I think they're old enough to know when they're having their leg pulled." He took two steps toward Charlie and leaned closer to Charlie's ear. "Or maybe not," he added in a sinister whisper. "See ya', Charlie." He grinned a self-satisfied grin and then headed back to the Abbey.

Charlie fought the chill that instantly shot up his spine and the urge to turn around and see if someone were watching him from the forest. He quickly hurried to catch up to Dominic.

HOWARD'S SECRET PLACE

Two days passed since Charlie had seen Abbot Ambrose. He was not at his usual place at the head table during their meals. Word around the dorms said he was fasting and praying over whom to select to be the new dean. After the prayer, Charlie took his usual seat at the table next to Howard in the refectory. They waited for the sound of the wooden block being hit against the head table, the signal that it was okay to speak.

"Have you found out anything yet?" Howard asked, placing his napkin in his lap.

"No," Charlie answered. His disappointment was obvious in his tone. "None of the Brothers I've asked seemed to know where he disappeared to, or they wouldn't tell."

"You don't think he's already made a decision on the new dean and doesn't want to face us, do you?" Howard asked.

"No." Charlie shook his head uncertainly.

"I just hope it's not Father Vicar," Howard offered as he watched the Brother with the serving tray of food make his way closer to Gus.

"I agree," Charlie nodded.

"You do, do you?" said a dry, cold voice from behind them.

Charlie jumped and looked over his shoulder. Father Vicar

was standing directly behind them, listening to them as they lamented. His bony face was its usual iciness.

"What?" Howard asked innocently as he looked at the prefect of Saint Peter dorm.

"Don't play stupid with me, Master Miller," Father Vicar's deep voice growled. "I overheard what you boys were saying." He bent down between Howard and Charlie so that he was even with their ears. "Well, let me break it to you boys right now," he said in a harsh, dry whisper. "Should Abbot Ambrose name me the new dean, not even Heaven itself will be able to save you. That I can promise you." He turned away and continued his walk around the refectory.

"How long was he standing there?" Charlie asked and kept an eye on Father Vicar.

"I don't know," Howard answered through clenched teeth. He looked across the table at Gus who was busy looking at his plate. "Why didn't you warn us?"

"What? How was I supposed to know he'd be walking around?" Gus shrugged and tried to defend himself.

"Because he had been doing it at every meal since Abbot Ambrose disappeared, you dolt!" Howard snapped.

Charlie frowned sternly at Howard. He elbowed him in the ribs.

Howard winced and grabbed his side. Ever since Charlie came to the Abbey, he's been trying to get Howard to be nicer to Gus but it seemed an almost impossible task. Howard sighed heavily.

"Oh, never mind," Howard said as the Brother placed a plate of food in front of him. "Thank you," he said politely to the monk.

The young monk smiled.

"One thing is for certain," Howard continued in a hushed voice once the serving Brother was gone. "You heard him, if Father Vicar becomes dean we're dead meat."

"Abbot Ambrose wouldn't do that to us," Gus said confidently with his mouth full. "Would he?" he asked, suddenly not so sure.

"I sure hope not. We thought Dougary and his goons were bad news. If Father Vicar's dean, they'll have free rein to terrorize us and everybody else. There'd be nothing we could do about it," Charlie answered. He glanced at the head table. Father Vicar was seated in his usual chair and keeping a strict watch on all of the boys as he slowly ate his lunch.

"Speaking of Dougary, anyone look at the list of courses for the summer?" Gus spoke up.

"Don't remind me," Howard growled. He was still unhappy about not being able to sign up for his first choice.

"I did," Charlie said with a nod. "Did you guys notice who else signed up for the pottery class?"

"Why on earth would I care?" Howard answered in the same disgusted tone. "I didn't even want to take that stupid class in the first place."

"Then it shouldn't bother you that Dougary and his two half-wits are also in our class," Gus sneered and took a big bite of his hamburger. The ketchup oozed from around the edges and plopped back onto his plate, just missing the sleeves of his red surplice.

Charlie shook his head and smiled to himself at the sight.

"Well, isn't that just perfect!" Howard folded his arms across his chest and slid down in his chair. "Could this summer get any worse?" he pouted.

"Careful what you say," Gus said ducking his head and looking around.

"Oh, you're such a superstitious dork!" Howard's tone still sounded annoyed.

Charlie shook his head. No matter what he or Gus said to cheer Howard up, Howard was not having it. It was beginning to seem that their summer was going to be void of any fun.

"So, what're we gonna do this afternoon?" Charlie asked to change the subject.

"You guys want to go watch them clear away more trees for the new building?" Gus asked with bulging cheeks.

"No!" sneered Howard.

"Want to go swimming?" Charlie tried to sound enthused.

"Nah," Gus shook his head. "We did that yesterday. Besides, too much chlorine dries out my skin and makes me itchy," he said and scratched the back of his neck.

"Hey, I know," Howard said, sounding a bit more enthused. "After lunch, I'll show you guys my new secret place."

Charlie looked at Gus and then they both looked at Howard. "New?"

"Yeah." Howard nodded as he took a bite of his hamburger. He chewed and swallowed quickly, washing it all down with a big gulp of his milk. "Since all that trouble in the attic, Abbot Ambrose asked me to find another place to go. He doesn't want anyone in the attic anymore."

"He never did," Gus reminded him in a snotty know-it-all tone, very unlike his usual mousiness.

"I know, Gustav," Howard retorted. "You sound like Rick." He glared at him. "Anyway, I've found an even better one. But you have to wait for me right after lunch. You game?"

"Sure," Charlie agreed.

"Me too?" Gus asked eagerly.

Howard looked at Gus for a moment and hesitated. From the corners of his eyes he could see Charlie's 'be nice' look. "Sure," he answered. "I did say you guys."

Immediately Gus grinned happily and took another oversized bite of his burger.

"Thank you," Charlie whispered at Howard.

The rest of the meal passed by uneventfully. Once they were dismissed, Howard excused himself, saying he needed to do something before they could go to his secret place.

As Charlie waited with Gus at the foot of the stairs on the main floor, he glanced down at the mail slots that hung on the wall of the landing between the first floor and the basement. Something strange and different caught his eye. It had been a long time since he checked his mail slot. "What's the point?" he told himself. For the past six months, someone had been stealing his letters. He had become so used to it that he gave up looking altogether, saving himself the disappointment. But today, there it was. He raced down the stairs without a word to Gus and grabbed the white envelope from his mail slot. He looked at it and read the return address. It was a letter from his grandmother. He smiled to himself and headed back up the stairs.

"What's that?" Howard asked as Charlie reached the first floor.

"It's a letter from my Grandmother," he answered. He could not hide the excitement in his voice.

"Wow," Gus gasped in surprise. "I don't believe it."

"You realize what this means, don't you?" Howard said as he looked at them both.

They looked at him with blank expressions on their faces.

Howard sighed and shook his head. "I can't believe you, of all people, the great detective," Howard mocked, "don't see? It means whoever is taking your mail is a student here. It has to be someone who's gone home for the summer."

"That's right!" Gus said as though a light went on in his head. He looked at Charlie and then back at Howard. "So, now we just have to figure out which one it is."

"Unless," Charlie said with a note of suspicion in his voice, "That is what he wants us to think." He nodded as he watched for Howard's reaction. "I just know it has to be Dougary or one of his goons," he shrugged and turned back to his letter.

"Exactly!" Howard agreed. "And the only one of Dougary's goons that's gone is Austin Fuller."

"It can't be him," Charlie said and looked up from the letter in his hands. He shook his head. "No."

"And why not?" Howard snapped disgustedly.

Charlie looked at him. He knew how Howard felt about Austin's warning.

"Think about it, Charlie," Howard said, trying to reason with him. "He had ink on his hands." He held his open palms out in front of Charlie's face to emphasize his point.

"I know," Charlie admitted and brushed Howard's hands away. "But he said he broke his pen in Brother Vincent's class."

"And you believe him?" Howard asked in a tone that sounded more shocked than inquiring.

"I don't know." Charlie shrugged.

"His story is easy to verify," Howard said reassuringly. "We just need to ask Brother Vincent."

"Ah," Gus spoke up hesitantly. "That may be harder than you think, Howard. Brother Vincent is leaving tomorrow morning. I heard some of the older guys saying that he and another Brother are being sent to Rome to go to school there for something."

"I guess that doesn't give us much time. I'll have to catch him before he leaves tomorrow morning."

"I don't think it's him," Charlie tried to sound positive.

"Why?" Howard sighed loudly and looked at Charlie. "Because he warned you that Dougary and his goons are out to get you? Charlie, we already know that. It's just a trick to get you to lower your guard."

"I don't know," Charlie sighed as he looked at his as yet unopened letter.

Howard shook his head disgustedly. "When are you going to realize that not everyone has some good in them? Some people are just rotten to their core. I tell you what, I'll check out Austin's story with Brother Vincent. Then you'll see."

Charlie did not answer. He knew Howard was right, but he wanted to believe what his grandmother always said, that given a chance, the good in everyone would shine through. "Some just take longer to shine than others," she told him.

"Well, don't just stand there," Gus interrupted, changing the subject. "Open your letter!" He gave Charlie's arm a gentle nudge.

"Oh, yeah." He smiled and the three sat down on the stairs.

Charlie carefully tore open the envelope and pulled out a single piece of white linen stationary. His grandmother always wrote on the nicest paper, he thought. He opened the folded letter and two five-dollar bills fell out. He quickly grabbed for them but missed. Howard retrieved them from the floor. Charlie turned his attention to his letter. His eyes skimmed over the familiar handwriting, not really reading it as much as looking at it and thinking about his grandmother.

"Well, let's go." Howard said impatiently, sounding bored with this whole letter-stealing thing. He handed Charlie his allowance and headed up the stairs toward the fourth floor.

Charlie quickly stuffed the money into his jeans pocket underneath his black cassock and then the letter back into its envelope as he stood up. He made a mental note to read his letter later as he tucked it into the pocket of his cassock.

"So, where are we going?" Gus asked as he and Charlie hurried to keep up with Howard.

"You'll see."

As they reached the fourth floor, Charlie and Gus started for the fire doors that separated the stairwell from the hallway.

"Where are you guys going?" Howard asked as he stood at the top of the stairs.

"What?" Charlie asked and turned around.

"This way." Howard said and motioned with his head toward the small door in the wall opposite the fire doors.

The small door looked more like a cupboard door really. It was about the size of the top half of a normal door. Howard looked around making sure no one else was watching. Cautiously he opened the door.

"In here," he said and crawled inside. He turned back. "It's okay, come on."

Charlie looked inside the dark room. The floor was even with the bottom of the door but it was still about three feet up from where Charlie stood. Slowly he pulled the hem of his cassock up and tucked it into the belt around his jeans underneath so he could climb easier. Cautiously he climbed up with Howard's help.

Howard turned back to Gus who was staring uncertainly at the small room through the doorway. Gus' eyes were wide with fear.

"I—I don't like dark places," he said.

"Come on, Gus," Howard urged, and held out his hand to help him.

Gus looked around the stairwell as though searching for an excuse to stay where he was.

"It's okay, Gus," Howard continued to coax. "Charlie did it."

"Charlie also went into the attic," Gus reminded him. "And was almost thrown out of the window by Dougary's father."

Howard frowned and stretched out his hand again at Gus.

With a heavy sigh, Gus took Howard's hand. With one quick tug, Gus was inside the room and kneeling next to Charlie. Howard closed the door and the room went pitch dark.

A shiver ran up Charlie's spine as all of his muscles tensed. A sudden fear swept over him as he lost his sense of up and down. His head started spinning. His pulse quickened. He felt as though he could not breathe.

Slowly, his eyes became accustomed to the darkness and the room began to come into view. Charlie could feel his fears grow as he looked around the room.

The three boys were crouched in what appeared to be a square room about fourteen feet wide. To their right, a rickety wooden staircase hugged the wall and spiraled upward. Five heavy ropes hung through the ceiling above them, and dangled through a large hole in the center of the bare wooden floor to somewhere below.

Cautiously Charlie inched his back up against the wall, away from the center of the room. He could not shake the feeling that at any moment he would be sucked down through the hole in the floor. The wooden fence that surrounded the hole did not look strong enough to save him, Charlie was sure.

Suddenly the feeling that the floor was beginning to slope toward the hole caused his fears to increase. Frantically he groped blindly for anything to hold onto as he fought hard to calm the panic that was beginning to overwhelm him. His breathing became shallow as he panted in fear. Desperately, he looked at Howard and Gus.

Gus, who had been afraid at first, was standing up with Howard and looking around. As they walked around, Charlie could feel the floor wobble beneath him. He gasped and grabbed at the wall behind him for something to hold onto, sure that at any moment the floor would give way.

In the dim light, Howard saw the fear in Charlie's eyes and rushed to him, causing the floor to shake even more and Charlie's fear to increase.

"It's okay, Charlie," he said in a reassuring voice as he knelt down on one knee beside him. "You're safe."

"Wh-where are we?" Charlie's voice trembled as he spoke.

"We're in the bell tower," Howard reluctantly told him. He had wanted to keep it a secret a bit longer.

Howard's answer seemed to do the trick. Charlie felt his fears begin to ease. Howard reached out his hand to him and slowly, cautiously, Charlie struggled to get to his feet. Once standing he immediately flattened his back against the wall and began to pant. His fears had stirred once again inside of him.

"Take a deep breath," Gus urged as he stood beside Charlie and held onto Charlie's right arm. "You'll be okay. We're here. We won't let anything bad happen to you."

Charlie looked at Gus, surprised at how this boy who was afraid of the attic and hesitant about the dark bell tower was perfectly comfortable now. He looked at Howard, who stood beside him holding fast to his left arm.

"Is this your new secret place?" Charlie asked, in a somewhat calmer, less quivering voice.

"No," Howard answered and looked at Gus with a worried expression. "Not exactly."

"What do you mean, not exactly?" Charlie asked and began to pant again.

"It's up those stairs," Howard admitted and nodded at the rickety stairs behind Gus. "Do you still want to see it?"

Charlie looked at the stairs, then at Gus, and then back at

Howard. "Give me a moment to catch my breath," he said uncertainly.

"Sure," Howard said, giving him an understanding smile.

Charlie took two, slow, deep breaths, and each time he felt a little stronger, though his legs continued to tremble.

"You'll be okay," Howard said again, trying to reassure him. "I'll be beside you."

Charlie smiled. "Okay. I think I'm ready."

Slowly the three boys approached the stairs. Charlie stayed next to the wall, still not totally sure the floor was strong enough to hold him, let alone Howard and Gus.

Howard stayed right by Charlie's side and held onto his arm to reassure him. He knew Charlie disliked heights, and after almost being dropped out of the attic window on his head, Charlie liked them even less.

"It is so cool up there," Howard said, trying to make small talk to ease the heavy silence. "The view is awesome. Just wait until you see it."

The three moved around the walls as they climbed the stairs. Soon they reached the top where the stairs met the ceiling. Howard released Charlie's arm and raised his hand, pushing against the ceiling. Slowly, the trap door opened. Howard kept pushing. Immediately the bright light of the afternoon sun illuminated the room around them. Charlie covered his eyes to shield them until they adjusted to the light.

"This is it," Howard said and stepped up into the top room of the bell tower. He turned around and offered Charlie his hand and helped him up. Gus, strangely brave, bounded up into the room before Howard could offer to help him. Immediately, Gus turned around and started to shut the heavy door.

"No!" Howard yelled and lunged at Gus. He grabbed the door before it could move. "Don't ever close that door when you're up here. Otherwise you'll be trapped, and believe me, you don't want to be up here when these bells start to toll. I was told that your eardrums would burst if you were this close to the big bell when it rings. We have to be very careful not to be here when that happens."

Charlie looked at the huge, iron bells that hung from the beams over their heads in the center of the room. His eyes followed the ropes as they dropped through the floor where, instead of a large hole in the floor like below, they disappeared through a much smaller, cloth lined opening. He felt himself relax for the first time since he climbed into the tower. Slowly he turned his attention to the walls. The walls were made of brick, just like the rest of the tower. There were four, arched, half-moon, window openings. One faced north, another south, one east, and one west. The windowsills were nearly chest high, which made Charlie, feel a lot safer.

"Look at this view!" Howard said excitedly as he looked out toward the north. "You can even see the main road from here, Charlie."

Charlie cautiously approached the window, his heart pounding in his chest. He reached out his hand and took hold of the windowless sill and looked out. It *was* a beautiful sight, he thought to himself. From there he had a clearer view of the main road up the hill than the view he had from his dorm window. He would really be able to see when his parents came for him. Maybe this isn't such a bad place after all, he thought. He looked at the window on the east wall.

Gus rushed over to it first and looked out.

"Wow," he breathed. "We're even higher than the tops of those trees." He pointed out at the forest below. "You can really see a long way from up here," he added.

Charlie and Howard slowly moved around to the east window. Together they looked down at the forest below. Charlie watched two boys walk past the cemetery and the grotto of Our Lady of the Subway. The boys nicknamed the statue of Mary that because behind her was the opening of the tunnel that led to the garages. The boys continued down the service road and path toward the swimming pool, its roof barely visible through the trees.

Suddenly Charlie saw a dark shadow move deep in the

woods. Every muscle in his body tightened and he froze, unable to move. His nightmare flashed in his mind.

Out of the corner of his eyes, Howard noticed Charlie stiffen in fear.

"What is it? What's the matter?" he asked.

Charlie struggled to speak as he kept his eyes fixed on the shadow in the forest. It appeared to be a man, but he was not sure. The shadow stopped moving. Could it be watching me, Charlie wondered. As his fear grew, he began to tremble.

"Charlie, what's the matter? What are you looking at?" Howard asked. His fear and concern for his friend was evident in his panicked voice. He turned and looked out at the forest trying to see what Charlie was seeing. "I don't see anything," he said and turned back to Charlie.

"Th-the shadow," Charlie stammered, slowly raising his shaking hand to point. As soon as he did, the shadow disappeared.

"What?" Howard asked and looked in the direction Charlie was pointing. "I don't see anything."

"What was it?" Gus asked, still trying to see whatever it was they were looking at.

Charlie suddenly turned away from the window and flattened himself against the wall beside it. He panted as he tried to catch his breath.

"I-I don't know," Charlie said as he struggled to compose himself. "It was dark, like a shadow, the shadow from my dream."

Howard turned away from the window. "It was probably just one of the Brothers or a construction worker. That's all," he said, putting his hand on Charlie's shoulder to reassure him. "You're safe, Charlie. Abbot Ambrose will make sure no one is going to bother you."

"But what about Doug—" The words stuck in Gus' throat as he caught Howard's sharp, disapproving glare. "He's right," Gus said, trying sound more positive in order to recover from his mistake.

"No." Charlie shook his head. "You were right the first time, Gus." Charlie's tone became stronger and angrier. "I'm tired of being afraid. It's time Dougary and his goons were afraid."

"That's more like it." Howard nodded with a smile. "That's the old Charlie. Come on, look over here," he said as he headed for the south window.

Charlie pushed himself away from the wall with a burst of defiant bravery, but it disappeared as soon as he passed in front of the east window. He glanced out at the trees, not seeing anything, as he hurried over to the south window.

The view from the south was a lot different from the other directions. The forest seemed not as close, and they could see further. In the distance, Charlie noticed a clearing on a smaller hilltop not far away.

"What's that?" he asked and pointed toward the area.

Howard looked in the direction Charlie was pointing.

"Oh, that's Black Butte," he said nonchalantly. "It's part of the Abbey's property. They even own those farm fields you see way over there and the orchards over there." He pointed in the distance toward the west of the butte.

"I can't believe I've been here all this time and I never knew about Black Butte," Gus said in amazement. "Hey, can we go there?" he asked excitedly.

"No!" Howard snapped sharply. "It's off limits."

"Why?" Charlie asked, more curious about why Howard had reacted so sternly. He did not act that way when they found out about the tunnel.

"I don't know." Howard shrugged. "It just is."

"Since when has that ever stopped you?" Gus teased.

Howard gave Gus a stern look. "We are forbidden!" he repeated emphatically, then walked over to the west window.

Charlie's curiosity was piqued. He stared at the clearing on Black Butte, and wondered what was out there that Howard did not want them to see. Slowly, he followed Howard and Gus.

Silently, they looked out at the rooftop of the Abbey.

Charlie turned away as he remembered his ordeal in the attic; when Dougary's father had held him out of the broken window by his ankles. He could have died had it not been for Brother Simon. Gus and Howard continued to laugh and talk as they looked out at the view. Charlie stared at the bells and ropes. Suddenly the ropes moved.

"Ah, Howard," he said, his eyes watching the ropes intently. "What time is it?"

"Oh my god!" Howard gasped as he looked at his watch. "We've got to get out of here. The bells are going to ring for Vespers any minute!"

The three quickly hurried to the trap door. Suddenly Charlie's fear came rushing back. He froze. He had never thought about having to climb down from the bell tower when he was climbing up.

"Gus, you go first, but not too fast," Charlie said, putting his hand on Gus' shoulder. Slowly, cautiously, the two started down the stairs together. Charlie blinked hard trying to get his eyes to adjust to the dark. Suddenly, there was a flash of light below them just as Howard closed the door above them. Charlie dismissed the thought as he concentrated on getting down the stairs safely.

Once all three were safely back in the hall of the fourth floor and heading for their dorm, the bells began to ring out, alerting the monks that it was time for evening prayers. Charlie looked at Howard.

"That was close."

"Oh, we had plenty of time," Howard scoffed. "Hey, Gus, what did you think of my secret place?"

Gus shrugged and smiled. "It was pretty neat."

"Well, you were sure brave up there," Howard smirked. "I thought you'd have chickened out on me, like you did about helping me prepare for our stake out in the attic."

Gus glared at him. "Well, it's different in the tower."

"Yeah, right." Howard nodded mockingly. "Well, just don't tell anyone about it. Otherwise we could get into trouble and I'll have to find another secret place."

"Gus won't tell," Charlie said, looking at Gus intently. "Will you?"

"Even Dougary and his goons couldn't drag it out of me!"

"Drag what out of you, pig boy?" An all too familiar voice greeted them from behind.

Howard clenched his teeth and doubled up his fists as he spun around to face Dougary and his two dim-witted goons, Travis and Larry.

"Never mind," Gus spoke up defiantly from behind Howard.

"Woo," Dougary mocked. "Well, you girls can go ahead and keep your little secret. But I'd be worried if I were you. Once Father Vicar is appointed Dean, even old Simple Simon won't be able to protect you," Dougary said smugly. "You'll finally get what's coming to you, MacCreepy."

"Don't count on it, dog breath," Charlie said through clenched teeth as he stepped in front of Howard. "Your father didn't scare me, and I'm certainly not afraid of a low-life like you. Word of warning, don't cross me or you'll be joining your father in the nut house."

Dougary's face turned red with anger. He seemed flustered for a moment, then blurted out, "I've something special in mind for you, MacCreepy. You just wait. Your days are numbered."

"Not if I don't get you first. You'd better keep looking over your shoulder," Charlie threatened. "Come on Howard, Gus, we've better things to do then talk to these morons."

The three turned around and left Dougary silently seething.

"You shouldn't do that, Charlie," Gus said fearfully as he looked over his shoulder at Dougary and his goons.

"Don't listen to him, Charlie," Howard shook his head and grinned proudly from ear to ear. "You did good, but you aren't really serious about getting Dougary, are you?"

"I'm serious," Gus interrupted, grabbing Charlie's arm before Charlie could answer. He turned Charlie around to face him.

The smile faded from Charlie's lips as he looked first at Gus and then at Howard.

"Why?" Howard asked for Charlie.

"Because Dougary could really hurt you, that's why," Gus answered and looked directly at Charlie. "Oh don't look at me like that. I'm serious. If Dougary's dad is nuts and tried to kill you, then maybe it runs in their family. And another thing, Dougary has nothing to lose. So he ends up in some juvie home, it's not as if he has anywhere else to go."

A chill ran up Charlie's spine as he realized that Gus was right. He put his arm around Gus' shoulders. "Thanks, Gus. I'll keep that in mind and be more careful," he tried to reassure him while his mind began to formulate a plan.

"We'd better get ready for dinner. Our clothes are a bit dirty from the dust in the tower. Come on." Howard said.

"I'm not that dirty," Gus protested as he looked over his robes.

Howard glared at him as he held the door to their dorm open for them. Gus silently obeyed and entered.

The three walked over to their lockers that were built into the south wall of the dormitory, on either side of the doors. Gus' locker was at the end, in the corner. Howard's and Charlie's lockers were beside each other and just one locker away from Gus'. Charlie opened his locker and looked at his long black cassocks. At first when he came to Saint Michael's he was not sure what he thought of their strange uniforms, but now, he gave it little thought as he slipped his arms into the long sleeves and began buttoning up the front of his clean cassock. He grabbed one of his freshly cleaned, white surplices, the color worn by all members of the Altar Boys Club, and slipped it over his head. His arms found the big bellowing sleeves with ease. He stuffed his dirty cassock and surplice into his laundry bag and closed the closet door.

Howard finished looking at his thick, curly, black hair in the small mirror he hung on a small nail on the inside of his locker door. He closed his closet door and glanced at Gus.

Gus closed his locker and snapped his new padlock shut. He froze when he saw Howard's frown.

"Wha-?" he asked.

Howard shook his head, as he looked Gus over. Gus' red surplice, the color of Saint Nicholas dorm members, was not on straight, the wide collar band was draped over his right shoulder. He had also skipped a button on his cassock so the hem was uneven at the bottom.

"Honestly, Gus," he said, and walked over to him. "Do I need to get you a mirror?" He straightened Gus' surplice.

"No," Gus answered smugly. "I'll do it," he said, and pulled away as Howard stooped to re-button his cassock.

"Okay," Howard said standing back up. "Hey, I've got something to do. I'll see you both downstairs."

Before either of them could say another word, Howard disappeared out the door.

"So, where is he going in such a hurry?" Gus asked as he finished buttoning his cassock. He did not really expect an answer, but he was glad Howard had left. He hated the way Howard always made him feel so stupid.

"Come on," Charlie sighed. "Let's go to dinner."

The two boys headed back down the hallway and stairs to the refectory on the first floor.

IT WAS A DREAM

The dormitory was dark. Charlie sat, curled up, in the corner of his bed. Only the soft sounds of sleep could be heard. Even though the room was cool, tiny beads of sweat dampened his hair and ran down his cheeks. He stared at the darkness around him, searching for the shadow that had awakened him again.

"It was a dream," Charlie whispered out loud, trying desperately to convince himself. But it seemed so real, he thought. He felt his neck where the shadow had touched him. There was something odd about it. The hand was neither cold nor warm when it touched his throat. "It was a dream," Charlie repeated, feeling more assured.

"What?" Howard stirred in his bed. He groggily looked over at Charlie and tried to focus his eyes without his glasses.

"Nothing," Charlie said and started to slip back down under the covers.

Howard realized what Charlie was not telling him. He propped himself up on one elbow. "It was that dream again?" he said and rubbed his eyes.

"Yeah," Charlie nodded and admitted. "It just seemed so real. When I opened my eyes, the shadow was standing over me again. But this time his hands were around my neck. It was so odd. It was like I could almost feel his hands but yet they didn't feel real. I jumped and suddenly the shadow was gone. It disappeared."

"Maybe you should talk to someone about it? Maybe talk to your counselor or how about Prior Emmanuel?" Howard suggested.

"No, he's too busy." Charlie shook his head. "Besides, they would only tell me it's just my imagination."

"True." Howard nodded and then lay back down on his bed. "Well, we can talk about it in the morning. Try to get some sleep." He yawned.

"Hey, Howard," Charlie said, while he continued staring blindly at the ceiling.

"Yeah?" Howard looked at him.

"Have you ever heard anyone talk about the novice that ran away?"

"Ran away?" Howard repeated, almost asleep.

"Yeah, I overheard Dominic telling a bunch of the guys about this novice who had to guard the cemetery chapel and how he was frightened away when the dead monk's body sat up in its coffin."

"Oh, that." Howard yawned again. "It's just another one of those spooky stories the older guys like to scare the younger ones with." He brushed it off.

"Do you think it is true?"

"No," Howard answered confidently. "You can verify it with Abbot Ambrose, when we see him." He yawned again and turned over. "Try to get some sleep, Charlie. Don't think so much!"

"Okay," Charlie sighed. As he lay down, he scooted back against the wall. From there he could see the dormitory doors. Even though his mind was sure it was a dream, there was part of him deep down that was not and was frightened.

FATHER ICHABOD

Abbot Ambrose stood behind the head table as the boys filed quietly into the refectory behind their prefects. First, Brother Conrad and the boys from Saint Sebastian dorm; next, Brother Simon and Saint Nicholas dorm; after them, Brother Owen and the boys form Saint Thomas and, finally, the boys from Saint Peter entered without their prefect Father Vicar. Charlie glanced up at as he passed in front of Abbot Ambrose. The Abbot did not seem to notice, apparently too distracted by his thoughts to see him.

Please, Charlie pleaded silently as though his great-uncle could read his mind, do not name Father Vicar as our new dean.

Charlie took his place behind his chair and waited silently with the rest of the boys. The familiar clap of the small wooden block against the head table signaled the beginning of Grace. Charlie bowed his head as Abbot Ambrose said the prayer. Afterward, another clap of the block signaled they could speak.

Howard and Charlie quickly sat down. The brothers assigned as servers made their way around each table with plates of French toast and scrambled eggs with ham. Gus eyed his plate hungrily, and once it was set before him, began eating as though he were starved.

"You never said where you went last night before dinner," Charlie said to Howard.

"I went to see Brother Vincent," Howard confessed, pouring himself a glass of orange juice.

Gus looked up from his food, a bit of maple syrup dripping down his chin. Charlie motioned for him to wipe it off before it fell on his robes. Gus quickly cleaned it off with his napkin.

"Well, what did he say?" Charlie asked eager to hear whether or not Austin had told him the truth.

"He said that Austin did break his pen in class," Howard reluctantly admitted before taking a big gulp of his juice.

"So, it wasn't Austin who's been stealing my mail?" Charlie asked. Part of him was pleased at the news. He liked Austin and wanted to believe him.

"I'm confused. If it wasn't Austin, who else could it be?" Gus asked.

"I don't know!" Howard snapped. "Why are you asking me?" He pushed his plate away angrily.

Gus stopped chewing and looked as though he had been scolded and was about to cry.

"Don't worry about it, Gus." Charlie smiled at him reassuringly. "I guess we still have a mystery to solve."

"Oh, no." Howard shook his head. "Leave me out of this. I'm tired of the whole missing mail thing."

Charlie knew why Howard was upset. He was so certain Austin was guilty, and he hated being wrong. Charlie looked at Howard and fought the urge to say, I told you so. He picked up his orange juice and took a drink.

Gus stuffed the last bite of his French toast into his mouth. After he finished, he sat eyeing Howard's and Charlie's plates. Neither had touched their French toast.

"Okay," Charlie sighed and cautiously slid his plate across the table. "You may have my French toast."

"Thanks," Gus said, and pulled the two slices onto his plate. He quickly slid Charlie's plate back across the table.

Out of the corner of his eyes, Charlie saw Howard frowning at him.

"What does it hurt?" He turned to Howard and shrugged.

"At least it's not going to waste."

"Yeah," he agreed. "But still, Gus shouldn't eat so much. It's not healthy."

"He'll burn it all off by lunch going back and forth to class," Charlie added and picked at his scrambled eggs with his fork. "Speaking of class, where is it going to be?"

"I heard ol' B. S. say that it's gonna be in the old stone building just beyond the pool house," Howard answered.

Charlie gave Howard a frown. "You shouldn't call him that," he said.

Howard rolled his eyes. "Okay, Brother Simon," he corrected himself and slid his plate over to Gus. "We have to be down there right after breakfast."

The rest of the meal passed quietly. The clap of the wooden block silenced what little talking there was. Abbot Ambrose rose to his feet. He looked at all of the young faces in front of him and smiled.

"We all have a busy day ahead of us," he began. "I trust that each of you has his class assignments. If you do not, you can see your prefect for them."

Slowly, he walked around to the front of the head table, and began to stroke his white beard.

"Several of you boys have been asking me about the new dean. I'm pleased to inform you that I have reached a decision. In fact, I was hoping to be able to introduce him this morning, but regrettably, he has been detained. As soon as he arrives, I assure you, I will make the announcement. So, don't worry yourselves over it, just enjoy your classes and enjoy your summer.

"Now remember, let's not be late this morning. We don't want to keep the Brothers waiting," he said as he walked back around the table. "That is all."

Once the concluding prayer was offered, they were dismissed. Charlie, Howard and Gus rushed out the back door of the Abbey.

"Hurry up, Gus!" Howard shouted impatiently. "I want to

get there before you-know-who so we can make sure we all sit together. Or don't you want to sit with us?"

"Yes!" Gus answered and plodded along after Howard and Charlie.

"So whadaya think of Abbot Ambrose's comment?" Howard asked as the three hurried down the path.

Charlie shrugged. "Nothing. Why?"

"It doesn't sound like Father Vicar got the job, that's why." Howard smiled to himself.

"Oh, I don't know." Charlie shook his head. "He wasn't there for breakfast this morning. We're still not out of the woods yet."

"Gee, I hope it isn't him," Gus sighed. "I don't know what I will do if it is."

"There's not much we can do," Howard said. "Unless you know a way to get adopted out of here, you're stuck like the rest of us."

Charlie smiled at Gus. "So, are you excited about the class?" he asked and changed the subject.

"Are you kidding?" Howard asked, sounding exasperated. "I wanted to take the photography class. It's just not fair. Every year it's the same thing. Those jerks in Saint Peter get to the list and they take all the good classes."

"Then why did Dougary and his goons take this one?" Charlie asked. "I wonder if it has something to do with Austin's warning?"

"Oh, you aren't still falling for that are you?" Howard groaned. "He may not have been the one who took your mail, but I still wouldn't trust him."

"But Austin seemed genuinely concerned when he warned me," Charlie said.

"That's right, Howard," Gus gasped like it was a new thought. "And remember Dougary did threaten to get Charlie."

"And Charlie threatened to get Dougary," Howard added. "But I still wouldn't believe anything any of them have to say. They're all a bunch of low-life creeps. Besides, he's probably just trying to scare you and ruin your summer."

Gus' mouth dropped open. "I never thought of that," he breathed. "But I'd still be careful around Dougary," he warned Charlie. "I know how mean he can be."

Charlie was silent. He heard what his friends said, and he remembered how, for a short time, Gus was a member of Saint Peter dorm. Still, he had a feeling deep down that Austin was not as bad as they both thought.

"Hey, did ya get a chance to see who Father Ichabod is?" Howard grinned and asked Charlie.

Charlie looked at Howard with a blank expression. Lost in his thoughts about Dougary, he did not really hear a word of what Howard said.

"Our teacher," Howard repeated and gave an exasperated sigh. "Did you meet him yet?" He grinned fiendishly.

"No." Charlie shook his head.

"Well, you will soon enough. Then you'll know what I mean," Howard gave a slight laugh.

Charlie looked at Gus and rolled his eyes as he shrugged.

"Well, don't believe me. See if I care!" Howard said, and stopped. He folded his arms over his chest and pouted. "Ya know I'm not the only one who thinks Father Ichabod is strange," he said in his own defense.

"Okay, I'm sorry. I believe you." Charlie said, although he was not really sure. "Now can we go to class?"

Howard took a deep breath. Reluctantly, he gave in, and they continued on their way down the path.

The old, stone building was just a few yards from the pool house, just as Howard said. It was built into the side of the hill with ivy covering most of its front. No wonder I've never seen it before, Charlie thought as he looked at the building.

As they drew nearer, Charlie noticed an elderly monk, his back bent over from age, standing beside a bench near what appeared to be a sliding, wooden barn door.

"Now you'll see I'm right," Howard said as they approached the building. "That is Father Ichabod."

"He doesn't look so bad." Charlie shrugged.

Father Ichabod kept his back to the boys while he snuffed out his cigarette in the dirt. He quickly unlocked the heavy wooden door and slid it open.

"Good morning," he greeted them.

Charlie froze in his tracks. Father Ichabod's face looked like it was molded out of reddish-brown clay. It was thin, almost skeletal. His cheeks were sunken. His eyes were red like fire behind his thick glasses. His short hair and mustache were completely white except for the yellowish nicotine stain just under his big nostrils. He smiled warmly at them.

"I told you so," Howard whispered into Charlie's ear and took him by his arm. "Come on."

As Charlie drew nearer, he could smell the thick stale odor of cigarette smoke. Charlie forced a smile.

"Come in, come in," Father Ichabod greeted and held out his hands to welcome them. Charlie fought to keep his shock from showing in his eyes as he looked at Father Ichabod's hands. The old monk's hands and palms were the same reddish-brown as his face. His fingers were long and thin. His fingernails were thick, curled and yellowed like an eagle's talons.

No, it couldn't be him, Charlie thought. Still, he avoided shaking Father Ichabod's hand and slipped into the pottery studio.

"Okay, you're right," Charlie whispered to Howard. Father Ichabod did give him the creeps but not for the reason Howard thought.

"Just take any seat you wish," Father Ichabod instructed them. His voice was raspy. "I'll be there in just a minute." He coughed an awful cough that sounded as though he was about to expire right then and there as he held onto the door.

Charlie looked around the room. He was surprised by how dirty the room appeared in contrast to the cleanliness of the rest of the Abbey and its buildings. Three of the four walls were made of stone and mortar; the fourth was of rustic, rough wood painted in a gray wash. There were no windows at all. The only source of light, other than the two fluorescent shop lights that flickered as they came on above their heads, was a skylight cut into the ceiling. Its opaque glass was covered by a layer of dirt, making it impossible to see the outside.

Cautiously, Charlie made his way into the room. Two odd-looking devices stood near the far wall. They resembled a large spool turned on end and were suspended above the floor by a wooden frame. Built into one rail of the frame was a small bench seat. The spool was also odd. The circular end on the bottom was quite large while the opposite one on the top was flat and much smaller. Charlie turned to Howard.

"What're those?" he asked, pointing at the strange contraptions.

"Pottery wheels," Howard answered. "I saw one of the monks using one once. They're really cool," he added and grinned.

Charlie gave Howard a curious, disapproving look. He could tell Howard had something up his sleeve, but he did not want to think about it at the moment. Instead, he continued looking around the room. In the center of the room eight stools surrounded a long, heavy, wooden table. As with the rest of the room, a layer of dust coated its top. Charlie frowned at the thought of getting his clothes covered by it.

Three coat trees stood to the right of the door. On them were rust colored, artist smocks of various sizes. Beside them was a long counter complete with a sink. Above the sink on a rack, much to Charlie's surprise, hung a row of clean, white hand towels.

Against the remaining stone wall, also coated in dust, stood three sets of cinderblock and wooden plank shelves. There were four shelves per set. Against the opposite wall, the rustic wooden wall, there were more shelves. On these shelves, boxes of pots and goblets of various shapes and sizes were placed. Their rich, colorful glazes with flecks of gold and silver sparkled in the light and fascinated Charlie. Also against that same wall were two large metal barrel-like objects.

"Those are the firing kilns," Howard told Charlie. "They're ovens that bake the clay. You'll see."

"Sit here," Howard said, quickly taking the stool at the end of the table nearest the kilns. Charlie hesitated a moment as he looked at the dusty stool beside Howard. Howard smiled at Charlie and brushed the dust away with his hand. "Go ahead."

Charlie took his seat.

Gus left an empty stool between him and Charlie and sat on the one at the end of the table, away from Howard. He did not want Howard to watch him and criticize him all summer.

"We're going to have a nice big class this year," Father Ichabod said with a raspy cough as he walked into the room. "That means we'll have lots and lots of new goblets and pots. Oh, this is going to be a good summer." He grinned and excitedly rubbed his hands together.

"Didn't I tell you?" Howard said and looked at Charlie. He rolled his eyes and stuck his tongue out of the corner of his mouth.

"I already said, you were right," Charlie whispered. "Be nice."

A loud commotion outside caused Charlie, Howard and Gus to look at the door. As Howard had dreaded, in walked Dougary, Larry and Travis, all wearing their distinctive purple surplices of Saint Peter dorm. They were laughing about something or at someone, Charlie thought, knowing they were up to no good.

A few moments later, Dale, a boy about Charlie's height and weight with brown eyes and freckles, from Saint Sebastian dorm, walked through the door. His brown hair was mussed and a small twig of pine needles was tangled in it. His blue surplice was dusty. Probably from being tripped or pushed down, Charlie suspected, and glared at Dougary.

Dale took the seat across from Howard; Travis and Larry were still wandering around the room looking for trouble. When they noticed where Dale was seated, they both rushed over to the table and stood intimidatingly behind him. Dale looked up and his eyes met Dougary's icy glare. Submissively, he moved to the stool between Charlie and Gus. Dougary smiled and took the seat across from Charlie. Travis sat across from Dale and Larry sat across from Gus.

"Well, I see we're all here," Father Ichabod beamed. "Let's get started, shall we?"

"Let's not and say we did," Dougary sneered under his breath but loud enough for all to hear.

Father Ichabod pretended not to hear and moved to the end of the table between Gus and Larry. "I see a couple of new faces with us. So why don't we get started by introducing ourselves to each other? Just say your name, what dorm you're in, and whatever else you'd like us to know about you.

"I'll begin," he smiled. "My name is Father Ichabod. I have been teaching pottery for nearly thirty-six years. It's been a very fulfilling assignment, and I'm proud to say that the Abbey has profited by its fruits."

"You got that right," Howard whispered out of the corner of his mouth to Charlie. Charlie nudged him with his elbow and frowned at him.

"Okay, now it's your turn," Father Ichabod said. He turned to Howard. "Master Miller, why don't you go next?"

Howard looked a little put out by having to go first but he took a deep breath. "My name is Howard and I'm a member of Saint Nicholas dorm. The best dorm in the whole school," he added, and looked directly at Dougary.

"Oh my," Father Ichabod said with a light chuckle. "I see we're very proud of our dorm. And you?"

"I'm Charlie and I, too, am from Saint Nicholas dorm."

"Charlie?" Father Ichabod repeated and put a bony finger to his lips as he thought to himself. "You wouldn't happen to be the Master Charlie MacCready the whole Abbey has been talking about these past few weeks, are you?"

Charlie could feel his face redden as all eyes turned toward him. He nodded quickly and hoped that Father Ichabod would move on.

"Well, I'm happy to meet you," he beamed. "Such a brave young man you are."

His smile faded quickly as he looked at Dougary. "Oh, don't worry, Master Duggan," he said in a cold tone, "the Abbey has been talking about you, too. But I have to admit, not so favorably."

Charlie and Howard looked down and held their breaths to keep from laughing. Dougary glared at Father Ichabod, and then at the rest of the boys.

"Well, let them talk," Dougary sneered. "The whole school is talking about you, too. About how stupid you are and you stink!"

Father Ichabod recoiled slightly upon hearing Dougary's venomous words.

"Oh, my, my, I see we have some serious anger issues," Father Ichabod said with a smile, a smile that quickly turned cold as ice. "Be careful, boy," he said, his raspy voice deepening. "You don't know to whom you are speaking."

Charlie subconsciously rubbed the goose bumps from his arms as he watched Father Ichabod. His mind flashed to the shadow from his dream. He looked at Howard. He wanted to tell him right then but he dared not.

"And you, young master?" Father Ichabod smiled and looked at Dale. "Tell us about yourself."

All eyes turned to Dale. Dale could feel his pulse speed up. His mouth became dry and his throat tightened. He looked around at their faces and then at Father Ichabod. His hands began to shake.

"M-m-my name is D-d-dale K-k-kaufman," Dale spoke in a nervous voice. "I'm a m-m-member of S-s-saint S-s-sebastian's dorm," he added and quickly looked down at the table.

Instantly a faint snicker rose from the end of the table. Larry and Travis covered their mouths as they continued to laugh. Charlie clenched his teeth and glared at them, but they paid no attention. Father Ichabod appeared not to have noticed.

"My name is Gustav Kugele, Gus," Gus spoke up quickly. He, too, appeared angered by Dougary's goons. "I'm from Saint Nicholas dorm."

"Thank-you, Master Kugele." Father Ichabod nodded. His smile faded to a very dry, serious expression as he looked at the seven of them. "Before we continue, I have a few words to say. While you are in my class there are some rules you are all required to obey. Violation of any of them will result in work crew. And I promise you, you will not like it," he hissed. "Rule number one," he raised his voice and turned his back to them as he began to pace. "You will show each other respect. There will be no laughing at the shortcomings or weaknesses of others. Now, we all know who you are, Master Duggan. You, you are next," he said, looking directly at Travis.

Travis quickly said his name and the name of his dorm. Larry did likewise, not wanting to anger Father Ichabod further.

"Thank you." Father Ichabod nodded and continued to pace. "Now, as I was saying, the rules."

He spun back around and looked directly at Dougary in a fixed stare. "Secondly, you are all to stay away from the kilns at all times. Only I will open them. None of you are to touch them, ever. They get very hot and can seriously injure you.

"Next, there will be no wasting of clay. Clay costs money and we waste neither here. The last rule is," he smiled at them, "have fun and be creative." He lifted his hands into the air in a big circular motion. "Any questions?"

He paused and looked around the room.

"Now, let us begin," he said as he resumed his pacing. "Pottery can be divided into two categories, pottery for a purpose or use and pottery for art. Forming clay into pots, bowls and other utensils has been around for centuries. Why, even the smallest of fragments have given archeologists a wealth of information about early civilizations.

"However." Father Ichabod stopped his pacing again and smiled his stained, toothy smile. "I'm not expecting anyone here to produce such greatness. By the end of this course, though, all of you will be well on your way."

Father Ichabod walked over and leaned against one of the pottery wheels. He looked at his students to be sure they were all paying close attention to what he was saying.

"On a very serious note," he continued. "The Abbey has come to rely on the sales of our pottery to help with the expenses in running the Abbey and the school. The goblets, mugs, vases and bowls we make here will be sold at the Oktoberfest and in our Abbey's gift shop. Your taking seriously this class will greatly help our Abbey and will be useful to you later in life."

"I doubt that," Dougary whispered, half under his breath, but loud enough for everyone to hear.

"Master Duggan." Father Ichabod fixed his gaze sternly on Dougary. "I am quite well aware of your personal situation here. So I suggest you keep your mouth in check."

Though Howard and Charlie tried hard not to laugh, their pleased expressions did not go unnoticed by Dougary. He quietly slumped down on his stool and glared back at them.

"Before we begin, there are a few housekeeping items I want to go over with you," Father Ichabod continued. "You will notice that there are smocks hanging on the coat racks. When you come in, you'll remove your surplices and put on one of the smocks. We want to keep you as clean as possible." He smiled again. "Since our time together is only two and a half hours a day, we'll have one ten-minute break. The closest restroom facilities are at the swimming pool. As you boys become more comfortable working with the clay and the wheel, you'll be permitted to spend some of your own time here, unsupervised as long as you work." Again, he smiled as he looked at them. "But that will be at some future time. You're not ready yet."

"Duh." Howard leaned back toward Charlie and whispered with a slight laugh.

Charlie playfully nudged him and tried to hide his smile.

"Before we get started, go ahead and change into your smocks," Father Ichabod instructed.

The first half of the morning seemed to drag. Even Charlie found it hard to listen to Father Ichabod's lecture about the different types of clay and their composition, so much sand and so much earthy clay. He was glad when it came time for their break. Father Ichabod told them not to stray too far from the building, as they would begin promptly in ten minutes and anyone returning late would receive work crew.

As they stood up to leave, Charlie invited Dale to join Howard, Gus and him. The four walked over to a tall fir tree a short distance from the stone building. From there they could keep an eye not only on the door, but also on Dougary and his goons who were busy chatting with some of the other boys from Saint Peter dorm by the swimming pool building.

"Don't pay any attention to Dougary and his goons," Charlie was the first to speak.

"Yeah, they aren't as smart as they think they are," Howard added.

"Th-th-thank-you guys for not laughing at m-m-me in ca-ca-class," Dale stuttered.

"There wasn't anything funny. Those guys are just blockheads." Charlie shrugged dismissively.

"So, have you always talked like that?" Gus asked, much to Charlie and Howard's shock. They both looked at him with wide eyes and gaping mouths.

However, Dale did not seem to mind the question. "No. It s-s-started after m-m-my mom and d-d-dad d-d-died."

Charlie noticed how red Dale's face became when he spoke. He wondered if Dale was embarrassed by his stutter.

"Isn't there something the doctors can do about it?" Howard asked.

Dale shook his head, apparently not wanting to speak.

"So, have you decided to talk to someone about you know what?" Howard asked Charlie.

Charlie looked at him and shook his head. He did not want to discuss it in front of Gus and Dale.

"What?" Gus spoke up as he noticed the way Charlie

reacted. "Talk to who about what?"

"Oh, it's nothing, really." Charlie turned to Gus and tried to reassure him.

"What do you mean nothing?" Howard jumped in. "You haven't slept. Those nightmares you're having aren't only keeping you awake but me too."

"Nightmares?" Gus questioned.

"Oh, it's really nothing," Charlie said to Gus but clenched his teeth and glared at Howard.

"Fine," Howard said, holding up his hands in surrender. "Have it your way. I was only trying to help."

"I'm sorry. I do appreciate it, Howard," Charlie's tone softened.

Gus looked at both of them. He knew they were keeping a secret from him and he did not like it. He looked at Dale.

"So, who do you think the new dean will be?" he asked and tried to make his annoyance obvious by not looking at the other two.

"I d-d-don't know." Dale shook his head. "I just hope it isn't F-F-Father Vicar." He glanced over at Dougary just in time to see him heading toward them.

Howard noticed Dale's worried expression, and he turned around to see what made Dale so uneasy.

"Oh, great," he sighed. "Here they come, the goon squad."

Charlie and Gus looked over their shoulders and then turned around to face their rivals.

"Hello, ladies." Dougary grinned as though he knew something the others did not.

"What do you want, dog breath?" Howard snapped.

"Oh, nothing." Dougary continued to act smug. "I just heard the news that Abbot Ambrose is going to announce our new dean at lunch and you girls are going to be so surprised."

"Oh yeah?" Gus spoke up in a defiant tone from behind Howard and Charlie. "How do you know?"

"I can't tell you, that." Dougary mocked offense and put his hand over his heart. "What would Abbot Ambrose think of me if I spoiled his surprise? He'll be making the announcement at lunch so you'll just have to wait. Then you'll know." He and his buddies began to laugh.

Howard glared at them. He hated Dougary laughing at him almost as much as he hated not knowing what they knew. He was just about to snap at Dougary when Father Ichabod stuck his head out of the doorway. He called to them all that it was time to return to class. Charlie rushed Howard, Gus and Dale back into the pottery room before anyone could say another word.

As he sat down on his stool, Charlie looked at the mound of red-brown clay on the table in front of him. He looked around the table and each of them had a matching lump before them.

"Now," Father Ichabod greeted them and started his lecture. "The trick to working with clay is to kneed it and work it until it gets pliable. Then you can begin to shape it into whatever you want. If the clay begins to get a bit dry, dip your fingertips into the little bowl of water that you each have before you. Take care not to get the clay too wet. Just a few drops will revive it," he cautioned as he walked around the table. "Also, be sure not to have any air bubbles trapped inside your pots. An air bubble is your enemy. It will cause the pot to crack or in the case of being fired in a kiln, explode."

Charlie looked at Dougary and his goons. For a moment he was sure he saw their eyes light up and a slight fiendish smile spread across their lips. When Dougary noticed Charlie looking at him, he glowered back.

"Now, you may begin kneading your clay," Father Ichabod instructed. "As you do, think about what you want to make out of your clay. Whether it's a goblet, bowl, mug, it's up to you as the artist and the clay."

The boys began to pound and work their mounds of clay. Gus seemed to be having a bit of trouble with his. He furrowed his eyebrows as he pushed his fist into the reddish-brown clay. Charlie smiled while he struggled with his own mound.

"Don't forget your water bowls," Father Ichabod reminded

them.

"Oh," Travis said, and dumped his water bowl on his mound of clay. He then took his fist and slammed it into the clay. Muddy water showered the boys and Travis let out a laugh. Dougary and Larry immediately joined him as they wiped the droplets of muddy water off their faces.

"Master Bleckinger!" Father Ichabod shouted. "Need I remind you that anyone wasting clay will be spending their free time in the hop fields with the Brothers."

The smiles quickly faded from Travis's, Larry's and Dougary's faces.

"Yes, Father Ichabod," Travis answered. "I mean, no. I mean, I understand," he stammered as he tried to stop the puddle of water from dripping off of the table.

Howard smiled and continued to work his clay.

"Once you've made your clay pliable, you can begin to create whatever you and the clay decide. There are several methods you might want to employ. One method is what I call the snake coil. You take your clay and roll it out into a long rope and then begin to coil it into either a cup or bowl. Once you have the shape you want, wet your fingertips and then smooth out the inside.

"Another method you can use is what I refer to as the pinch and pull method. You begin by flattening your clay and then you start to pull it and pinch it into the shape you want.

"No matter how you work your clay, remember that air bubbles are not our friends. They will destroy your piece. So be sure to work the air bubbles out." Father Ichabod continued to pace around the table glancing over the boys' shoulders as he instructed them.

"I'm going to make a bowl," Gus announced as he began to roll out his clay into a long rope. His tongue stuck out of the corner of his mouth as he concentrated on his work.

"Very good, Master Kugele," Father Ichabod commended.

Charlie kept working his clay while he struggled to figure out what to make. He looked at Dale who was forming his clay into a rather crude goblet. He turned toward Howard. He was busy making a rather flat bowl. Still, no inspiration came to Charlie as he pounded his clay flat on the tabletop.

"I'm going to step outside for a moment," Father Ichabod announced to the class. "I'll be right outside the door so no monkey business."

Charlie watched Father Ichabod pull a cigarette out of the pocket in his dusty habit. He slid open the door and stepped outside. He pulled a lighter from another pocket in his habit and lit his cigarette. A puff of white smoke bellowed from his mouth and clouded his face. Suddenly, Charlie had an idea and began to shape his clay quickly.

The second hour of the class seemed to go by quickly. Charlie just finished shaping his clay when Father Ichabod told them to begin cleaning up.

"Now, let's go around the table and tell the class what you've made," Father Ichabod said curiously eyeing the crude shapes on the table before him.

"I made a bowl," Howard said in a rather depressed tone as he looked at his flat bowl with crimped uneven edges.

"I made a bowl, too." Gus said proudly as he looked at the lopsided coiled bowl in front of him.

"A ca-ca-cup," Dale stuttered. His was actually the only one that turned out to resemble what it was.

"I m-m-made a plate," Travis mocked Dale as he looked at the oddly shaped flattened blob in front of him.

"That will be enough of that, Master Bleckinger!" Father Ichabod snapped. "And you, Master Hertz? What do you call that?"

Larry looked at his mound of clay. "I call it a paperweight," he said and then began to laugh out loud.

"That is not funny," Father Ichabod's tone sounded as though he were losing his patience with them. "If you are not going to take this course seriously, then I will be happy to talk to Abbot Ambrose on your behalf. I'm sure the brothers could use the extra help in the fields, since quite a number of them have been reassigned to the new building project."

The room fell deathly silent as the boys looked at each other and their clay creations.

"Well, I agree with you, Father Ichabod," Dougary spoke up in a rather superior tone. "I think some people in here need to be more serious. It's so distracting for the rest of us. I made you an ashtray," he said boastfully, smiling and puffing out his chest.

"My, my," Father Ichabod smiled to himself. "How very thoughtful of you, Master Duggan, and very nice work too."

Charlie shook his head and looked at the ashtray he made. He now wished he had thought of something else to make.

"Master MacCready?" Father Ichabod looked at him. "What have you made?"

Just as Charlie opened his mouth, the bells rang out signaling the end of class. The boys jumped to their feet. Father Ichabod quickly moved aside.

"Before you go, be sure you put your clay creations on the drying shelves and don't forget to wash your hands before changing back into your surplices," he spoke in a loud voice as the boys scrambled about.

Gus and Dale hurried to catch up with Charlie and Howard as they headed back to their dorm.

"What's the hurry?" Gus panted as he caught up to them.

"Nothing," Charlie shrugged. "I just didn't want to let Dougary get a head start on us. Can you believe that brown-noser?" he said disgustedly.

"What? That ashtray thing?" Howard scoffed.

"Yeah," Charlie answered. "That and his comments. I was about to hurl."

"M-m-me too," Dale added, and nodded.

"So, what did you make?" Gus asked Charlie.

Charlie could feel his face redden. "Oh, it was just a bowl," he answered and gave a slight shrug.

Howard smiled as he looked at his best friend. He knew Charlie did not make a bowl. He knew an ashtray when he saw one, but he was not about to speak up. He just let it go.

"Slow down," Gus panted as he tried to keep up with them. "I haven't had anything to eat since breakfast and I'm feeling weak."

"You're always hungry," Howard shook his head. "Come on." He took Gus's arm and hurried him along. "Abbot Ambrose is going to make the announcement about our new dean, and I don't want to be late."

THE NEW DEAN

The refectory was buzzing with noisy whispers and chatter as the boys ate their lunch. Howard and Charlie did not say much as they took turns looking at the head table. Seated beside Abbot Ambrose was seated a monk neither Charlie nor Howard had seen before. He was a blonde-haired man with a square, stern-looking jaw. His eyes were blue, like Charlie's grandmother's, behind his gold wire rimmed glasses. Charlie could not explain it, but there was something about the new monk that made him uneasy.

When the meal was finished, Abbot Ambrose clapped the small block of wood against the head table. The room immediately fell silent and all heads turned toward him. He smiled his usual, friendly smile.

"I trust all of you enjoyed your classes this morning," he said more than asked. "I'm pleased to say, I did not hear any reports of any problems," he added glancing at Dougary and the rest of the Saint Peter boys. "Let's keep it that way, shall we?

"As a reminder, none of you are allowed beyond the fences around the baseball fields. That area is for the construction workers only. There is a lot of machinery and things for boys, such as you, to hurt yourselves on and none of us want that. That goes for the actual construction site as well. It is off limits.

"Now, I know you're all wondering who our guest is this afternoon," Abbot Ambrose nodded at the monk seated beside him. "And I am well aware of the rumors going around that the new dean has arrived." He glanced over at the boys at Saint Peter table.

Charlie looked across the room at Dougary. As their eyes met, Charlie glared. Dougary turned up his nose and looked away.

"At this time," Abbot Ambrose continued. "I would like to introduce to all of you, Father Mark. He has been a member of our Order for nearly twenty-nine years. For the past ten years, he has been serving the parishioners of Our Lady of Sorrow's Parish in Forest Heights as their associate pastor and vice principal of their school." Again, he motioned to the monk beside him. "After much persuading, I am pleased to announce he has accepted the position of Dean of Men."

Abbot Ambrose turned to Father Mark and led the boys in a brief welcoming applause. Howard nudged Charlie and gave a sigh of relief as they clapped their hands.

Father Mark smiled and stood up. Charlie was surprised to see how tall he was. Father Mark stood as tall, if not a bit taller than Abbot Ambrose.

"Over the next few weeks, as Father Mark gets settled into his new position, he will also be getting to know each of you boys better. I would appreciate your making him feel welcome." Abbot Ambrose turned and looked directly at the boys at the Saint Nicholas table. "To start things off, Father Mark has asked to meet with the members of Saint Nicholas dorm this afternoon. So once the meal is concluded, I would appreciate it if you boys would gather in your dorm."

Again, Charlie glanced at Father Mark. His body tensed when he noticed Father Mark staring at him. Charlie slumped a bit in his chair and looked away. He had a bad feeling about the new dean. *Why does he seem so familiar?* he wondered.

After the prayer, the boys filed out of the refectory. Though

Charlie did not look, he could feel Father Mark's eyes on him as he passed in front of the head table. Once in the hall he turned around and took Howard aside.

"I don't think I like Father Mark," he whispered.

"Why? We haven't even met him yet," Howard asked, with a puzzled look on his face.

"I know but he keeps staring at me." Charlie looked over his shoulder toward the refectory.

"Oh, you're just imagining it."

"No I'm not," Charlie insisted. "He was staring at me."

"Charlie," Howard sighed. "I think you worry too much. Father Mark seems okay. Come on; let's get back to the dorm before all the other boys take the chairs."

Charlie took a deep breath. He glanced over his shoulder at the refectory just one more time before following after Howard. *Maybe Howard's right. Maybe I am being a bit paranoid.* Charlie quickened his pace and caught up with Howard.

The dormitory was quiet when Charlie and Howard walked through the doorway. With the students gone, there were only the five residents left. Gus looked up from his seat in one of the overstuffed chairs. His smile quickly disappeared when he looked at Howard. Sheepishly he stood up and moved over to the sofa. Howard dropped down in the chair.

"Thanks, Gus," he said and glanced at Charlie who was frowning at him. "What?" he shrugged innocently. "He moved. I didn't say anything." Howard defended himself.

"Oh, never mind," Charlie said. He shook his head and sat down on the sofa next Gus.

"I'm so glad Father Vicar wasn't named the new dean," Gus said in a slight whisper. "He's so mean. You remember when I was a member of Saint Peter dorm? Father Vicar made me clean toilets during work crew."

"Don't remind me," Charlie said, remembering how Gus and Dougary's goons had dunked his head in one of those toilets.

"I hope Father Mark is nice," Gus said wistfully.

Howard ignored the bit of conversation and looked at the other boys. As the one who'd been a member of Saint Nicholas dorm the longest, he had seen them all come to Saint Michael's, knew their stories. He knew all about them and felt protective of them even though two were older than him.

Before anyone could say another word, the doors to the dormitory opened, and Father Mark walked into the room. He smiled at the faces of his new charges as they nervously looked up at him. Gus and Todd jumped to their feet to stand in a line as Brother Simon had insisted they do but Howard's silent glare sat them back down.

"Good afternoon," Father Mark greeted them.

No one said a word. Father Mark did not seem to mind.

"As you just heard, I've been away from the Abbey for many more years than I would've liked, but we do as we are assigned." Again he smiled and clasped his hands in front of his stomach. "Now, I've heard that Brother Simon, though a dear Brother, is very strict with you boys and that he has many rules. While I agree with the principle of having rules, I don't think we need to be such sticklers, so I will talk to him. After all, boys will be boys, won't they," he said as he looked at each of them. He stopped when he came to Charlie, his gaze fixed on him. "And this is your home."

Howard's smile faded as he looked back and forth at Father Mark and Charlie. For a moment it seemed as though the new dean was only talking to Charlie. Howard shrugged it off and relaxed a bit more.

Charlie felt an uneasiness growing inside of him. It gripped his chest and caused dizziness in his head. He looked away, breaking their stare.

The rest of the meeting with Father Mark seemed to go fine for the other boys. They laughed and joked with each other while they showed Father Mark their cubicles and their most treasured possessions. Charlie could not shake his feeling of uneasiness. He did not know what it was, but something about Father Mark was disturbing. While the group kept Father Mark busy across the dorm, Charlie quietly slipped through the doors and into the hall.

"Cha-Cha-Charlie," the unmistakable voice called to him as he approached the stairs.

Charlie turned around and smiled. Dale hurried after him.

"Wa-wa-wait up," he said almost out of breath. "Where are you g-g-going?"

"Nowhere really. I just had to get out of there," he answered and nodded toward his dorm. "There's just something about Father Mark that gives me the creeps." He looked over his shoulder in the direction of his dorm again. "Say, do ya wanna go for a walk with me? Check out how they're coming on the new building?" He turned back to Dale.

Dale nodded with a smile and the two headed off.

The warm afternoon sun had already begun its descent in the clear blue summer sky as the two boys headed across the front grounds. Suddenly a chill ran up Charlie's spine. He stopped. The feeling that someone was watching him paralyzed him with fear. Slowly, forcibly, Charlie turned his head toward the forest. His eyes narrowed as he strained to see in the shadows of the trees. Suddenly, he let out a gasp. Standing beside a tree was a dark figure. One moment it was there, and the next it was gone.

Dale stopped and turned around. He looked at Charlie curiously. Charlie stood frozen, his eyes wide and unblinking as he stared at the forest. Dale looked at the woods and then back at Charlie.

"Wha-wha-what is it?"

Charlie glanced at Dale then quickly returned to searching shadows in the forest. "Did you see that?" he asked in a hushed whisper.

"S-s-see wha-wha-what?" Dale answered him with a question, and looked at the dark woods again.

"Someone's out there," Charlie answered.

"I don't s-s-see anyone." Dale said as he searched the shadows. "Are you sh-sh-sure?"

"Yes," Charlie said flatly.

"M-m-maybe it was one of the wa-wa-workers?" Dale offered as an explanation.

"Never mind, come on," Charlie's tone was a bit annoyed, because Dale sounded as though he did not believe him.

The sound of heavy machinery and the buzz of chainsaws broke the silence of the hilltop as the two boys approached a clearing. Quite a distance away from the construction site, Charlie spotted Larry talking to one of the workers. Charlie looked at the man. He was a tall man, dressed in dark blue coveralls. He was wearing a hard hat but Charlie could see that he had short blonde hair.

"Who's that?" Charlie asked Dale.

"M-m-m," Dale struggled to speak. He felt frustrated that the words seemed to be stuck in his throat. He pulled at the roman collar of his black cassock. "Larry's dad," he blurted out all at once.

"His dad?" Charlie asked. "Are you sure?" He looked at Dale.

Dale nodded. "He wa-wa-works for a ca-ca-construction company. I overheard Fa-fa-father Emmanuel and Abbot Ambrose talking. Abbot Ambrose di-di-didn't s-s-sound too happy that Fa-fa-father Emmanuel had hired the ca-ca-company M-M-mister Hertz works for."

Charlie looked back at Larry and his father. He could not help but remember when he saw Dougary talking to his father and what happened when Dougary's father had snapped in the attic, almost throwing him out the window. Charlie shivered.

"Come on," he said to Dale. They continued toward the clearing a safe distance away from the construction area.

"Wow," Dale gasped as he looked at the construction site.

Where once tall pine trees stood was now a large clearing covered with wood chips and ruts from the big tires of the log trucks. Charlie and Dale watched as the men loaded the last of the fallen trees onto a truck. Once the truck roared down the road and out of sight, the boys returned to their dorms.

"So where did you disappear to?" Howard asked as Charlie plopped down on his bed across from him.

"I just went for a walk with Dale," Charlie answered. "We went to see how they're coming with the new building." He paused for a moment and wondered if he should say anything to Howard. "I saw it again," he said in an almost whisper.

Howard gave him a puzzled look.

"The shadow," Charlie added, "in the woods. It was watching me from the edge of the woods on the front grounds."

"It's probably just the sunlight playing tricks on you." Howard shook his head. "Besides, if there were someone out there in the woods, I'm sure one of the brothers would know about it by now."

Charlie just looked at Howard for a moment not sure what to think. Could he be right? Could it have been just the sunlight?

"So, where's Father Mark?" he asked, scanning the dorm.

"Oh, he left quite a while ago," Howard said. He flipped the page of one of his favorite comic books and looked at the pictures.

"Good," Charlie answered flatly. He lay on his back and stared at the ceiling.

Howard put his comic book down and rolled over onto his side to face Charlie. He propped himself up on one elbow. "So, what's the matter with Father Mark?"

Charlie looked at Howard. "I don't know. He just gives me the creeps."

"There you go again," Howard sighed then swung his legs around and sat up. "First, you're worried Dougary's out to get you, then this shadow, and now Father Mark too?"

"Dougary *is* up to something," Charlie insisted. "I just know it. And the shadow is real. I'm not just making it up."

Howard shook his head. "Honestly, Charlie, you've got to get a grip on yourself and relax. Not everyone is out to get you."

"I wish I could be sure," Charlie sighed. He looked back up at the ceiling. "It's just that there's something about Father Mark—"

"It's always something," Howard interrupted in a disgusted tone much like the one he used with Gus and Rick. He slapped his thighs and stood up. "You're wrong about Father Mark. He's a nice guy. You haven't even given him a chance. You like ol' B. S. and he's a million times worse in my book. So if I give B. S. a chance, why won't you lighten up on Father Mark?"

Charlie did not say a word. He could tell that Howard was becoming angry with him and he did not want to fight with his best friend. Instead he turned over, picked up his writing tablet from the windowsill, and began writing a letter to his grandmother. Howard shook his head in frustration and walked out of the dorm.

THE SHADOW

The July sun beat down on the four boys as they headed toward the pottery studio. Tiny beads of sweat already dotted Gus's forehead. He tugged at the collar of his black cassock.

"Honestly, I don't think I can take another day like this," he panted.

"You'll be fine," Howard assured him, and shook his head. Howard did not seem to mind the heat, but then he did not seem to mind anything.

"I'm wa-wa-with Gus," Dale stammered. "It's t-t-too hot." He wiped the sweat from his brow with the back of his hand.

Charlie frowned as he tagged along. He was not really following their conversation. His thoughts were elsewhere. Even though it had been nearly a month since he mentioned the shadow to Howard, he was still plagued by the nightmares. And as they walked along the path, he could not shake the feeling that he was being watched. It was a fear he kept to himself.

It had also been just as long with Father Mark as their new dean. Charlie was careful to avoid him. Even at their Altar Boys' Club meetings where Father Mark stood in for their sacristan, Charlie was successful in not being caught alone with him. His uneasiness grew even more when he wrote his grandmother about Father Mark, and she responded that she did not know a priest by that name. She asked him for a description of Father Mark, so Charlie sent off his reply that morning. He glanced at Howard as he walked beside him. How he wished he could talk to his best friend about this, but he knew it was not a good idea. His thoughts changed to Rick.

"Only seven more weeks 'til Rick and the others are back," Charlie spoke up.

"Yeah," Gus agreed, continuing to tug at his collar. "Seven more weeks of this miserable weather, too. I can't wait for summer to be over."

"Oh, stop whining!" Howard snapped.

Charlie smiled and shook his head. He did not care for the heat either, but knew it was no use complaining. He glanced into the woods as they headed down the dirt path. Suddenly a shadow darted behind a tree. The familiar numbing rush of fear swept over Charlie. He froze in his tracks.

"What was that?"

"What was what?" Howard asked and turned around.

Suddenly Charlie realized he had actually spoken. He looked at Howard and then back into the trees.

"Ah, over there," he answered hesitantly and pointed at the woods. "Someone or something moved out there."

Howard looked to where Charlie was pointing. He did not see anything. "Charlie, you're just seeing things. There's nothing out there. Come on before we're late," he said not even trying to hide his irritation.

"No, I'm not just seeing things, Howard," Charlie protested as the four resumed their walking. "There was something out there."

"As I told you before, it's probably just a shadow caused by the sun shining through the trees," Howard answered and raised his hands in gesture at the sunlight and shadows over their heads. He continued walking at a faster pace, obviously annoyed with Charlie.

"It wasn't the sun," Charlie insisted, the hurt caused by his best friend not believing him was evident in his voice.

Howard stopped and turned around. He looked at Charlie and frowned.

"I'm sure it's not what you're thinking. It's nothing. Come on," he said and put his arm around Charlie's shoulders. It was his way of apologizing.

"What d-d-did it look like?" Dale asked as his own fears began to rise. He remembered their day on the front grounds when Charlie said he saw a shadow.

Charlie thought for a moment and then shrugged. "I don't know. I didn't really get a good look before it was gone."

"Was it a bear?" Gus asked in a hushed whisper as he looked over his shoulder fearfully.

"Howard's right," Charlie answered with a bit of uncertainty still in his voice. "It's probably nothing."

Gus shivered. "Let's hurry up. I'm getting scared."

Before either Charlie or Howard could say anything, Gus and Dale took off in a run toward the studio. Howard, not wanting to admit he was spooked too, walked after them but quickened his pace.

As they neared the studio, Howard's fears subsided. He slowed his pace. He looked at Charlie and felt a different fear growing inside him. Ever since the incident in the attic, Charlie had been acting strangely. He thought about talking to Father Mark about it, but he knew Charlie would be upset with him if he did. He wondered if he should say something to Abbot Ambrose. Charlie seemed to be closest to the Abbot, perhaps he would not mind. Howard dismissed the thought as he entered the pottery studio.

"Well, good morning boys," Father Ichabod greeted them as they stumbled into the pottery studio. "It's nice to see a group so enthused about their pottery lesson." He smiled broadly.

"Oh," Howard scoffed while took off his surplice and hung it on the coat rack. "Charlie just spooked Dale and Gus, that's why they were running."

Father Ichabod did not appear to have heard Howard. He

was busy taking a batch of bowls and mugs from the kiln and placing them on the table.

"Wow," Gus breathed as he took his seat. "Charlie, look at your bowl. It's beautiful."

Charlie smiled proudly as he looked at the orange and yellow speckled glaze that covered his bowl.

"Yes, Master MacCready, it is." Father Ichabod nodded as he took the last of the contents from the kiln. "In fact, the majority of the class's work turned out extremely well. I think we will be able to fetch a good price for them at Oktoberfest."

The smiles on their faces slowly vanished as the boys remembered their work was not theirs to keep.

"Oh, come, come now," Father Ichabod said as he pulled the hot mitts from his hands. "Why such long faces? Before any of the pieces are sold, each of you will have the opportunity to select a piece from your work that you would like to keep. Remember, we have to pay for our keep and the sale of our pottery helps."

Just as Father Ichabod finished speaking, the door to the studio slid open. Dougary entered followed closely by Larry and Travis. The three were noisily laughing and punching each other in the shoulders as they stomped over to the coat rack. They traded their purple surplices for their pottery smocks and then took their seats.

"So nice of you boys to join us." Father Ichabod frowned at them as they continued laughing. "Perhaps Master Duggan would like to share with the rest of the class what is so funny?"

Dougary looked at Charlie, Howard, Gus and Dale. They were all looking at him intently. His smile faded instantly. "No," he said dryly. "I'll pass."

"Then that will be the end of it," Father Ichabod said and broke into a raspy coughing bout. When he was through, he looked at the boys. "Let us begin.

"Now, today we're going to continue working with the wheel." Father Ichabod walked over to one of the pottery wheels and placed a hand on its flat surface. "Over the last few weeks

I've been guiding you as you worked on the wheel. Well, today I think you're ready to work on your own.

"You will all begin with a simple vase shape," Father Ichabod instructed while he drew an outline on the portable chalkboard he moved beside one of the wheels. "Think of a drinking glass," he said. "To make this shape, gently begin by pressing your thumbs in the center of the mound as the wheel is turning and then move one of your hands to the outside of the cup and gently draw it up. Remember to wet your hands from time to time but don't overdo it. You want your clay to remain stiff. Too much water and it won't hold its shape.

"Master Duggan and Master Kugele take your place at the wheels. The rest of you boys gather around."

A look of panic came over Gus's face as he nervously walked over to one of the pottery wheels.

"Don't worry, Gus," Charlie smiled encouragingly. "You'll do just fine."

Gus pulled his cassock up to his waist and slid onto the small bench of the pottery wheel. Dougary took his place at the other pottery wheel facing Gus. The rest of the boys moved in closer.

"Now begin by giving your bottom wheel a kick with your left foot. This will get your top wheel spinning. You need to keep the wheel spinning rapidly while you work with your clay. Coordination is a must here," continued Father Ichabod.

Gus pushed the large wheel beneath his feet and the small flat wheel in front of him began to spin. He continued to kick his feet moving the wheel faster and faster.

"Very good, Master Kugele," Father Ichabod smiled revealing his yellow, smoke stained teeth. "Now, once you feel comfortable with the speed of your wheel, wet your hands a bit and then take a ball of clay. This is the hardest part of using the wheel and the most critical, so take your time. First find the center of your wheel and then forcefully slam the ball of clay down. Don't worry if you don't get it the first time. Just stop your wheel and then start over."

Gus dampened his hands in the water barrel next to his wheel and then grabbed a big fistful of reddish-brown clay. He nervously formed it into a ball. He looked at his spinning wheel. Tiny beads of sweat began to dot his forehead again. He leaned over to dampen his hands again, but the ball of clay slipped from his hands and fell into the bowl of water. He quickly scooped it up, hoping that no one noticed.

Dougary slammed his clay down on his wheel with a loud thud. Tiny droplets of dirty water spun off the wheel and splattered the front of his smock. He smiled proudly seeing he hit the center of the wheel on his first attempt.

The panicked look returned to Gus's face and he glanced over at Howard and Charlie.

"Don't worry," Howard tried to reassure him. "You can do it."

Gus's heart pounded nervously in his chest. The clay in his hands was very soft. He looked at Dougary and then back at his wheel. He raised the dripping clay ball over his head and then slammed it down on the rapidly spinning wheel. To his horror, he had missed the center of the wheel and the overly wet clay began to splatter on the boys.

"Stop! Stop!" Charlie shouted and turned his face away from the flying clay. He put his hands up in a feeble attempt to shield himself.

"Gus!" Howard shouted and ducked, covering his head as globs of clay flew through the air.

Dougary, Larry and Travis roared with laughter as they, too, tried to shield themselves.

Gus' face turned red as he leaned over his wheel and tried to stop the clay from flying off. He flattened his feet against the large wheel and slowly the spinning stopped.

"Master Kugele," Father Ichabod shook his head and smiled kindly. "I think you should clean up a bit before you give it another try."

Gus hurried over to the sink with Charlie and Howard to wash up.

"Master Duggan." Father Ichabod turned his attention to Dougary. "You stopped your wheel," he said coldly. "Please resume."

Dougary coughed as he tried to stop from laughing. "Yes, Father Ichabod," he said and gave his wheel a kick.

"I can't believe what a mess I made," Gus moaned as he wiped the front of his smock with a paper towel.

"Don't worry about it," Charlie tried to console him and handed him another paper towel.

"But did you hear them laughing at me?"

"Pay no attention to them," said Charlie. He put his hand reassuringly on Gus' shoulder.

"What a mess," Howard groaned as he tried to wipe the dirty water spots from his glasses. "You are such a klutz, Gus."

Gus looked at Howard and tears filled his big brown eyes. His chin began to quiver and then the tears began to fall.

"I'm sorry," Gus sobbed.

Charlie looked at Howard in disbelief. "Howard!" he snapped.

"What?" Howard gave Charlie an innocent look. "He is a klutz. Just look at us."

"Be nice," Charlie said harshly and then turned back to Gus. "Gus, stop crying. You didn't do it on purpose."

"He-he's right," Gus's voice quivered as he continued to cry. "I'm a loser. I-I can't do anything right."

Suddenly Howard felt guilty. He looked at Charlie, who was still frowning at him. "Gus, I'm sorry. You may be a klutz, but you're our klutz. Besides, this could've happened to any of us. Just wait 'til I have my turn at the wheel." He forced a smile. "Everyone'll need a shower by the time I'm through."

Gus' tears slowly stopped and he dried his cheeks. He smiled at Howard.

The rest of the class period passed uneventfully. After two more attempts, Gus finally hit the center of the wheel. He beamed proudly as he turned out a nice vase. Even Father Ichabod commented on how fine it looked. Gus carefully carried his vase over to his drying shelf. He stood back and admired it for the rest of the period.

After class, the four boys hurried back up the path to the Abbey. They talked among themselves about what they were going to do for the rest of the afternoon. Suddenly Charlie stopped in his tracks. His eyes were wide and his mouth dropped open.

Howard turned around and looked at him. "What's wrong?"

"Very slowly look over your shoulder into the woods," he whispered.

A cold chill ran up Howard's spine. He knew there was nothing there, but with being in the woods and the way Charlie was acting, he could not help but get the creeps. Slowly he turned his head to look. His fears vanished as he looked into the empty woods. He turned back to Charlie.

"You saw it?" Charlie gasped and pointed over Howard's shoulder. "Now do you believe me?"

"Yes," Howard lied. His heart sank as he looked at his friend. "Let's get out of here!"

The four boys raced back to the Abbey. No one bothered to look back or stop until they were safe in their dorm.

"So," Charlie panted. "What do you think it was? A bear, like Gus said?"

Howard tried to slow his breathing. "I don't think so," he answered and shook his head. "It looked more like one of the monks," he lied and hoped the conversation would end.

"You don't think it could be the missing monk, do you?" Charlie asked in a whisper.

"No!" Howard answered a bit too quickly. "It couldn't be. Someone would've seen him years ago and why would he stay around here all this time? Anyway, we don't even know if that story is true."

"What story?" Gus asked and looked that the two of them. "You guys are scaring me."

"It's nothing." Charlie shrugged and shook his head. "It's

probably like Howard said, just one of the brothers."

"Yeah, just one of the brothers," Howard added, trying to convince his friend and stop Gus from worrying.

Charlie sat down on his bed and looked out his window. He was not as sure as Howard that it was one of the brothers. Why would one of the monks be lurking around in the shadows?

THE PHOTOGRAPH

Howard lay on his bed and read the same tattered comic book for the fifth time that summer. He sighed and sat up, bored by the silence. He tossed the comic book back onto the stack on the lower shelf of his nightstand. He glanced across the dorm at Rick's empty bed.

"I wonder what Rick's doing," he said with a heavy sigh.

Charlie looked up from writing another letter to his grandmother. He glanced at Rick's empty cubicle in the opposite corner of their dorm.

"I don't know." He shrugged.

"Well, I hate to say it, but I can't wait 'til he comes back." Howard said.

Charlie smiled to himself. "Why Howard, you care."

Howard looked at Charlie with a funny expression. "What? No, I don't," he said indignantly. "It's just that I'm gonna go nuts. I'm bored and there's nothing to do."

"Correction," a deep voice boomed from around the end of their cubicle wall.

Charlie and Howard looked up as Father Mark walked into view. He smiled kindly at both of them, then fixed his gaze on Charlie. "You boys have plenty to do. There will be a meeting of the Altar Boys' Club this evening after dinner. You boys will be meeting downstairs in visiting room five."

Charlie looked nervously at Father Mark and then turned away.

Father Mark turned around to leave, but then paused. He slowly turned back around and looked directly at Charlie. "Master MacCready, I was wondering if we might have a word this afternoon, after the noon meal?"

Charlie looked at Howard in wide-eyed panic. Howard frowned at him. Charlie looked back at Father Mark.

"Sure," he answered.

"Good." Father Mark smiled and nodded. He turned around, tucked his hands beneath his robes, and walked out of the dorm.

Lunch seemed to drag on. Charlie was hungry, but soon lost his appetite when he saw the bowl of green split pea soup set before him. It actually smelled inviting, but hearing one of the boys on the other side of the refectory refer to it as cow's snot left an image in Charlie's mind that he could not stomach. He had a slice of bread with blackberry jam instead.

After lunch, Charlie told Howard, Gus and Dale he would catch up with them later. Reluctantly, he headed off to Father Mark's office.

Father Mark's office was across the hall from Abbot Ambrose's. Charlie paused and looked at the Abbot's door. Part of him wanted to knock on the Abbot's door and tell him about his fears, but he already knew what his great-uncle would say. He turned away and lightly knocked on the door, hoping Father Mark would not hear and he could leave. If asked, he would honestly claim that no one had answered his knock.

"Enter," came Father Mark's voice from the other side of the door.

Charlie's heart sank. Slowly he turned the doorknob, opened the door, and stepped inside. The room still looked like the other visitation rooms with its marble faux-fireplace on the west wall and tall windows on the north wall. The sofa was replaced with an oak desk. The two winged back chairs were moved around to the front of the desk. Oak bookcases were set up against the east wall and were covered with books, photos and plants. In fact, Father Mark was busy watering a big plant that sat on a stand under one of the tall windows behind his desk.

"Master MacCready," he smiled over his shoulder. "Please, have a seat. I'll be just a second. Plants have to eat, or drink, too."

Charlie sat down in the chair closest to the door. Father Mark finished emptying the small watering can into the soil around the plant and then dried it with a small towel that he kept in the bottom cabinet of one of his bookcases.

"There," he smiled as he turned around. He picked up a file from the top of his desk and then took a seat in the chair beside Charlie. "So, how have you been?" he asked to try to break the ice.

Charlie shrugged. "Okay."

Father Mark nodded to himself. He could tell from his years of dealing with children that Charlie was going to be a tough boy to reach.

"It's such a nice day out, what do you say we go outside for a little walk," he said, and stood up.

"Okay," Charlie shrugged again. Actually, he was relieved at the thought of getting outside in the open, where people could see him and he could run in case his suspicions about Father Mark were correct.

Charlie followed behind as Father Mark led the way through the front doors of the Abbey. The August sun was bright in the clear blue sky. Even though there was a cool breeze, in his black cassock and white surplice, Charlie felt the heat. He looked around for some shade and hoped Father Mark, in his black habit, would have the same idea.

Father Mark obviously did not. He directed Charlie toward the lush green front grounds.

"I noticed that you slipped out of the dorm on my first day," Father Mark began as they walked across the lawn in no particular direction. "I've given you some time and granted you some leeway, but now I would like to know where you went."

Charlie felt even hotter as he grew more nervous. He did not look at Father Mark, but stared blindly ahead. His mind raced back to the day Father Mark came to the Abbey nearly two months ago. He struggled to remember. Finally it came back to him.

"Oh, I met up with Dale from Saint Sebastian," he finally answered with a shrug as though it were no big deal.

"I see." Father Mark nodded. "Since you left early, you missed hearing about my plans. I would like to get to know each of you boys individually; find out what your likes and dislikes are; your hopes and dreams. I thought that I would start by having a talk with each of you, and I have already met with the other boys."

Charlie listened without saying a word. He silently wished for some way to just slip away.

"Abbot Ambrose has given me your file. I must admit that there is not much in it. I understand you are the newest member of the dorm and yet the most famous. The entire Abbey is talking about the brave boy who uncovered the ghost in the attic, but I want to get to know you personally myself."

The more Father Mark spoke, the more nervous Charlie became. He thought and thought and tried to figure out why Father Mark seemed so familiar.

"I read that you are from Hillsborough," Father Mark continued. "That is near the town where I was assigned. In fact, several of my former parishioners were from there."

Charlie gave Father Mark a dry look that told him he was less than impressed.

"I read that your grandmother is Ophelia Zenner," Father Mark smiled. "I remember your grandmother, a very nice lady."

Suddenly Charlie felt a jolt and the muscles in his back tightened. He almost stumbled on the lawn. He stopped and looked at Father Mark. That was it, he remembered. He looked like the man his grandmother described. The man his Uncle

Chester had brought with him when he came to see her at Shady Meadows Retirement Home.

Father Mark stopped and looked curiously at Charlie. "Is something wrong? You look a little flushed."

Charlie shook his head, afraid if he spoke his voice would give his fear away.

"I met your grandmother through your cousins. Your Uncle Chester's boys were students of mine," Father Mark explained and smiled.

"Ah-h-h?" Charlie hesitated a moment.

Father Mark gave Charlie another curious look. "Is everything okay?" he asked. "Perhaps we should sit down over there."

He directed Charlie toward the bench by one of the many ponds that dotted the front grounds. The bench was shaded by a big dogwood tree. Around the pond's edge was a well-tended, colorful, flower bed in full bloom. Father Mark sat down and motioned for Charlie to sit next to him.

"There now," Father Mark said, folding his hands on his lap. He gave Charlie quick look. He could tell from the odd look in Charlie's eyes that something was troubling him. "Better?" he asked, to try to draw Charlie out.

Charlie simply nodded. He tried not to tremble as he sat next to the man his grandmother had warned him about. What was he to do now? He looked up at the top of the bell tower barely visible above the tree. He wished he could be there with Howard right at that very moment.

"So, what would you like to talk about?" Father Mark asked, his tone revealing his frustration by Charlie's silence.

Charlie looked at the priest. Questions flashed in his mind but he dared not ask them. "Whatever you want," he answered.

"Okay," Father Mark nodded. "Tell me, what is your most favorite thing, your most prized possession? Perhaps it is something your grandmother may have given you?"

Every muscle in Charlie's body tensed. He instantly thought about the key and medal his grandmother gave him, but he was not about to tell Father Mark.

"I don't know," he said with a slight shrug.

"Well, what about your checkerboard game that Master Miller made for you?" Father Mark asked.

"Yeah, I guess that would be it." Charlie nodded and relaxed a bit. He was relieved the conversation moved into a different direction. His key and medal were safe, for now.

"That was a wonderful Christmas gift," Father Mark continued.

"Howard's my best friend," Charlie said. He kept glancing up at the bell tower and then back down at the goldfish in the pond.

Father Mark was aware that Charlie seemed distracted. He looked up at the bell tower and then back at Charlie. "Is there something wrong with the bell tower?"

"No," he blurted.

"Then, why are you staring at it?"

Charlie began to fidget. "I was just looking at it. It's really tall, isn't it?"

Father Mark smiled and nodded. "Yes, it is."

"I don't like heights." Charlie shivered.

"I don't blame you," Father Mark said. "After what you've been through, I'm not surprised. Are you okay about what happened? Do you want to talk about it?"

"No, I'm fine," Charlie answered much too quickly to sound believable; but it was true, at least, for the most part.

An awkward silence fell between them. Father Mark noticed Charlie's uneasiness and decided that it was time to end their first conversation. He glanced at his wristwatch.

"Oh my goodness," he gasped in a feigned panic. "I almost forgot I have another appointment. I hope you don't mind cutting our visit short. We can pick it up later. What do you say?"

"Yeah, sure," Charlie nodded.

Father Mark stood up. He held out his hand for Charlie to shake.

"See you at dinner," he said.

"Okay." Charlie stood and took Father Mark's hand. The two parted without another word.

Charlie waited by the bench and watched Father Mark return to the Abbey before he ran around to the back door. He couldn't wait to tell Howard his suspicions of Father Mark. Cautiously he entered the backdoor. He looked around to be sure it was clear, then hurried to the stairs. He darted up the stairs taking them two steps at a time. He was out of breath by the time he reached the fourth floor. A quick look in the dark bell tower said what he needed to know. He hurried down the hall to Saint Nicholas dorm.

Sure enough, Howard and Gus had returned to their cubicles. Gus was already asleep, napping on his bed. Howard was busy reorganizing his stack of tattered comic books.

"That was sure a long talk," Howard said as Charlie sat down on his own bed across from him.

"Actually, Father Mark did most of the talking." Charlie admitted, still slightly out of breath. "But I finally figured out why he bothers me." Charlie looked at Howard with wide eyes.

Howard rolled his eyes and let out an exasperated sigh. He slapped the last comic down onto the stack and looked at his best friend. He froze. He could tell by Charlie's expression something was up and that he dared not say a word.

Charlie waited for a moment and tried to ignore Howard's reaction. Finally, he spoke in a whisper. "A few months ago my Uncle Chester showed up at my grandmother's with a man. Grandma couldn't remember his name, but she told me what he looked like. She said he was tall like Uncle Chester but bigger and gruff looking. He has a square jaw." Charlie paused and looked at Howard. "He has blonde hair and wears gold wire rimmed glasses." Again, Charlie paused becoming annoyed by Howard's blank expression.

Howard shrugged his shoulders and shook his head, a look that told Charlie he was not getting it.

"Don't you see?" Charlie sighed. "It's him. It's Father

Mark."

"Maybe, but maybe not," Howard said. "Didn't you say so yourself that your grandmother doesn't know him."

"I know, but it is him," Charlie insisted. "He told me himself."

"He did?" Howard gasped.

"Well, not in so many words," Charlie admitted a bit sheepishly. "But he told me my cousins went to the school he was at. Also, he said he knows my Uncle Chester and met my grandmother."

From the look on his face, Charlie could tell that Howard beginning to believe him.

"He fits the description and he knows them. It has to be him," Charlie said earnestly.

Howard thought for a moment and then shook his head. All signs of believing Charlie were gone. "No, Charlie, I don't think it is him. Abbot Ambrose wouldn't have a man like that as our new dean."

Charlie started to protest, but then stopped as Howard's words sunk in. He was right, Abbot Ambrose would not do that. For the first time Charlie did not feel so sure.

"Well, there's one way to find out for sure," Charlie said. "We need to get a picture of Father Mark to send to my grandmother. Do you know anyone who has a camera we can use?"

"Rick has a Polaroid camera," Howard answered. "It was a present from his parents for his birthday last summer," he added in a snooty voice, sounding a bit jealous. "It's in his nightstand. I'll show it to you." He jumped up and rushed over to Rick's cubicle, looking over his shoulders to be sure no one was watching. Moments later he returned with the small, odd shaped camera.

"Have you ever used one of these things?" Howard asked.

"Only in commercials," Charlie admitted, shaking his head and staring at the camera. "How does it work?"

"I saw Rick use it once," Howard said turning the camera

over and around as he examined the square camera. "Once you take the picture, it comes out here," he said confidently and pointed to the long slit under the lens on the front. "But I'm not sure which button you push to take the picture." He turned the camera around to look at the front.

"What does this button do?" Charlie pointed to a button on the side with a red dot on it.

Before Charlie could stop him, Howard pushed the button. Instantly there was a bright flash and a whirling sound. Sure enough, just as Howard said, a small, square white card popped out of the slit. Howard blinked as he tried to see. He reluctantly handed the card to Charlie.

"I don't think it's working," Charlie said. "There's no picture."

"I better put it back before anyone sees me with it. I didn't break it and I don't want to get blamed."

Charlie sat back down on his bed and stared at the white card while Howard returned the camera to Rick's nightstand. He could not help feeling disappointed. They were so close to being able to solve the mystery. He tossed the card onto Howard's nightstand and then something caught his eye. The center of the card began to darken. He picked it up and turned the card toward the light. The dark spaces began to take shape and the picture became visible.

"Wow!" he said as he watched the picture develop before his eyes.

"What?" Howard asked as he returned to the cubicle.

"I don't think the camera is broken after all," Charlie said and handed him the photograph of a rather surprised Howard.

"Cool," Howard said with a smile. "I'll get the camera."

"Wait." Charlie stopped him. "Don't you think we should we wait for Rick to come back and ask him?"

"What for?" Howard scoffed. "He'll just whine a lot and end up letting us have it anyway. This way we don't have to listen to him."

Charlie followed Howard over to Rick's cubicle and

retrieved the camera. The two boys then set out to find Father Mark.

"Hold it a second," Charlie said, just before they were to start down the stairs. "We can't just walk up to him and snap his picture. We have to be sneaky. He can't know we took his picture."

"And how do we do that?" Howard asked.

Charlie thought for a moment. His brow furrowed as he tried to figure out a plan.

"I've got it!" he said and looked back at Howard. "We can wait until tonight and then I can take his picture at the Altar Boys' Club meeting. We can say we want a picture of him with the other boys, only you can focus it just on him."

"Good idea," Howard agreed.

After dinner Charlie and Howard told Gus and Dale they'd catch up with them at the swimming pool after their meeting. They parted ways. Howard and Charlie headed off to Visiting Room Five.

"You have the camera?" Charlie asked Howard as they stood outside the door.

"Yes," he nodded and took the camera from beneath his surplice. "Now, at the end of the meeting, we'll ask if we can get a picture."

"You better do the asking, I don't think that I can," Charlie quickly added.

Howard frowned. He was planning on asking Charlie to do the same thing. Reluctantly he nodded and gave in.

The visiting room was just like the others on the main floor with its tall ceiling. The walls were painted a sterile off-white. Lace curtains with deep burgundy drapes adorned the tall windows on either side of the electric fireplace. Two matching wingback chairs sat in front of the windows. A tall mirror in an ornate gold frame hung above the fireplace and reflected the large, silk flower arrangement that set on the mantle. A camelback, burgundy and cream striped sofa was placed in front of the fireplace, its back to the door. A cherry wood coffee table sat in the center of the room. On the other three walls were hung paintings of Saints. Charlie was not sure what their names were.

Howard quickly sat down on the sofa. Charlie sat down next to him. The rest of the Altar Boys filed into the room. There were not as many of them since three had graduated last spring and three had gone home for the summer. Only six remained of the twelve.

The room immediately fell silent when Father Mark walked in. Charlie swallowed as a feeling of nausea rose in this throat. He watched Father Mark walk over to the fireplace and turn around to face the group. He at them and seemed to look at each of them as though taking a silent roll call.

"It's good to see you're all punctual," Father Mark began. "I know I must have said it a dozen times but I am so thrilled that Abbot Ambrose put me in charge of the Altar Boys for the summer. I know he's still making the decision on who becomes an Altar Boy, and on your assignments but." He grinned. "I'm just so thrilled."

Charlie and Howard looked at each other and rolled their eyes.

"Once Master Troyer is back in a couple of weeks," Father Mark continued. "He will take over conducting these meetings and I will be meeting only with him. Until then, I just wanted to check in with each of you and see how things are going.

"I can't begin to tell you what memories this brings back for me. Some of my fondest memories were of my days as an Altar Boy. I hope you boys appreciate the experience as much as I do." He looked around the room.

"Now for our first order of business, I would like to hear how each of you is doing with your assignments. Any concerns or things you need help with?" He turned to Charlie. Charlie instantly froze. "Master MacCready, I understand that you have been assigned to Father Elijah. How are you two getting along?"

Charlie looked around the room. All eyes were on him and he began to feel very self-conscious. "Fine," he said flatly.

"Any concerns?" Father Mark asked.

"No." Charlie was quick to answer as he shook his head.

Father Mark nodded and moved around the room, asking each of the boys the same questions. He frowned as all of the boys answered with the same short answers as Charlie. No concerns, and everything was fine.

"Well," he gave a heavy sigh and folded his arms over his chest. "I guess we'll move on to our next order of business. We need to discuss some of the brothers' concerns. It seems that even though most of you are doing well, a few of the brothers have some matters they want addressed. All of the brothers have expressed to me that, from time to time, they have a few errands that need to be run, but you boys have been too quick to rush off. It would be appreciated if you would take a little extra time to assist them and not be in such a hurry to get out and play."

The boys looked at one another, seeming to say the counsel was not meant for them.

"Also, there is to be no gum chewing," Father Mark announced and looked directly at Curtis, a boy from Saint Thomas dorm. "That goes for you, too, Master Hoyt. Please do not chew gum when you are with Brother Xavier. Your incessant snapping gets on his nerves."

Curtis shrugged indifferently and continued snapping his gum even louder. Charlie suspected since this coming school year would be his senior and last year there, the rumors about Curtis were true. He did have a bad attitude. Charlie looked back at Father Mark.

"I guess, that will conclude our meeting unless any of you has a question?" Father Mark said looking a bit sad.

Charlie turned to Howard who sat staring at the coffee table, and elbowed him. At first, he gave Charlie a confused look and then remembered. He raised his hand.

"I have a question."

Father Mark turned and smiled at Howard. "Yes, Master Miller?"

"Well, actually it's more of a favor. I was wondering if, perhaps I could get a picture of you and the guys here." Howard looked around the room.

"What on earth for?" Father Mark asked. His tone sounded a bit defensive and he eyed both Howard and Charlie suspiciously.

"I just wanted to have a group picture of our meeting with you," Howard answered. It was not really a lie.

"I see," Father Mark said. He looked at Charlie again just long enough to cause the butterflies in Charlie's stomach to stir. "Sure. I guess it wouldn't hurt."

"Great," Howard said and took the camera from under his surplice.

"Shall we all stand over here in front of the fireplace?" he asked.

Charlie looked at the mirror and remembered the flash of the camera. "Maybe we should all sit on the sofa here and Howard stand in front of the fireplace," he suggested, trying not to sound too bossy.

Father Mark smiled and glanced at the mirror. "Okay, Master MacCready."

He walked over to the sofa and sat down between Charlie and a boy from Saint Peter dorm. Curtis Hoyt stood behind the sofa next to his fellow dorm mate and continued to snap his gum.

Howard took his place across the room in front of the fireplace. He focused on Father Mark to the exclusion of the boys around him. "Okay," he said as he steadied the camera. "Watch the birdie." Flash. Whirl. The white card ejected from the slit below the lens. Howard quickly grabbed it before it could fall on the floor.

"Well, I hope this will give you what you are looking for," Father Mark said and stood up. "I have to be going for now."

Charlie waited until Father Mark left the room before he jumped to his feet.

"Let's see it," he said anxiously and took the photograph from Howard. He stared at the photograph, growing impatient as it slowly developed. Finally, it was finished. Howard had done an extraordinary job. He had zeroed in on Father Mark perfectly.

"Now, all we need to do is send this to my grandma and wait for her answer," Charlie whispered excitedly.

"Come on," Howard said and started for the door. "We need to get this back upstairs to Rick's nightstand. Then we're supposed to meet Gus and Dale at the pool, remember?"

The two hurried up the stairs.

BROKEN POTS

The rumbling of the heavy construction equipment rattled the entire hilltop. The air was thick with diesel exhaust. Charlie covered his nose and mouth with his surplice while he, Dale, Gus and Howard hurried down the path to the pottery studio. Today was their last official class. Gus, seemingly oblivious to the dust in the air, rambled on to Dale about something. Charlie really was not paying attention. He was thinking about the letter from his grandmother he just received that morning.

"What did she say about the photo?" Howard asked impatiently. His voice sounded muffled with his mouth covered.

"She said she's not sure it's him," he admitted. "She said he could be. He resembles the guy, but she's not sure. The man she remembers wasn't wearing a monk's robes."

"Ah-ha! I knew it!" Howard laughed out loud and slapped Charlie on the back. "There, Father Mark is not the guy. He's okay."

"No!" Charlie protested, stopping in his tracks. He pulled the letter from his pocket and shook it at Howard. "Her exact words were 'in his habit, it is hard to tell.' We need to get a picture of him in regular street clothes." He stuffed the letter back into the pocket of his cassock

"And how do we do that?" Howard asked. "He's always in his habit."

Charlie thought for a moment. It was true. Since Father Mark had returned to the Abbey, Charlie could not remember ever seeing him in street clothes. He thought harder.

"Hey," Gus spoke up. "Don't the brothers wear regular clothes when they work in the fields?"

"Yes," Howard nodded.

"Well, I overheard Brother Conrad and Father Mark talking about helping out the brothers in the fields this Saturday. You could get a picture of him then," Gus informed them.

Charlie's mouth dropped open and he smiled, excited by the thought.

Howard looked at Charlie and cocked his head. "Ah, and just how do you plan on doing that? The only way we would see him is if we had work crew."

"Then we have to get into trouble," Charlie answered nonchalantly.

"Have you lost your mind?" Howard protested. "It's hot and I don't want to spend the afternoon working in the fields just for a stupid picture."

"Fine, then I'll do it myself," Charlie said, in a bit of a huff. He walked past Howard and continued on to the pottery studio.

Howard looked Gus and Dale and then at his best friend. He shook his head and hurried to catch up with Charlie. Gus and Dale followed close behind.

"Okay," he sighed. "If we can't figure out another way, I'll go with you."

Charlie looked at Howard and smiled. "Thanks."

As they entered the pottery studio, Charlie could not help but think about their first day. It did not seem possible that nine weeks could pass so quickly, but they had. He remembered how Howard protested the most, and yet he turned out to be the best potter of them all.

"Good morning, Father Ichabod," the boys greeted as they walked into the studio.

Father Ichabod did not say a word. Silently he emptied a dusty cardboard box of broken pottery pieces into the garbage can by the front door.

Charlie shivered as he passed by the monk. He still did not feel comfortable around Father Ichabod. Images of the dark monk from his nightmares flashed in his mind every time he saw the priest. Charlie quickly donned his smock and took his seat at the table.

"What's going on?" Howard whispered to Charlie when he took his seat at the table.

Charlie shrugged and continued watching Father Ichabod. Father Ichabod placed the empty box on top of the stack of other empty boxes next to the finished pottery shelves.

"What are you guys whispering about?" Gus asked out loud.

Howard clenched his teeth and strained his neck as he stared wide-eyed at Gus.

"We were just wondering what was going on," Charlie answered.

"I'll wait until the rest of the class arrives," Father Ichabod answered sullenly, looking straight at Charlie. For a moment their eyes met then he looked away.

Howard noticed Father Ichabod's pained expression and turned to Charlie. "What was that about?"

"I don't know," Charlie answered as he watched Father Ichabod return to his desk beside the pottery shelves. Charlie looked around the room. Something was different, but he could not say what. Suddenly it struck him. "Oh no," he quietly gasped.

"What?" Howard looked around the room.

"All of my bowls and mugs," he whispered. "They're gone."

Howard looked at the pottery shelves. It was true. Not one of Charlie's creations was on his shelf.

Just then, in their usual noisy flare, Dougary and his two clumsy oafs burst through the door. They lazily changed into their smocks and took their places at the table. Father Ichabod stood by his desk watching them intently, his arms folded over his chest.

"Are you boys quite through?" he asked.

Dougary opened his mouth to start to answer but closed it when he saw the look in Father Ichabod's eyes. The room fell silent.

"Then we shall begin?" Father Ichabod said. He walked back to the table and stood at the head. "I don't know which one of you boys is responsible but I want whomever it is to know that I will find out and you will be punished severely. What you have done is nothing short of biting the hand that feeds you!" He slammed his fist down on the table.

Gus and Dale jumped. Gus looked at Howard and Charlie, confused. Charlie frowned at him and motioned ever so slightly with his head toward the pottery shelves. Gus did not understand. Charlie looked back at their teacher.

"What're you talking about?" Dougary spoke up without raising his hand first.

"I'm talking about the person or persons who used their pass key to come in here last night and smash all of Master MacCready's pottery!" Father Ichabod snapped.

Gus and Dale gasped and looked at the pottery shelves and then back at Charlie.

"Those bowls and mugs were to be sold at the Abbey's booth at Oktoberfest next month. Not only is it a loss of money from the sales of those items, but it is also a waste of clay, glazes, electricity and the last nine weeks of hard work. So help me, when I find out which of you boys—" Father Ichabod clenched his fists and shook. "Turn in your keys at once! All of you!" he ordered, and held out his bony hand to receive them.

Slowly, reluctantly the boys began to dig in their pockets searching for their keys. Howard was the first to pull his key out. Father Ichabod held out his hand. Charlie reached out his key too, but Father Ichabod pulled his hand away.

"No, Master MacCready, you may keep your key. You are

welcome to come back anytime you like," he said and turned to Gus. Gus dropped his key into Father Ichabod's palm.

Charlie looked across the table at Dougary. Something appeared to be wrong. He was frantically searching his pockets for his key.

"Master Duggan." Father Ichabod held out his hand. "Your key."

"Ah," Dougary stammered. His face went pale and he looked scared.

"I'm waiting," Father Ichabod breathed impatiently.

"I-I can't find it," Dougary admitted sheepishly.

Father Ichabod closed his fist around the five keys and shoved them into the pocket of his robes. He walked over to the kilns and turned around.

"You have one hour to get me that key, or we will see what Abbot Ambrose has to say about this. Do I make myself clear, Master Duggan?"

"Yes, Father," Dougary answered, and looked at Travis and Larry.

"Usually I wait until the end of class to have each of my students select a piece of their work to keep," Father Ichabod continued. "But today I want you all to do it now and bring it back to the table."

Obediently the boys, except for Charlie, rose and quickly selected a pottery piece from their shelves. They returned to the table and took their seats. Gus frowned when he looked over at Charlie. He felt awful for Charlie, who sat with nothing in front of him.

Slowly Father Ichabod walked around the table and looked at the boys' pottery pieces. Gus leaned protectively over his lopsided bowl, afraid that at any moment Father Ichabod would smash it in a fit of rage.

"Now, get out of my sight!" Father Ichabod hissed as he completed his inspection. "Leave! Take your piece of pottery and get out of here!"

The boys quickly changed back into their surplices and

hurried out of the door. Father Ichabod slammed the heavy door behind them.

"What a freak!" Travis sneered as he looked over his shoulder at the door.

"Just wait until I tell my dad," Larry said smugly. "He'll see to it that old Icky never teaches another class again."

"That guy needs to be locked up in a home!" Dougary shook his head.

"Yeah, you should know," Howard glared at Dougary. "You're the resident expert on crazy people."

"What was that?" he asked challengingly, taking a step toward Howard.

"We all know who smashed Charlie's pottery. You aren't fooling anyone." Howard glared and stood his ground. "'Oh, I can't find my key'," he mocked in a whimpering voice.

"What makes you think I'd do something like that?" Dougary scoffed. "If I wanted to get even, I wouldn't take it out on a bunch of dried up clay." He glared at Charlie.

"I don't believe you," Howard snapped back.

"Well, I don't care," Dougary sneered. "Believe what you want, How-weird. I haven't got time for this. Come on." Dougary turned around and left with Travis and Larry hurrying after him.

Charlie watched them leave. "Do you think he could be telling the truth?" he asked.

"No," Howard answered in disbelief at Charlie's doubts. "I don't think the truth and Dougary have ever met."

"Who d-d-do you th-th-think d-d-did it?" Dale asked as the four boys began to walk up the path.

"I think Dougary did it," Howard answered without hesitation.

"I don't know," Charlie shook his head in answer to Dale's question.

"Well, one thing is certain," Gus spoke up. "I think Father Ichabod is beyond angry. Did you see how red his eyes were?"

Charlie froze as the image in his nightmare flashed before

his eyes. The dark, shadowy figure with fiery red eyes tightened his grip on Charlie's arms, lifting him off the ground. Charlie could feel the shadow's hot breath against his face. He shook his head as if to erase the memory and then hurried to catch up with the other boys.

"So, what are we gonna to do 'til lunch?" Gus asked when they reached the Abbey.

"Let's go see how they're coming with the new building," Howard suggested.

"Okay," they all agreed.

Charlie waited while Howard, Gus and Dale rushed upstairs to put their pottery away. The main hall was quiet. Charlie walked over to the stairs and leaned against the rail.

Suddenly a commotion down the hall caught Charlie's attention. He pushed away from the rail and looked down the hall just as Father Mark, Abbot Ambrose and Father Ichabod walked through the main entrance with Dougary, Travis and Larry. Charlie walked a little closer.

"But I didn't do it!" Dougary insisted.

"Forgive me if I do not believe you," Father Ichabod said. "But it *is* common knowledge that you and Master MacCready aren't the best of friends."

"But that doesn't mean I did it!" Dougary raised his voice. "I told you that someone stole my key!"

"Please lower your voice, Master Duggan. We are not deaf," Abbot Ambrose said calmly. "Master Bleckinger, what do you know about this matter?"

Travis shook his head and shrugged his shoulders. "I don't know nothing."

Abbot Ambrose frowned at Travis's language. "Anything, Master Bleckinger, you don't know anything. And that is certainly not news, is it?" He turned to Larry. "And you?"

"I was nowhere near the pottery studio, I swear," Larry answered.

"There won't be any need for that." Abbot Ambrose shook his head. "The two of you may go, but don't think this matter is closed," he warned them.

Larry and Travis quickly disappeared through the main doors before Abbot Ambrose, Father Mark, or Father Ichabod could change their minds. Dougary stood alone with the three monks.

"Why won't anyone believe me?" Dougary shook his head. "I didn't do it. This isn't fair."

"What isn't fair, Master Duggan, is that all of Master MacCready's hard work for the last nine weeks is ruined, not to mention the financial loss to the Abbey," Father Ichabod spoke up. "And it is my opinion, Father Abbot, that the person responsible should pay dearly for it." He glared at Dougary.

"I agree with you, Ichabod." Abbot Ambrose nodded. "I will handle this matter from here."

"Yes, of course." Father Ichabod nodded obediently.

"Master Duggan, wait here," Abbot Ambrose instructed. "Mark, Ichabod, please step into my office."

Charlie watched as the three disappeared into Abbot Ambrose's office and closed the door behind them. Slowly he crept closer, staying close to the wall. Dougary paced back and forth in front of him, shaking his head and muttering something to himself. At one point he stopped and leaned against the wall opposite the Abbot's office and wiped his eyes. Is he crying? Charlie wondered. At that moment Charlie felt sorry for Dougary. To his own surprise, he found himself beginning to believe Dougary was not the one who smashed his pottery.

"I believe you," Charlie heard himself say.

Dougary jumped and stood away from the wall. He sniffed and wiped his eyes then glared at Charlie.

"What?"

Charlie walked over to him. "I said, 'I believe you.' I don't think you had anything to do with it."

"You don't know that," Dougary sneered. He folded his arms over his chest and glared at Charlie. He was obviously embarrassed and annoyed by Charlie's sympathy.

"I do know," Charlie said confidently. "If you wanted to,

you could've broken my pots any time. After all, your shelf was right above mine. It would've been easy for you to knock them off the shelf pretending it was an accident. But you didn't."

Dougary thought for a moment. "Shows what you know, MacCreepy. What if I told you I did do it?"

Just then the door to the Abbot's office opened. Dougary looked up shocked.

"Ah-ha!" Father Ichabod gasped. "You heard him. He just admitted he did it."

"Master Duggan, I would like to see you in my office." Abbot Ambrose said sternly. "Master MacCready, is there something I should know about?"

Charlie looked at Father Mark and Father Ichabod. Both were staring at him intently, causing him to feel very nervous. He looked at Dougary who looked worried about what was going to happen next, but as soon as their eyes met, he glared at Charlie.

"I don't think Dougary did it," Charlie said. "I don't know why, but I don't think he did."

"What need have we for witnesses?" Father Ichabod turned to Abbot Ambrose. "We heard him admit to it. All that needs to be done is administer the punishment."

"I will handle this, Ichabod. You may go," Abbot Ambrose said in a stern but loving tone. "Master MacCready, thank you for your input. Why don't you run along? Now, if you will excuse me," Abbot Ambrose nodded and returned to his office. He closed the door behind him.

"Nothing's going to happen to that boy!" Father Ichabod said coldly. "And it's all because of you!" He turned his head sharply and glared at Charlie. "Perhaps I was wrong letting you keep your key."

Charlie stepped back and looked at Father Ichabod, at his red eyes and long, bony finger pointing at him. His heart began to beat faster. He looked at Father Mark as though for some sort of help.

"Now, Ichabod," Father Mark stepped forward. "I'm sure

Abbot Ambrose knows the value of what was lost and will deal with the situation. Let's not jump to conclusions."

"Well, until I get my key back Master Duggan will have an hour of work crew every day from me," Father Ichabod snapped at Father Mark. "At least I have that much authority in this matter. You'll have my formal reprimand on your desk this afternoon."

"Very well," Father Mark nodded.

"And as for you, Master MacCready." Father Ichabod stepped closer. His eyes still burned with anger. "Don't make me regret allowing you to keep your key," he warned. Charlie winced as he felt Father Ichabod's hot breath against his face. "I'll be watching you very closely," Father Ichabod hissed.

"Hey, Charlie," Howard called from the foot of the stairs. "Come on."

Father Ichabod turned around sharply, his black robes bellowed out. Then suddenly he disappeared through the main foyer doors.

Charlie glanced over his shoulder and then back at Father Mark. "I-I better be going," he said nervously. He cautiously took two steps backward before he turned and hurried to meet Howard at the foot of the stairs.

"What was that all about?" Howard greeted Charlie.

"It's him!" Charlie panted.

"Him?" Howard looked at him confused. "Him, who?"

"The shadow," Charlie answered. "It's Father Ichabod!"

"What makes you think that?" Howard asked in disbelief.

Charlie shivered. "His eyes were red and bloodshot and his breath was hot, just like in my dream."

"Whoa!" Howard said, holding up his hands as he stopped. Charlie stopped and turned around. "Your dream? Charlie, you can't go around accusing people because of your dream. You need solid evidence. No one is going to believe you and they'll be locking you up in the nut house next."

Charlie thought for a moment. "I guess you're right."

"Come on."

The two walked through the backdoor and around to the front of the Abbey. They met up with Dale and Gus on the front grounds.

"So, what made Father Ichabod so angry?" Howard asked.

"Because I don't think Dougary smashed my pottery."

"What?" shrieked Howard and looked at Charlie. "Are you out of your mind? Of course he did it. You've been saying all summer how Dougary's out to get you. What do you mean, he didn't do it?"

"I know," Charlie agreed. "But he was crying. I don't think he did it."

"Crying?" Gus said with surprise. "Dog-breath was crying?" He let out a laugh that shook his round belly.

"Yes," Charlie nodded, frowning at Gus.

"Well, even if he d-d-didn't da-da-do it," Dale spoke up. "He'll ga-ga-get what he d-d-deserves."

"That's right, Charlie," Howard agreed. "Don't feel sorry for him. He's done enough stuff to all of us and got away with it. So, if he didn't do it, his being punished for it will make up for all those other times."

"Well, Father Ichabod doesn't seem to think Father Abbot will punish him," Charlie admitted.

"Why?" Gus asked, clearly disappointed.

"Because I sort of told Abbot Ambrose, I didn't think Dougary did it," Charlie answered sheepishly.

"You did what?" Howard gasped. "Oh, I don't believe this." Howard shrieked. He threw his hands in the air as though pleading with heaven. He shook his head and turned around in a circle. "Why on earth would you do that? Isn't this what you've been wanting all summer, to get even with Dougary before he does something to you?"

Charlie did not answer. He just stared at his friends. He understood their being upset. He did want to get even, but he seeing Dougary cry changed everything. He could not stand by and let Dougary take the fall for something he did not do. It would not be right.

"So, what's Father Ichabod going to do now?" Gus asked looking at the Abbey behind Charlie.

"He's giving Dougary an hour of work crew a day until he returns his key. Dougary said someone stole it so I'm afraid he'll have work crew for a long time," Charlie frowned.

"Well, that's more like it!" Howard said. "Let's go see the construction."

The boys started down the road that bordered the west edge of the great lawn. The new building was being constructed right at the edge of the hillside where the road turned toward the Abbey.

"Have you seen the drawing that Prior Emmanuel has of the new building?" Howard asked as they walked.

"No," Gus answered.

Dale shook his head.

"Did you see it?" Charlie asked.

"Last night," he answered. "I stopped by Prior Emmanuel's office after dinner and he showed me. He told he really misses all of us and wishes we would come to see him. He's really different. He doesn't seem happy anymore."

Charlie could tell Howard was worried. The news worried him too. He could not help but remember the last time he saw Prior Anselm. He said he was only tired, but the next day Charlie found out the elderly Prior had died. Suddenly, Charlie felt a twinge of guilt. He was so preoccupied with solving his mysteries that he had not gone to see his former prefect. He thought about the first time they met. Prior Emmanuel was then just Father Emmanuel. Though he was dressed in the black habit of the monks, Father Emmanuel reminded Charlie of Santa Claus minus the white beard. Charlie's smile faded as he remembered the tears in Father Emmanuel's eyes when he told them he was appointed Prior of the Abbey, second to the Abbot, and they would be getting a new prefect.

Charlie looked at Howard as they walked.

"He'll be okay. He's just been busy," he tried to reassure Howard but he knew his voice did not sound too convincing.

"He has been working really hard on this project."

"I know," Howard agreed. "It's just I've never seen him so depressed."

"We'll look in on him," Charlie said, and continued to walk.

"So, what did he say about the new building?" Gus asked.

"He said they hope to have most of the exterior done before winter. That way the Brothers can work on the inside when the weather is bad," Howard explained. "He and Abbot Ambrose hope it'll be completed by next summer or fall." Howard grinned fiendishly. "I can't wait to see the look on Rick's face when he comes back next week."

"I can't wait to see Rick, period," Gus spoke up. "We don't always get along but he's still my friend."

The three paused in the shade of a dogwood tree. They stared in awe at the progress on the new building. They watched as men in blue coveralls and hard hats worked at putting up the walls of the first floor with help from a large crane. The boys watched in silence.

Charlie looked away for a moment. Suddenly his attention was drawn away to a white pickup truck parked away from the others. Standing beside it in the shadows, almost out of sight, were Larry and his father. They appeared to be arguing. Charlie noticed a tree near them, one where he could hide. Stealthily he slipped away.

The tree was one of a cluster of three fir trees beside the road. Charlie slipped under its branches and hid behind the thick trunk. Cautiously he peeked out.

"I don't care if he *is* your friend," Mister Hertz said in a stern tone. "You don't need to be getting into any more trouble."

"But, dad, the key—"

"Will you keep your voice down and watch what you say!" Mister Hertz cut Larry off. "I cannot afford to lose this job. We all have to do things we don't like. It's time for you to grow up, be a man. Sometimes we have to sacrifice our friends for the good of the family."

"Yes, sir," Larry answered, less than enthused.

"Now, get back to the Abbey before someone sees you over here," Mister Hertz ordered. "We both have jobs to do. Let me know when you've finished yours."

"Yes, sir." Larry nodded. He turned around quickly.

Charlie gasped as Larry looked straight at him. He quickly ducked behind the tree and held his breath and waited. Nervously he glanced over at Howard, Gus and Dale. They had spotted him hiding in the tree and were walking toward him.

"Oh no," Charlie silently groaned, fearful that he was about to be caught by Larry.

"What are you doing in there?" Howard asked as the three approached.

"Shhh!" Charlie panicked and stayed flat against the tree.

"Oh, if you are talking about Larry," Howard snickered. "He's already gone."

"What?" Charlie said and looked around. Sure enough, Larry was nowhere in sight. Charlie sighed and relaxed as he emerged from under the tree and joined the other three.

"So, are you going to tell us what you're doing?" Howard persisted.

"I saw Larry and his dad talking behind that truck over there. I think they're up to something. Larry's dad told him to finish his job and then let him know. Larry said something about a key," Charlie explained with a raised eyebrow.

"Honestly, Charlie," Howard shook his head. "Sometimes I think you're being a little paranoid."

"I am not!" Charlie took offense. "I didn't say they were after me. Dougary said his key was stolen."

"So you think Larry took it?" Howard asked sarcastically. "Larry has one, or did you forget?"

"No, I *didn't* forget," Charlie snapped back. He did not appreciate Howard's tone.

"Well, we'd best be getting back. It's almost lunchtime," Gus interrupted.

"I suppose so," Howard agreed.

The four boys headed back to the Abbey.

THE RETAKE

Charlie lay quietly on his bed, staring up at the ceiling. He could not shake the fear that had awakened him in the middle of the night. It was from the same reoccurring nightmare he had been having for the past two and a half months. Voices in the dark forest were calling him. He called out to them but they just kept calling his name as though they could not hear him. He strained to see in the darkness, but he could not find them. Then suddenly, the shadow appeared in front of him, its eyes glowing red and its breath hot, like an oven. It grabbed him, lifting him off the ground. The dreams always seemed to stop there and he would wake up. What could it mean? Who was calling him? Why? What did they want?

Charlie felt the key that hung around his neck. Why would she not tell him what it was for? What was so dangerous about knowing?

Charlie looked through the window. If he looked to the west, he could see the large crane over the tops of the trees at the building site. He wondered if he would still be able to see the road clearly from his window in the new building. Perhaps when his parents came for him, they would tell him what the key was for.

"Charlie!" Howard rushed into their cubicle, out of breath. "Where's the camera?"

Charlie quickly jumped up and retrieved the camera from the drawer in the nightstand in Rick's cubicle.

"Why? What's happening?" he asked handing the camera to Howard.

"We have to hurry," Howard answered and turned around sharply.

"Why?" Charlie repeated, quickly following after him.

"I saw Father Mark in street clothes talking to one of the construction workers," Howard explained as they hurried down the hall. He headed down the stairs, taking them two at a time. "If we hurry, we can get a picture of him so we won't have to do work crew."

"Great," Charlie smiled and ran faster.

They crossed the front lawn in record time. Sure enough, Father Mark was still there. Charlie froze when he saw the construction worker. He quickly ducked into the shadow of a nearby tree and watched from a distance. Howard approached the two men and said something to them. Charlie could not hear but they seemed agreeable. They smiled and nodded. Howard took a few steps back and the two men stood closer together. Father Mark put his arm over the worker's shoulders. Howard aimed the camera. The men smiled. The camera snapped and whirred; a card emerged from the bottom of the camera and Howard caught it.

"Thanks," he called to the men and waved to them as he started to leave. His smile faded to a look of confusion as he searched for Charlie.

"Charlie?" he said and approached the shadow of the tree.

Charlie stepped out and gave Howard a start.

"What are you doing?" he snapped.

"Nothing," Charlie answered.

"Then why didn't you come with me?"

"Because," he answered. "Do you know who that man with Father Mark was?" Charlie asked.

"Oh, not this again," Howard shook his head. "No. I don't and I don't care."

"It's Larry's father, Maxwell Hertz," Charlie answered. "Dale told me Father Emmanuel hired Mister Hertz' construction company to work on the new building."

"So," Howard shrugged again.

"So, remember I saw them talking yesterday? I didn't want him to see me again. He might get suspicious."

"Suspicious of what?" Howard asked. By the tone in his voice, Charlie could tell Howard was becoming impatient. Charlie ignored it.

"Wondering why we want a picture of Father Mark," Charlie answered. "He could've let Father Mark know we are onto him."

"Oh," Howard nodded his head sarcastically. "And we are concerned about that, because?"

"Never mind," Charlie snapped.

"Look, Charlie," Howard pleaded. "Your grandma doesn't think Father Mark's the guy. I'm only doing this to prove to you you're wrong about him. He's a nice guy."

"Well we'll just see about that," Charlie said indignantly. "Where's the picture?"

Howard handed it to Charlie. Charlie looked at the photograph and smiled.

"This is perfect," he said more to himself than to Howard. "Nice and clear and close enough to really see his face."

"I would've moved in closer but I had to get Mister Hertz in the shot too. Otherwise he would've become suspicious," Howard said.

Charlie looked at Howard and smiled.

"I'll get this off to my grandmother right away."

The two boys headed back to their dorm. Charlie quickly wrote a note to his grandmother while Howard returned the camera to Rick's nightstand.

"Oh," Howard said walking back into their cubicle. "You should ask your grandmother for some money to get Rick some more film. I'm afraid we used the last one."

"Good idea," Charlie said, and quickly added it to his note. He stuffed the letter and the photograph carefully into the envelope and sealed it. "There. I'll just drop this in the outgoing mail before dinner, and hopefully she'll get back to me right away."

"I hope so," Howard sighed. "I really think you're wrong about Father Mark."

"We'll see."

SISTER MARGARET MARY

The night air blowing through the slightly open window above Charlie's bed felt cool against his cheeks. Gradually he began to pass through the veil of sleep to wake.

Suddenly he felt the presence of someone next to his bed. A warm feeling radiated from his chest down his arms and legs, paralyzing him. Was this a dream? Was he awake? He did not know. Slowly, he opened his eyes just enough to peek. His heart skipped a beat. Standing over him was a dark, shadow. Its bony hands, with long fingers and nails like an eagle's talons, slowly reached for Charlie's throat.

Charlie screamed for Howard, at least he thought he did, but the hands moved closer. Charlie opened his eyes wide. Suddenly, the weight that was holding him down was gone. He screamed and sat up in his bed. Quickly, he scooted into the corner of his bed, and drew his knees to his chest. He stared, wide-eyed, into the dark dorm. The shadow was gone, but this time, he knew it was real.

Howard woke the instant he heard Charlie's scream. He leapt from his bed, tripping over his slipper and falling against Charlie's bed.

"What's going on?"

"Who screamed?"

"What time is it?"

Voices came from every corner of the dorm.

"What is it? What's the matter?" Howard asked in a panic. "What's wrong? Are you okay?"

"Y-y-yes," Charlie answered. "Did you see it?"

"See what?" Howard asked, picking his glasses up from the floor and putting them on.

"Th-the shadow," Charlie stammered and shuddered.

Howard turned and looked over his shoulder. His heart sank when he saw nothing but the empty dormitory. He turned back to his best friend.

"There's nothing here."

"There has to be!" Charlie insisted. "I didn't imagine it."

"It was a dream, a nightmare," Howard said quietly. He reached out his hand and touched Charlie's. Instantly Howard pulled his hand away. "What's on your hand?" He turned on to the small lamp on his nightstand. The dim light illuminated the cubicle. Howard noticed something white on the floor. Cautiously he bent down and picked it up. He raised the surplice up to look at it. His eyes immediately focused on the mud smears, still damp. He looked at Charlie, at his hands. "Your hands—there's blood—are you hurt?"

Charlie looked at his hands. In the dim light, he could see that the backs of his hands were smeared with mud and blood. Clumsily he crawled out of his bed, careful not to touch his sheets or blankets for fear of getting them dirty. He stared at his hands, confused and bewildered.

"I-I don't know," Charlie answered.

Howard looked at the tag on the surplice. "If it isn't your blood, then whose is it?"

"Whose is what?" a groggy voice yawned from the foot of Howard's bed.

Howard jumped up and spun around. "Don't do that!" he said looking at Gus.

"What's going on?" Gus asked with a yawn. He wiped the

sleep from his eyes.

"Nothing," Howard answered and quickly put the surplice behind his back. "Go back to bed."

"What's that?" Gus asked and cocked his head to see what Howard was trying to hide.

"Nothing, I told you! Now get back to bed!" Howard snapped but Gus did not move. He looked at Charlie.

"What's all over your hands, Charlie?" he asked.

"I, I don't know," Charlie answered.

"It's nothing," Howard interrupted. "He had a nose bleed, that's all."

"Oh," Gus said in a tired voice.

"Now will you please go back to bed," Howard pleaded. He stepped toward Gus ushering him out of their cubicle.

"Okay." Gus relented. He returned to his cubicle on the other side of the partition. "You better turn off that light before Brother Simon sees it," he warned. The partition shook as he lay back down on his bed.

Howard quickly switched the light off.

"Do you think I really had a nose bleed?" Charlie whispered as Howard sat on the edge of his own bed, facing him.

"I don't know," he answered.

Charlie's breath became shallow and he felt nauseated. "I think I'm going to be sick," he groaned, and sat back down on the edge of his bed.

"Oh no you don't!" Howard jumped to his feet and grabbed Charlie's arm. "You're not gonna puke in here!"

Howard held onto Charlie as he hurried for the doors. Before leaving the dorm, he paused and dropped the muddy surplice down the laundry chute just inside the dormitory doors. Quickly and quietly they rushed to the sinks.

The feeling of nausea seemed to fade the closer they came to the bathroom. Charlie slowed, pulling against Howard's grasp but on look at his hands and the feeling rushed back.

"Here, wash your hands," Howard ordered.

Charlie quickly stuck his hands under the warm water. He tried not to look at his hands as he washed away the mud and blood.

"What about that surplice?" Charlie stopped and turned to looked at Howard.

"Just keep washing your hands," Howard instructed. He handed Charlie a bar of soap.

Slowly, Charlie rubbed the soap on his hands and stuck them under the warm water. As he became more awake, his mind filled with questions he could not answer.

"There," Howard said, handing Charlie a towel. "It's all gone. Feel better?"

"Yeah, I guess so," Charlie answered. He took a deep breath and then nodded more sure.

"Let's get back to the dorm."

"Howard," Charlie said as they walked down the hall. "Whose surplice was that?"

Howard stopped. He looked at Charlie and then at the floor. "It was yours."

Charlie's eyes widened. "So, my nightmares aren't just dreams. They're real?"

"I didn't say that. When I woke up the only person I saw was you. No shadow. No one else. Nothing."

"We should tell Brother Simon," Charlie said.

"No!" Howard snapped and looked at his friend. "We can't tell anyone."

Charlie looked at Howard confused. "But why?"

"How're you going to explain all of this?" Howard turned to him. "You're seeing shadows that no one else sees. You have blood on your hands and mud on your surplice. Who's going to believe you?"

"But you—"

"Charlie, I didn't see anything. Not the other day in the forest. Not even tonight. There wasn't anyone or anything there," Howard explained. "It's all in your head."

"But what about that surplice?" Charlie insisted. "How do

you explain—"

"Charlie, it was yours," Howard answered.

Charlie looked at Howard and tears filled his eyes. For the first time he realized that Howard did not believe him. "I'm not losing my mind, Howie. Say you believe me."

Howard looked at the tears in Charlie's eyes. His stern expression softened. "Charlie, I don't know what to believe, but you're my best friend," he sighed. "If you say it's true, then I believe you. But convincing ol' B.S. or even Father Mark isn't going to be easy. Why don't you write your grandmother and tell her about it. Ask her what we should do?" Howard suggested. "And while you're at it, you can ask her again about the photograph."

Charlie nodded and wiped his eyes. "I will."

The two walked quietly into the dorm.

"Howard," Charlie whispered. "I'm not going crazy, am I?"

Howard looked at Charlie, glad for the darkness of the dorm. Over the past two months the thought had occurred to him that he could be losing his best friend. Perhaps that night in the attic, when Charlie hit his head, it did something to his mind. Howard felt his throat tighten as his eyes filled with tears. "No." he answered in a shaky breath. "Try to get some sleep."

"I don't think I can sleep," he said, and stared at the ceiling.

"What time is it?" Howard asked as he lay facing the partition.

Charlie looked at the clock on Howard's nightstand. "It's almost time to get up," he sighed.

"Well, I'll stay awake with you if you want me to," Howard offered. "I don't think I could sleep much anyway."

Charlie smiled to himself, relieved that he would not be awake alone. "Thanks, Howard. I'm really sorry."

"For what?" Howard asked.

"Because I think whoever it is that's doing this is after my key," Charlie said, and felt the key under his pajama top.

"Your key?" Howard turned over and faced Charlie in the

darkness. "Why do you think that?"

"Because every time I've seen the shadow over me, he's reaching for the chain around my neck," Charlie answered.

"Why would someone want your key? What's it to?" Howard asked, confused.

"I don't know." Charlie shook his head.

"Well, I doubt anyone is after it," Howard yawned.

"I hope you are right," Charlie sighed and looked around the room.

The two boys lay in silence listening to Gus quietly snore as they waited for the morning bell. Once it rang, the dorm lights came on and the room came alive. Charlie and Howard quickly showered and dressed for breakfast.

"You know what today is?" Charlie asked as they headed down the stairs to breakfast.

"Yes, it's pancakes and sausage day," Howard teased.

"No," Charlie said, and gave him a nudge. "Today Rick comes back."

"Duh!" Howard laughed. "I hate to say it, and I'll deny it if you tell anyone, I'm actually glad he's coming back. Maybe things will get back to normal."

The mood was unusually quiet as the two reached the first floor. The boys stood, single file, in their dorm lines. All eyes were focused ahead. No one looked around. Charlie gave Howard a curious look as they took their places in line.

The refectory doors opened and the prefects walked into the hall. Brother Simon slowly walked down the line of Saint Nicholas boys. He seemed to look them over more carefully than usual. Charlie glanced over his shoulder at Howard.

"Turn around," he whispered, then frowned.

Silently the boys filed into the refectory and took their places behind their chairs. Abbot Ambrose stood at his usual place behind the head table with Father Mark, to his right. Then one by one the prefects took their places at the head table. It was just like normal, Charlie thought, but something still did not feel right.

As the boys stood behind their chairs, Abbot Ambrose walked around to the front of the head table. His blue eyes were damp and he looked tired. His normal smile was replaced by a serious look of concern.

"Please, be seated," he invited in a quiet tone.

The boys quickly took their seats. Not a word was spoken as they watched Abbot Ambrose step down from the raised platform.

"Boys," he began softly. "I have some news to tell you, but I don't want to cause you alarm. Sister Margaret Mary, from our kitchen, is in the hospital."

Charlie gasped and covered his mouth. He looked at Howard but he just stared toward the front of the refectory. A feeling of dread began to grow inside Charlie. He thought about the last time he talked to Sister Margaret. It was the night before, just after dinner. She was working late baking some extra special cookies and pastries for her returning boys. She was so excited.

Sister Margaret Mary always reminded Charlie of his grandmother. She was short and stout. Her gray hair was barely visible under the edges of her short, white veil. Her smile was so kind and her eyes were gentle.

"As she has done for years since she began working in our kitchen," Abbot Ambrose continued. "She was walking down the hill by the pig barns on her way back to her convent. She was found unconscious early this morning when the Brothers went to feed the pigs. As of yet, she has not regained consciousness and the doctors fear the worst.

"Now I know this is a shock to you boys," Abbot Ambrose said as he looked at their stunned faces. "But I wanted you to hear the news from me. Let's just keep Sister Margaret in our prayers and hope for the best."

Suddenly, Charlie did not feel much like eating. Again, he looked at Howard and this time Howard looked back. Howard took a deep, unsteady breath and shook his head in disbelief at his friend.

"Please, stay seated," Abbot Ambrose said as he took his place behind the head table. "Let us pray."

After saying Grace, the serving brothers emerged quietly from the kitchen with their carts. They began setting their hot plates of pancakes and sausages before the boys. Charlie just sat and stared at his plate of food. He could not believe how life was going on without Sister Margaret in the kitchen.

"I can't believe it," he sighed. He looked at Howard. Howard seemed to be lost in his thoughts. Gently Charlie nudged him in the ribs.

Howard winced and grabbed his side. He looked at Charlie with an annoyed expression. "What?" he snapped but Charlie did not seem to notice his tone.

Charlie leaned closer so no one else would hear him. "Do you think I should tell Abbot Ambrose about the shadow in the forest?"

"Why?" Howard gave him a confused look.

"Because maybe the shadow attacked Sister Margaret Mary."

Howard looked at Charlie curiously. "Or she could have stumbled or had a stroke or something. No," Howard said flatly. "Remember what I said? If you go to the Abbot and tell him that you, and only you, saw a shadow in the forest, he'll ask you what it looked like. What are you going to tell him? It looked like the shadow of a monk or something? Charlie, the hill is crawling with monks if you haven't noticed. Besides, no one is going to believe you and it will only make you look guilty."

Charlie looked at his best friend and hesitated. "Guilty? Do you think I did it?" he asked.

"What?" Howard looked at Charlie in surprise.

"You know, the blood, my hands, my surplice?" Charlie answered.

"No," Howard answered sharply, and gave Charlie a disgusted look. "There's no way you could've done it. But if you go telling anyone else, they may think you did. Just stay calm." He looked away. His expression did not seem as convincing as his words, Charlie thought. The look in Howard's eyes as he picked at his breakfast seemed to say otherwise.

Charlie looked at his plate and thought about what Howard said. Howard was right. He really did not have any idea who or what or even if the shadow was real. And telling the Abbot about his surplice would make him look guilty. He turned back to his plate and pushed it away.

"Oh, how can you eat?" Howard groaned as he looked across the table at Gus.

Gus looked up from his plate, his mouth full of pancake and syrup. "Wha—?" he asked, looking at one and then the other.

"Oh, gross." Howard grimaced and covered his eyes. "Don't talk with your mouth full!"

"Never mind, Gus," Charlie spoke up. "Go ahead and eat your breakfast."

"Well, I can't," Howard said flatly and pushed his plate away.

"Is there something the matter with your food this morning, Master Miller?" Abbot Ambrose asked as he stood behind Charlie.

"No, Father Abbot," Howard said sheepishly, his cheeks turning red. "I just don't feel too much like eating."

"Me either," Charlie added. "I can't stop thinking about Sister Margaret Mary. What do you think happened to her? Could she have had a stroke like Howard said?"

"I do not know, son," Abbot Ambrose sighed. "The doctors will determine what happened. Now, the last thing she would want is for you two to skip breakfast. So, why don't you both try to eat something?"

Charlie looked at Howard. "I'll try, if you will."

Howard thought for a moment and then pulled his plate back in front of him. "Yes, Father Abbot," he agreed.

"That's my boys," Abbot Ambrose nodded. "Oh, I almost forgot, you'll be happy to know that Rick has arrived."

"Rick's back?" Gus gasped with his mouth full.

"Yes, Master Kugele," Abbot Ambrose frowned. "Wipe your chin," he instructed in a hushed voice, as he wiped his own bearded chin. "You can see him after the meal." Without another word, he returned to the head table.

After breakfast, Charlie, Howard and Gus hurried up the stairs and back to their dorm. Charlie could not wait to hear about Rick's summer and to tell him about theirs.

Rick was busy unpacking his trunk with his back to the dormitory doors as Howard, Charlie and Gus slowly crept up behind him. Howard fought hard to keep from laughing out loud while he anticipated scaring the daylights out of Rick. On the other hand, Gus had to be quieted several times by Howard's stern glares as they tiptoed closer. Once they were right behind Rick, Howard held up his hand and silently counted down. Three, two, one

"Rick!" the three shouted at once.

"Aaah!" Rick screamed a high-pitched scream. He spun around and he fell onto his bed. "Don't do that!" he cursed. He was obviously embarrassed because his face was bright red.

"I'm so glad you are back," Gus said, wrapping his arms around Rick's skinny body in a tight bear hug that nearly knocked the glasses from the end of Rick's nose.

"Me, too," Charlie agreed with a big smile. He looked at Howard.

"Guess your plane didn't crash," Howard teased, sounding disappointed and trying to play it cool.

"Nice to see you, too, Howard," Rick said peeling himself free of Gus' arms.

"So, tell us, how was your trip?" Charlie urged and sat down on Rick's bed.

"Do you really want to hear?"

"Yes," Gus said.

"Sure," Howard shrugged indifferently and rolled his eyes. "If you must."

"It was so much fun, you wouldn't believe it!" Rick ignored Howard and began excitedly. "It was like no carnival

I've ever been to. The rides were out of this world. They have this one pirate ride. You go into what looks like a house on the outside but inside it is like an old bayou with a dock and rowboats, but you don't row them. You just get in and the boat drifts along. Then without warning it goes down these waterfalls into a cave. When you come out, you're between a pirate ship and a Spanish village. The pirates are firing their cannons at the village and the water splashes all around. It's so cool."

Charlie and Gus listened intently as Rick explained ride after ride. Howard pretended to be indifferent and cool, but Charlie noticed that he too was hanging on Rick's every word.

"Oh, I bought you guys something," Rick suddenly remembered. He reached into his trunk and pulled out a small, soft package. "This is for you, Gus," he said and handed it to him.

"For me?" Gus beamed in disbelief. 'Thank you." He grabbed the brightly colored package and immediately tore through the wrapping. He dropped the wrapping paper onto the floor and held up a sweatshirt. On the chest was a silk-screened picture of Mickey Mouse. "Wow!" he gushed.

"You'll notice that it's even signed by the mouse himself," Rick said proudly and pointed to the scribbled signature just under the image. "It wasn't easy getting him to sign it either."

"Thank you." Gus reached out to hug Rick again, but froze when Rick pulled away and pointed his finger at him.

"And here, this is for you," Rick said handing Charlie a smaller box.

"Thank you." Charlie grinned. He felt a twinge of guilt as he looked at the box. "But I didn't get you a gift," he said quietly.

Rick smiled. "That's okay. Open it," he urged.

Charlie carefully opened the box and took out a small figurine of a fairy. He recognized it immediately. "Tinkerbelle," he said, though it sounded more like a question. He smiled and tried to act grateful.

"Do you know why I bought it for you?" Rick asked.

"It better not be because you think I'm a fairy?" Charlie glared.

"No," Rick laughed, but the look in his eyes said otherwise. "I'll explain in a moment. This is for you," Rick said turning to Howard and handing him a slightly larger package.

Howard took the package, trying to act cool but inside he was as excited as though it were Christmas. He opened the box and carefully took out a figurine of Peter Pan. "Thanks," he said in a slightly confused voice.

"You're welcome," Rick said. "Now for the explanation."

"What? You actually thought about this?" Howard asked, giving the figurine a puzzled look.

"Yes," Rick answered in a slightly annoyed tone. "Like Peter Pan, Howard, you'll never grow up. You'll always be a boy. And like Peter Pan, who had no parents either, you're the leader of the Lost Boys, us."

Howard looked at Rick with a surprised expression. He smiled. "Well done."

"Now as for your present, Charlie," Rick said, turning back to look at Charlie. "I bought Tinkerbelle for you because like Tinkerbelle is to Peter Pan, you are to Howard, sort of his sidekick."

Charlie smiled. He was actually okay with his souvenir and he knew just where he was going to put it, on the windowsill above his bed.

"Hey, did you hear the news?" Charlie spoke up and changed the subject.

"What news?" Rick asked.

"Well, you weren't the only one who had an exciting summer," Gus spoke up with a smile. He gave Rick a complete and lengthy run down on everything that had gone on that summer. Rick listened intently and shook his head in disbelief.

"I can't believe he's our prefect," he said as he sat down on his bed.

"He's not all that bad." Gus shrugged. "In fact, he's lightened up on us a lot since Father Mark became Dean."

"Hey, let's go check out the new building." Rick changed the subject and jumped to his feet.

"Sure," the three boys nodded.

"It beats sitting around here listening to Gus," Howard whispered to Charlie.

"Howard," Charlie warned, but had to agree.

Rick quickly changed into his robes and the boys headed for the front grounds.

"So, you say this Father Mark is nice?" Rick asked as they walked into the hall.

"Yes," Gus answered. "But Charlie doesn't like him."

Rick gave Charlie a curious look.

"It's not that I don't like him," Charlie defended himself. "It's just there is something about him that makes me uncomfortable. That's all."

"I see," Rick nodded and dropped the subject. He was too excited about being back and hearing the news about the new building to be bothered with Charlie's paranoia.

Just as the boys reached the first floor, Charlie glanced to his left, toward the Abbot's office. He stopped and grabbed Howard's arm when he saw Abbot Ambrose and Prior Emmanuel talking with two uniformed policemen from town. Howard saw them, too, and told Rick and Gus to go on ahead; they'd catch up with them outside. The two waited until Rick and Gus were gone before they slowly inched their way down the hall toward the visitors.

"Thank you for letting us know," Abbot Ambrose said as he shook the hand of one of the officers. "She's such a dear Sister and loved by everyone here at the Abbey. It's hard to believe that someone would've done such a thing. You're sure she just didn't just fall or trip?"

"I'm afraid so, Father Abbot," the elder policeman answered. "At this point we're treating it as an assault."

A chill ran up Charlie's spine as he turned to Howard. Howard looked at Charlie; his eyes were wide behind his black-rimmed glasses.

"We're still following up on a couple of tips," the officer continued as he released the Abbot's hand. "But to be honest with you, Father Abbot, we don't have much. Unless we get more information, I seriously doubt we'll be able to close this case."

"We understand," Abbot Ambrose nodded.

"But we'll keep patrolling the area. My advice," the officer continued glancing at Charlie and Howard standing down the hall. "Be sure your boys don't wander off alone and keep them inside after sundown."

Abbot Ambrose noticed the officer was preoccupied with something behind him. He glanced over his shoulder and saw Charlie and Howard. He turned back to the officer. "You can rest assured," he answered.

"We'll be in touch." The officers nodded and then left.

Abbot Ambrose turned around and looked down the hall. "Master Miller and Master MacCready," he called to them in a disapproving voice.

Howard and Charlie jumped. They looked at each other, then turned back toward the Abbot.

"Yes," they answered in unison.

"I would like a word with the two of you, please." Abbot Ambrose inhaled deliberately and he folded his arms over his inflated chest. "In my office, now."

Prior Emmanuel frowned and slowly shook his head.

Charlie glanced at Howard as they both continued down the hall and into Abbot Ambrose's office. Abbot Ambrose and Prior Emmanuel followed and closed the door behind them.

"Please, have a seat, boys," Abbot Ambrose said as he walked around his deck and sat down in his chair.

Howard and Charlie sat down in the two empty chairs off to the side of the desk. A tall floor lamp sat between the chairs. Prior Emmanuel turned it on and then stood by the door. He tucked his arms inside his robes.

"We didn't hear a thing," Charlie blurted out before he thought. The look in Abbot Ambrose's eyes sent pangs of guilt though him. "We didn't hear much," Charlie corrected. "But we won't tell anyone, honest," he quickly added.

"I see," Abbot Ambrose nodded. "You boys know better than to eavesdrop. It is not polite and can get you into serious trouble."

"Father Abbot," Howard spoke up hesitantly.

Abbot Ambrose turned his attention to Howard. "Yes, Master Miller?"

"We heard you talking about Sister Margaret," he said nervously. "Is there any more news?"

Abbot Ambrose looked at Prior Emmanuel. There was a pained look in his blue eyes. He turned back to the boys. "Yes," he sighed and gave a nod. "The doctor has determined that Sister Margaret's injuries appear to have been caused by an attack. So they notified the authorities. The policemen were just telling us that they found a piece of a tree limb with blood on it in the mud nearby where Sister Margaret was found."

Charlie turned sharply and looked at Howard. His thoughts flashed with visions of his blood-smeared surplice and the mud and blood on his hands. For the first time the thought that he might have attacked Sister Margaret Mary raced into his mind. But how?

"No," he said softly and shook his head.

Abbot Ambrose rushed to Charlie's side and put his arms protectively around him. "It's okay," he assured Charlie. "The doctors are taking good care of her. She will be okay."

Charlie continued to look over the Abbot's shoulder at Howard. Howard did not move. It was as though he could read Charlie's mind. He just stared at Charlie.

DOUBTS

"So, there you are," Howard said as he climbed into the bell tower. "I've been looking all over the hilltop for you."

Charlie did not turn around. Instead he stared out at the front grounds, at the shadows of the trees that stretched toward the east. The sky glowed pink and orange as the sun began to set. Charlie's mind was numb and his eyes were red and damp with tears.

"Are you okay?" Howard asked, while he walked over to Charlie.

"I don't know," Charlie's voice quivered slightly. It was apparent to Howard that Charlie had been crying. "I feel like I'm losing my mind."

"Charlie," Howard sighed. "You are not losing your mind."

"Then how come I'm the only one who sees the shadow? How come I have the same nightmare over and over again and I wake up seeing someone standing over me?"

"I don't know," Howard admitted. He looked out at the front grounds.

"Howard," Charlie spoke softly but didn't take his eyes off the front lawn. "Do you think it's possible for a person to have done something so horrible that they can't remember it?"

Howard looked at Charlie curiously. "What are you talking about?"

Charlie looked at Howard. "I think I might have attacked Sister Margaret." The words nearly stuck in his throat as his eyes welled up with tears again.

"Why would you say such a horrible thing?" Howard said even though he was thinking the same thing. "You couldn't have."

"But the surplice," Charlie protested. "The blood. And remember Gus' surplice? It was muddy from the pig barns and that's where they found Sister Margaret. Don't you think that's odd?"

Howard thought about what Charlie had said. He had forgotten all about Gus' surplice. Charlie was right. It was very odd indeed.

"That doesn't mean you did it," Howard said trying to sound convinced but failing miserably. "Wait a second, I know a sure way of telling if you did it or not."

Charlie looked at his best friend and for a moment there was a glimmer of hope in his eyes, a hope that he had not committed a serious sin.

"Let me ask you one question and this will determine whether or not you did it. Where are the pig barns?" Howard asked, and looked at Charlie.

Charlie thought for a moment. He looked around the grounds and then back at Howard. He shook his head.

"I don't know," he answered, and smiled.

"There," Howard said, with a proud nod. "You couldn't possibly have done it. You don't even know where the pig barns are. You are innocent. Case dismissed." From the look in Howard's eyes, he seemed as relieved as Charlie. "Why didn't I think of it sooner?" he said, more to himself than to Charlie.

"I didn't do it," Charlie repeated to himself confidently. He turned and looked out at the forest. The smiled quickly faded from his lips; he looked at Howard with wide fearful eyes. "Oh, my God," Charlie gasped.

Howard furrowed his brow as he looked at Charlie.

"That means he's still out there," Charlie said, and looked back at the forest.

THE FRESHMEN

The loud clap from the small block of wood against the head table in the refectory signaled the end of breakfast and for the boys to be quiet. Father Mark stood up behind his chair. He looked at the boys and smiled.

"I know you are all excited to begin your first day of classes, but there are a few announcements to make first." He turned to Brother Conrad. "I know it is early, but the head of the Halloween committee would like a few words with you this morning. Brother Conrad," Father Mark nodded toward the monk to his left.

Brother Conrad quickly stood up. He smiled nervously. "There'll be a meeting of the Halloween committee this afternoon after classes in the common area on the fourth floor. Please be on time since we have a lot to discuss." He nodded to Father Mark and quickly slipped back into his chair.

"I would also like to add that there will be a meeting of the Altar Boys' Club this evening after study hall. Father Abbot will be attending so punctuality is strongly recommended," Father Mark said. He looked directly at Howard and Charlie. "And now for the last item on my list but the most important. I know with all of the excitement of the new building, a new school year, seeing old friends, that you may tend to forget, but this is extremely important. So, please pay attention. The police have asked for our full cooperation since they still have not been able to find Sister Margaret's attacker. No one is to leave this building without first checking in with your prefect and having someone with you. And absolutely no one is permitted outside after sundown. Last night more than one boy was found outside, Master Hertz," Father Mark looked directly at Larry. "This is a very serious matter. Anyone caught disobeying this curfew will be dealt with severely. Any questions?"

Instantly Rick's hand went up in the air. Father Mark turned to him. "Yes, Master Walters?"

As Rick stood up beside his chair, Howard and Charlie both lowered their heads and sank down in their seats. They braced themselves for another one of Rick's embarrassing questions.

"When you said severely," Rick asked in a tattletale voice as he glanced at Howard and Charlie. "What kind of punishment are you talking about? Work crew?"

"Oh, here we go again," Howard whispered to Charlie.

"Well, Master Walters." Father Mark nodded to himself. "That is definitely an option, but rather than looking at the punishment, why don't you focus on being obedient?"

"But," Rick started to protest. He caught the stern look in Brother Simon's eyes and quickly sat back down in his chair.

Charlie held his breath and tried not to laugh. He continued to look down at his lap, fearing to look up at Rick seated across from Howard.

Howard raised his hand.

"Yes, Master Miller?" Father Mark called on him.

Howard stood up and cleared his throat. "Has there been any news about Sister Margaret's condition?"

Father Mark looked at the floor and then back up at the boys.

"I'm afraid not. While her injuries are healing, she still has not regained consciousness. But, remember boys, it has only been a week and Sister Margaret is not as young as she once was."

Howard quietly sat back down in his seat.

"Let us not forget how serious your obedience is in this regard," Father Mark continued. "Now, try to remember what I've said, keep Sister Margaret in your prayers and also, enjoy your day."

After the prayer, the boys were dismissed.

"I can't believe we are stuck with Brother Simon as our prefect," Rick sighed and shook his head once he reached the hall.

"Get over it, Rick," Howard said as they all walked down the stairs to their first class as freshmen. "He's here to stay."

"I know," Rick said in a disgusted tone. "But it doesn't mean I have to like it."

"Hey," Charlie said as he looked at his mail slot. He quickly grabbed the letter. "It's from my grandmother."

"Well, it's about time," Howard said as they stopped on the landing between the first floor and the basement.

Gus, Rick, Dale and Howard huddled around Charlie as he quickly tore open the envelope.

"Maybe now we'll find out about the photograph of Father Mark that you sent her," Howard said.

"You sent her a picture? Where did you get a camera?" Rick asked.

Howard's eyes widened behind his black-framed glasses as he realized he just spilled the beans on himself. He sheepishly looked at Rick. "We sort of borrowed your camera. It was nice of you to let us use it," he smiled and slapped Rick on the back.

"Nice my foot!" Rick snapped and pulled away from Howard.

"Don't worry," Charlie spoke up as he read the letter. "Here's the money to buy more film." He handed Rick the bill that was enclosed in the letter. "My grandmother sent me the money to pay for the pictures."

"Pictures? You mean there were more than one?" Rick

glared at Howard and then looked at the money. "Oh, keep it." He shrugged and handed it back to Charlie.

"So, what did she say?" Howard probed as Charlie quickly read the letter. "It's not him! I was right!" Howard smiled knowingly, not giving Charlie a chance to answer.

Charlie's eyes widened and his mouth dropped open. The smile on Howard's face faded as he looked at Charlie.

"What?" he asked quietly.

"She said that it's definitely him," Charlie answered. His voice was hushed. A warm feeling blanketed him and paralyzed him as he became afraid.

"What guy? Who?" Rick asked confused.

"Last year a man went with my Uncle Chester to see my grandma. She couldn't remember his name, but told me what he looked like. From her description, the man sounded just like Father Mark," Charlie explained. "So, Howard and I borrowed your camera and took his picture. We sent it to her."

"I don't believe it's him." Howard shook his head in denial.

"Read it for yourself," Charlie said and handed him the letter.

Howard read the letter and shook his head.

"Well?" Charlie said.

"I guess it's true," Howard answered.

"Oh my god," Charlie gasped. "You don't think he could have—"

"No!" Howard interrupted. "Why would he hurt Sister Margaret?"

Charlie thought for a moment.

Howard handed the letter back to Charlie. He was not totally convinced of anything anymore.

Rick, Gus and Dale looked at each other in silence as they listened to Charlie and Howard.

"Come on, we better get to class," Gus finally spoke up. "I don't want to be late on our first day."

The boys walked into their new homeroom, which was across the hall from last year's homeroom. It was the same room they sat in many times the year before, but this year it was different. This year it was *their* homeroom, the high school freshmen's homeroom. They walked a little taller as they entered and took their seats.

"One good thing about this year." Gus leaned forward and poked Charlie in the back. "No Dougary and his goons."

"Yeah," Charlie nodded. He had forgotten that this year they would not have any classes with Dougary, Larry, Travis or even Austin. Charlie clenched his teeth as he thought about Austin and his false warning about the summer. Since Austin's return, Charlie had not spoken a single word to him even when they passed in the hall.

"Good morning," came the cheerful greeting as Brother Paul entered the room. He was a rather short man with a potbelly that hung over the belt around his waist. He had a cheerful smile and warm gray-blue eyes. His hair, what little was left of it, formed a white ring around the back of his head, from ear to ear. He wore glasses, similar to Howard's, perched on the end of his rather bulbous nose. He seemed to bounce as he walked over to his desk at the front of the room and set his black leather satchel down. He looked curiously at the boys as they sat rigidly in their chairs.

"Is that how you greet your teacher?" he asked and cocked his head to one side. "Now, stand up beside your desk. All of you. Come, come now. Snap to it." He clapped his hands to hurry the boys out of their seats. "Your first lesson in classroom etiquette. Whenever your teacher enters the room, the polite thing to do is to stand quietly beside your desk. When he says, 'Good morning' then you reply in kind. Shall we try it again?" He looked at the class. "Good morning, students."

"Good morning, Brother Paul," they returned in unison.

Brother Paul smiled. "Let us begin with a prayer."

The boys followed Brother Paul's lead as he led them in reciting the Hail Mary. Once they were through, they took their seats and silently watched as Brother Paul reached into his satchel and took out his teacher's guide. He pulled his long robes up a bit then sat down on the end of his heavy metal desk. Then he reached across the desk and moved a small, desktop podium over to him. He placed his book on it.

"Now, before we begin, let me go over your schedule with you." He looked over the top of his glasses at them and smiled, which made his thin lips curl at the ends in an odd sort of way. "You will begin each day here for your English class. Algebra and then World History will follow it. After lunch, you will report to either the choir room or the band studio located in the stone building next to the swimming pool. You know the one," he gestured, waving his hand in the air as though shooing away an invisible fly. "Next to the pottery studio. Anyway," he sighed. "We shall all meet again in the typing room for fifth period. It will alternate every other day with your study period. Your last class will meet here. On Monday, Wednesday and Friday it will be Health and on Tuesday and Thursday you will dress down and meet on the front lawn for Physical Education. This will be the only time you will be permitted out of uniform. However, the dress code for P.E. will be strictly enforced. Be sure to wear your yellow shorts and matching tee shirt. Anyone not in proper attire will find himself with Saturday work crew. Any questions?" He paused and looked around the class. No one raised his hand. "Good." Brother Paul smiled again. "Let us begin. Please open your English 101 books to chapter one."

Their first day of classes passed quickly. Gus could not wait to get out of typing class. He rubbed his sore knuckles and looked over his shoulder to be sure Brother Paul was not following him with that vicious pointer stick as he headed back to his homeroom.

"He told you not to touch your typewriter," Rick said smugly as he noticed Gus' red hands.

"Well how was I to know that he would actually hit a person with that thing?" Gus spoke up in defense of himself.

"He told us, that's how!" Rick answered a little bit louder.

"Never m-m-mind him," Dale said to Gus. "Da-da-did he hurt you?"

"Nah, it just stings a bit." Gus shrugged.

Charlie smiled to himself as he and Howard silently walked with the others. It was actually very comical to see their Brother Paul lose his temper when Gus jammed the keys of his typewriter instead of following along in his book. Brother Paul had warned all of them, in fact Gus, several times. But even after the first time being hit by the pointer stick, Gus did it again. The temptation was just too strong, and Brother Paul was quick with his stick.

"I think I'm going to like typing class," Howard said, with a rather fiendish grin.

"Oh, be nice." Charlie smiled back at him. "Oh now what?" Charlie sighed when he noticed Austin walking toward them.

"Just ignore him," Howard said, turning his head away.

"Hi guys," Austin greeted them. "Have you heard the news?"

No one answered.

"The police are upstairs talking with Abbot Ambrose and Father Mark. They want to start questioning some of us about Sister Margaret."

A chill ran up Charlie's spine and he looked at Howard.

"Well, I'd be careful if I were you." Howard sneered at Austin. "You know Dougary and your other pals might not like you talking to us."

"Oh, they don't scare me." Austin shrugged.

"They should." Gus stepped forward. He puffed up his chest and glared at Austin defiantly.

Austin looked at Gus and then at the rest of them and shook his head. "Losers," he muttered. He turned around and walked off to his next class.

"Way to go, Gus," Rick said, with a near-laugh in his voice.

Gus shrugged and shook his head as though it was not a big deal. He followed the others into their classroom.

"Pssst, Howard," Gus whispered, and leaned forward over his deck. He tapped Howard on the back.

Howard turned around.

"What?"

"What if the police want to talk to me?" he asked, sounding a bit panicked.

"Why would they want to talk to you?"

"Well, wasn't Sister Margaret attacked the same night you and Charlie were out of bed? You remember you said Charlie had a bloody nose."

Howard nodded. He remembered. How could he not?

"But I didn't see any blood on his pillowcase," Gus continued.

A jolt swept through Howard, his entire body stiffened. "They're not gonna wanna talk to you. But if they do, just keep your mouth shut," he ordered in a stern whisper. He glared at Gus a moment to make his point but it only made Gus' eyes widen more.

"He hurt Sister Margaret, didn't he?" Gus whispered and looked at Charlie.

"No, he didn't!" Howard snapped. "And don't you ever say that again!"

"What are you guys up to?" Gus asked.

"Nothing. Now just keep your nose out of where it doesn't belong," Howard answered and turned around.

Charlie glanced at Howard and Gus. While he could not hear what they said, from the look on Howard's face, it must not have been good.

The bell rang and signaled the start of their last class. As their teacher entered the room the entire class jumped to their feet and stood beside their desks. Charlie was surprised to see that it was not a monk or a nun.

"Good afternoon, boys," the man greeted them. "My name is Clifford Brown."

"Good afternoon, Mister Brown," they returned.

"Please take your seats." Clifford smiled warmly at them as he set his leather briefcase on the metal desk. True to his name, his eyes were brown behind his round, wire-rimmed glasses. The thick hair that covered his head and forearms was also dark brown. He was clean-shaven, but Charlie suspected had he a beard or mustache it too would have been brown.

Mister Brown looked younger than the other teachers, Charlie thought. He wondered if this was his first teaching assignment right out of college.

"As you have noticed, I am not a monk." He continued to smile. "In fact, I am not even a Catholic."

A faint gasp rose from some of the boys. They looked at each other confused.

"It's okay." Clifford laughed at their reaction. "The Abbot knows and is fine with it. Let's begin with a few introductions and then we'll get into our book."

Charlie was so absorbed in the class when the bell rang out forty-five minutes later; he jumped and nearly dropped his book on the floor. He quickly stuffed his book into his desk.

"Howie," Charlie called in a hushed voice. He leaned across the aisle and grabbed Howard by the arm before he had a chance to stand up.

"What?"

Charlie watched and waited until Gus, Rick and Dale left the room. "What did Gus want?"

Howard looked over his shoulder at the classroom door and then back at Charlie. "He just wanted to know what to do if the police wanted to question him. That's all." He shrugged indifferently.

"Well, what if he tells them about my surplice?" Charlie asked in his hushed voice. "He saw us that morning, remember? Will he talk?"

"No, I told him not to," Howard answered confidently but then a worried look came over his face. "At least I don't think he will."

"But what if the police get him in a room and start hammering him with questions," Charlie asked, feeling extremely nervous.

Howard shook his head warily, not wanting to actually say his next words and regretting it already. "I guess we will just have to find out who is doing this before that happens."

"I think we both know who it is," Charlie said.

Howard looked at him. "But proving it is another thing."

"We just have to set a trap for the shadow," Charlie said, already thinking of a plan.

"Whatever we do, we have to keep it quiet. No one can know what we are up to," Howard cautioned.

"Agreed."

Moments later, in their cubicle, Howard and Charlie quietly sat quietly on their beds, thinking up a plan that would work. Howard had dismissed Charlie's original plan of a rabbit snare like trap, but his idea of a bear trap would get them both into more trouble.

"How does one catch a shadow?" Charlie asked, scratching his head in frustration. He fell back on his pillow and stared at the ceiling. Before he knew it he was asleep.

A thick fog moved through the tall trees of the forest. Slowly Charlie crept along the path leading to the pottery studio. He glanced over his shoulder but could no longer see behind him. The fog was all around him.

"Charlie," a voice called to him.

He spun around. No one was there.

"Charlie," another voice called.

"Where are you?" Charlie called back, turning in circles, searching the foggy mist.

Suddenly a dark figure appeared.

Charlie froze.

Slowly it reached out its hand with long gnarly fingers and yellowed claw-like nails. Just as its eyes glowed red, its hand grasped Charlie's shoulder.

"Charlie."

Charlie lunged and sat up in his bed, screaming as he looked into Howard's shocked face.

"It's okay. It's okay," Howard repeated. "You were having a bad dream."

Charlie panted as he tried to calm his rapidly beating heart.

He looked around the empty dorm and then out the window to his left. The sun was already beginning its descent. Long shadows from the forest were starting to stretch across the great lawn.

"Come on," Howard urged. "Or we'll be late for dinner." He cautiously took hold of Charlie's arm again and pulled him to his feet.

The two boys quickly joined the last group and headed down the stairs.

"You wanna talk about it?" Howard asked as they rounded the first landing.

"It was the same as before," Charlie answered and gave a noticeable shudder.

"The shadow again?"

"Yeah."

Dinner seemed to drag on. Charlie barely touched his mashed potatoes and chicken-fried steak. He kept thinking about his dream and about the police questioning them. He glanced at the head table, but when he noticed Father Mark looking at him, Charlie quickly looked away. His heart pounded. He looked at Howard. Howard appeared to be having the same trouble eating as him. Charlie suspected why. Howard was probably thinking about their previous conversation about Gus. Charlie looked across the table at Gus.

"Okay, that does it," Rick snapped. "Why are you two so quiet tonight?"

"Whadaya mean?" Howard sneered at Rick.

"What're you two up to?" Rick leaned forward and pried. "Come on, you can tell us."

"What makes you think we're up to anything?" Howard scoffed.

"Because you're always up to something." Rick sat back in his chair. He glanced at Gus who was busy eating, seemingly oblivious to everyone around him.

Charlie and Howard looked at each other.

"A-ha! So, you are up to something!" Rick said, looking

back at them. "If you won't tell me, maybe Gus will."

Gus looked up with his mouth still full.

"No!" Howard snapped and reached his hand across the table as if to stop Rick. He looked at Charlie for help, but Charlie just shrugged his shoulders as though to give in.

"All right," Howard sighed, then tightened his jaw. "But you have to keep this quiet. We think that Father Mark is trying to frame Charlie for the attack on Sister Margaret."

Rick cocked his head. "Really?" He tried to look concerned but the tone in his voice sounded more like a laugh of disbelief.

"It's true," Charlie spoke up. "We didn't want to say anything because we knew you'd act like this."

"Well, come on," Rick said. "How do you know Father Mark attacked Sister Margaret? And if he did, why would he try to frame you? What makes you so special?"

"Look, you stupid little twit," Howard leaned across the table and glared intently at Rick. "It's true and if I hear anything about this from anyone else, I will personally rearrange your face."

"You don't scare me, Howard," Rick said trying to put on a brave face, but everybody knew, Rick was no match for Howard.

"Rick," Charlie spoke up. "I'm asking you to please keep it quiet. If you don't want to help us that's fine but please don't say anything."

"Who said I didn't want help you?" Rick protested. "I'll help you. So, what's the plan?"

Charlie looked at Howard and frowned. "We haven't figured that out yet."

"Well, tell me what you have and let me see if I can figure out a plan," Rick said.

Charlie glanced at Howard and Gus and then quietly filled Rick in on his nightmares and the shadow. Rick listened. He did not appear to be as convinced as they were that Charlie's shadow was real, let alone, Father Mark was involved in it.

"I'll think of something," Rick said confidently. He really

did not have a clue but he was not going to let Howard know it.

The serving brother set Rick's dessert in front of him. Rick wrinkled up his nose at the square piece of pound cake with half of a canned peach on top. Thick peach syrup dripped down the sides of the yellow cake. He picked up his spoon and poked the peach. "Yuck," he shivered.

"Thank you," Charlie said to the monk who served him his dessert. He watched the monk disappear through the doorway to the right of the head table.

"So, any ideas yet?" Howard asked.

"First we need to find out if the shadow that is paying Charlie a visit at night is real or not," Rick answered.

"Well, duh!" Howard said and rolled his eyes.

"But how?" Charlie asked earnestly, ignoring Howard's comment. "Whenever I wake up, it disappears."

"And since I can't see anything without my glasses, I'll never be able to see it," Howard spoke up.

"We do have a problem," Rick sighed and thought for a moment. He glanced over at Gus and watched Gus sprinkle powdered sugar on his already too-sweet peach. Rick visibly gagged at the sight but then his expression changed. An idea came to him and he grabbed the shaker of powdered sugar from Gus.

"Hey! I'm not through with that," Gus protested.

"I've got it!" Rick said a bit too loudly. Heads all around him turned and looked at him. He smiled at them, a bit embarrassed and handed the shaker back to Gus.

"What we need to do is—" Rick leaned across the table and whispered his plan to Charlie and Howard.

CURFEW

After dinner, the boys had a half an hour to brush their teeth and get to their homerooms for forty-five minutes of study hall. Even though it was their first day of classes, some of their teachers felt the need to assign them homework. Charlie could not remember when he had been assigned so much to do. Brother Paul assigned them to study two lists of twenty words. One list was for spelling and the other was for vocabulary. Charlie looked at the lists and shook his head. He would never be able to remember all of these, he thought. Father Martin, their Algebra I teacher, assigned them fifty problems and the "nice Mister Brown" assigned them to read two chapters, twenty pages, in their Health book by their next class in two days. Charlie set his Health book aside and tried to focus on his Algebra assignment.

The forty-five minutes flew by and Charlie still had two more problems to do. Howard waited impatiently by the door for him to finish. When he had, the two headed back to their dorm.

When they entered the dorm, they immediately spotted Gus and Dale in the lounge area in the center of the dorm. The two were seated on opposite arms of the sofa facing each other with their stocking feet on the cushions.

Charlie and Howard gave each other a worried glance. Casually they walked over to them.

"So, what's going on?" Charlie asked trying to act calm but inside he was panicking, afraid that Gus was talking about their plan with Dale. It was not that he did not trust Dale. It was just that the fewer people who knew about it, the better their chances of catching the shadow.

"Well," Gus grinned. "I—"

"Boys?" the familiar deep voice touched their ears.

Howard and Charlie jumped and turned around as Brother Simon walked over to them.

"Feet off the furniture, Master Gustav and Master Kaufman," he said in his usual stern tone. Gus and Dale immediately complied. "Aren't the two of you supposed to be in a meeting?"

"Oh!" Charlie gasped. He had completely forgotten all about the Altar Boys' Club meeting. "Yes, Brother," he answered.

"I suggest you both hurry," Brother Simon said in a tone that was meant as a warning. "Do not keep the Abbot waiting."

Charlie and Howard hurried off without as much as a "see you later" to Gus.

Visiting Room Five was quiet when the two entered. Abbot Ambrose stood in front of the white stone fireplace with his arms folded over his chest. He was not smiling as he looked at the two tardy boys. With their heads ducked, they took a seat in the last two folding chairs behind the sofa. Charlie glanced up.

"So kind of you both to make it," Abbot Ambrose said as he looked over the top of his half-moon spectacles at them. Charlie's eyes met with the Abbot's for a brief moment. Charlie could tell that his great-uncle was not in a good mood. He looked down at the floor.

"The reason I have called this meeting is that we need your help. I know that we do not have all twelve members of the Altar Boys' Club yet, but the eight of you will be enough for now.

"The police have informed us that they have little to go on in apprehending the person who attacked Sister Margaret Mary. As a way of cooperating with them we have instituted a curfew, as you are all well aware. We now need your help in making sure the boys adhere to it. Last night several boys disobeyed the curfew were outside after sundown, alone. I don't need to tell you how serious that can be.

"What we would like you boys to do is, in pairs of two; make sure all the boys are accounted for. You will be assigned to check the grounds just before sundown and make sure all the boys are back in the building. Once inside, you will give your report to your prefects. If you have any problem getting any of the boys to comply, you have the authority to assign them work crew. This is a very serious matter."

Charlie looked at Howard and then at Abbot Ambrose.

"We, that is Father Mark, Master Troyer, and I, have assigned you into pairs. Master Troyer will hand out your assignments now."

Robert Troyer, the sacristan and student head of the club, stood up. In what Charlie thought a rather haughty manner, Robert handed each of the boys a sheet of paper. Charlie quickly scanned the list to see who he was partnered with. His heart sank as he read the name next to his, Sean Adkins. Sean was an okay boy, a sophomore, but he was a member of Saint Peter dorm. They were assigned to cover the parking lot and garage area across the front grounds. He glanced at Sean.

Sean stared sternly at Charlie. His crew cut, dark brown hair and even darker brown eyes made him look even more menacing. Had it not been that the two were the same height and build, Charlie would have been more nervous. Instead, Charlie glared back at Sean, daring him to look away.

"Master Troyer will hand out flashlights to each of you. Be very careful and do not lose them. If you need batteries, please don't hesitate to ask. Are there any questions?" Abbot Ambrose asked and looked directly at Rick.

Rick did not raise his hand. He was too upset at being

paired off with Howard. They were assigned to check the swimming pool and pottery studio buildings.

Abbot Ambrose looked around the room and then smiled for the first time. "Well, that is good. Your duties begin immediately and unless Master Troyer has anything further to discuss with you—" Robert shook his head. "This meeting is adjourned."

Everyone stayed in his seat and waited for Abbot Ambrose to leave the room before they stood.

"I can't believe this," Rick moaned and shook his head. "You'd better not get me into trouble out there," he sneered at Howard.

Howard did not hear him. He was busy looking at Charlie's assignment sheet.

"I got stuck with the bookworm," Howard lamented. "Who did you get?"

Charlie opened his mouth to answer.

"Hey, MacCreepy," Sean called from the doorway. "Get the lead out. I don't want to be up all night."

Charlie rolled his eyes. "See you later," he said to Howard, and met Sean at the door. Robert handed each of them a large flashlight and the two set out.

"Don't take all night, guys. Be quick about checking your areas and then get back to your dorms. It's already late, and Father Mark wants us all in bed on time."

"Come on, MacCreepy," Sean sneered.

The two headed off across the front grounds toward the parking garage. As they reached the middle of the lawn the overwhelming feeling that someone was watching them made Charlie feel uneasy. He stopped and flashed his light at the dark shadows of the forest.

"What's the matter with you?" Sean barked, shining his light in Charlie's eyes. "The garages are this way," he said and turned around.

Charlie blinked as he tried to readjust his eyes. He quickly followed Sean.

They quickly inspected the parking lot and met at the entrance door of the garage.

"Hey, Mac Wimpy, you afraid of the dark?"

"No," Charlie answered in an offended tone.

"Fine, then you check the basement."

"No problem," Charlie agreed without hesitation. He was not afraid of the basement. He'd been down there several times in the past year.

Sean walked Charlie to the basement door. Trying to hold his light steady in his trembling hand, he watched as Charlie descended the stairs. Once Charlie was out of sight, Sean turned around and pressed his back against the wall. Slowly he shone his flashlight beam around the garage. Four of the five bays were occupied with the various cars of the Abbey, all black and all very eerie looking in the dark.

"Well," Charlie said confidently as he came up the stairs. Sean jumped, nearly dropping his flashlight. Charlie smiled to himself. "The basement is clear."

"All clear up here too," Sean said quickly. "Let's get back to the dorm."

It was well after lights out by the time Charlie made it back to his cubicle. Howard was already fast asleep when Charlie finally slipped into bed. All thoughts of their plan to catch the shadow left his mind as his head reached his pillow and he drifted off to sleep.

A DAY IN THE LIFE OF A FRESHMAN

The hallway was quiet when Charlie and Howard left the shower room. All around them the boys, still half-asleep, brushed their teeth and combed their hair.

"So what time did you get in last night?" Howard asked while he and Charlie headed back to their dorm. He dried his dripping hair with the towel around his neck.

"About eleven I think," Charlie answered. "Sean kept blinding me with his flashlight. I had to check the garage by myself because Sean was too afraid. You and I need to work together."

"I don't know how we can arrange that," Howard answered and opened his closet door. "It would have to be approved by Robert, Father Mark and Abbot Ambrose. And I get the feeling Robert doesn't like us very much."

"Me, too," Charlie agreed.

The two quickly dressed and made their way down the stairs to the refectory. After the prayer, Father Mark instructed the boys to be seated while the announcements were made. Brother Conrad reported that the Halloween committee had decided in addition to the annual costume contest there would be a talent show. Each grade would have to come up with a skit and perform it at the party on Halloween night. Then Brother Owen announced the names of the seniors who would be working at the Abbey's Oktoberfest booth, and he reminded everyone to be on their best behavior, as the Abbey would still be offering tours to the public.

After all the announcements were made, Father Mark and the prefects left. The serving brothers entered and began making their rounds. Howard groaned as he looked at the bowl of oatmeal that was set before him. He hated oatmeal almost as much as he hated canned prunes. He took a slice of warm toast from the middle of the table and buttered it.

"So, when are we going to put our plan into action?" Rick whispered across the table.

Charlie looked at Howard and shrugged. "That's the problem. I never know when the shadow's going to show up."

"Then we'll just have to keep setting the trap," Rick answered. "Sooner or later we're bound to catch him."

Charlie looked at Howard and frowned. He did not like having Rick involved in their plan. He still was not sure he could trust him.

After breakfast was finished, Charlie rushed upstairs and grabbed his books. The first period bell rang just as he took his seat. Brother Paul bounced in right on schedule and began the prayer. After the prayer, the boys took their seats.

"Good morning," Brother Paul greeted in his usual cheerful voice.

"Good morning, Brother Paul," the boys responded together.

"I understand we need to come up with a skit for this year's Halloween party," Brother Paul continued with a twinkle in his eye. "As your home room faculty member, I have been given the assignment to help you put together your presentation. So, for the next few minutes, let's hear some ideas." He looked at the eleven blank faces staring at him. "Oh, come, come now. This is going to be so much fun," he said in an even more animated voice. "Master Miller, how about you?"

Howard sat straight up in his chair as though it had been electrified. "Ah," he stammered and shook his head.

"Master Kugele?" Brother Paul asked hopefully.

Gus looked like a deer caught in the headlights of an oncoming car. His mouth was open but no sound came out.

"Oh, please," Brother Paul sighed and pouted. "Surely one of you must have an idea." He looked around the room and then smiled. "Master Walters, thank you. I was beginning to think I was in the wrong class."

Rick stood up next to his desk. "Why don't we do something with a Halloween theme?" he said and sat down.

The smile quickly faded from Brother Paul's thin lips. "And just what did you have in mind?" he asked in an exhausted tone.

"Oh, nothing," Rick answered without standing up. "That was all."

Howard and Charlie looked at each other, rolled their eyes and laughed.

"Well, we're almost out of time this morning," Brother Paul said as he looked at the clock. "Your assignment for tomorrow is to come up with ideas. We've been given a twenty-minute time slot on the program," he said as he reviewed the notice. "Halloween is only a few weeks away and that doesn't give us much time.

"Now, let's begin with our spelling quiz wiz." Brother Paul smiled as he took out his black binder and opened it to the test section. Reluctantly, Charlie took out a piece of paper and put his name in the upper right corner. He wished he had taken a few minutes that morning to review the spelling words.

The bell rang none too soon, signaling the end of the first period and time for everyone to prepare for their next class. The boys all remained seated and watched Brother Paul gather his things and leave the room.

"Great," Howard sighed. "It's not as though we don't have enough to think about already. I don't know anything about skits and acting and junk like that."

"I'm not surprised," Rick said in his usual superior tone. He slipped his English book back into his desk and took out his binder. "The theatre is for cultured people."

"If you stick your nose any higher in the air, I'm gonna let you have it," Howard warned, clenching his fists.

"My parents have taken me to several operas and plays," continued Rick, ignoring Howard's threat. "Why just last summer we caught Godspell, Jesus Christ Superstar, Faust-"

"Oh, pardon me," Howard jeered as he put his hand over his heart and gave a slight bow. "I didn't realize we were in the presence of high society."

"Maybe if you weren't so busy chasing shadows, you'd learn something," Rick growled back at Howard.

The words struck Howard like a slap in the face. He reached across the aisle and grabbed Rick's bony arm tightly. "Watch your mouth you idiot! You're supposed to keep that a secret."

"What?" Rick winced and tried to pull free. "I didn't say anything."

"Howard, just let him go," Charlie said in a defeated tone. "Rick knows if he breaks his word and blabs, then that's it, we're done with him."

"Yeah," Rick said still struggling in Howard's tight grip.

Howard let go and sat back behind his desk. Charlie leaned over to him.

"You have to apologize," he whispered.

"Are you nuts?" Howard objected and gave Charlie a disgusted look.

"No," Charlie answered. "Think about it. We need Rick on our side. We need his help with the shadow. He's the only one with access to the stuff we need."

Howard thought for a moment. Charlie was right. He glanced at Rick who was rubbing his arm and then back at Charlie. Charlie nodded, urging him to go ahead and apologize.

"Oh, all right," Howard said and stood up. He stepped across the narrow aisle and stood beside Rick's desk. Rick pretended to be busy. "I'm sorry about that," Howard apologized quietly.

Rick looked up. "I'm sorry, did you say something?"

Howard could feel his face redden and his jaw tense as he clenched his teeth. He glanced again at Charlie and then back at Rick. "I said I'm sorry."

"I see," Rick sighed melodramatically. "And?"

"And what?" Howard answered and looked confused.

"Well I guess it's really not your fault you haven't been exposed to more cultural things," Rick added.

Howard's shoulders slumped. He looked over his shoulder at Charlie. Charlie could see the burning anger in Howard's eyes. He smiled and nodded for Howard to stay calm. Howard turned back to Rick.

"Just be careful," Howard said in a very controlled voice. "We can't let it get out about the 'you-know-what'."

"I know," Rick answered hastily. "I won't say anything."

Howard nodded to himself and then returned to his desk. He looked at Charlie and nodded as though to say, there, I did it.

Charlie smiled and nodded in return.

The afternoon sun shone brightly in the clear summer sky, but there was still a nip in the air as Charlie and Howard walked across the front lawn.

"Do you think Rick will really come up with a skit?" Charlie asked.

"I don't know," Howard shrugged. "But I thought of one."

"You did?"

"Yes," Howard answered a bit offended by Charlie's surprised tone. "I thought we could enact a typical freshman school day. You know two of us could be freshmen and the rest of us could be the faculty. We would start with waking up, breakfast, then first period. You could impersonate Brother Paul, you do him so well!" Howard was beginning to get excited and laughed as he imagined the skit in his mind.

Charlie listened as they walked. He liked Howard's idea.

Suddenly, the feeling that someone was watching him caused the hairs on the back of his neck to stand up. Charlie stopped and slowly looked around.

Howard took a couple steps and then realized Charlie was not beside him. He turned around and saw the worried expression on Charlie's face.

"What is it?" he asked, walking back over to Charlie.

"I don't know," Charlie answered. He continued to search the shadows in the forest. "I just had that feeling again, that someone was watching us."

"The shadow?" Howard asked and looked around.

"I'm not sure." Charlie shook his head.

"Well, I don't see anything," Howard admitted, looking one last time at the forest's edge.

"I guess I'm just overreacting," Charlie sighed.

Just then, in the darkness of the forest, a shadow moved. Charlie saw it and he looked at Howard. By the look on Howard's face, Charlie knew he had seen it too.

"What was that?" Howard breathed.

"I don't know," Charlie answered.

Before either said another word, they both took off in a run back to the Abbey. They were out of breath as they sat down on the front steps of the main entrance.

"We have to put our plan into action," Howard panted. "Tonight."

Charlie nodded in agreement and continued to gasp for air. "Let's go find Rick and Gus."

The two hurried up to their dorm. As they passed by Saint Peter dorm, they noticed Dougary and his goons picking on a new boy from Saint Thomas dorm.

"Let it go," Charlie told Howard and grabbed his arm. "We have work to do. Besides, here comes Father Mark."

Howard picked up his pace and hurried after Charlie.

Rick and Gus had their heads together, talking in Rick's cubicle as Howard and Charlie walked into the dormitory. Rick quickly silenced Gus when he noticed the two walking toward them.

"What are you two out of breath about?" Rick asked.

"We need to talk about our plan," Charlie said in a hushed voice.

"We need to set the trap tonight," Howard added. "Do you have everything?"

"Yes," Rick nodded.

"Great! Then we're all set. After lights out we'll set it up," Howard said.

~§~

The next morning, Howard and Charlie hurried down the empty stairwell as fast as they dared. It had taken them extra time cleaning up their cubicle after breakfast, leaving them only a few minutes before first period.

"I can't believe it." Charlie shook his head. "For the first time in weeks I slept all night."

"Yeah." Howard frowned. "I'm happy for you. Just don't let it happen again. We can't be late to class every day."

Charlie smiled at Howard's sarcastic tone.

The classroom was silent when the two walked into the room. The clock above the chalkboard said they still had five minutes before Brother Paul would arrive.

"We had better tell Rick about your idea for our skit," Charlie whispered to Howard. "Otherwise we could get stuck with whatever he's dreamt up, and you know the parts we'd get won't be good."

"I guess you're right," Howard nodded. He took his seat at his desk between Charlie and Rick.

"Hey, Rick," he greeted.

Rick looked up at Howard and glared. "Come to grovel and beg me to come up with a skit for the class?"

"No, but if you're gonna have that attitude, I'm not going to tell you what I was going to."

"Howard," Charlie groaned. He reached over and nudged

him in the shoulder. "Come on, be nice."

"Yes, Howie, be nice," Rick mocked in a pouting voice.

Howard clenched his teeth and looked at Charlie, then back at Rick.

"I just wanted to tell you that if you haven't come up with an idea for our skit—"

"Oh, but I have," Rick interrupted in an excited voice. He smiled smugly.

"You have?" Charlie asked, failing miserably to hide his disappointment.

"Yes, I have but you'll just have to wait until class to hear it." Rick turned up his nose at them both.

"Well, I like Howard's idea and I think we should go with it," Charlie quickly spoke up.

"I see. Well tell me all about your scathingly brilliant masterpiece, Mister 'I-don't-know-anything-about-the-theater,'" Rick mocked. "I'm all ears."

Howard shot a look of dread at Charlie that seemed to say, what's the use. Hesitantly he began to explain his idea to Rick. As he did, the rest of the class began to huddle around him. They all became excited at Howard's skit and began volunteering to play the different parts before Howard had a chance to finish.

"So, what do you think?" Charlie asked Rick as Howard finished.

"I like Howard's s-s-skit," Dale spoke up.

"Me, too," the other boys added.

Rick looked around the classroom at the other boys. He was not pleased that they were so quick to accept Howard's idea for their skit.

"I'll go along with it on one condition," he said looking directly at Howard. "Howard plays Sister Lillian."

"What?" Howard shrieked. "There's no way I'm wearing a dress!"

"A habit," Rick corrected. "Nuns wear a habit."

"It's still a dress and I'm not wearing it!"

"It's either that or we let Brother Paul decide when he gets here." Rick smiled, knowing he had Howard just where he wanted him.

Howard looked at Charlie for help.

"It can't be any worse than wearing these," Charlie said as he pulled out the sides of his cassock.

Howard thought for a moment. Charlie did have a point, but a nun's habit? Him? "Okay," Howard sighed. "Deal."

The bell rang just as Brother Paul bounded into the room.

The day felt long to Charlie and Howard. Classes seemed to drag on as though the clocks were purposely slow. Charlie's mind was so filled with ideas and plans about their skit that there was no room for thinking about anything else, let alone the shadow and Sister Margaret Mary. Just as Charlie and Howard started up the stairs to their dormitory, Austin walked up behind them.

"Hey, guys," he greeted the two.

Charlie stopped and turned around midway up the flight of steps. He looked at Austin coldly.

"What do you want?" Howard blurted and took a step down, closer to Austin.

"I'm looking for Gus," he answered. "Abbot Ambrose wants him to come to his office immediately."

Charlie shuddered and looked at Howard. Austin gave him a curious look but did not ask any questions.

"Why does he want him?" Howard asked.

"How should I know?" Austin snapped and gave Howard a disgusted look. "I was just asked to find him. So, have you seen him?"

Howard looked at Charlie whose eyes were wide with fear. He turned back to Austin. "Last I saw him, he, Rick and Dale were headed to the pool."

"Great! Thanks!" Austin answered and then hurried off to find them.

"Howard," Charlie said in a fearful voice. "What if the laundry monks said something to the Abbot about my muddy surplice?"

"Charlie, has anyone ever told you, you worry too much. If they had, you would've been called into Abbot Ambrose's office long ago."

"You sure?" Charlie asked, not totally convinced with Howard's reasoning.

"Yeah, come on," Howard said and the two continued up the stairs toward their dorm.

As they reached the fourth floor, Howard held open the heavy metal fire door for Charlie. "You have to go with me when I ask Sister Lillian if I could borrow her habit," he said.

"Okay," Charlie agreed. "Then you'll have to help me ask Brother Paul for one of his."

"Deal," Howard said and nodded. They shook hands to seal their deal. "I'll get us checked out of study hall tonight so we can work on writing the script for our skit."

That evening, after dinner, Charlie and Howard met in their homeroom for study hall. True to his word, Howard had arranged for them to be able to go to the typing room to work on their skit. The minutes ticked away as the two of them worked. They were so busy that they did not notice the clock strike nine.

"Boys?" a voice came from the doorway.

Charlie and Howard jumped. They turned around to see Father Mark standing in the doorway.

"Shouldn't you two be checking your assignments outside?" he asked.

They both looked at the clock.

"Oh my—" Charlie gasped. "We're sorry, Father Mark. We were just working on our class skit and lost track of the time." He quickly gathered up his books and papers.

"That's no excuse," Father Mark said coldly, his arms folded over his chest. "Being an Altar Boy is a privilege not to be taken lightly. This is the second time the two of you have been late, not to mention I've had a couple reports from your assigned partners."

"We're truly sorry, Father Mark," Howard spoke up. "It

won't happen again."

"See to it that it does not," Father Mark answered sharply and stepped to the side to let them pass. "You both can be replaced."

"Yes, Father," Charlie nodded sheepishly as he rushed by Father Mark. They stopped by their homeroom and dropped off their books then ran up the stairs to the first floor.

"Figures," Charlie said when he caught sight of Sean standing outside Father Mark's office.

"I'll catch you later," Howard said.

"Hurry up, Mac Tardy," Sean yelled. His voice echoed throughout the cold, empty hallway. "We don't have all night."

"Sorry," Charlie apologized but in the most insincere voice he could muster.

When the two stepped outside, Charlie suddenly remembered he had forgotten his flashlight.

"Forget it, Mac Stupid. I'm not waiting. Come on," Sean groaned and started across the front grounds.

Charlie quickly followed him, not wanting to be left alone in the dark.

The two headed across the front grounds while crickets chirped in the distance and frogs croaked all around them. The beam from Sean's flashlight did little to illuminate the grounds around them. They had just enough light to see a few feet ahead of them. Sean kept swinging the beam from the left to right as they walked, trying to see as much as he could. He did not want to let on that he was actually afraid of the dark, but Charlie already figured it out.

Suddenly in the distance, just out of the light beam's range, a twig snapped. Sean froze in his tracks, causing Charlie to bump into him. He shone his flashlight beam in the direction of the sound. The beam dimly illuminated a small patch of the forest just beyond the parking garage. Sean slowly moved the beam as he searched the edge of the woods. He struggled to keep his hand steady as he gripped the flashlight.

"Who's there?" Charlie shouted into the darkness. He felt

strangely braver knowing that Sean was afraid.

There was no reply, just silence. Even the crickets and frogs were silent. Sean began to move the beam of light slowly to the right and then back to the left. The sound of the garage door slamming shut caused them both to jump.

"There is definitely someone out here," Charlie whispered. He stayed close to Sean and the flashlight. "We had better go check it out," he added, in a tone that said he really did not want to. "Come on."

Slowly the two made their way over to the garage. They could see light shining through the cracks in the doors.

"Hello?" Sean nervously called ahead of them.

Suddenly the light inside went out. Sean stopped and looked at Charlie. He was glad it was dark; he did not want Charlie to see the fear in his eyes.

"Did you see that?" he asked in a high-pitched whisper.

"Yes," Charlie whispered. "Let's go." He tried to make his voice as deep and angry as possible to hide his own fear.

"The light switch is just inside the door," Charlie told Sean as they approached the door. "Shine your light to the left, the switch is on the wall."

"Okay," Sean answered. He gripped the flashlight with both hands to try to steady its beam.

Charlie took a deep breath, then swung the door open boldly. Sean quickly shone his light on the wall as instructed and Charlie quickly flipped the lights on. The fluorescent lights flickered as they came on and the once-dark parking garage lit up. Both boys gave a brief sigh of relief. They slowly walked around the inside of the garage, pausing to look under the parked cars. To Sean's relief, there was no one to be found.

"You did see the light, did not you?" Sean asked, as he began to doubt himself.

"Yes," Charlie nodded.

Just then the sound of an empty can hitting the concrete floor caused both of them to jump. They looked at the basement door across the garage.

"That came from downstairs," Sean said. His voice quivered uncontrollably but he didn't care.

"We have to check it out," Charlie said, but hoped Sean would object.

"Here," Sean said, handing Charlie the flashlight. "I'll keep a look out up here and you check it out downstairs."

"Me?" Charlie protested.

"Well, you aren't chicken, are you?" Sean challenged.

"No!" Charlie snapped back. "But what about you?"

"Me? Seniority has its privileges. I'll stay up here in case someone tries to come up the stairs."

Charlie glared at Sean. He gripped the flashlight tightly in his hand. The beam flickered, distracting him. He shook the light sharply and the beam became stronger.

"You need to get the batteries replaced," he snapped.

He turned toward the open basement door. Carefully, Charlie made his way down the stairs. The air was cold and musty. The smell of motor oil and dirt was thick. Charlie shone the light all around the basement. The large oil drums in the center of the room were covered with dusty canvas tarps. Nothing looked out of place. Charlie continued down the stairs until he reached the floor.

"See anything?" Sean called down to him.

"No. There's nothing here," Charlie reported back as he continued to shine his light about the room.

Along the east wall of the basement was an old workbench. Above it, hanging on old rusty nails pounded into the rafters, were old dusty kerosene lamps. The wooden closet in the middle of the south wall marking the entrance to the tunnel stood open. Charlie figured whoever was down there must have gone into the tunnel. There was no other way out of the basement, but there was no way he was going in there with a dying flashlight. He turned around and headed back up the stairs.

"There was no one down there," Charlie reported. "It must have been a rat or something. Let's get back to the Abbey."

The two boys turned off the lights and shut the garage door

tightly. They quickly headed back to the Abbey as the light from the flashlight grew dim. They gave their report to Robert, who was waiting at the main entrance. As Charlie left them he heard Sean report that his flashlight was in need of new batteries.

The dormitory was quiet when Charlie entered. The overhead lights were out but several of the boys still had their nightstand lights on in their cubicles. Charlie quickly changed out of his cassock and surplice and into his pajamas before heading to his cubicle.

Howard was already in his bed looking at their script when Charlie walked up.

"You're never gonna believe what happened tonight," Charlie whispered as he crawled into his bed.

"What?" Howard asked stuffing the script into the top drawer of his nightstand. He listened as Charlie quickly told him about the shadow, the garage and the tunnel.

"Who do you think it was?" Howard asked.

"I don't know," Charlie answered and thought. "I have a feeling it was 'the shadow,'" he whispered.

"You do?" Howard sat up on the edge of his bed. "Did you say anything to Robert?"

"No way!" Charlie shook his head. "He would've made us go back out there or worse, he would've told Father Mark. There's no telling what would happen then."

"Good," Howard said with a nod. "After lights out I'll set the trap again."

"Okay," Charlie agreed. "Hey, what happened with Gus?"

"Oh, nothing." Howard shook his head. "He wouldn't say a word. But I think it had something to do with the Altar Boys' Club. Remember last year when Gus gave up his spot for Rick?"

"Yeah," Charlie nodded. "You don't think he asked Gus to give up his place again, do you?"

"I don't know." Howard put the papers on his nightstand.

"I hope not," Charlie yawned. "Well, good night and don't forget to set the trap," he said before turning over to face the window.

"I won't," Howard assured him.

THE TRAP

Charlie was restless as he tried to sleep. Images of the light shining through the cracks in the garage doors kept flashing in his mind as he lay on his side in his bed. He glanced over at the clock on Howard's nightstand. Two o'clock in the morning it read. He rolled over onto his back and stared up at the ceiling. Sleep finally came without Charlie realizing it.

A cold misty fog surrounded Charlie. Voices called to him from deep in the forest. "Where are you?" he called back and began to run. He stumbled over fallen branches. The voices kept calling him. "I can't see you," he yelled as he stopped and looked around. He tripped over the hem of his cassock and landed on his hands and knees. The ground was damp. His fingers dug into the mud. He looked up and suddenly there it was, the shadow standing above him. With one hand, it reached down and grabbed him by his throat. The fingers tightened making it hard for him to breath. He grabbed the arm as it lifted him off the ground. He felt the hot breath and then saw the fiery red eyes.

Charlie opened his eyes only to look up at a dark shadow bent over him. He did not scream. He did not move. He watched as a bony hand slowly reached for the chain around Charlie's neck.

He's after my key, Charlie thought. He tried to move, but he could not. The warmth of adrenaline coursed through his paralyzed body. "No!" he tried to shout, but his mouth would not cooperate.

The hand drew closer. Charlie's heart beat faster. He could feel the chain lift from around his neck. The medal and locket fell along the chain behind his neck. He watched the bony fingers search for the key.

"No!" Charlie tried to scream but no sound came from his lips.

The shadow's hand closed into a fist and it gave a sharp tug against the chain around Charlie's neck.

"No!" Charlie screamed and sat straight up in his bed.

He grabbed the old brass key that hung from the chain beneath his pajama top. His heart beat rapidly and he tried to catch his breath as he panted. It had seemed so real.

Howard woke instantly and grabbed his glasses from his nightstand. He looked at Charlie who was silhouetted in the glow of the moon.

"Charlie?" he whispered as he propped himself up on his elbow.

Charlie looked at Howard. Slowly his breathing returned to normal as he looked around the darkened dormitory.

"I'm sorry," he apologized. "Just another nightmare."

"Quiet down!" someone groaned from across the dorm.

"Quiet down yourself," Howard said in a loud whisper back to the voice. "You okay?" he whispered to Charlie.

"Yeah." Charlie nodded. "I'm sorry." Charlie lay back down in his bed and turned onto his side. Sleep came quickly.

"Charlie, wake up!"

Slowly Charlie opened his eyes. The sun was just beginning to rise outside and cast its glow though the window beside Charlie's bed. He rolled over and looked at Howard, who was sitting up in his bed across from him.

"What?" Charlie yawned as he tried to wake himself.

"Don't get out of bed," Howard said.

Charlie felt the rush of adrenaline as he remembered their trap. Suddenly he was wide awake. He turned and leaned over the edge of his bed.

"Oh my god," Charlie gasped as he looked at the floor.

There on the floor, in the white talcum powder Howard spread out the night before, were clear shoeprints beside Charlie's bed. The prints entered their cubicle and then left trailing toward the dormitory doors but fading before they reached them.

"He was here last night," Charlie breathed. "He is real."

"What's going on?" Gus asked, rubbing his eyes and yawning.

"No! Stop!" Howard and Charlie screamed at once.

They were too late. Gus walked into their cubicle and all over the shoeprints in his bare feet.

"Gus," Charlie groaned.

"What?" Gus asked. "What did I do?"

"You just ruined our evidence, you idiot," Howard said and stood up.

"What?" Gus asked and looked at the floor. "Oh," he gasped as he saw the powder. "I'm sorry." He started to turn around to leave.

"No!" Howard snapped and grabbed Gus' arm. "Stay still."

Howard carefully made his way around Gus and out of their cubicle. He looked at the white powdery shoeprints that trailed away toward the dormitory doors.

"I think we have a good print over here," he announced. "Gus didn't ruin them all."

"Good," Charlie sighed with relief.

"I'm really sorry," Gus said, his lower lip quivering slightly.

"Oh, don't cry," Charlie consoled him. "You didn't know. It's okay."

Charlie joined Howard and Rick in the middle of the dorm. Rick had already snapped a photograph of the shoeprint with his

Polaroid camera as Howard held a ruler beside it. Rick then wrote down the figures in a black notebook.

"What's that?" Charlie asked Rick and pointed to the book.

"This?" Rick closed the notebook. "Just something I bought from the bookstore to keep track of our clues."

"I see." Charlie nodded suspiciously.

"Well, judging by the size of the print, it looks like our shadow wears a ten and a half shoe," Howard announced as he stood up.

"How do you know that?" asked Gus.

"Because the print measures ten and a half inches," he answered and rolled his eyes warily.

"Now we just need to find out what size shoe Father Mark wears," Charlie said. He watched as Rick made more notes in his black book.

"Got it," Rick said as he finished writing and looked up. "How do we do that?"

"I don't know," Charlie shrugged.

"Well, I can't come up with all of the good ideas all of the time," Rick sighed and looked at Howard.

The other boys in the dorm began to huddle around them. Howard quickly swiped the shoeprint with his foot, smearing it beyond recognition.

"What's going on?" they asked one at a time.

"Nothing," Howard answered. "Just go get dressed."

"Yes," came a voice behind them. "You don't want to be late for breakfast."

Charlie, Howard and Rick gasped as they looked up at Brother Simon. Slowly Brother Simon walked closer to them, staring at the white powder on the floor.

"My, my," he said thoughtfully. "What do we have here?" His eyes followed the powder back to Howard's and Charlie's cubicle.

"What is going on here?" he asked in a tone that told the boys he was not pleased.

"Howard spilled his talcum powder," Rick quickly

answered.

Brother Simon's eyes squinted as he looked intently at each of the boys. None of them dared say a word. Charlie could tell that Brother Simon was thinking about whether or not to believe Rick's half-truth.

"So be it," he finally spoke in his usual cold, stern voice. "Master Miller, get it cleaned up immediately. Master Walters, get dressed. Master MacCready, I want to see you in my office right away."

"Yes, Brother Simon," the three answered. They watched in silence as he turned around and left the dorm.

"Good thinking, Rick." Gus smiled at his friend. "I think he bought it."

"I think you're the only one who does," Charlie said fearfully.

"You better get dressed and into B. S.'s office before he comes back in here. Rick and I will—hey, where are you going?" Howard called to Rick who was heading back to his cubicle.

Rick turned around. "You heard him, I'm supposed to get dressed and you're supposed to clean up that mess."

"But—" Howard started to protest and then clenched his teeth. "Quick thinking indeed!" He glared at Rick who was already back in his cubicle changing.

"I'll help you," Gus offered eagerly.

"No! Stand still," Howard yelled, holding up a halting hand as he looked at the floor and the trail of new tracks leading from his cubicle.

Gus turned and looked at the tracks he had just made. He looked at the bottom of his feet covered in white powder.

"I'm sorry," he said trying to balance on one foot as he tried to wipe the powder from his other. He wobbled and stumbled backward, falling to the floor.

"Stay put," Howard ordered. He rushed to his closet and quickly returned with a towel. "Use this," he said and tossed it to Gus.

Gus wiped his feet while Howard retrieved a dust mop and waste pan from the janitor's closet.

Cautiously, Charlie knocked on Brother Simon's door. He tried to calm the butterflies in his stomach as he waited for the answer. For a moment he even entertained the idea that maybe Brother Simon was not in, but that idea vanished as the door opened.

"Good, come in," Brother Simon greeted him coldly.

Charlie entered and stood while Brother Simon closed the door behind them.

"Please, have a seat," he invited, motioning toward the two chairs beneath the window.

Nervously, Charlie took a seat. He looked around the office. It was a lot different from the way Father Emmanuel had things. The bookshelves were still covered with books, but there were not any photographs or plants. The only decoration on the walls was a crucifix hung beside the door.

"So, Master MacCready," Brother Simon said as he sat down behind his desk. "Do you mind telling me what you and Master Miller are up to?"

"Nothing," Charlie answered quickly. "It's just like Rick said, Howard spilled his powder. That's all."

Brother Simon sat forward in his chair and rested his elbows on the desk. He put his chin in his hands and stared expressionless at Charlie.

Charlie began to feel the butterflies flutter uncomfortably in his stomach. He looked away from Brother Simon's stare and then back again.

"I see," Brother Simon breathed. "Well, let me tell you what I think. I know Master Miller did not accidentally spill that powder. Where he acquired it is another matter, but as I have never known him to use talcum powder before, I say that you two are up to something. Remember what I said, Charlie," Brother Simon's tone sounded gentler and mixed with a bit of worry and concern. "Be careful."

"I am, Brother Simon. Honest," Charlie tried to reassure

him.

"All right, then," Brother Simon nodded. "You may go."

"Thank you," Charlie said and stood to leave.

"By the way." Brother Simon looked at him. "You may inform Master Walters, Master Kugele and Master Miller they have work crew this weekend for two hours. That will be all."

"But—" Charlie protested.

"That is all," Brother Simon said and opened his notebook.

The morning bell rang, signaling it was time for breakfast, as Charlie left Brother Simon's office. He quickly glanced into their dorm, then hurried downstairs to meet up with Howard, Rick and Gus.

"So, what did you tell him?" Howard whispered as Charlie took his place in front of him.

"I didn't tell him anything," Charlie said with a shrug and continued to stare straight ahead.

"And he was okay with that?" Howard persisted.

"Yeah."

"What else?"

"He said to tell you, Rick and Gus that you all have two hours of work crew this Saturday," Charlie murmured.

"What!" Howard gasped.

"I'm sorry," Charlie said.

Howard clenched his teeth and stared straight ahead as though Charlie was not there. Slowly, Charlie turned back around.

ALL HALLOW'S EVE

Charlie checked his reflection in the mirror as he dressed in the hooded habit he had borrowed from their serving brother, since Brother Paul's habit was too big. He smiled as he looked at himself. A feeling of calm filled him. For the first time since he came to Saint Michael's, he wondered what it would be like to be a monk and have the Abbey be his home. Actually it was more like a flash than a full-fledged thought. It was there for a moment and then it was gone, replaced with thoughts of the Halloween dinner only minutes away, but the calm feeling stayed with him. He walked over to the bathroom stall door and leaned against it.

"Are you ready yet?" he asked and looked up at the ceiling.

"No!" Howard yelled. "I'm not coming out."

"Honestly, how bad can it be?" Charlie turned around and spoke at the closed stall door.

"I look ridiculous."

"This skit was your idea; you can't let everyone down," Charlie tried reasoning with him. "Think of the prize. We can't let Dougary and his goons win it again."

"But everyone is going to laugh at me," Howard protested.

"They are going to laugh at all of us," Charlie assured him.

"That's the idea. Come on, Howard, please?"

"Okay, but don't *you* laugh at me."

"I won't, I promise," Charlie said, and stepped away from the door.

Slowly the door opened. Charlie fought hard not to even smile. He tired several stone-faced expressions before he bit his tongue and stared straight ahead.

Howard slowly stepped out from behind the wooden door of the bathroom stall. With Sister Lillian's veil and long hoodless scapular over his cassock, he looked the part. He held out his hands as if to say, here I am.

"You look perfect!" Charlie smiled.

"Don't laugh," Howard warned.

Charlie quickly wiped the smile from his lips. "Don't worry, I wasn't going to. Come on let's get downstairs."

As they walked past the row of sinks, Howard glanced in the mirror at his reflection. He stopped and looked at himself. Charlie stopped too and looked at Howard's reflection. Howard tucked his arms under the scapular and folded them just the way Sister Lillian always did and turned sideways. He turned the other direction and studied at his reflection.

"See, Howard," Charlie spoke up. "You'd make a great nun."

"Yeah," Howard agreed but frowned. "Dog breath is never gonna let me forget this one." He turned away from the mirror and headed for the stairs. Charlie quickly followed him.

"I wonder what Rick's up to?" Howard asked to change the subject as they walked down the stairs.

"I don't know," Charlie shook his head. "This was supposed to be a class skit. I don't know why he backed out."

"Well, it's a good thing we convinced Gus not to quit. I think the skit will still work just fine," Howard tried to sound reassuring.

As they rounded the last landing and started down the final set of stairs Howard stopped. He looked at the flurry of costumed boys below and suddenly he felt nervous again.

Charlie turned around and looked at his friend and then at the boys gathered outside the refectory.

"See, Howard," Charlie said pointing at another boy in costume. "You aren't the only one here dressed like a nun."

Howard took a deep breath. "Okay," he said and started down the stairs again.

"Hey, Rick," Howard beamed as he took his place in the Saint Nicholas line. "Nice costume. Oh, wait! I'm sorry, you aren't wearing one."

"Very funny, Sister Howie," Rick sneered.

"What's the matter, boycotting Halloween again?" Howard returned, ignoring Rick's tone.

"No, I'm not, if you really must know," Rick answered. "You'll see."

The refectory doors opened slowly and a cloud of fake fog bellowed into the hallway. Noisy cackles and loud shrieks echoed from inside. Slowly the boys filed into the darkened room. Flickering jack-o-lanterns and five-candle candelabras placed alternately down the center of each table provided the only light.

Charlie ducked sharply as he saw something swoop past him.

"What the—" he gasped and jumped behind Howard.

"It's only a rubber bat on a string," Howard laughed.

"Oh," Charlie laughed and stood behind his chair. He looked up at the head table. It was moved off the platform and set in the corner. Bundles of cornstalks and bales of hay were stacked around the wall behind the table. In the corner was a life-sized scarecrow on a pole.

"Cool," Howard breathed as he looked at the decorations.

"Where are all of the prefects and Father Mark?" Howard asked.

Just then, a loud scream came from the back of the refectory. Everyone jumped and moved away. Charlie smiled when he noticed that even Dougary was startled by the scream and had sought safety behind Travis.

Everyone stared at the dark corner, their heads turned away from the head table. The sound of the wooden block hitting the head table caused everyone to gasp and jump again.

Charlie laughed to himself as he looked at the four prefects now in their places. Brother Simon was dressed as a vampire, with fake blood dripping down his chin. Father Vicar was dressed like the Grim Reaper. Brother Conrad was dressed like the Easter Bunny, very out of season Charlie thought until he saw the fake axe sticking out of the back of the rabbit costume. Brother Owen looked even thinner wrapped up as a mummy. Slowly, Charlie leaned over to Howard.

"Okay, so where's Father Mark?" he asked.

Just then, the scarecrow in the corner moved. Charlie gasped and took a step back as did the rest of the boys. Then suddenly, the room exploded with laughter and applause.

After the prayer, the serving brothers brought out trays of pizza, hamburgers and French fries and pitchers of cold, foamy root beer. The boys ate eagerly.

"So, Gus," Charlie said as he put ketchup on his hamburger. "Tomorrow is All Saints' Day. You know what that means." He grinned.

Gus looked up and smiled. "I just hope Abbot Ambrose will remember."

"He'll remember," Howard spoke up. "He never breaks his promises."

"I don't recall Gus ever saying that Abbot Ambrose actually promised him anything," Rick said in his usual snotty tone. "Isn't that true, Gus?"

"Well, not in so many words," Gus answered. "But he knows how much I want to be an Altar Boy. Surely he has to remember that."

"He'll remember," Howard glared at Rick. "After all, he let Rick in."

"Well, I, for one, hope he remembers," Charlie tried to sound positive.

The dinner plates were cleared away and then the dessert

trays were brought in. Candied apples on sticks, sucker trees, pastries and bowls of candy corn and chocolates of all kinds were brought to each table to the delight of the boys. As they ate their treats they laughed and talked noisily.

Unnoticed, Brother Conrad stepped to the center of the platform and tapped his spoon against the side of his glass to get the boys' attention. Gradually, the room fell silent.

"I would like to welcome all of you to this year's Halloween party. We have decided to do things a bit differently this year. Instead of awarding a winning dorm, we have decided to award a winning class, through our talent show. Tonight, our judges are Abbot Ambrose, Prior Emmanuel and Father Mark. We will begin with our freshmen class, followed by our sophomore class and so forth, in just a few minutes."

"This is it," Howard sighed, looking around the table.

"I guess so," Charlie agreed. He suddenly regretted stuffing himself with pizza, root beer and candy.

Moments later, the refectory doors opened and Abbot Ambrose and Prior Emmanuel entered. Both were dressed in their habits, no costume. They took a seat with Father Mark at the head table. Abbot Ambrose gave Brother Conrad a nod that they were ready to begin.

Brother Conrad smiled and raised his hands. The room fell silent.

"Tonight, we are in for a real treat from the youngest members of our Abbey. I've watched them rehearse and I must say they are a talented group. Their skit is entitled 'A Day in the Life of a Freshman.'"

The lights dimmed and when they came up, Gus lay in a table made up to look like a bed. Off stage a bell rang and Gus groaned. Dale, dressed in Charlie's white surplice, rushed in.

"Ge-ge-get up and da-da-don't be late," Dale said.

Gus pulled himself off the table and slowly walked off the stage in his pajamas. The blankets were stripped from the table and two chairs were set up to it. Two bowls of cereal were placed on the table with silverware. Gus, dressed clumsily in his cassock and red surplice, and Dale walked back on stage and stood by their chairs. The boys paused for a moment and then sat down. Gus kept dozing as he pretended to eat his cereal. Then to everyone's surprise, he fell face first into his bowl. Cereal and milk splashed out over the table amid roaring laughter from the audience.

The lights dimmed then came back on. The table was cleaned and set up like a desk. A portable chalkboard stood behind it. In front of the fake desk were two chairs. Dale and Gus sat with their backs to the audience. Charlie gripped the leather satchel and tried to calm his nerves as he started up the center of the hall toward the stage. Almost immediately the audience burst into laughter. When Charlie started his prayer, mimicking Brother Paul's voice and mannerisms to a tee, the laughter was deafening. Charlie was so thankful when the lights dimmed and his part was over. Soon the boys were finished and back in their seats.

"You were great!" Howard leaned over and whispered into Charlie's ear.

"Thanks," Charlie smiled. "So were you. Did you hear them laugh?" Charlie looked across the table at two empty chairs. "Hey, where're Gus and Rick?"

Howard looked around the refectory. "I don't know," he answered.

The sophomores' skit began with three boys playing guitars and singing. Charlie thought they were really good, but he felt confident their skit could beat them. Even when the audience roared with applause as the boys left the stage, Charlie's confidence did not waver.

Brother Conrad walked back onto the stage.

"Next, we have a late entry in tonight's entertainment list," Brother Conrad announced. "Now, doing their own rendition of one of my favorite old songs, we have Masters Walters and Kugele."

Charlie and Howard looked at each other as the lights dimmed and came back on. Their mouths dropped open as Rick and Gus walked awkwardly onto the stage dressed in a pair of three legged overalls with two bibs and an extra wide shirt.

"I don't believe it," Howard gasped.

"Siamese twins?" said Charlie and cocked his head.

The music started. Gus and Rick began to sway.

"Me and my sha-a-a-dow," they began to sing and dance.

The smile immediately left Charlie's lips. He looked at Howard who sat with his mouth open, glaring at the stage.

"How could he?" Charlie whispered.

"Oh, this isn't funny." Howard shook his head. "He's dead meat."

The room filled with applause as the two took their bows and left the stage. They returned to their seats, putting their chairs together before sitting down. They looked across the table at Charlie and Howard. Gus beamed, oblivious to Charlie's and Howard's shocked expressions. Rick grinned proudly.

"I did it," Gus breathed. "I was so nervous."

"I don't believe you," Howard leaned across the table and hissed at Rick.

"What?" Rick feigned innocence.

"You know perfectly well, what," Charlie said and turned away. For the rest of the show, he did not look at either of them.

"Now has come the moment we've all been waiting for," Brother Conrad announced. "The announcement of this year's winning act. Abbot Ambrose?" he invited.

Abbot Ambrose stood up and walked to center stage. He looked at the boys in front of him and smiled.

"I am so impressed with all of you." He smiled under his long white beard. "I never knew how talented you all are. If I could, I would award you all as winners, but Brother Conrad and the Halloween committee have told me I cannot."

A playful booing rose from the boys.

"The winning act belongs to our sophomore class," Abbot Ambrose announced, and began the applause. "Congratulations. The sophomores are invited to wait after the meal for your prize.

"It is also my pleasure to announce the winner of this year's costume contest. While I know all of you worked hard on your costumes, and may I add, you all outdid yourselves this year, there can only be one winner."

Brother Conrad quickly approached Abbot Ambrose and whispered into his ear as he handed him the envelope. Abbot Ambrose nodded and smiled as he took the envelope. He waited until Brother Conrad had left the stage.

"I guess I spoke too soon," he said. "This year we have a tie. The winners of the best costume award are Master Walters and Master Kugele."

"What?" Howard gasped and pushed away from the table.

After the announcements the party was concluded. All except the sophomores were excused from the refectory. Howard and Charlie headed back to Saint Nicholas dorm to change their clothes.

"Charlie, Howard," Gus called as he and Rick hobbled after them as quickly as they could. "Please, wait," he begged.

Charlie and Howard stopped when they reached the stairs and turned around.

"What?" Howard snapped at them.

"We really didn't mean anything by our skit," Rick began.

"No, we didn't." Gus added.

"We've had this planned since last year," Rick tried to explain.

"Yeah, right, but for some reason I don't believe you," Howard smirked. "Come on, Charlie."

The two turned around and started up the stairs.

"It's true," Gus said. "This had nothing to do with the shadow that is bothering you, Charlie. You have to believe me. We're friends."

Charlie stopped. It was true they were friends. He looked at Howard and then turned back around to face the two-headed boy.

"I believe you, Gus," Charlie said and looked directly at him. He turned and looked at Rick for a moment, then turned around and continued up the stairs.

When Howard and Charlie reached Saint Nicholas dorm, they ignored the bowls of candy and goodies in the middle of the dorm, and headed straight for their closets. Howard could not wait to get out of the nun get-up. He quickly pulled off the veil and set it aside. After he took off the scapular and folded it neatly, he placed it and the veil in the paper sack that Sister Lillian had given to him.

"It feels good to be back in my own clothes," Howard said as he and Charlie walked over to the lounge area in the center of the dorm.

"It wasn't so bad." Charlie shrugged.

"Not for you," Howard answered. "You weren't dressed up like a girl."

"I still can't believe we didn't win," Gus said as he walked over to the lounge, freed from his twin.

"I liked your adlib of putting your face in your cereal," Rick laughed. "That was so funny. What made you think of that?"

"I don't know." Gus shrugged while everyone laughed again.

The dorm doors opened and Brother Simon walked in.

"Good evening boys," he greeted them with his arms tucked under his robes in his usual manner. "Have any of you seen Master Kaufman?"

"Dale?" Howard asked, looking at Charlie and then the other boys. They all shook their heads. "Not since our skit. Why?" Howard added.

"Brother Owen reported that Master Kaufman isn't in his dorm," Brother Simon answered. Charlie noticed the genuine concern in Brother Simon's cold eyes. "Father Vicar can't seem to find Master Duggan and Master Hertz either." Brother Simon continued. "Master Walters, Master Miller and Master MacCready, please change your clothes and meet the rest of the Altar Boys at the main entrance. We need to search the grounds." Not waiting for an answer, Brother Simon quickly turned around and left the dorm.

"Yes, Brother Simon," the three answered as the doors closed behind him. They quickly returned to their closets to change.

"Did you notice how worried Brother Simon seemed?" Gus asked as he followed Charlie and Howard over to their closets.

"What?" Howard scoffed. "Him? Worried? I think you're seeing things, Gus." He quickly threw his cassock on over his head.

"I wonder where he could be," Charlie said as he slipped back into his cassock.

"Ol' B. S.?" Howard asked.

"Dale!" Charlie snapped. "And Dougary and Larry." He pulled his surplice over his head and put his arms through the sleeves.

"Wherever they are, I'm sure they're up to no good." Howard answered indifferently. He closed his closet and ran his hand over his curly dark hair.

"Don't forget your flashlights," Gus reminded them. "Oh, I hope they aren't being mean to Dale," he lamented.

"I wouldn't worry too much," Rick spoke up as he joined them at the doors. "We'll find them."

"Yeah, Gus," Charlie agreed. "He'll be okay."

The three boys walked through the doors, leaving Gus and the rest of the boys behind to enjoy their party. They quickly hurried down the stairs to the front lobby. Waiting for them were the rest of the Altar Boys, Abbot Ambrose and the prefects. Charlie was surprised at the concerned look on Father Vicar's usually stony face, but he was more surprised that Father Mark was nowhere to be seen.

"You boys are to take extra care this evening," Abbot Ambrose instructed. "It's extremely dark out due to the clouds. Be sure to check thoroughly. Report back to me when you're finished. I would appreciate it if you brothers would search the Abbey wing and the cloister. That is all." Abbot Ambrose dismissed them.

The late October night air was cold as Charlie and Sean made their way across the front grounds toward the parking lot and garage. Neither said a word. Sean swung his flashlight beam annoyingly to the right and left as they walked. Charlie tried not to let it get to him.

"I'll check the basement," Charlie said as they entered the garage. He knew the routine; there was no way Sean would go downstairs even with Charlie.

"Make it quick, I want to get back to my Halloween party," Sean gloated.

Charlie slowly started down the stairs. Without warning his flashlight beam flickered and went out. He shook it hard and the beam came back on. He continued down the stairs moving the beam slowly around. Suddenly, there was the sound of metal crashing to the floor across the basement. Charlie jumped and quickly shone his flashlight in the direction of the noise just in time to see a shadowy figure disappear into the tunnel.

"Hey!" Charlie shouted.

"What? What are you screaming about, MacCreepy?" Sean called down from upstairs.

"Go get Abbot Ambrose," Charlie instructed. "Quick! I'm going after him."

"Who?" Sean asked.

"Just go!" Charlie yelled. He could hear the sound of the garage door slamming shut as Sean ran out. Charlie quickly headed across the basement toward the tunnel entrance. As he drew closer, his flashlight beam died. Again he shook it hard and it came back on, but weaker. Not wasting any time, Charlie grabbed one of the kerosene lanterns from the hook above his head. "Empty," he said as he shook it. He set it down and grabbed another and then another. "Aha!" he gasped as he heard the sound of sloshing inside. "Now, matches, matches," he muttered to himself as he shone the flashlight beam at the row of old lockers against the wall. He quickly opened the first locker and looked through the pile of old, dirty tools. He slammed it shut and opened the next. To his relief, on the rusted shelf was a box of wooden matches. Charlie lit the lantern just as his flashlight died.

Charlie quickly entered the tunnel. The glow of the lantern was bright and lit up the tunnel around him. Charlie hurried to catch up to the shadow ahead of him. From his brief glimpse of the shadow, Charlie could only tell that he was dressed in a cassock. He did not get to see much more.

"Dale!" Charlie called ahead of him. He listened for an answer. Nothing. The smell of fresh dirt filled the air as Charlie approached the new fork in the tunnel. Now he wished that Howard and he had checked out the tunnel earlier, as they talked about doing. Charlie had no idea where it went. Howard thought it was headed in the direction of the town.

Charlie looked down the tunnel, with its bare stone and dirt walls, as far as he could. He held the lantern away, to the side, so the tunnel in front of him was dark. Just as he had hoped, in the distance ahead of him he saw a faint glimmer of light. Without thinking, Charlie quickly headed down the new tunnel.

The air was not as fresh as it was in the old tunnel. Charlie glanced up at the ceiling. The thick roots from the trees held the dirt securely in place. However, there were no air pipes like in the old tunnel. Charlie wondered why the brothers had failed to dig them. Then a chilling thought occurred to him. What if the brothers had not dug the tunnel, but someone else had? Charlie stopped dead in his tracks as fear gripped him. He shivered.

"Don't panic," he said out loud to himself, and shook his head. He quickly set out again.

The smell of fresh dirt suddenly changed. It smelled different. It smelled like a barnyard. I must be getting close to the end of the tunnel, Charlie thought as he hurried after the shadow.

Sure enough, the tunnel opened up in the side of the hill. A curtain of thick ivy and roots veiled the entrance. Charlie swept them aside with his free hand as he exited the tunnel. The smell of a barnyard was strong. Charlie quickly covered his nose. He shone his lantern in all directions, but nothing looked familiar.

He had no clue as to where he was. He had never been to this part of the hill before, and even though Howard had not shown him where the pig barns were, he figured he must be close to them. Slowly he walked away from the tunnel. Old twigs snapped beneath his feet.

"Dale!" he called out into the night.

"Ch-Ch-Charlie?" A faint voice called back from the darkness behind him.

Charlie spun around.

"Dale!" he called out again.

"Ch-Ch-Charlie," came the weak reply.

Charlie quickly moved in the direction of the voice.

"Charlie?" A voice called from behind him.

Charlie spun around sharply. He looked into the darkness and a chill ran up his spine. It all seemed too familiar; the trees, the voices, the darkness.

Suddenly, in the distance a flashlight beam appeared.

"Hey, MacCreepy?" the voice called again. This time Charlie recognized the voice. It was Larry Hertz.

"Ch-Ch-Charlie," groaned the voice in the opposite direction.

Charlie quickly turned around and headed toward the voice.

"Dale!" he gasped as he nearly tripped over him. "What happened to you?"

In the glow of the lantern, Charlie could see that Dale had been badly beaten. He was still dressed in Charlie's white surplice but now it was soiled and bloody. Charlie knelt down beside Dale and took his hand.

"I'm here," he told Dale.

Dale's face was smeared with blood and dirt. His hair was matted on one side. Tiny twigs and leaves were tangled in his hair. Charlie could not imagine who would have done this to his friend. The images of Dougary and Larry flashed in his mind just as Larry walked up to them.

"What have you done?" he accused Charlie and he knelt

down beside Dale.

"What have I—? I didn't do anything!" Charlie snapped and glared at Larry.

"Dale, what happened?" Larry asked, ignoring Charlie. "Who did this to you?"

"Ch-Ch-Charlie," Dale stammered and tightened his grip on Charlie's hand.

Larry pulled back and looked at Charlie suspiciously. Charlie glanced up and saw the look.

"He doesn't know what he's saying," Charlie protested.

Just then the sound of footsteps on gravel came through the forest. Charlie looked up. The beams of two flashlights drew closer.

"Dale!" Howard called out.

"Howard!" Charlie shouted. "Over here!"

Charlie watched as the two beams began to bounce wildly. The sound of running on gravel meant Howard and his partner Rick were on their way.

"What are you doing here?" Rick panted as they left the gravel road and climbed up the steep slope to where Charlie, Larry and Dale were.

Charlie did not answer. He just shook his head in disbelief that Rick would even ask such a stupid question.

"Dale's hurt bad," Charlie told Howard.

Howard pushed Larry aside and knelt down next to Dale, across from Charlie. He looked at Dale's battered and bloody face. In the glow of the lantern's light, he could see a large bump on the side of Dale's head.

"Rick, go get Abbot Ambrose!" Howard ordered over his shoulder. "And hurry!"

Rick hesitated for a moment. He did not like being told what to do and he really did not want to be alone in the dark. He looked at Larry who was standing away from the group.

"Come on, Hertz," he said. "Let's get help."

Larry did not object. He seemed relieved to get away from there. He quickly followed Rick back to the Abbey, leaving

Charlie and Howard alone with Dale.

"You'll be okay," Howard tried to reassure Dale. "Just lay still. Help is coming." He looked at Charlie. He grimaced as he took a deep breath, smelling the stench from the pig barns. "I thought you didn't know where the pig barns were?"

"I don't," Charlie answered in a slight whisper. "I mean, I was checking the basement in the garage when I saw the shadow run into the tunnel. So, I grabbed a lantern and followed. By the way, the new tunnel leads to just over there." He pointed up the hillside. "When I came out of the tunnel, I found Dale here."

"What about Larry?" Howard asked. "Where was he?"

"He was over there." Again Charlie pointed. "Back in the trees by where I spotted you and Rick. He was walking this way."

"Ch-Ch-Charlie," Dale said in a groggy, tired voice.

"I'm here," Charlie answered and held onto Dale's hand.

"You have to stay awake," Howard instructed. "Help is coming, Dale." He looked at Charlie again. "I heard Brother James say if you've been hit in the head really hard you shouldn't go to sleep."

Charlie nodded in agreement. He was glad Howard seemed to know what to do.

"Who did this to you?" Howard asked.

"Ch-Ch-Charlie," Dale repeated.

Howard looked at Charlie again but this time with a questioning expression.

"I didn't do it," Charlie protested. "That's all he will say."

"Boys!" a voice called from the road below.

Howard and Charlie looked up as Father Mark hurried up the slope toward them.

"What happened?" he asked as he looked down at them and Dale.

Just then the sound of one of the Abbey's trucks on the gravel road drew closer. The beams of its headlights lit up the road and the forest on both sides. The truck came to a stop just below them.

"They're here," Charlie told Dale.

Abbot Ambrose and Brother James quickly hurried up the hillside to them. Howard stood up and moved aside to let Brother James help Dale. Charlie tried to release Dale's hand but Dale would not let go. He just tightened his grip.

"Did you find Dougary?" Howard asked.

"Yes," Abbot Ambrose nodded as he gave Father Mark a curious look. "He wasn't outside, after all. He was in the Abbey Church talking with Brother Zechariah. So, how did you get over here? Aren't you supposed to be with Master Adkins checking the garage and front lawn?"

"Yes," Charlie admitted. "But, I told him to go get help."

"I see," Father Mark nodded.

"We will talk about this later," Abbot Ambrose interrupted.

"Let's get Master Kaufman into the truck and to the infirmary right away," Brother James said and stood up. "There's a stretcher in the back of the truck."

"I'll get it," Howard volunteered and headed down the slope to the waiting truck.

"I'll give you a hand," Father Mark offered and went with him.

Moments later, Dale was safely loaded onto the bed of the truck and headed back to the Abbey with Brother James at his side. Father Mark was behind the wheel with Howard and Rick in the cab beside him.

Charlie and Abbot Ambrose watched as the truck drove off then slowly the two started walking up the gravel road. Abbot Ambrose carried Howard's flashlight to light their way.

"Are you all right?" Abbot Ambrose asked in his gentle fatherly voice.

"Yes," Charlie nodded. "I think so. I'm just worried about Dale. Why would someone hurt him?"

"I don't know," Abbot Ambrose answered as he thought. "I will talk to him when he's better. But there's something else troubling you, isn't there? Do you want to tell me?"

"Uh—" Charlie shrugged, remembering Howard's words

that no one would believe him. "There's nothing bothering me."

"I see," Abbot Ambrose nodded. He was not fooled by Charlie's lie. He knew there was something going on, but he was not going to pressure Charlie about it. Not yet, anyway. The two finished their walk back to the Abbey in silence.

ALL SAINTS' DAY

Thick dark rain clouds blocked the morning sunlight. The dorm felt cold. Charlie wished he could stay beneath his warm covers all day, but the morning bell rang.

All through the dorm, boys scurried about making their beds and straightening up their cubicles. Some even took extra time combing their hair and washing their faces. Today was All Saints Day and that meant it was Open House, the day when prospective parents would come to look over the boys and spend the afternoon. Though Charlie thought it was nice for the resident boys, those boys without parents, he was not looking forward to that. Today was also the day the new members of the Altar Boys' Club would be announced at breakfast. Charlie looked at Howard's bed. His shoulders slumped in disappointment when he saw the neatly made bed. Howard was already up and gone.

Charlie threw his covers back and climbed out of bed. In no time he was showered and dressed in his clean cassock and surplice. Fearing Brother Simon's wrath, he quickly made his bed. There was not a lot of time before the breakfast bell would ring and he had to find Howard. He knew just where he'd start his search.

The infirmary was located in the monastery wing and just one floor down, on the third floor. It was not far from Saint Nicholas dorm, for which Charlie was grateful. Quietly he entered the long hallway and immediately spotted Howard coming out of the infirmary's door.

"What're you doing here?" Howard asked Charlie coldly.

"I was just looking for you and I wanted to see how Dale is," Charlie answered in a confused whisper.

"The doctor was here all night watching over him. Dale's a bit bruised and battered but Brother James says that he'll be okay." Howard answered.

"Did he say who beat him up?" Charlie asked.

Howard looked at Charlie coldly with his arms folded over his chest. "He just repeats your name," Howard answered. "We'd better go."

"It had to have been Larry," Charlie said sure of himself. "He was the only other person out there."

"Well, Larry claims he saw your light and was going to check it out when you called out to him," Howard replied as they started back toward their wing. "I'm afraid it's your word against his. So now it's up to Dale. Guess you'll just have to hope he remembers what happened and tells Abbot Ambrose."

Charlie stopped and watched Howard walk away without looking back. The realization that Howard did not believe him anymore and suspected that he was the one who beat up Dale left him feeling alone. A great sadness filled his chest at the thought that he lost his best friend. Slowly, Charlie headed for the refectory.

The first floor suddenly fell silent when Charlie came down the last flight of stairs for breakfast. All heads turned and watched as he walked over and took his place in the Saint Nicholas line. Howard and Rick avoided eye contact with him. Even Gus seemed to ignore him. Charlie glanced at Dougary, Travis, Larry and Austin in the Saint Peter line. Dougary had his usual half grin-half sneer expression on his lips, a look that Travis and Larry had learned to imitate perfectly. Charlie turned back to face the front of the line.

The refectory doors opened and the boys filed inside. After the prayer, they took their seats. The serving brothers began making their rounds in their usual silence but today, for Charlie, it felt more deafening. They set a steaming bowl of oatmeal in front of each boy. Howard groaned and rolled his eyes.

The clap of the wooden block against the head table signaled that it was okay for the boys to talk.

"So, how's Dale?" Rick asked as he spooned brown sugar onto his oatmeal.

"He's going to be okay," Charlie informed him.

Rick ignored Charlie and looked straight across the table at Howard. "What was he doing out there in the first place?" He shook his head.

"I'd like to know what Larry was doing," Charlie answered. "It seems awfully strange that he just happened to be there."

"Let's change the subject," Howard interrupted. "Have either of you two heard anything about who's going to be named to the Altar Boys' Club?"

Charlie looked at his three friends as they ignored him. He looked at his bowl of oatmeal and suddenly did not feel like eating.

"Oh, I'm so nervous," Gus said and pushed his empty bowl away.

"You're a shoo-in," Rick assured him, and bumped his shoulder with his playfully. "Don't be nervous."

"He's right, you know," Howard agreed.

"No, I'm not," Gus admitted and frowned.

"But Abbot Ambrose promised you last year," Rick spoke up.

"I know," Gus nodded. "But he could still change his mind."

"Is there something you aren't telling us?" Howard asked, and leaned over the table in Gus's direction. "What did the Abbot want the other day when he called you into his office?"

Gus looked at Howard and then at Rick. His eyes filled with tears and he looked down at the table in front of him.

Charlie did not hear Gus's explanation. His attention was drawn to the head table. Abbot Ambrose sat between Father Mark and Brother Owen. Brother Owen seemed agitated about something as he talked to his superior. Every now and again he cast a glaring glance at Charlie. It did not take a brainiac like Rick to figure out what Brother Owen was saying. It was the same thing Howard and everybody else were thinking. But they're wrong! They're all wrong! Charlie thought and tightened his jaw for fear of crying.

The serving brothers quickly gathered the cereal bowls.

"You didn't eat your oatmeal," the young brother said, picking up Charlie's bowl.

Charlie did not answer.

Moments later the brothers returned with plates of pancakes, scrambled eggs and sausages.

"Now this is more like it," Howard said with a smile. He watched the monk make his way around the table setting the plates down gently in front of each boy.

"Thank you," Charlie said to the brother when it was his turn.

The monk did not acknowledge him. He dropped the plate onto the table in front of Charlie, sending the two sausage-links rolling off the plate onto the table. Charlie quickly retrieved them and glanced at the brother, only to receive a cold glare in return. Charlie's throat tightened. He struggled to keep from crying. Several times he looked at Howard, but Howard continued to ignore him. He looked at Abbot Ambrose. Their eyes met and Abbot Ambrose smiled slightly, understandingly.

The rest of the meal seemed to drag on for Charlie. He tried to eat but had trouble swallowing. He picked at his food and waited. He had no desire to be there, but had no place else to go. He wished he could go back to his bed and start the day over. Finally, Father Mark clapped the small block of wood against the table and the room fell silent. Charlie felt relieved.

"Good morning," Father Mark began. "As I am sure you've all heard, last night one of our students was attacked. To ensure your safety, we've had to tighten up some of the rules. Beginning today, absolutely no one will be permitted outside after dinner."

Immediately hushed groans filled the refectory. Abbot Ambrose gave a disapproving look and the room fell silent again.

"Additionally, during the day, no one is to leave the building without an escort and without first checking in with your prefect. There will be no exceptions. Are there any questions?"

Immediately a hand went up at Saint Peter table.

"Yes, Master Wilson," Father Mark addressed him.

The thin boy with short, coal-black hair and cold, dark eyes stood. "Wouldn't it be easier to just lock MacCready up?"

"And why is that?" Father Mark asked and folded his arms over his chest.

"Well," Ted Wilson said and looked at the members of his table for support. "Everybody knows he beat up Kaufman. He was the only one there."

"Yeah," echoed the rest of the Saint Peter boys.

"I see." Father Mark nodded, and looked at Charlie.

Charlie sat with his head ducked low and his teeth clenched as he fought to keep from crying. He could not believe his friend and former dormmate had turned on him so quickly. He glanced at the head table and caught Brother Simon's eyes. Brother Simon sat back in his chair and motioned with his head for Charlie to sit up and hold his head high. When Charlie did, Brother Simon nodded approvingly.

"And just where were you last night, Master Wilson?" Father Mark asked, not taking his eyes off Charlie.

"I was in my dorm."

"Yes, that is correct." Father Mark nodded and looked at Ted. "So, how could you possibly know what happened outside? Now, take your seat. It seems there has been a lot of gossiping going on. I am here to tell you, we are not taking this matter lightly. Father Abbot, the authorities, and I are all looking into it. As of yet we do not know who is behind this. We would appreciate your cooperation and not stirring up conflict between one another. Are there any more questions?"

No one dared raise his hand.

"Now, as for the rest of the day's events," Father Mark continued. "After Mass we will be hosting our open house. The brothers will be on alert to ensure everyone's safety, so be on your best behavior. And now Father Abbot has an announcement to make." Father Mark nodded to Abbot Ambrose and then sat back down in his seat.

"Oh, god," Gus groaned. "This is it."

"Don't worry," Rick patted him on the back.

Abbot Ambrose stood up and walked around to the front of the head table. Brother Owen and Brother Simon stood up and waited at one end of the raised platform and Father Vicar and Brother Conrad waited at the other end. Father Abbot folded his arms under his robes.

"This year," he began. "There will be four new members to our Altar Boys' Club. As you know, being an Altar Boy is a privilege. One that can be taken away. With it comes a lot of responsibility. Not only will you be assisting the priests of the Abbey with serving at Masses; you will be assisting Brother James with some of our older members.

"Our first new member, I am pleased to announce is Master Duggan."

A collective gasp rose from all four tables as all eyes turned to Saint Peter table. It was obvious that no one was more surprised than Dougary, himself. He sat frozen in his chair. His eyes were fixed in a blind stare and his mouth dropped open.

"Oh, I can't believe this," Rick seethed. "Why him? Why?"

"Master Duggan," Abbot Ambrose smiled. "Please come forward and receive your new surplice."

Slowly Dougary stood up. Abbot Ambrose led the rest of the boys in applause. Dougary made his way over to Father

Vicar and Brother Conrad. They helped him out of his purple surplice and into his new, white surplice with lace around the hem. Charlie could have sworn he saw a slight smile on Father Vicar's lips.

"Our next Altar Boy," Abbot Ambrose continued. "Is Master Hertz." Abbot Ambrose did not wait for Larry to stand up as he began the applause.

Larry was obviously pleased. He bounded up to the front of the refectory and took his place beside Dougary.

"Oh God, oh God," Gus groaned. "I don't think I can take it."

"Relax," Howard said as he leaned across the table. "Breathe." He smiled at his friend.

"Master Fuller." The third name was called.

"What?" Rick gasped indignantly. "Oh, I don't believe this!" He shook his head and folded his arms over his chest in an angry pout.

Austin smiled proudly as he took his place next to Dougary and Larry. He glanced at Howard and Rick and his smile became a smirk.

"Our last member and definitely not our least," Abbot Ambrose turned and looked directly at Gus. Gus sat with his eyes closed tightly and all of his fingers crossed which caused Abbot Ambrose to chuckle out loud. "Master Gustav Kugele."

"Me?" Gus gasped and opened his eyes. "He said my name! I made it!" Gus jumped to his feet so quickly he knocked over his chair. It hit the floor with a loud crash. Suddenly the room began to spin and his vision blurred. Without warning, he collapsed onto the floor.

Rick jumped to his feet as did Howard and Charlie. Brother Simon rushed to Gus's side as Gus opened his eyes.

"Oh," Gus groaned as he lay on the floor. "What happened?"

"You ninny," Rick laughed. "You passed out."

"Master Walters!" Brother Simon snapped sternly. "Take your seat!" He turned back to Gus. "Are you okay, Master

Kugele?"

"I think so," he answered.

Brother Simon slowly helped Gus to his feet.

Certain that Gus was okay, Charlie sat back down in his chair. Silently he watched as Brother Simon and Gus walked to the front of the refectory. Gus changed into his new white surplice. He smiled proudly and mouthed the words, "I made it," to Rick and Howard.

As the room applauded the newest members of the Altar Boys' Club, Charlie sat quietly. He was happy for Gus but at the same time, he felt hurt that his friends did not believe him. Even though the room was filled with boys, Charlie felt alone. He thought of his grandmother and wished he could talk to her. She would be able to make it better. She always did, he thought.

After the prayer, the Altar Boys huddled around the head table to congratulate their newest members. Charlie stood apart from the group and watched silently. Rick and Howard congratulated Gus, patting him on the back. Howard, a little too hard.

Rick glared when he looked at Larry and Austin. "I can't believe this," he complained to Howard.

"That makes two of us," Howard added. "What could Abbot Ambrose possibly be thinking to allow the likes of them into the Altar Boys' Club?"

"I thought we were finally rid of them since we don't have any classes with them this year." Rick grumbled.

Out of the corners of his eyes, Charlie noticed Abbot Ambrose standing by the refectory door talking with Dougary. Slowly he walked closer; wanting to speak with Abbot Ambrose after Dougary was finished.

Dougary appeared to be troubled by something. He was not his usual gruff self. He was more like the way Charlie saw him that day outside of the Abbot's office, normal.

"I don't understand why you chose me," Dougary said. His voice was quiet and unlike his usual tough tone.

Abbot Ambrose smiled and stroked his white beard.

"Because, whether you believe in yourself or not, I believe in you. You aren't as tough as you try to put forth, Master Duggan. Deep down, I know, you have a good heart beating in there." He tapped Dougary's chest lightly with his long, thin index finger. "I'm just hoping you'll give it a chance to be seen by the others."

Dougary stood silently looking at Abbot Ambrose, apparently thinking about what the Abbot said. He looked at the floor and then back up.

"What if I don't want to be an Altar Boy?" he asked. "Can I quit?"

"That is your choice." Abbot Ambrose nodded and tucked his arms under his robes. "But I don't think you're a quitter."

Again Dougary appeared to think for a moment. He opened his mouth as if about to say something but then closed it and walked back over to the rest of the boys.

Charlie quickly followed his great uncle into the hall.

"Father Abbot," he called.

Abbot Ambrose turned around. "Yes?" he smiled at Charlie.

"May I talk with you for a moment, please?"

"Sure," Abbot Ambrose answered. "Walk with me and tell me what's troubling you, son?"

Charlie looked over his shoulder at the refectory doors. He turned back around.

"I didn't do it," he said. "I didn't beat up Dale. When I came out of the tunnel, I heard Dale groaning and then I saw Larry. He could've done it and started to leave; but when he saw my light he could've turned around and pretended he was just walking up."

"I see," Abbot Ambrose said.

"I don't care if everyone else won't believe me," Charlie said and glanced over his shoulder again. "But Howard...." Charlie's throat tightened and tears welled in his eyes. "That hurts."

"I know, son," Abbot Ambrose said, putting his arm around Charlie's shoulders. "Give him time."

"Abbot Ambrose," Brother Owen said as he rushed up to them. "Oh, Master MacCready, good." His voice sounded bitter and cold. "You might as well hear this, too."

"Hear what, Owen?" Abbot Ambrose asked and tucked his arms back under his robes.

"I want to talk with you about the Altar Boys' Club," he answered and looked at Charlie again. "And particularly about Master MacCready."

Abbot Ambrose looked at Charlie and then back at Brother Owen. "Go on."

"One of the bylaws of the Altar Boys' Club is to maintain fine conduct."

"I am quite well aware of the rules," Abbot Ambrose answered. "What is your point?"

"I've talked to the other prefects and the consensus is that Master MacCready should be removed," Brother Owen said, and nodded smugly to himself as he looked at Charlie's shocked face.

"And why is that?" Abbot Ambrose asked.

Brother Owen looked at the Abbot again. "It has come to my attention that Master MacCready has been late on more than one occasion to the Altar Boys' meetings and also in fulfilling his duties checking the grounds."

"I see. Anything else?" Abbot Ambrose urged as he listened.

"Yes. There is the matter of Master MacCready being the prime suspect in the vicious attack on Master Kaufman. I feel it is a disservice to the rest of the Altar Boys to allow him to remain among them with this sort of reproach."

"Yes," Abbot Ambrose nodded. "Is that all?"

Brother Owen nodded and tucked his hands under his robes.

"Owen, thank you for your input. Your feelings have been duly noted," Abbot Ambrose answered. He turned around to open his office door.

"Forgive me, Father Abbot," Brother Owen spoke up.

"Aren't you going to remove him?"

Abbot Ambrose slowly turned around. "Tell me, what are Brother Simon's feelings on the matter?"

Brother Owen looked away, avoiding Abbot Ambrose's eyes. "He doesn't think Master MacCready is guilty," he answered quietly. "But he's the only one."

"He is not the only one," Abbot Ambrose answered.

"You can't possibly—" the words stuck in Brother Owen's throat as he saw the look in his superior's eyes. "Forgive me. I was out of line."

"Yes, you were," Abbot Ambrose answered firmly, yet not without compassion. "I have noted your feelings on the matter but until we have more facts I am withholding any decisions. That will be all." He turned to Charlie. "We will speak again." With that, he entered his office and closed the door behind him.

Charlie looked at Brother Owen.

"You may have fooled him," Brother Owen snarled. "But you don't fool me. You're a little troublemaker and you can bet that I'll be watching you."

A chill ran up Charlie's spine as he watched Brother Owen walk away. In his year at Saint Michael's he had never seen Brother Owen so upset or act so mean.

The bells began to ring out, signaling that Charlie was once again late for Mass. He quickly rushed into the Abbey Church and to the sacristy behind the sanctuary.

"Well, it is about time, MacCready," Robert snapped at Charlie. "Grab the thurible and get a charcoal lit, fast."

"Yes sir," Charlie answered and rushed to the incense closet. He opened the door and immediately the overpowering smell of the incense took his breath away. He grabbed the brass incense burner from hits hook and set it on the counter. He returned to the closet, lined with fireproof walls, and opened the drawer at the bottom. He took out a charcoal disc and grabbed the tongs and matches. He quickly lit the charcoal.

"Hurry up, MacCready," Robert impatiently urged as the music began to fill the church.

Charlie quickly closed the cover on the thurible and returned the matches and tongs to the incense closet. He grabbed the small incense bowl and spoon and closed the closet door. Picking the thurible up by its long chains, took his place in line just as the altar boys began the processional.

"Lucky for you, you made it," Robert whispered as they walked into the church sanctuary.

Charlie did not respond.

After the Mass was concluded, the embers in the thurible were extinguished and the thurible safely put away. Charlie slipped away to the top of the bell tower to be alone.

The autumn air was chilly. The morning's clouds had vanished and the sun's rays felt warm against Charlie's face. He stood by the arch that overlooked the front grounds. Below, several boys mingled with the visitors, their laughter reaching up to the top of the tower. Charlie was glad he was not down there. He did not want to be adopted because he was not an orphan, no matter what his Uncle Chester thought. His parents were coming for him; he just knew it deep down in his heart. Today, he just wished they would hurry up.

He turned his head away and looked at the forest. Suddenly he spotted a shadowy figure behind a tree. It appeared to be searching the crowd. A burst of anger and adrenaline filled Charlie.

"Oh no you don't!" he said out loud. "You're not getting away this time."

Quickly Charlie made his way down the wooden stairs of the bell tower and into the hallway on the fourth floor. He descended the stairs, two at a time, and quickly rushed out the back door. He ran around to the front grounds. He stopped and searched the woods, his anger still filling him with boldness. He spotted the shadowy figure standing behind the tree with its back toward him. Carefully Charlie crept into the woods. The laughter and noisy chatter of the crowd on the front lawn covered up the snap of the twigs beneath Charlie's feet. He drew closer, his eyes intent on the shadow behind the tree.

"Master MacCready!" A voice shouted sternly from the crowd.

Charlie recognized it immediately and stopped. He looked at the crowd on the front lawn. Brother Owen was heading toward him in an almost run.

Charlie looked back at the shadow, but it was gone.

"Come out of there this instant!" Brother Owen ordered. He stood with his arms folded over his chest.

"You know the forest is off limits to you boys. Just what on God's green Earth, do you think you're doing?" he demanded as Charlie emerged from the woods and walked over to him.

"I was," he began as he glanced over his shoulder in the direction of where the shadow was lurking. He sighed and he looked back at Brother Owen's angry eyes. "I thought I saw someone over there."

Brother Owen squinted and looked in the direction Charlie had pointed. "A likely story," he said, not seeing anything. "Perhaps Father Abbot will listen to me now. Come on." He grabbed Charlie by the arm and gave it a sharp jerk that nearly knocked Charlie off balance. Brother Owen briskly led him through the crowd.

Charlie felt his face turn red with embarrassment when he noticed the boys and guests all looking at him. He spotted Gus with a couple off in the distance. They appeared to be laughing. For a moment Charlie pulled against Brother Owen's grip but Brother Owen gave Charlie's arm a sharp tug and moved him along.

Moments later they were standing in Abbot Ambrose's office. Charlie listened as Brother Owen made his second appeal.

"And he claims he saw someone lurking in the shadows but I didn't see anyone except him," Brother Owen concluded.

"I see," Abbot Ambrose said. He turned to Charlie. "Is this true? You were in the woods, alone?"

"Yes, Father Abbot." Charlie nodded sheepishly.

"Charlie, you disappoint me." Abbot Ambrose shook his head. "You know the rules. No one is allowed in the forest and especially alone. You will report for an hour of work crew this Saturday."

"An hour?" Brother Owen gasped. "But—" Again the words stuck in his throat as Abbot Ambrose gave him a stern look.

"That is the punishment for a student's disobedience," Abbot Ambrose said. "That will be all."

"Yes, Father Abbot," Brother Owen answered and walked out of the office.

Charlie silently followed him and returned to his dorm to wait for the lunch bell.

When the bell sounded, Charlie slowly walked down the stairs toward the refectory. He was not looking forward to lunch, anticipating that it would be the same as breakfast. Charlie spotted Howard in line. Their eyes met briefly and Howard looked away. With a heavy sigh, Charlie walked over and took his place in line.

"Hey, Charlie," Gus gushed as he stepped out of line. "You aren't going to be—" The words stuck in his throat as he noticed Howard's pursed lips and stern glare. "But Howard, this is exciting," Gus pleaded. "Father Mark located my dad's cousins. They came to visit me today. They're going to talk to the Abbot about adopting me."

"That's great!" Charlie smiled at his friend. "Were they the people I saw you with on the front grounds?"

"Ye—" again the words stopped when Gus looked at Howard. Slowly he took his place in line.

"Hey, MacCreepy!" Travis called from his place in the Saint Peter line.

Charlie looked over at him. He regretted it the moment he did it, but it was a reflex.

"Heard the news?" Travis snickered.

Charlie looked at him with a blank expression on his face.

"Kaufman was transferred to the hospital. You really know

how to treat your friends," he laughed.

Charlie glanced at Howard and then turned back around.

Lunch began the same as breakfast with the serving brother dropping Charlie's plate onto the table in front of him. The fries and a hamburger bounced off the plate and onto the table causing Charlie to jump and grab his food before it fell onto the floor. Rick and Howard ate quietly, not looking up. Gus kept his head down but occasionally snuck a look at Charlie. He frowned compassionately at him.

"Please pass the ketchup," Charlie asked Howard as he noticed the bottle to Howard's right.

Howard did not move. Neither did Rick.

"Would you please pass the ketchup, Howard?" Charlie asked directly.

Again, Howard pretended not to hear and continued eating his hamburger. Charlie looked at Rick.

"Rick?"

Rick did not move.

Anger began to replace the hurt Charlie felt inside. He turned and looked directly at Howard.

"You are such a hypocrite!"

"What?" Howard finally spoke and looked at Charlie.

"You once told me that we were friends," Charlie continued angrily. "But how quickly you believe the likes of Larry over me. Some friend you turned out to be."

Charlie turned back to his lunch. His body trembled. He took a deep breath to try to steady his nerves. He picked up his fries and began to eat them plain.

Howard sat quietly and thought about what Charlie said. Charlie was right; he was too quick to believe Larry. Slowly he took the bottle of ketchup and set it in front of Charlie.

Charlie looked at the bottle and then Howard. "I don't want it anymore!" he snapped and slammed the red plastic bottle back in front of Howard, causing ketchup to erupt from the pointed spout on top. Howard jumped back.

After lunch, Charlie returned to the bell tower. He was still angry with Howard and did not want to be around anyone. Abbot Ambrose's reassurances that Dale would be back in the infirmary in a couple days, after all the medical tests were completed, did little to ease his mind. He looked across the front grounds as people milled about. Suddenly Charlie felt the presence of someone behind him. He turned around sharply and looked at Howard.

Howard appeared a bit nervous as he looked at Charlie. "I'm sorry," he said quietly

"Sorry?" Charlie smirked and turned his back to Howard.

"I mean it, Charlie. I'm sorry." Howard repeated.

"I don't understand you." Charlie shook his head. "All summer you wouldn't believe me about Austin, but suddenly you believe the likes of Larry over me? You actually believe I would hurt Dale?" Charlie said. He looked at Howard. "Dale's my friend! I would never intentionally hurt a friend." Charlie turned back around and blindly looked at the scene below on the front grounds.

"I know," Howard admitted. "It's just that I don't know what to think."

"But you do now? Why the sudden change?" Charlie asked without looking at Howard.

"I don't know," Howard shrugged.

"I thought we were friends," Charlie said. He turned around. "But I guess I was wrong about that." He started for the trap door.

"We are friends," Howard said and grabbed Charlie's arm to stop him from leaving. "I know I haven't acted like it," he continued. "But you *are* my friend and I am truly sorry."

Charlie looked at Howard, at his dark eyes. He could tell that this time Howard really meant it. He nodded, then gave a slight shrug. "So, now what?"

"I don't know," Howard answered, and shrugged. "Guess we still need to find out who's behind this."

"That's easier said than done." Charlie walked back to the window and looked at the forest below.

UNMASKED

Saint Nicholas dorm was nearly deserted. Charlie and Howard sat quietly facing each other on the sofa in the lounge with the checkerboard between them. Howard stared at his pieces, contemplating his next move. The doors opened with a bang, causing both boys to jump and upending the game. Rick and Gus rushed into the room.

"There you are. You're not going to believe this," Rick panted excitedly. He had his black notebook and a wooden ruler in his hands.

"Ok, I give," Howard answered and continued picking up his pieces.

"Gus and I were walking outside by the construction site when we noticed Father Mark talking with Mister Hertz," Rick explained.

"And?" Howard prodded impatiently.

Charlie put his pieces back into their box and listened.

"I'm getting there," Rick answered. "Don't rush me."

"Oh, this is exciting!" Gus added rubbing his cold hands together.

Charlie raised his eyebrows uncertainly at Gus.

"After they left," Rick continued. "I noticed there was a

perfect shoeprint in the mud where Father Mark had been standing. So, I took my ruler and measured it." He held up his ruler for all to see.

"You did?" Howard sat forward and tried to see what Rick had written in his book.

Rick pulled it away. "I'll tell you," he said and looked offended. "The print was a perfect size ten and a half!"

"I don't believe it." Howard fell back on the sofa in shock. "It can't be him."

"Now what do we do?" Rick asked. He plopped down in of one of the overstuffed chairs.

Charlie looked at Howard. "Go to the Abbot?"

"Definitely not!" Howard gasped. "So far all we know is that his shoes are the same size as those worn by the shadow. That doesn't prove anything. We need more."

Rick threw his hands in the air and shook his head. "I don't believe this," he said. "I'm through with this." He slammed his notebook closed and stormed off to his cubicle.

"What more do we need?" Charlie asked.

"Well, you said so yourself that Larry was the one who attacked Dale. Father Mark wasn't there until much later. And we still don't know who attacked Sister Margaret."

"Well, maybe I was wrong about Larry." Charlie could not believe he just said that out loud. By the shocked look on Howard's face it was obvious that he did not either. "I said, maybe," Charlie added. "Remember Father Mark wasn't at the meeting on the front steps the night Dale was attacked. And he did show up right after Rick and you."

"So?" Howard shrugged.

"Well, maybe instead of Larry doubling back, it was Father Mark instead."

Howard thought for a moment. "No, it can't be him." Howard shook his head. "It's time for bed." He stood up and walked back to his cubicle.

Charlie sat and watched Howard for a moment. He knew Howard liked Father Mark and convincing him would be hard.

If he just had more proof, surely Howard could not ignore the evidence.

The glow from the harvest moon shone through the window above Charlie's bed and filled his cubicle. The cold night air softly whistled through the tiny crack in the opening cooling Charlie's face while he slept.

"Char-lie!"

Charlie turned around and holding his lantern higher to illuminate the dark forest in the direction of the voice.

"Charlie!" It called again from the opposite direction.

Charlie spun around but saw nothing. Suddenly he felt a hand on his shoulder, gently turning him around. Charlie dropped the lantern as he came face to face with the shadow. He could not run. He could not move.

Slowly, the shadow reached out its bony hand and took hold of the chain around Charlie's neck. Without thinking, Charlie grabbed the hand and woke up.

He gasped as he looked up at the shadow above him, his hand wrapped around the shadow's wrist. The wrist felt strange, neither warm nor cold. The shadow began to pull away. Charlie felt the wrist bones twisting beneath its skin. Then suddenly it was free, shedding its skin, and disappeared.

Charlie screamed, but only a faint moan escaped his lips. He threw the boneless hand away from him. It dropped on the floor next to Howard's bed. Frantically, Charlie retreated to the corner of his bed, pulling the covers up to his chin.

Howard stirred and turned over in his bed. He opened his eyes and bolted straight up when he saw Charlie. Quickly grabbing his glasses from his nightstand, he put them on.

"What is it?" he asked.

"Th-th-the shadow," Charlie panted. "Its hand." He pointed at the hand on the floor.

Howard turned on the lamp on his nightstand so he could see. Cautiously he crawled out of his bed.

"Charlie," he said as he picked it up. "It's rubber."

"What?" Charlie asked as he tried to understand.

"It's a costume hand," Howard explained.

Suddenly they heard the sound of the dormitory doors opening. Howard dropped the glove. He quickly jumped back into his bed. Brother Simon entered and walked directly toward the lighted cubicle. In his tight grasp he held the arm of someone dressed in a monk's black hooded choir robe.

"Master Miller and Master MacCready," Brother Simon greeted them sternly. "Would either of you mind telling me what is going on here?"

"Ask him," Howard nodded to the person in Brother Simon's grip.

"He's been trying to get my key," Charlie spoke up angrily. He pulled the chain from under his pajama top and looked at the old tarnished key between the smaller key to the pottery studio and the Saint Christopher medal his grandmother had given him.

"Here, I think you forgot something," Howard said, picking up the glove. He held it out for Brother Simon to see.

Brother Simon looked at the hooded person in his grasp. "Well, let's see who we have here." He pulled the hood off the person's head only to reveal a rubber mask of an old man. He gave a start and then quickly yanked the mask off.

"You!" Howard gasped. He threw the rubber glove at the boy.

"Larry?" Charlie looked at him, confused. He was expecting to see Father Mark.

"Master Hertz," Brother Simon spoke in an angry tone. "What have you to say for yourself?"

Larry glared at Charlie and Howard as he twisted in Brother Simon's tight grasp. "I wasn't trying to get your stupid key," he hissed.

"Then what were you doing?" Brother Simon tightened his grip and asked.

"I was after the key to the pottery studio," Larry grimaced. "Ouch! You're hurting my arm!"

"I'll do more than hurt your arm, young man," warned Brother Simon. "Now, why were you after the studio key?"

"Because, if you must know, I lost mine."

"But I thought Dougary was the only one missing his key," Howard spoke up.

"That's because I took his key," Larry admitted. "I didn't want Father Ichabod mad at me. So when Dougary went to shower, I took his key. I didn't know he'd get in so much trouble."

"So, what's with this get up?" Brother Simon asked.

"I overheard Charlie telling Howard about seeing shadows, so I thought I would have a little fun while I was at it."

"Well, Master Hertz," Brother Simon continued. "We'll see what Father Mark has to say about this in the morning. I suggest you get back to your bed and stay there!"

"What about my things?" he asked, looking at the glove and mask.

"I will be keeping them," Brother Simon answered, then looked directly at Charlie. "We will continue this talk in the morning. I suggest you both go back to sleep."

"Yes, Brother Simon," Charlie and Howard answered at once.

They watched as Brother Simon led Larry out of the dorm. Howard turned off his light and crawled back into his warm bed. He tossed and turned until he found a comfortable position. He looked over at Charlie. Charlie was still sitting up in his bed, staring at the doors.

"What's the matter?" Howard asked.

"Do you believe him?" he asked.

"Larry?" Howard looked at Charlie, confused. "About what?"

"That story about Dougary's key and that he wasn't after my key?"

"Sure, I guess," Howard said. "Why not?"

"Because if he wasn't after my key, then there is still someone out there, the real shadow."

"What are you talking about?" Howard yawned.

"Remember the first time I saw the shadow? It was before

we even signed up for the pottery class."

"Good point," Howard said. He propped himself up on his elbow and stared at Charlie. "So if Larry's not *the* shadow, you still think it's Father Mark?"

Charlie nodded.

Howard lay back down and rolled over, facing the partition.

Charlie lay back down and stared up at the dark ceiling. His head began to hurt as he tried to sort out his thoughts. Soon he was fast asleep.

The autumn sky was clear and the bright sunlight filled Saint Nicholas dorm as the boys returned to their cubicles after breakfast. Rick plopped down on the sofa with his arms folded over his chest.

"Well, someone is in a bad mood," Charlie said, as he sat down in the overstuffed chair across from Rick.

"Don't mind him," Howard shook his head. "He's just upset about Gus being gone this weekend."

"Oh like you aren't," Rick sneered. "Have you ever thought about what would happen if those people adopt Gus? He'll be gone, that's what!"

"Like that's gonna happen," Howard smirked. He looked away so Rick would not see just how worried he really was.

"We should be happy for Gus," Charlie said.

"I am happy for him," Rick said bitterly. "I'm just—never mind. Let's talk about something else. So what happened last night?"

Charlie glanced at Howard while recounting the events from the night before. Rick sat quietly and listened.

"So, whadaya think?" Charlie asked.

Rick flipped through the pages of his little black notebook, occasionally glancing up at Howard and Charlie. He squinted as he reviewed the facts he had written down.

"Well?" Charlie asked again. He looked at Howard who just shook his head.

"You're right," Rick answered finally.

"What? You're agreeing with me?"

"That's right," Rick answered smugly. "Larry couldn't possibly be the real shadow. For one thing, his feet are too small. When we all, that is except for you, had work crew, Larry was working with us. We had to put on boots and he wears a size...." He consulted his notes. "Nine and a half. So, it can't possibly be him."

Charlie looked at Howard; his eyes were wide as he realized Rick was right.

"Then it has to be Father—"

"Master MacCready," Brother Simon called from the door, interrupted him. "I would like you to come with me to see Father Mark."

Charlie looked at Howard with a fearful expression, his mouth still open.

"Today, Master MacCready," Brother Simon insisted. "And you too, Master Miller."

Howard and Charlie jumped to their feet. Nervously, they followed Brother Simon down the hallway to Saint Peter dorm.

"What are we going to do?" Charlie whispered to Howard. "We can't tell Father Mark about the shadow."

"I don't know." Howard shrugged.

"If Father Mark finds out we're onto him we'll never be able to catch him," Charlie added.

"Simon, you're just wasting your time!" Father Vicar greeted when Brother Simon stopped outside Saint Peter dorm.

"We shall see what Mark thinks of these," Brother Simon said holding out the mask and gloves. "Not to mention, Master Hertz was out of his bed after lights out."

"Oh, come on, Simon. It was a joke," Father Vicar scoffed.

"Forgive me, Vicar, but I'm not laughing."

"It seems to me that a person who lives in a glass house shouldn't throw stones. What of Master MacCready?" Father Vicar said and glared at Charlie. "Wasn't he guilty of the same just a few months ago?"

"That was different," Brother Simon defended Charlie.

"It's only different because it's one of your boys, Simon." Father Vicar looked down his long, crooked nose at Brother Simon. "Come along, Master Hertz."

Larry stepped from behind Father Vicar and glared at Charlie. He quickly followed close behind his prefect.

"Pay them no mind," Brother Simon said and led Charlie and Howard down the stairs to Father Mark's office.

"Enter!" Father Mark called from inside his office.

Father Vicar opened the door and ushered Larry inside. Brother Simon held the door for Charlie and Howard, then followed them.

"Good morning," Father Mark greeted them from his seat behind his large oak desk. "Please have a seat, boys." He motioned to the three chairs off to the side, in front of the fireplace. "Okay, what's this about, Simon?" he asked.

"Last night, around one in the morning, I heard a noise in the hallway. When I went to see what it was, I found Master Hertz wearing one of our black choir robes and these." He handed the mask and gloves to Father Mark.

Father Mark looked them over for a moment and then looked back at Brother Simon. "Go on."

"From the direction Master Hertz was headed it was obvious he had just come from my dormitory," Brother Simon continued. "So, I took him back into the dorm where I found a light on in Master MacCready's and Master Miller's cubicle. It was then that we unmasked Master Hertz and he admitted he had been trying to steal Master MacCready's key to the pottery studio."

Father Mark looked at Larry. His disappointment was evident in his expression. "Is this true, Vicar?" he asked turning back to the gaunt prefect.

"Mark, Mark," Father Vicar shook his head and gave a crocked half-smile. "It was a simple misunderstanding. That's all. A silly teenage prank. There was no real harm done."

Father Mark thought for a moment. "But he was still out of bed and in another dorm after lights out," he reasoned out loud.

"Yes, he was," Father Vicar agreed. "Just as were Masters Miller and MacCready on several occasions over this past year. I'm sure you've read the reports in their files."

Father Mark nodded slightly in response.

"Anyway, Master MacCready still has his key," Father Vicar pointed out.

"True," Father Mark said with a heavy sigh.

The sigh sent shivers up Charlie's spine. He did not like the way Father Mark looked at him. Could Father Mark and Larry be working together? Suddenly his hand found the keys that hung from the chain beneath his robes. He glanced at Howard.

"I'm afraid that I cannot do anything about Master MacCready's or Master Miller's indiscretions prior to my becoming dean," Father Mark said after much thought. "However, I can put a stop to any further violations," he continued as he looked at Father Vicar. "It will be duly noted in Master Hertz's file, and in light of the punishment handed out to an innocent Dougary, he shall receive one hour of work crew with the brothers each Saturday for the remainder of the school year."

"I knew Abbot Ambrose made a mistake choosing you as dean!" Father Vicar hissed. "If I were dean—"

"But you're not," Father Mark said through clenched teeth, and glared at Father Vicar.

"Things can change!" Father Vicar returned just as coldly. "Master Hertz, get up!" he snapped and turned around sharply. He tucked his hands under his robes, which made his chest appear even more puffed up than before. Larry quickly opened the door for his prefect.

"This is not over, Mark!" he said as he walked out of the office.

"Is there anything further?" Father Mark turned his attention to Brother Simon.

"No." Brother Simon answered, then turned around. "Come, boys."

Howard and Charlie, who were biting their tongues to keep

from laughing triumphantly, jumped to their feet and quickly followed Brother Simon out of the office.

"You were great in there," Howard said with a smile to Brother Simon.

Brother Simon stopped in his tracks and looked at Howard dryly. "I beg your pardon?"

The smile quickly faded from Howard's lips. "Ah, never mind," he said.

"Master Miller," Brother Simon spoke without emotion. "One should never take delight in the misfortune of others. Is that clearly understood?"

"Yes, Brother Simon," Howard answered sheepishly. Brother Simon nodded and for a split second, smiled before he continued on his way back to his office.

Howard looked at Charlie in surprise and the two laughed quietly.

DOUGARY

The December 1st wind was cold against Charlie's cheeks as he and Howard looked out of the bell tower at the front grounds. To their left, they could see the large crane at the construction site lowering the huge domed skylight onto the roof of the new building. On the grounds, in the distance toward the parking garage, the novices and Larry raked up the last of the fallen leaves.

"There's Steve," Howard said, and pointed.

"I sure wish he were still our sacristan," Charlie lamented. "I don't think Robert likes me very much."

"Give him more time. The rumors are still out there," Howard said. "It's only been a week since Dale came back from the hospital."

"I know," Charlie sighed. "Father Abbot said Dale still won't talk about what happened. When I've tried to stop by the infirmary to see Dale, Brother James wouldn't let me in."

"I know," Howard said. "But try not to take it personal. He's only following orders from Brother Owen."

"I know, but that's just as upsetting," Charlie said.

"There you are," Gus panted as he crawled up through the trap door in the floor of the bell tower.

Charlie and Howard turned around.

"Why? What's up?" Howard asked.

"You won't believe this," Gus continued as he tried to catch his breath. "They just brought Dougary to the infirmary."

"What?" Charlie gasped. He looked at Howard and then back at Gus.

"Two of the brothers were raking leaves over by the garages and found him lying under a tree. He was beaten up pretty bad, even worse than Dale."

"Oh my God," Charlie gasped.

"Is that all?" Howard asked indifferently.

"No, I overheard one of the brothers telling Abbot Ambrose that when they found Dougary, he kept repeating Charlie's name," Gus said and looked at Charlie.

Howard looked at Charlie.

"It wasn't me." Charlie shook his head.

"This time, I can vouch for you," Howard spoke up and turned back to Gus. "Charlie and I have been up here all afternoon. There's no way he could've done it."

"I have to go see Dougary," Charlie insisted.

Before Howard could say a word, Charlie was at the trap door. Howard quickly rushed over to him. "Okay, we'll all go," he said and went down the stairs first.

"Hey Charlie," Gus said as the two hurried after Howard.

Charlie stopped as they reached the fourth-floor stairwell. He waited for Gus to crawl through the small door.

"I guess this proves you didn't beat up Dale either?"

Charlie thought for a moment. "Yeah," he answered. "But I'm more concerned about Dougary right now?"

"What do we care? He's always been mean to us," Gus asked.

"But that doesn't mean I want to see him hurt," Charlie said. "Besides, he's an Altar Boy, now."

Howard quickly opened the fire door and the three headed down the hallway toward the stairwell between the Abbey's wing and theirs.

"Where do you guys think you're going?" a voice asked as they passed by Saint Peter dorm.

Charlie stopped and looked at Austin. "To see how Dougary is doing, if it's any of your business."

"Do you think that's such a wise idea?" Austin asked in a near whisper as he looked around to be sure that no one was watching him talk to Charlie.

"Why?" Charlie asked.

"Because I heard how you threatened Dougary many times over the summer. It's common knowledge since his father tried to throw you out of the attic that you've had it in for Dougary," Austin answered.

"Oh, you don't know anything," Charlie shook his head. Part of him wanted to believe Austin but he just was not sure. He turned away and started down the hall.

"For your information, Howard was with Charlie all afternoon," Charlie heard Gus tell Austin.

Charlie caught up with Howard as they reached the door to the monastery wing.

"What did Austin want?" he asked and pushed the fire door open.

"To cause trouble," Charlie answered looking over his shoulder. "But Gus took care of him."

"Wait for me," Gus called as he ran after them.

The three hurried down the flight of stairs to the third floor. Howard opened the door to the monastery wing. The hallway was silent even though a gathering of brothers and Altar Boys huddled around the Infirmary doors halfway down the hall. Slowly the three joined them.

"Well, I must say that I am surprised to see you," a brother said when he saw Charlie. "You have a lot of nerve showing our face around here after what you just did."

Charlie looked at the monk. He recognized him. It was his serving monk from the refectory.

"I haven't done anything to be ashamed of," Charlie said, with a bit of anger in his voice.

"Time will tell," the young monk said.

"Look Brother," Howard spoke up. "Charlie was with me all afternoon. He didn't do anything to Dog breath."

"That's right," Charlie agreed a bit more boldly.

"Forgive me if I don't buy it," the monk said, then turned around sharply and walked away.

The infirmary doors opened, and Abbot Ambrose walked into the hallway with novice Stephen. Abbot Ambrose whispered something into Stephen's ear and Stephen rushed off.

"Ah, why am I not surprised to see you boys here?" Abbot Ambrose greeted Howard, Charlie and Gus. He folded his hands over his stomach.

"How's Dougary?" Howard asked.

"Brother James has called the doctor. He's been worked over pretty well, I'm afraid." A worried look filled Abbot Ambrose's eyes.

"He's going to be all right, isn't he?" Charlie asked.

"I certainly hope so, son," Abbot Ambrose said, glancing behind him at the door.

"Is it true that he keeps saying Charlie's name over and over?" Gus asked.

Charlie looked at Gus curiously.

"Yes," Abbot Ambrose nodded. "Master Duggan has been asking for him, but he's not in any shape to talk right now. Why don't you boys run along for now. Father Mark will keep you posted on Master Duggan's condition."

"Yes, Father Abbot," Howard said.

The three turned around and headed back to the student wing. Just as they reached the door, Charlie looked back at the Abbot. Father Mark emerged from the infirmary.

"Mark, I want to speak to the brothers who found Master Duggan, and also anyone else who was working near the area where he was found this afternoon, in my office right away."

"Yes, Father Abbot." Father Mark nodded as they both parted company.

Charlie turned back around and returned to his dorm.

"Where have you guys been?" Rick demanded when Charlie, Howard and Gus walked over to the dorm lounge. "Haven't you heard about Dougary?"

"Yes," Howard answered, as he stretched out in his favorite overstuffed chair.

"We were just talking with Abbot Ambrose," Gus added as he flopped down on the sofa.

"Brother James is taking Dougary to the hospital," Charlie added. "It's really strange. The other attacks have all happened at night, but not this time."

"So, what difference does that make?" Howard asked.

"A big difference," Charlie continued. "It means that someone had to have seen something. At least Abbot Ambrose thinks so. As we were leaving, he told Father Mark to have anyone who may have any information see him at once."

"Wow!" Gus breathed.

"Well, I saw him," Rick announced impatiently.

"You what?" Howard gasped and sat up in his chair. All three boys looked at Rick in opened-mouth surprise.

"Well, I didn't actually see what happened to him," Rick admitted. "But earlier today I was walking over by the construction site when I heard someone yelling at someone. So, I took a peek from behind a tree and I saw Dougary. But I couldn't see who he was yelling at. A stupid truck was blocking my view."

"What was he yelling about?" Charlie asked.

"I didn't catch all of it. He did say Dale's name," Rick answered, flipping the pages in his notebook.

Charlie looked at Howard. He could not believe what he was hearing.

"What exactly did Dougary say?" Howard pressed. "You said he was yelling. You should've heard something."

"The crane was too loud," Rick explained.

"Well, was he upset that Dale was beat up?" Charlie asked.

"Yes, I think so," Rick said, nodding his head. He paused and read his notes. "Yes, he was." Rick sounded more positive this time. "But I had the feeling there was something more, that there was more to it than just Dale being beat up."

Charlie looked at Howard and then back at Rick. "You know what this means, don't you?"

Howard and Rick looked at each other and shrugged.

"It means that Dougary knows who's behind this," Charlie answered for them.

As the realization that Charlie was right sank in, Rick stood up. "This is big! We have to tell Abbot Ambrose."

The four boys jumped to their feet and headed for the doors. The hallway outside their dorm was noisy. A group of boys huddled around, talking all at once. Howard walked over to Ted.

"What's going on?" he asked.

"An ambulance just took Dougary to the hospital," he answered.

"What?" Howard gasped. "Where's Abbot Ambrose?"

"He and Father Vicar went to the hospital," Ted answered, eyeing Charlie suspiciously.

"That doesn't sound good," Charlie sighed.

The boys turned around and returned to their dorm. Howard sat down in his favorite overstuffed chair facing the dorm doors. He slumped down, resting his arms on the arms of the chair and pressing his hands on either side of his head. Charlie and Gus sat down on the sofa, while Rick claimed the other overstuffed chair. Rick pulled out his notebook and began quickly writing down what he heard and saw.

"So, what do we know?" Howard asked, watching Rick.

"We can eliminate Dougary as a suspect, for starters," Charlie said.

"I didn't know he was even being considered," Rick said, looking at Howard, then Gus.

"Yeah," Gus nodded.

"So, any ideas who it could be?" Howard asked.

"I still can't help but think Larry is involved in this somehow," Charlie answered.

"Why Larry?" Rick asked. "I thought we already determined that he can't be the shadow."

"I know," Charlie agreed. "But what if he is working with Father Mark?"

"Why would he do that?" Howard asked. It was plain, Howard was still not as certain as Charlie that Father Mark was the shadow.

"And why would either of them beat up Dougary?" Rick asked.

"To keep him from going to the Abbot?" Gus spoke up.

Rick and Howard looked at Gus in surprise.

"Or maybe Dougary found out that Larry stole his pottery studio key?" Charlie speculated. "And Dougary started the fight?"

"And he ended up getting the worst end of it," Rick continued the line of thought.

"It sounds possible," Howard agreed. "But how do we prove any of it?"

"We can't talk to Larry," Gus thought out loud.

"But we can talk to Austin," Charlie suggested.

Howard turned sharply and looked at Charlie. "I wouldn't believe anything that comes out of that jerk's mouth."

"What other choice do we have?"

"I don't know," Howard shrugged. "But talk to him if you want. I just think you'd be wasting your time."

Charlie did not say another word. He already knew Howard would react as he did, so there was no point in talking about it or trying to convince him otherwise. The boys fell silent as they avoided each other's eyes and looked around the dorm.

TIME IS RUNNING OUT

Winter seemed to set in overnight. Snow covered the ground in a blanket of shimmering, white. It frosted the tall, fir trees of the forest and traced the bare branches of the trees on the front grounds. Charlie smiled as he looked out at the scene from his fourth floor window.

"Howard, isn't it beautiful?" he exclaimed as he continued to marvel at the sight.

"Sure," Howard shrugged as he glanced out the window. "We better hurry up if we want to see Dale. He gets out of the infirmary today, remember?"

"That's right," Charlie said. He jumped off his bed and grabbed his books. He quickly straightened his bedspread, then rushed after Howard.

"And just where do you two think you are going?" Brother Owen asked, folding his arms over his chest as he stood guard at the door of Saint Sebastian dorm.

"We just wanted to see Dale," Charlie answered.

"There is no way I am going to let either of you anywhere near him," Brother Owen said looking directly at Charlie. "And especially you. Now get to class."

"You have no right," Howard snapped.

"You're wrong, Master Miller. I have every right," Brother Owen spoke coldly. "I have been appointed to protect and care for the boys in my dorm and that is exactly what I intend to do. Unless you two want work crew, I suggest you stay away from Master Kaufman."

Howard and Charlie looked at each other and then turned away. Slowly they started down the hall toward the stairs.

"Can you believe that?" Charlie shook his head. "He still thinks I did it."

"No," Howard disagreed. "If that were the case, he would've let me in to see Dale. No, he's not sure who did it."

"Well, he can't stop us from seeing Dale in class," Charlie said, and looked over his shoulder.

"Yeah," Howard agreed. "So, what did Austin have to say when you talked to him about Larry?"

"He said I'd have a hard time convincing anyone else that Larry would beat up his best friend," Charlie admitted. "Yet everyone's so quick to believe I would beat up Dale." Charlie shook his head. "Talk about a double standard."

"True," Howard said. "But what if it isn't Larry or Father Mark?"

Charlie looked at Howard as though Howard had lost his mind. "What?" he asked. "It has to be one of them. I already told you. Larry was the only other person there the night I found Dale. And Father Mark showed up out of nowhere just after you and Rick."

"I know they were the only two you *saw* there that night." Howard said.

A chill ran up Charlie's spine as the thought slowly occurred to him that someone else could have been lurking in the shadowy darkness, watching everything he did.

"Thanks, Howard." He shuddered. "But I still think I'm right about Larry and Father Mark."

Just as they reached Saint Peter dorm, the doors opened. Larry and Austin walked into the hall wearing their clean white surplices. Travis followed closely behind them, wearing the dark purple surplice of his dorm. The three stopped when they spotted Howard and Charlie.

"Well, if it isn't Tweddle Dumb and Tweddle Dumber," Larry sneered in his usual tone.

"Back off, Hertz," Charlie warned and took a step toward Larry. "Mask or no mask, you don't scare me," he said and glared directly into Larry's eyes.

Larry glared back and then nervously looked away. "Come on, guys," he said to Austin and Travis as he walked away.

"Be careful," Austin quietly warned Charlie as he passed him.

The words echoed in Charlie's ears as he watched the three disappear down the stairs.

"I hate them," Howard seethed as they stood at the top of the empty stairwell. "Come on, let's get to class."

As the two reached the landing between the first floor and the basement, Charlie noticed Howard glance up at his mail slot. It was empty, as usual. It occurred to Charlie, in the last year and a half that he had known Howard, Howard had never received any mail. A feeling of sadness for his best friend came over him. He knew the feeling of excitement he had when he received a card or letter from his grandmother. Suddenly he realized it had been weeks since he received anything. He glanced at his mail slot. Empty.

The two continued down the stairs to their homeroom. As they walked through the door, Gus came rushing up to them. His eyes sparkled and his cheeks were pink with excitement.

"You are never going to believe this," he gushed.

"What?" Howard asked.

"Father Mark has given his permission for me to spend Christmas with my cousins!" he said and giggled. "I can't believe it. I'm going to have a *real* Christmas."

"That's great," Howard smiled and patted Gus on the back.

Charlie caught the look in Howard's eyes. Even though his mouth said he was happy, Howard's eyes said differently. Charlie could see his sadness.

"I'm happy for you, Gus." Charlie smiled at his portly friend.

The bell rang just as Howard and Charlie took their seats. Brother Paul bounded into the room and took his seat on his desk.

"Good morning," he greeted the class.

"Good morning, Brother Paul," they replied.

After the prayer, the boys took their seats again.

"Today looks as though it is going to be a busy day," Brother Paul began. "You will have semester exams in Algebra and English. The choir is going to have an extended practice for the Christmas concert this afternoon instead of this morning. So your Health exam has been moved to just before lunch."

Groans rose from the boys. Even though Charlie had studied for hours, he still felt he was not ready. There was just too much to remember, and he was still having his nightmares and not sleeping well.

As Brother Paul was concluding his announcements, novice Dominic quietly walked into the room and handed him a note. Dominic glanced over at Charlie and then left the room. Brother Paul read the note and then folded it up and tucked it into the pocket of his robes.

"Master MacCready, please report to Abbot Ambrose's office," he said.

Charlie gave Howard a confused look as he stood up.

"Take your things with you," Brother Paul instructed.

Charlie picked up his books and headed out of the classroom. As he reached the classroom door, he glanced over his shoulder at Howard. Howard could not help but see the worried look on Charlie's face. He smiled back at his friend.

Charlie slowly walked up the stairs and wondered what the Abbot could possibly want. As he turned down the corridor toward the Abbot's office, the office door opened and a boy from Saint Thomas dorm and a member of the Altar Boys' Club came out.

"Hey, Gary," Charlie called to him as they passed each

other.

"What?" Gary stopped and turned around. He stood about a head taller than Charlie, with dark brown hair and just as dark, brown eyes.

"The Abbot called me to his office. Do you know what he wants?" Charlie asked.

Gary looked back at the office door then at Charlie. He leaned a bit closer to Charlie and whispered. "Archbishop Gavin is here. He, Abbot Ambrose and Father Mark are questioning everyone in the Altar Boys' Club about the attack on Sister Margaret Mary. It seems that she has remembered a bit about the guy that attacked her in the woods. She thinks it was an Altar Boy."

A feeling of panic rushed over Charlie as he remembered his white surplice. His heart beat faster. He fought the urge to run away.

Gary noticed the fear on Charlie's face. "What's the matter?" he asked, giving Charlie a curious look. "You know something! Don't you?"

"No!" Charlie blurted and shook his head.

Gary continued to eye Charlie curiously which made Charlie all the more nervous. He wondered if he answered too quickly to be believed. Slowly Gary relaxed and turned away. Charlie waited until Gary was gone before he continued down the hall to Abbot Ambrose's office.

Charlie knocked lightly on the door. It opened quickly, causing Charlie to jump back. Father Mark smiled at him.

"Take a seat, Master MacCready," he said in a cheerful tone that did little to ease Charlie's fears. "We'll be with you in a moment."

Charlie sat down in the chair next to the Abbot's door as the door closed. He leaned back in the chair and rested his head against the wall. The hallway was deafeningly quiet. Charlie could hear his nervous heartbeat in his ears. He tried not to think about it, to think of something else, anything. Then suddenly he began to hear voices from inside the Abbot's office. He strained to listen.

"You know you have the Abbey's full cooperation in this matter. We are taking this very seriously," Abbot Ambrose said.

"I understand and I commend you," the deep voice of the Archbishop answered. "But unless we get to the bottom of this and quickly, I'm afraid the Diocese has no option but to close the school down."

"No!" Father Mark protested sharply.

"Mark, I understand your reluctance," Archbishop Gavin said compassionately. "But we have to think of what is best for the boys. They have to be safe."

"But—"

"Mark," Abbot Ambrose interrupted him. "We understand Your Eminence."

Charlie jumped when he heard the hall door to the main foyer open. Suddenly he could no longer hear the voices in the office as he watched two uniformed policemen enter the Student Wing. Charlie recognized the shorter, gruff-looking officer. He had been to the Abbey before, just after Sister Margaret Mary's attack.

The officers stepped up to the Abbot's door and gave a sharp knock. Charlie did not realize he was staring at them until the younger officer, who stood to the right of the older one, looked down at him and smiled. Charlie smiled nervously back, then looked away.

"Yes?" Father Mark greeted the officers as he opened the door.

"We're here to see the Abbot and the Archbishop," the older, gruff officer replied.

"Oh, yes," Father Mark sounded flustered. "Please come in."

The policemen walked into the office. Father Mark closed the door behind them. Charlie leaned back, closer to the wall and strained to listen. At first he could not make out what was being said. He imagined it was just introductions but then the gruff officer's voice became very clear.

"Unless we're able to interrogate these boys down at headquarters, I don't think we're going to get anywhere with any of them."

"That is out of the question!" Archbishop Gavin spoke firmly, yet calmly. "These are children. They are *not* criminals."

"I assure you, they are innocent until proven otherwise," the officer spoke again. "But you have to admit, your Eminence, with your presence here; these boys are going to hold back. Sister Margaret described her attacker as a male, wearing a cassock and white surplice. Due to her stature, the assailant could be any one of the members of your Altar Boys' Club. We need to be able to make them talk."

"How?" Father Mark asked defiantly. "By bullying them?"

"Mark!" Abbot Ambrose spoke up.

"I'm sorry, Abbot Ambrose, but I know something about how the police force operates. I remind you, Officer, these are children."

"Children that are capable of assaulting an old woman not to mention put two of the other boys in the hospital," the officer snapped. "We have the juvenile records of at least ten boys here that are capable of committing such a crime. No, these are not innocent little babes, as you would like to have us think. These boys are juvenile delinquents and only understand one thing." There was a long pause. Charlie cocked his head to the side and pressed his ear against the wall. "This is getting nowhere. Think it over and let me know your decision. You do realize I can get a court order."

"We are quite well aware of that," Abbot Ambrose said sternly. "We will be in touch. Good day!"

The office door opened and Charlie jumped to his feet. The two police officers walked back into the hall with their hats in their hands. They walked right past Charlie. Neither one paid him even a passing glance. They disappeared through the main doors of the Abbey.

"Master MacCready," Father Mark spoke up.

Charlie jumped and turned around.

"You may go back to your class," he instructed.

"Yes, Father," Charlie nodded as the office door closed shut. Instead of rushing back to class, Charlie listened again.

"Ambrose," Archbishop Gavin spoke. "I'm afraid this changes everything. You have to find out who is behind these attacks, and soon. Otherwise, I'm afraid the Church isn't going to be able to protect these boys. The officer was right, some of these boys, sad as it is, are not as innocent as we would like to believe. You don't have much time."

Charlie heard enough. He hurried back to his class.

The classroom was quiet when Charlie returned to his seat. Everyone was busy taking a test. Slowly Father Martin, a tall, thin, balding monk, walked over to Charlie.

"Master MacCready, you have fifteen minutes to finish your exam. I hope you have studied well," he whispered.

"But—" Charlie started to protest.

"Fourteen minutes, now," Father Martin said pointing at the clock on the wall at the front of the classroom. He returned to his desk and to reading his thick book.

Charlie quickly looked over the test of twenty-five math problems. He wrote his name in the top right corner of the page and began. After working through the first five problems, he relaxed. The test was not as hard as he thought it would be. By the time Father Martin rang the small brass bell he carried in his briefcase, Charlie had finished twenty-three of the problems. He was assured of at least a C grade, he thought.

The boys quickly passed their test papers forward amid quiet moans and groans. Gus was the loudest in his despair. He hesitantly passed his paper to the boy in front of him and then buried his face in his hands as he groaned.

"Master Kugele," Father Martin said as he collected the papers. "Is something the matter? Did you not study for the test?"

Gus looked up. "Yes, Father Martin, I did study," he answered.

"Then I will have no more of that noise," Father Martin

said sternly. He returned to his desk, stuffed the papers into his black leather briefcase, and snapped it closed. Without another word and as soon as the period bell rang out, he left the room.

Howard turned and faced Charlie once they were alone.

"What did Abbot Ambrose want?"

"I don't know," Charlie shrugged. "I didn't get to see him, but I did hear something."

"Really? What?" Howard asked eagerly.

Charlie looked around. "Not here. Come on."

The two boys rushed up the stairs and moments later stood in the chilly air that blew through the bell tower.

"You remember Sister Margaret Mary thinks her attacker was an Altar Boy?" Charlie explained.

"I heard the rumors," Howard answered. "So?"

"She remembers seeing her attacker wearing *my* surplice!"

Howard pulled his head back in surprise and looked at Charlie more intently. "Did she say that?"

"Not in so many words," Charlie reluctantly admitted. "But think about it. It had to have been mine. But it wasn't me. Anyway, the Archbishop told Abbot Ambrose he didn't have much time to find out who's behind all of this; otherwise they're gonna close the school down."

"No!" Howard gasped.

"But that's not all," Charlie continued, ignoring Howard's interruption. "Two policemen from town came in. One wants to question all the members of the Altar Boys' Club down at their station. For now Abbot Ambrose refused, but Archbishop Gavin doesn't think he can stop them." Charlie paused and looked at Howard.

Howard seemed to be deep in thought.

"So, now what?" Charlie asked.

"That doesn't give us much time," Howard answered. "It won't be long before they find out about your surplice. So, we have to act fast. Since whoever attacked Sister Margaret was wearing your surplice, that means the person would be someone with access to our dorm."

"But remember Dougary's dad?" Charlie reminded Howard. "Dougary helped him."

"That's true," Howard agreed.

"I still think it had to have been Larry."

"I hate to admit it," Howard shook his head. "But you could be right about that. He does have access. But, I don't know."

"The policeman said something else that was very interesting. He said there are ten boys, juvenile delinquents he called them, capable of attacking Sister Margaret Mary, Dale and even Dougary. So that should narrow the list down. Larry would be one of those guys on that list. I can't think of anyone else it could be if it's not him," Charlie said. "After all, he was there the night Dale was attacked. And don't forget, he was raking leaves just a few minutes before in the area where Dougary was found."

Howard was silent as he thought about what Charlie had said. Slowly, he nodded in agreement.

The refectory was noisy as the boys ate their tomato soup and grilled cheese sandwiches. Charlie filled Rick and Gus in on his morning in the hall. Rick quickly wrote everything down in his notebook.

"This shouldn't be too hard to figure out," Rick said. "We just need to go through the list of Altar Boys and see who was here this summer."

"Were you not listening?" Howard rolled his eyes and shook his head. "For being the smartest in the class, you're sure stupid." He leaned into the table toward Rick. "We already told you who it is."

"But Larry wasn't an Altar Boy," Rick defended himself.

"It doesn't have to be an actual Altar Boy. It just had to be someone who has access to our robes," Howard repeated.

"And Larry has access," Charlie added.

Rick looked at Howard with pursed lips, still upset at being called stupid. "I think you're wrong," he snapped. "I think it has to be one of the Altar Boys."

Charlie looked at Howard then back at Rick. "No, I'm

afraid you're the one who's wrong, but it's not your fault." he said.

"Then whose is it?" Rick snapped and looked at them both.

Howard looked at Charlie and nodded.

"It's my fault," Charlie admitted. He took a deep breath and then quietly explained about the night Sister Margaret was attacked and about finding his surplice and the mud and blood. As Charlie talked, Rick feverishly wrote every word down in his black book.

"Have you told this to Father Mark?" Rick gasped in wide-eyed shock.

"No! Are you nuts?" Howard snapped. "And don't you go telling him either," he warned.

"But they should know," Rick's voice returned to his usual superior tone. "You guys tampered with evidence. You could be in serious trouble for this."

"You'll be in serious trouble if you open that mouth of yours," Howard threatened coldly. He doubled up his fists as he leaned into the table.

Charlie glanced up at the head table. Brother Conrad was talking and laughing with Father Mark. Charlie turned and looked at Howard. He knew he had best say something before anyone at the head table noticed the arguing.

"Rick, we didn't know it was evidence at the time," Charlie spoke quietly. "And I will tell Abbot Ambrose when the time is right, but Father Mark is the last person that should know! I still don't trust him."

"If you say anything to him, he'll think Charlie's guilty," Howard explained.

"And you're so sure he isn't?" Rick answered and looked directly at Charlie.

Charlie's jaw tightened as his anger flared. He looked at Howard and then back at Rick. At that moment he did not care if the head table heard them or not, he wanted to jump across the table and punch Rick's lights out.

"Over the summer I read about sleepwalkers," Rick

explained quickly as he noticed the fire in Charlie's eyes and Howard's clenched fists. "The article said that they do all sorts of things and don't remember it the next morning."

Howard thought for a moment then slowly relaxed his fists. "That would explain why Charlie wouldn't remember Sister Margaret, but what about the attack on Dale? Charlie was wide-awake then. What about the attack on Dougary, that was in the daytime, and I was with Charlie that day?" Howard asked.

Rick shrugged his shoulders.

"Let me hit him!" Charlie said with clenched teeth as he glared at Rick.

"No!" Howard said and put a halting hand on Charlie's arm. He tightened his grip without taking his eyes off Rick. "No," he spoke up in Charlie's defense. "You're wrong again. Charlie couldn't have done it. We have to find a way to prove it was Larry before we tell anyone about the surplice. Otherwise, Charlie will be in trouble."

Rick thought for a moment and looked at both Howard and Charlie. He finally closed his booklet and tucked it into the pocket of his robes.

"Okay, but for the record, I don't like this one bit." Rick gave in and returned to eating his lunch.

As soon as Howard felt the muscles in Charlie's arm relax, he let go and returned to eating his meal.

"Are you excited about Christmas, Gus?" Charlie asked, to change the subject, but his voice was still tense and he continued to glare at Rick.

"Yeah," Gus nodded. He ducked his head when he looked at Howard.

Howard stopped eating. He looked at his plate and sighed quietly to himself.

"Don't worry," Gus said to him. "I'm not going very far. My cousins moved into a house in town, not far from here. So, I can still come up while on vacation."

Howard looked at Gus. "I know," he said. "It's just not gonna be the same here, that's all."

Gus smiled to himself. It was as close as he had ever come to knowing just how Howard really felt about him. He liked the thought that Howard would miss him, that Howard was really his friend.

CHRISTMAS

Before the boys knew it, the day of the Christmas Concert had arrived and it was a success. The applause seemed to go on longer than the previous year's. Charlie looked over his shoulder at Howard who stood in the bass section. He was clowning around with another boy taking bows and patting each other on the back while Sister Lillian, their conductor, was not looking.

After the concert the brothers served cookies and punch to the parents and guests. While the resident boys mingled and talked, the students quickly returned to their dorms and gathered their things to leave for the holiday. Charlie and Howard stood off by themselves, and watched the crowd.

"I wish this day were over," Howard grumbled with a heavy sigh. "Why can't the students just get their bags and get out of here? Why do we have to entertain their parents? It's like rubbing our noses in the fact that we don't have anyone and are staying here."

Charlie did not know what to say. Several times during the concert, he caught himself daydreaming about his own parents, and what it would be like to see them in the audience. He wondered what they would say. Would they be pleased? Before he knew it, he was daydreaming again.

"Charlie!" Howard nudged him, jarring him back to the present.

"What?"

"Those people, over there," he whispered out of the corner of his mouth. "They're staring at us."

Charlie looked across the room. For a moment his heart fluttered in his chest. Could they be...? But they did not look like the photograph of his parents. The man had dark brown hair and coal black eyes. He was shorter than Charlie imagined his father would be and a bit stockier, too. The woman did not resemble the photograph of his mother at all. Even though her hair was blonde and pulled back in a bun just like his grandmother's, she did not look like her either. Perhaps the years had changed them, Charlie reasoned as they drew nearer.

"Hello," the man greeted them with a heavy German accent. "You must be Howard." He reached out his hand to Howard.

Howard nodded. "Yes."

"We are Gustav's cousins," he explained. With his thick German accent, he pronounced his "W's" like "V's". "And you must be Charlie. We have heard so much about you."

Charlie felt a sinking feeling in the pit of his stomach. He was disappointed, and yet relieved at the same time. He smiled at the couple and shook their hands.

"It is a pity, what happened to poor little Gustav's parents," the man continued. "We live in Germany and lost contact with little Gustav's family years ago," he explained. "Now, we sadly know why."

"But we are so thrilled to have little Gustav with us," the woman spoke up with a big smile and a twinkle in her eyes. "It is going to be a wonderful Christmas this year," she beamed, then suddenly gasped and covered her mouth with her chubby hand. "Oh, I'm so sorry, boys," she apologized and took their hands into hers.

"Oh, they understand, Anna." The man playfully punched

Howard. Howard grimaced and rubbed his stinging shoulder.

"But Adolf, they are just boys," Anna said with a frown as she looked at them.

"It's okay," Howard said with clenched teeth as he glared at Adolf for punching him.

"So, Gus says that you have a place in town," Charlie spoke up.

"Oh, yes," Adolf said, nodding his head rapidly. "We will be staying for a while then we are going back to Germany."

"What about Gus?" Howard spoke up. His heart beat faster at the thought of never seeing Gus again.

"What about him?" Adolf shrugged.

Howard shook his head. As he looked at the man in front of him, he became confused.

"Will he be going too? You are going to adopt him, aren't you? I mean, Gus said you were," Howard said bluntly.

Adolf looked at his wife and then back at Howard. "It's a bit too early to say," he answered. "But we are considering it." He smiled.

Howard gave Charlie a worried look.

"There you are," Gus said as he walked over to them. "Cousin Adolf and Cousin Anna, I see you've met my best friends, Howard and Charlie."

"Yes." Anna smiled at Gus. "They are such nice boys."

"Are you ready to go?" Adolf asked Gus.

"Yes," he answered.

Gus said his good-byes. Charlie and Howard watched silently as he left the refectory with his cousins.

"I don't like them," Howard said out loud.

Charlie looked at him curiously.

"Why?"

"I can't put my finger on it just yet," he answered. "But something's not right."

Charlie smiled. "Now who's having hunches?" he ribbed.

Howard did not respond. Without a word, he walked into the hall and headed for his dorm.

~§~

Tiny flakes of snow drifted down from a white, hazy sky, blanketing the great lawn. The bells in the tower rang out, announcing Christmas morning and waking Howard and Charlie from their sleep. Howard groaned and put his pillow over his head. He was still tired from serving at midnight Mass only five hours before.

"Come on, Howard," Charlie said excitedly, and jumped out of his bed. "It's Christmas!"

"Who cares?" Howard groaned. "I wish this day were over."

"Come on, don't be a Scrooge," Charlie teased and lifted the pillow from over Howard's head. "Let's go unwrap our presents."

The dorm doors opened.

"Merry Christmas," Brother Simon greeted in a less jolly tone than Father Emmanuel did the year before. Carefully, Brother Simon set the serving tray of mugs filled with steaming hot cocoa with marshmallows and a platter stacked high with an assortment of Christmas cookies, on the trunk coffee table in the center of the dorm lounge.

"Hurry up, you two," Todd called impatiently to Charlie and Howard. "It's time to open our presents."

"Merry Christmas, Brother Simon," Charlie greeted as he tied the belt of his robe. He hurried over to the sofa and sat down. It was hard to keep his excitement concealed as he looked at the pile of gifts under the tree.

Howard silently walked over to the sofa and sat down beside Charlie. He stared at the plate of cookies and the cup of steaming hot chocolate. He leaned forward and took a gingerbread man from the plate and bit its head off as he sat back.

Christmas was just not the same without Gus. And though it was obvious that Brother Simon was trying, he was no Father

Emmanuel. Before he was made Prior of the Abbey, Father Emmanuel was their prefect and every Christmas would dress like Saint Nick, something Brother Simon would never do.

However, moments later, the floor all around the base of the Christmas tree and lounge was littered with pieces of torn wrapping paper, ribbons and bows. Brother Simon had returned to his office and Todd had gone to look for one of his friends from Saint Thomas dorm. Howard and Charlie sat opposite each other, quietly slumped back in the overstuffed chairs and sipped their hot cocoa.

"We did pretty good this year," Charlie said as he looked at his pile of unwrapped gifts. He was amazed at how kind the town's people were in giving them gifts.

"Yeah." Howard shrugged. He looked at the pottery mug Charlie made him. "Thanks again," he said.

"You're welcome."

"You know, you're pretty good at this pottery stuff. No wonder Father Ichabod was so upset when all of your pottery was smashed up last summer."

"Thanks," Charlie blushed. "You know, when I was making it, I overheard Father Ichabod talking with one of the novices. He was a bit upset because their booth at Oktoberfest didn't make as much as he hoped it would."

"Wow," Howard breathed. "Remind me to stay away from him for a while," he teased. "You don't suppose it was Larry who smashed your pottery, do you?"

"I think it's a very good possibility," Charlie answered, and nodded as he thought. "Thank you for the wooden bowl."

"Actually, Father Gregory did most of the work," Howard admitted. "But I sanded it out and stained it."

"It's beautiful." Charlie smiled.

"Oh, don't let me forget to tell your grandmother thanks for the baseball mitt and the knit hat and scarf. That was really nice of her."

"Sure," Charlie nodded. "She knitted it herself, you know?"

"Wow," Howard smiled.

As the two boys sat talking, neither of them noticed the dormitory doors slowly open. Quietly, Dale slipped into the dorm and stood with his back against the doors. He was watched Charlie and Howard for a moment and then took a step away from the doors.

"A-hem," he pretended to clear his throat.

Charlie looked over his shoulder in the direction of the noise. Instantly he jumped to his feet.

"Merry Christmas, Dale," he greeted his friend with a big smile.

"M-M-Merry C-C-Christmas," he returned.

"Come and sit down with us," Howard invited. "Have some hot cocoa and help yourself to the cookies. But I have to warn you, they're not as good as Sister Margaret Mary's."

Dale seemed to relax as he walked closer to the sofa. He took a cookie from the platter and sat down.

"So, how are you?" Charlie asked and sat on the arm of the sofa.

"Fa-fa-fine," Dale answered, and bit the leg off if his gingerbread man.

Charlie looked at Howard. Howard shrugged.

"Does Brother Owen know you're in here?" Howard asked directly.

Dale quickly sat forward, looking at the dormitory doors.

"He doesn't know," Charlie answered for Dale.

Dale shook his head.

Charlie looked at the side of Dale's face and noticed a thin red scar, an inch long, at his hairline. A feeling of sadness came over him.

"I'm sorry about what happened to you," he sympathized.

Dale looked at Charlie. "I know what the g-g-guys are s-s-saying," he struggled to speak. "But th-th-they're wrong."

"I know that I didn't do it," Charlie said. "But why did you keep saying my name?"

"I d-d-don't know." Dale shook his head. "I d-d-don't remm-m-ember."

"It's okay," Charlie nodded even though he was a bit disappointed. He hoped Dale would be able to tell him more.

"B-b-b-but," Dale continued. "Th-th-the g-g-guy who hit m-m-me, th-th-thought I was you. He ca-ca-called me by your na-na-name."

Charlie looked at Howard with wide eyes.

"Why didn't you tell the Abbot or the police?" Howard asked.

"Be-c-c-cause, he s-s-said he would k-k-kill m-m-me." Dale looked at them both with fear in his eyes.

Charlie felt numb. He looked back and forth at Howard and then Dale. The words *kill me* kept echoing in his ears.

"Why, Ch-ch-charlie? What d-d-does he want?" Dale asked and looked pleadingly at Charlie.

Charlie cast a worried look over at Howard. Slowly he pulled the key out from under his pajama top. "This," he said and held it up.

"A k-k-key?" Dale asked and looked confused. "What's it f-f-for?"

"I don't know," Charlie said, and shrugged.

Dale gave Howard a puzzled look. He bit the other leg off the gingerbread man and looked at the tree.

Charlie tucked the key back under his pajamas. "Dale." Charlie hesitated for a moment as he glanced at Howard. "Do you know who hit you?"

Dale looked at Charlie with fear in his eyes. Slowly he nodded.

Charlie smiled and became excited.

Howard sat forward in his chair. "Who is it?" he asked.

Dale looked at their faces and slowly shook his head. His hands began to tremble. "N-n-no!" he said. "I c-c-can't tell you."

"Or he'll kill you," Howard finished for him. Dale nodded again. Howard looked around, not knowing what to say but not wanting Dale to leave either. He picked up a bright yellow and red box, with a picture of a man on an operating table on its top, and opened it. "Hey, you wanna play my new game?" he asked.

The boys spent the rest of the morning playing Howard's game. Dale seemed more like his old self and relaxed a bit more the longer he played. He even laughed a few times when Howard caused the man's light bulb nose to glow red.

At dinner Howard, Charlie, and Todd sat alone at the Saint Nicholas table. The table was festively decorated with fir boughs, sprigs of holly and candles in gold holders. Small crystal bowls of whole cranberry sauce, orange spiced marmalade jam, butter, and black olives were placed on the table beside a gold, wire basket of warm dinner rolls. The serving brother set a plate piled high with freshly carved hot turkey, mashed potatoes, apple and walnut dressing, candied yams and green beans before each of the boys. Howard poured eggnog into his crystal goblet and then offered the pitcher to Charlie.

"Merry Christmas, Charlie." He smiled and looked around the room.

Charlie smiled. "You, too," he said and took a drink from his goblet.

As they ate, Christmas carols played from a stereo Father Mark set up behind the head table. Charlie liked hearing the music as he ate. It reminded him of the many Christmases he spent with his grandmother. She always played carols at Christmas dinner.

"What do you think about what Dale said this morning?" Charlie quietly asked Howard as he buttered his roll.

"What do you mean?" Howard asked with his mouth full.

"Remember when he was telling us about the guy that hit him?" Charlie asked. "He called him, 'the guy'."

Howard looked at Charlie and stopped chewing his food. His eyes widened. He quickly chewed and swallowed to clear his mouth. "That's right! You know what that means? It had to be a guy!" he said sarcastically. "Look around, Charlie. We're all guys here."

"Oh, I know that," Charlie said disgustedly. "What I mean is he must have been talking about Larry. We refer to each other as 'guys' but not the monks or an adult. If he had meant an adult had hit him then he would have said 'the man.' See?"

Howard looked at Charlie and started to shake his head. "I don't know. It sounds reasonable but I'm not so sure."

Charlie glanced at the head table. Father Mark and the rest of the prefects were busy eating and talking among themselves. No one was paying attention to the handful of boys seated at the tables in front of them.

"It would be a lot easier if Dale would just tell us," Charlie sighed. He looked across the room at Dale and the four other boys of Saint Sebastian.

"Have you figured out how we're going to trap Larry?" Howard asked. He took a drink from his goblet and then poured himself some more eggnog.

"No," Charlie shook his head while he continued to eat.

After dinner the boys cleaned up their dorm and put their gifts away. Charlie lay down on his bed and began to write a letter to his grandmother. Howard had his nose buried in one of the new comic books he received from Gus.

"That's it!" Charlie gasped and put his pen down.

"What?" Howard asked and looked at him.

"I figured out a way to trap Larry," Charlie announced. He turned around to face Howard. "Dale said *the guy* thought that he was me. And we also know he is after my key. So," he said, leaning closer to Howard to explain his plan. "Do you think it'll work?" he asked and sat back.

Howard slowly cocked his head as he thought about what Charlie said. "I don't know. It sounds pretty risky. Remember Larry threatened to kill Dale. Maybe we should just tell Abbot Ambrose and let him do the rest?"

"No! We can't," Charlie protested. "Larry will just deny it. No, you said so yourself, we have to catch him in the act," Charlie defended his plan. "And we're running out of time."

"I think you should ask your grandmother," Howard said

and motioned to Charlie's letter.

Charlie looked at the letter he had started. He frowned. "I need to ask her. I already know what she'll say. Besides, someone's still stealing my mail. I'd never get her letter anyway."

"That's true," Howard agreed.

"I'm going to do it whether you're with me on this or not," Charlie said with conviction.

Howard stared at Charlie for a moment. He knew it was useless to try to talk him out of his plan.

"Okay," he sighed. "But I think we should at least run it by Gus and Rick before we do anything, agreed?"

"Agreed." Charlie nodded with a smile.

CHARLIE'S PLAN

"It was so awesome," Gus sighed as he explained in detail his holiday with his cousins. Charlie and Howard listened while they sat on the overstuffed chairs in the dorm lounge. Rick sat next to Gus and half-listened, waiting for his turn to tell about his vacation. "They bought me this cool clock radio and lamp for my nightstand. They even said when they adopt me, I'll have my own bedroom and they'll buy me a new bicycle and—"

"Just don't count on it," Howard interrupted.

Charlie looked at Howard. He recognized the tone in Howard's voice, part concern and part jealousy. He frowned at Howard in an attempt to silently signal him to knock it off, but Howard would not look at him.

"What?" Gus asked looking confused.

"Grown-ups always make promises they never keep," Howard explained. His tone was unchanged. He folded his arms over his chest and looked bored.

"Well, not my cousins," Gus defended, becoming a bit annoyed at Howard.

"How well do you know these people? If they were so wonderful, why didn't they come for you long before now?"

"A-hem!" Charlie cleared his throat and gave Howard a

wide-eyed look.

Howard looked at Charlie and shrugged.

Without warning, Gus jumped off the sofa and stood in front of Howard with his hands clenched into fists and drawn up, ready for a fight.

"Take it back!" he warned.

Howard looked at Gus and laughed. "No. It's true. Grow up, Gus."

"Well, you're just jealous because my family wants me!" Gus blurted.

Howard shook his head as though he had just been hit. He looked at Gus with a look that was a mixture of anger and pain. Charlie sat stunned in disbelief at what he heard.

"What did you say?" Howard said. He slowly stood up.

Gus took a half-step backward and readied his fists. "Just because your dad doesn't want you doesn't mean my family doesn't want me."

The color drained from Howard's face as he looked at Gus. His whole body went limp. He looked at Charlie who had a pained expression on his face. He looked at Rick who was trying not to laugh unsuccessfully. He turned back to Gus.

"Believe what you want. I don't care," he said in a dismissive tone. He turned around and started for the doors.

"Gus!" Charlie snapped as he jumped up.

"Wha-?" Gus looked at Charlie.

"I don't believe you said that!" Charlie continued, and brushed past him.

"But he started it." Gus defended himself.

Charlie turned around as Howard disappeared through the doors. He took a step back toward Gus. "But you didn't have to say that. I know you're excited about having a family and your holiday, but you want to know something? While you were off with your cousins and having a wonderful time, Howard was miserable. He missed you. He really cares about you and hates the thought of never seeing you again."

Gus slowly relaxed his hands. His expression softened.

"I'm sorry."

"Don't tell me, tell Howard," Charlie said. He turned around and rushed out the door. He had an idea where he would find Howard. Effortlessly he crawled into the bell tower. Sure enough, the trap door in the ceiling was open. Charlie hurried up the stairs.

Howard sat in the far corner. His knees were pulled up to his chest and his head was down. He did not look up when he heard Charlie walking over to him.

"Howard," Charlie spoke quietly. "Are you okay?"

"He's right," Howard answered. Charlie could tell he was crying. "My dad doesn't want me. He doesn't love me."

"No, Howard, that's not true," Charlie tried to encourage him. "I'm sure your dad loves you."

"No, Charlie." Howard looked up and took off his glasses. He wiped the tears from his cheeks. "If he really loved me, he'd never have left me here. I was only seven years old. Why couldn't he love me? What was so terrible about me? What did I do wrong?" The tears fell from Howard's eyes.

Charlie did not know what to say. Slowly he sat down on the floor next to his best friend. The sound of someone climbing the stairs caught Charlie's attention. Gus sheepishly entered the tower and looked around. When his spotted Howard, he frowned.

"Howard, I'm sorry. I'm such a clod."

"Just leave me alone!" Howard said, the anger in his tone masking his pain.

"But I should never have said that about your dad," Gus continued to apologize.

"Are you deaf?" Howard snapped. He jumped to his feet. "I said leave me alone!"

"So, this is where you guys are hiding," Rick said as he stepped into the tower.

"Oh, that's just great!" Howard exhaled sharply as he looked at Rick. "It's not bad enough already and you ruin my secret place by bringing him here!"

Charlie quickly stood up. He was just as surprised as Howard seeing Rick there.

"I'm sorry," Gus quickly apologized. "He must have followed me."

Howard was not listening. He headed for the trap door.

"Does Father Mark know you guys are up here?" Rick scolded.

"No, he doesn't," Howard answered condescendingly. "But Abbot Ambrose knows if it's any of your business." He pushed passed Rick and started down the stairs.

"What's with him?" Rick asked.

"Just forget it," Charlie said, and followed Howard down the stairs.

~§~

Dinner seemed like torture for Howard and the rest of the four boys. Howard ate his meatloaf and mashed potatoes in silence. Rick's one attempt to start a conversation was met by Howard's icy glare. Charlie could tell Gus felt bad because picked at his food and kept looking at Howard with sad puppy dog eyes.

After dinner, Charlie followed Howard back to their cubicle. Neither spoke a word the whole evening. Once Gus peaked around the partition to see if Howard was there, but Charlie shook his head to warn him off.

Two weeks passed after Gus and Howard's fight. Charlie was worried about Howard but more concerned that they were running out of time for catching Larry. His attempts to talk to Howard failed miserably. Howard was in a funk and nothing was working to pull him out.

Charlie glanced out the window as he sat on his bed, just in time to see the Archbishop's car pull in front of the Abbey. Quickly, he jumped up and rushed down the stairs. When he came to the first floor, he cautiously peeked down the hall toward Abbot Ambrose's office. The hallway was empty.

Slowly, Charlie made his way down the hall, listening as he went. He slid into the chair outside Abbot Ambrose's office and leaned his head back.

"That detective is becoming a thorn in my side, Ambrose." Charlie could hear the Archbishop say from inside the office. "I received this just yesterday. He's wanting to question the boys on this list, beginning with Master MacCready."

Charlie jumped and his mouth dropped open. He quickly looked up and down the hall to be sure no one saw him. He turned his head back to the wall.

"He's a minor," Abbot Ambrose protested. "Isn't there something we can do?"

"I have a call in to the Archdiocese's attorneys, but I'm not sure there's anything we can do. It is a court order and they only want to question the boys." The Archbishop's voice sounded defeated.

"When do they want to begin?" Abbot Ambrose asked.

"Next week," Archbishop Gavin sighed.

Charlie heard enough. He had to find Howard right way. They had to put his plan into action which meant, like it or not, Howard had to get over it.

Howard was in the dorm lounge, curled up in his favorite chair thumbing through another one of his comic books. He looked up as Charlie rushed over to him.

"Howard," he panted. "I just came from Abbot Ambrose's office and we've got big trouble."

"What?" Howard put his comic book down.

"The Archbishop is here and he has a court order thing to force us to talk to the police. They want to start with me, next week!" Charlie explained as fast as he could. "We have to put my plan into action tonight."

"Charlie, you can't set yourself up as a decoy," Howard raised his voice.

"What's going on?" Rick asked as he and Gus walked into the dorm.

Howard looked at Gus and then picked up his comic.

"Howard, stop it!" Charlie snapped. "You have to start talking to them again. This is more important. I could be in big trouble."

Howard looked at Charlie and thought for a moment. "Okay, you're right."

Charlie proceeded to fill Rick and Gus in on what he overheard and his plan for trapping Larry. Rick kept glancing at Howard to see his reaction while he listened to Charlie's plan.

"So, what do you think?" Charlie asked them when he was finished.

"I already told him I don't think he should set himself up as a decoy. It's too dangerous," Howard told the group.

"I agree," Gus said.

Charlie looked at Gus. He knew Gus would have agreed with anything Howard said, just to get back in Howard's good graces.

"I hate to admit it, but he's right, Charlie," Rick added. "However, what if we just make Larry *think* Charlie is there but instead Howard will be there waiting to catch him."

"I think that would work," Gus nodded agreeably.

"Howard?" Rick asked.

"Yeah," he nodded after giving it a bit of thought.

"Charlie?" Rick turned to him.

"But it's my plan," he protested.

"If you want our help," Howard cocked his head. "You can watch from the bell tower but you have to stay out of sight."

"Fine." Charlie gave in.

"Then we'll put our plan into action tonight, just after dinner," Rick said and gave a nod.

Charlie cringed at Rick's taking credit for his plan.

After dinner, Rick and Gus distracted Brother Simon so Howard could slip out the back door of the Abbey. Then Charlie hurried up the stairs and into the bell tower. It was darker than usual; he had never been in the tower after nightfall. He sat with his back against the wall next to the small door so that he could hear what was happening in the stairwell.

"Hey, Gus," Charlie heard Rick's voice. "I overheard Charlie tell Howard he's going to sneak out of the building after dinner. He said he thinks he lost his key down by the pig barns where he found Dale on Halloween. He's going to try to find it."

"Doesn't he know no one's allowed outside after dark?" Gus said in a much-scripted response.

Charlie shook his head. No way was Larry going to buy that. He listened for more but there was only silence. He looked around blindly in the dark. As his eyes grew accustomed to the darkness, he could make out the stairs. He wondered if he should start up the tower.

"Pssst, Charlie," Gus whispered through the door. "The bat flies at night."

"What?" Charlie said and shook his head.

"The bat flies at night," Gus repeated.

"What bat?" Charlie asked, "What are you talking about?"

"The bat," Gus repeated.

"Speak English, Gus," Charlie interrupted.

"Fine!" Gus said indignantly. "Larry took the bait. Rick saw him sneak out the back door."

"Good," Charlie breathed and relaxed a bit. His plan was beginning to work. "Let me know when Howard gets back."

"I will," Gus said.

There was silence. Charlie thought about going to the top of the tower but decided to stay close to the door instead. He did not want to miss Gus when Howard returned with Larry in toe.

Minutes seemed to pass like hours as Charlie sat in the dark. Occasionally he could hear brief bits of conversation as boys passed unsuspectingly by the door. Charlie started to wonder if Gus left his post. He did not have to wonder too long.

"Master Kugele, what are you doing here?" Charlie recognized Father Vicar's icy voice.

"Nothing," Gus answered.

"Well, I suggest you do *nothing* down at your end of the floor and stop lurking around the stairwell."

"Yes, Father," Gus's voice sounded timid as usual.

"Now, Master Kugele!" Father Vicar said sternly.

Charlie heard footsteps fade away and he wondered what he should do. Cautiously he made his way around the wall toward the stairs. The night air was cold against Charlie's face as he stood at the east window. He looked down from the top of the bell tower at the dark forest below. The night was darker due to the cloudy sky. He could not see a thing. With a heavy sigh he turned around and headed back to the trap door.

Unable to take the silence any longer, Charlie slipped out of the tower into the bright lights of the stairwell. He dusted his robes off and headed back to Saint Nicholas dorm to find Gus and see what happened. As he passed the common area, he glanced up at the clock on the wall. To his surprise he had been in the tower for nearly two hours. He quickened his pace.

Gus was not in the dorm. Charlie began to feel panicked. He hurried back down the hall. Just as he was about to start down the stairs, Gus and Rick walked up.

"Where have you been?" he asked them. "Where's Howard?"

"He hasn't come back," Rick answered. Charlie could hear the fear in his voice.

"We were just coming to get you," Gus added. "What are we gonna do?"

"I'll handle this," Charlie said and hurried back to his cubicle to retrieve his flashlight.

Rick and Gus followed closely behind him. They grabbed their flashlights and tucked them under their robes. The three quietly hurried down the stairs and slipped out the back door. They waited until they were sure they would not be seen from the Abbey before they turned their flashlights on.

"I can't believe you waited this long," Charlie whispered disgustedly.

"We thought he'd be back but when he didn't show up, we didn't know what to do. We knew you wouldn't want us to go to Father Mark," Rick defended himself.

"But you could have come to me right away. Two hours?" Charlie shook his head.

The gravel crunched under their feet as they hurried down the road to the pig barns. Charlie kept the beam of his flashlight far out in front of him as he walked. Rich and Gus lagged behind a few steps searching both sides of the road for any sign of Howard or Larry. The smell from the barns was getting stronger as they drew nearer.

Suddenly Charlie stopped. Rick and Gus both bumped into him.

"Ouch!" Gus groaned as he rubbed his forehead.

"What's the matter?" Rick asked. He shone the beam of his flashlight in front of them.

"I think I just saw a shadow in front of us," Charlie answered in a whisper.

"Where?" Gus said and stepped behind Charlie again.

"It darted across the road up ahead and into the forest." Charlie shone his light into the forest.

Rick turned away and shone his light into the barnyard. "Stupid, stinking pigs!" he muttered out loud. Suddenly he froze as the beam of his light came across a dark object lying in the middle of the mud patch. "Charlie!" he nearly shouted. "Howard!"

"Where?" Charlie spun around. "Oh no!" he gasped.

Quickly he climbed over the wooden fence. The mud of the barnyard was slippery as he rushed to Howard. Howard lay motionless. Stinky mud and blood matted his hair and covered his once white surplice.

"Oh no! Howard, wake up," Charlie began to cry as he knelt down and wiped some of the mud away from Howard's face. He looked around for Howard's glasses and spotted them, broken in two.

Howard moaned. "Ch-Charlie?" he groaned in a daze. "La-Larry...fa-father..." Howard's head went limp as he lost consciousness.

"Howard!" Gus gasped as he reached them.

Charlie looked up at him. He turned and looked over his shoulder at Rick, who did not dare to enter the barnyard for fear of getting his robes dirty, let alone his shoes.

"Rick, go get Abbot Ambrose!" he yelled. "Get help, now!"

Charlie watched Rick hesitate for a moment and then turn around. The sound of the gravel crunching beneath his feet and the beam of the flashlight bouncing wildly ahead of him told Charlie that Rick was actually running. Charlie stood up slowly. He put his hand on Gus's shoulder to steady himself. "Stay here with Howard," he ordered. "I'm going after Larry!"

Before Gus could protest, Charlie was up and over the fence. He rushed across the gravel road and up the sloping bank into the forest. He tripped and fell over a fallen tree limb. His flashlight flew from his hand and he let out a yell. Angry and determined, he forced himself to his feet and quickly retrieved his flashlight. There was a burning pain in his left knee but he ignored it and pressed on.

"You're not gonna get away from me this time!" he breathed through clenched teeth as he hurriedly searched the forest.

He stopped when his light flashed on a figure slumped by the base of a tall fir tree. Slowly he approached. The figure appeared to be holding his arm and crying.

"Larry!" Charlie seethed as he shone the light in Larry's bloody face. "Looks like Howard got a few good licks in. Serves you right!"

"Miller didn't do this, MacCreepy," Larry spit back.

"He didn't?" Charlie looked at him confused. "Then who did?"

"None of your business," Larry sneered. "Get away from me!" he shouted angrily.

"What's your problem?" Charlie looked at him confused and stepped toward Larry.

"That's close enough, Master MacCready."

Charlie turned around and gasped. Unconsciously he held

his breath as his light shone in Father Mark's face.

"Turn the light away!" Father Mark ordered shielding his eyes from the light.

Charlie directed the flashlight beam toward the ground when he noticed Abbot Ambrose behind Father Mark. He began to breathe again.

"Father Abbot," he said while Father Mark rushed to Larry's aide. "Did you find Howard?"

"Yes," Abbot Ambrose nodded. "Mark, how is he?"

"I think his arm is broken, and he's going to have a pretty good shiner and fat lip for a while." Father Mark answered as he carefully examined Larry.

"Help him to the infirmary, will you Mark?"

"Yes, Father Abbot." Father Mark nodded. "Now, hold your arm tight against you," he instructed and gingerly helped Larry to his feet. "We'll take it slow. Watch your step."

Charlie watched as Father Mark led Larry past him. Larry jumped away from Charlie fearfully. Father Mark gave Charlie a stern look. Charlie stepped back.

"You've disappointed me again, son," Abbot Ambrose sighed.

Instantly Charlie was stabbed in the heart. The last thing he wanted to do was cause his great-uncle trouble. "But I can explain—"

"And explain you will. In my office in twenty minutes," Abbot Ambrose's tone was firm. "Now, back to the Abbey with you."

The walk back to the Abbey was quiet. Neither said a word. Instead of going to the back entrance Abbot Ambrose led Charlie to the main entrance. As they approached, several brothers were standing on the steps. There was a police car parked in the circular driveway.

"Father Abbot," Brother Conrad greeted as they drew nearer. "That policeman is here to see you."

"Who phoned them?" Abbot Ambrose asked as he mounted the stairs.

"I don't know." Brother Conrad shook his head and followed him up the steps. "He and his partner are upstairs in the infirmary right now."

Abbot Ambrose glanced up in the direction of the third floor of the Abbey, or Heaven, Charlie was not sure which, and then continued up the steps toward the front doors.

"Abbot Ambrose!" came an angry voice from the darkness behind them.

Abbot Ambrose turned around at the top of the stairs just as Maxwell Hertz came into the light of the Abbey's portico.

"Yes, Mister Hertz?" Abbot Ambrose greeted with his hands tucked under his robes.

"Where's my boy?" he demanded.

"I believe Master Hertz is in our infirmary," Abbot Ambrose answered kindly.

"What kind of school are you running here? What have you done to him? I want to see him!" Maxwell continued his demands.

"And see him you shall," Abbot Ambrose nodded. "Quietly, follow me, please." He turned toward Charlie. "Master MacCready, we shall talk in the morning."

"But I wanted to see Howard," Charlie sheepishly said.

Abbot Ambrose looked at Charlie's muddy robes and frowned. "Very well," he relented. "Try not to bring too much of the outside in." He turned toward the front doors and two brothers opened them for him.

Abbot Ambrose led Charlie and Maxwell into the lobby and up the stairs to the third floor. He paused at the door to the monastery wing and was about to instruct them both to be quiet, but decided it would be futile. Brother Conrad opened the door and held it for them. He avoided looking directly at Charlie, something for which Charlie did take notice.

Once in the hallway, Charlie immediately noticed Rick and Gus seated on chairs outside the infirmary door. They both stood up as Abbot Ambrose approached and looked at the floor.

"Master MacCready." Abbot Ambrose turned and looked

at Charlie. "Please wait here with your friends; I will let you know if Howard can have visitors. Mister Hertz, please follow me."

Abbot Ambrose and Maxwell entered the infirmary. Charlie craned his neck to see inside the waiting room. When his eyes met the officer's, he froze and the door shut between them.

"So, any word yet about Howard?" Charlie turned and asked Rick and Gus.

"No," they both answered and shook their heads.

"I saw Father Mark bring Larry in," Gus whispered. "What did you do to him?"

"That's just it," Charlie answered. "I didn't do anything. I found him leaning against a tree holding his arm and whimpering like a baby."

"Then how did your hands get all scraped up and your surplice ripped?" Rick asked.

"I tripped and fell," Charlie answered, slightly annoyed by Rick's tone.

"That's not what it looks like," Rick said suspiciously.

"Well, I don't care what it looks like. I didn't do it!"

The infirmary door opened and Brother Conrad stepped into the hallway. By the look on his face, he had heard their conversation and he was not pleased.

"I think you boys should return to your dorm and get cleaned up. Brother Simon will speak to you when he is finished talking with Brother James. Now, go."

"Yes, Brother," they nodded respectfully and headed back to their dorm.

The hot water of the shower felt good against Charlie's sore shoulders. He stood and let it the water massage his neck and back while he thought about the way his plan had fallen apart. He wondered what Abbot Ambrose was going to say when they talked. Then he thought about Brother Simon and his heart sank. He turned off the water and grabbed his towel.

Gus and Rick were already dressed in their pajamas when

Charlie walked into the dorm. Gus looked at Charlie and gasped at the sight of Charlie's bruised knee.

"Charlie, you should have Brother James look at your knee," he said. "It looks like it's swelling."

"I'm okay," Charlie shrugged. "Besides, Brother James has enough to deal with tonight."

"Well, I'm going to tell Brother Simon, then," Gus pressured him.

"Okay, I'll see Brother James in the morning after breakfast. I promise," Charlie lied.

Gus nodded and walked over to the lounge. Charlie quickly dressed in his pajamas so no one else would notice his injured knee. He joined Rick and Gus on the sofa.

"So, how much trouble do you think we're in?" Gus asked apprehensively.

"We'll get work crew, I'm sure," Rick answered. "Thanks a lot, Charlie."

"No one forced you to do anything," Charlie curtly answered back.

"That's good to know," Brother Simon said as he walked into the dorm.

All three boys jumped to their feet.

"I want to see you three in my office right now." His tone was cold, and bordered on angry. He turned around and walked out of the dorm, not looking back but knowing the three were following close behind. He unlocked his office door and opened it for the boys. Once everyone was inside, he shut the door and walked around his desk. The three stood in a line, shoulder to shoulder. Brother Simon sat down in his chair.

"Brother Simon, I just want you to know that this was all Charlie's idea," Rick blurted out.

"Master Walters, that will be enough!" Brother Simon slammed his palms down on his desktop.

Charlie jumped. Instantly he felt a painful stab in his knee but he tried not to let it show in his face.

Brother Simon looked at the three boys from head to foot.

With each passing second, Charlie became more nervous. He could tell that Gus was about to cry, as usual, but he was still managing to hold it in. Rick stood defiantly cool and smug.

"I will ask this just once and I want the truth. No games," Brother Simon said coolly. "What were you boys doing outside after curfew?"

No one spoke. They just looked at him with a blank expression.

"That is one hour of work crew," Brother Simon said as he watched the clock on the wall behind them. "For every second you delay, I will continue adding an hour to your punishment. Three hours."

"Charlie, tell him!" Rick spoke up and nudged him.

"Okay," Charlie flinched. "We were trying to set a trap for Larry."

"Master Hertz?" Brother Simon questioned. "Why him?"

"Well, remember when I found Dale on Halloween night?" Charlie asked, but didn't wait for Brother Simon to respond. "Larry was there too. I mean, he came up just as I found Dale. And when I talked to Dale over Christmas break, he told me the person who beat him up thought that he was me. And don't forget you caught him with the mask. So, I wanted to see if Larry was really telling the truth about the pottery key story. I came up with the idea to let Larry overhear Gus and Rick talking about me going back to the pig barns to look for the key. Only, instead of me, Howard would be waiting to catch him."

"And just what were you going to do once you 'caught' him?" Brother Simon asked.

"Well, bring him back here and tell Abbot Ambrose," Charlie explained.

"I'm sorry," Brother Simon said, and shook his head. "What exactly would this prove?"

Charlie thought for a moment. "That he was the one behind the attacks on Sister Margaret and Dale."

"Well, Master MacCready, your plan was flawed from the start," Brother Simon sighed. "Had it worked, the only thing it would have proven is that Master Hertz, as well as Master Miller, disobeyed curfew. But instead, we now have two more boys in the infirmary, and you three being caught outside after curfew."

Rick's mouth dropped open as he listened. He looked at Charlie and glared. "Way to go, MacCready!"

"That will be enough of that!" Brother Simon snapped. "By your own admission, no one forced you to go along with Master MacCready's plan. As punishment for disobeying each of you will spend an hour of work crew every afternoon this week immediately following your last class of the day."

Rick gasped, but refrained from saying anything. Charlie glanced at Gus who seemed to be taking it all very well. Gus was concentrating so hard trying not to cry in front of Brother Simon that he dared not say anything. But Charlie could tell by the look on his face that he was not pleased with the news of work crew.

"That will be all. You may go back to your dorm." Brother Simon dismissed them. "And Master MacCready, you will report to Abbot Ambrose's office right after breakfast tomorrow morning."

"Yes, Brother Simon," Charlie nodded as he closed the office door.

"Thanks a lot!" Rick punched Charlie in the shoulder.

Charlie instantly struck back, hitting Rick just as hard.

Gus walked straight to his cubicle and flopped down on his bed. He did not speak to either Rick or Charlie.

Charlie, careful of his injured knee, crawled into his bed and lay on his side, looking at Howard's empty bed. He wondered how badly Howard was hurt, and how long he would be without his bunkmate. Sleep found him but it was far from restful. He tossed and turned all night as the nightmares returned in full force.

Breakfast was quieter than usual as neither Rick nor Gus would speak to Charlie. They were still upset with him about their getting work crew. While Charlie ate his oatmeal with raisins and brown sugar, he glanced at the head table. Father Vicar was bending Father Mark's ear as they ate. Brother Owen appeared unusually smug as he stared at Charlie while sipping his coffee. Charlie looked away.

As the meal finally drew to a close, Charlie grew more and more nervous about his meeting with Abbot Ambrose. Slowly he walked down the hallway toward the Abbot's office trying not to limp since his knee continued to pain him. He knocked lightly on the door.

"Come in," Abbot Ambrose called out.

Charlie opened the door slowly and stepped inside.

"Ah, yes, son, come in," Abbot Ambrose greeted and put down his papers. He removed his half-moon spectacles, wiped them clean with a white handkerchief he kept tucked in a pocket of his robes and then put them back on. "Please sit down." He motioned to the chair in front of his desk.

Charlie gingerly set down, trying not to bend his sore knee if at all possible. Abbot Ambrose leaned a bit forward, over his desk, and looked at Charlie's leg.

"Is there something wrong with your leg?" he inquired.

"I tripped last night in the woods and hurt my knee," Charlie admitted.

"Has Brother James looked at it?"

"No, not yet."

"Well, after we're finished here, you're to go straight up to the infirmary and have it looked at," Abbot Ambrose instructed. "And you can check in with Master Miller while you are there. He's been asking for you."

Charlie seemed to relax a bit at the news of being able to see Howard.

"Brother Simon has filled me in about your conversation last night. He has already implemented your punishment for disobeying your curfew. I want you to know that I am in full agreement with him on that; however, there is another matter that needs to be addressed.

"You recall our conversation on the night that Master

Kaufman was injured? I had asked you if there was something you needed to tell me. Do you remember?"

Charlie nodded.

"And your response?"

Charlie nodded again. "I said there was nothing."

"That is correct." Abbot Ambrose leaned back in his chair for a moment. "But there was something more, wasn't there?"

Charlie began to grow nervous again. He did not answer for fear Abbot Ambrose would know he was lying.

"Son, we know all about your surplice," Abbot Ambrose said. "Why else do you think Father Mark, Archbishop Gavin and I have been fighting so hard to keep you from having to answer the detective's questions?"

"The Archbishop knows?" Charlie heard himself say.

"Yes, son," Abbot Ambrose nodded. "And he's on your side. None of us believe you had anything to do with what happened to Sister Margaret Mary or any of the boys."

Charlie let out a sigh and slumped back in his chair as the tension left him.

"However, that being said, we still have another matter to address."

The butterflies returned to Charlie's stomach. He sat back up.

"Son," Abbot Ambrose began again. "I know you are aware that some of the prefects are questioning me about why you are still a member of the Altar Boys' Club. I have been on your side all through this. However, I'm afraid after what happened last night, I can no longer turn a blind eye to what has been going on. A member of the Altar Boys' Club has to be exemplary among the other boys. He has to be truthful and display fine conduct. I'm afraid that I cannot ignore any longer your disobedience to the rules, your eavesdropping—Oh yes, I am fully aware that you were listening to my conversation with Archbishop Gavin the other day—and your lying."

Charlie's heart sank as he listened to the charges; all of which he knew were true. He imagined himself standing in front of a firing squad and wondered if that would be more preferable to what he felt at that very moment.

"That is why I am forced to suspend you from the Altar Boys' Club, effective immediately."

The words hit Charlie like a wall of bricks. He stared in shock as he noticed for the first time since he had entered the office the three red surplices that were draped carefully over the back of one of the chairs to the side of the desk.

"You will remove your white surplice right now and put on your dorm colors. I'm sorry to have to do this, son," Abbot Ambrose apologized. "But you have left me no other choice."

"But what about Brother Elijah?" Charlie asked.

"We will have one of the other boys look in on him and help him until a replacement is named, should it come to that," Abbot Ambrose explained and motioned for Charlie to begin changing into his dorm color surplice. "It is my hope that when this matter is finally put to rest that I will be able to lift the suspension and return you to the Altar Boys' Club." He sounded hopeful. "However, much of that will depend on you, son, and how well you adhere to the rules."

"I understand," Charlie nodded as he slipped the red surplice over his head.

"You can send your other surplices to the laundry and they will be set aside," Abbot Ambrose instructed.

"Yes, Father Abbot," Charlie nodded obediently.

"Now, as for your work crew, I understand that Brother Simon has given you boys one hour a day for a week. I am adding another week to your punishment."

Charlie's mouth dropped open in protest but he quickly closed it and accepted his sentence. It was better than a bullet, he figured, but not much.

"That will be all," Abbot Ambrose dismissed him. "Be sure to see Brother James about your leg straight away."

"I will," Charlie nodded and left his great uncle's office.

Just as he closed the door behind him, Father Mark opened his door across the hall. He nodded knowingly as he looked at

Charlie's red surplice.

"I see you've been demoted," he said with a hint of satisfaction in his voice. He folded his arms and puffed out his chest in an air of superiority.

"I've been temporarily suspended from the Altar Boys' Club," Charlie answered him back, stressing the word, *temporarily*.

"Well, we shall see how long it lasts," Father Mark added smugly. "By the way, I hope you didn't lose your key."

Instantly Charlie's entire body stiffened. He fought the urge to reach for the key that hung around his neck beneath his robes. Without answering, he turned away and slowly limped down the hall.

Carefully he climbed the stairs, holding fast to the handrail. His knee was becoming stiff and swollen and more painful to bend. He tried not to look at the snickering boys of Saint Peter dorm as he passed by them in the hallway. When he opened the door of his dormitory the stunned faces of Rick and Gus, as well as the rest of the boys greeted him. He quickly hung the red surplices in his closet and grabbed his remaining white surplice. He stuffed it into the laundry chute on his way back out the door.

He paused for a moment in the stairwell between the Monastery wing and the Student wing to compose himself. He never felt so humiliated in all his life. It was going to be hard getting used to not having the freedom to move about the Abbey building anymore. Normally the Monastery wing was off limits to the boys, the only exception being going to the infirmary, but not for those in the Altar Boys' Club. Also, he would no longer be permitted in the cloistered gardens behind the Abbey or in the sacristy of the Abbey church. It was not going to be easy.

He pushed himself away from the wall and down a flight of stairs to the third floor. Moments later he opened the door to the infirmary.

The infirmary took up two rooms on the north side of the Abbey building. The smaller of the two served as a waiting room and was divided in half by a long counter. Behind the counter was a desk where Brother James worked. Charlie walked up to the counter and leaned against it for support. Brother James looked up from his notes.

"Ah, Master MacCready," he smiled a toothy smile. "What can I do for you this morning?"

"I seemed to have hurt my knee last night in the forest," Charlie answered and felt his leg as the pain continued to throb.

Brother James stood up and walked over to the end of the counter and opened the small swinging door. "Well, let's have a look-see. Step inside and we'll get you fixed up."

He ushered Charlie behind the counter and through a side door into the larger of the two rooms. There were a total of eight old-fashioned hospital beds that lined the north and south walls, four on each. A privacy screen was placed around the bed at the end of the north wall. Charlie wondered who could possibly be behind it. In the bed opposite it was Larry looking thoroughly bored. Howard lay sleeping in the bed nearest the door on the north wall. Brother James directed Charlie to the bed on the south wall.

"I'll need you to take off your robes and your pants, leave your underwear on," Brother James instructed as he washed his hands in the small sink built into an old antique dresser against the wall separating the two rooms.

Charlie did as he was instructed, then sat down on the bed. He looked at his bruised and swollen knee. It looked worse than it had the night before. Brother James dried his hands then turned around.

"Oh my," he said as he looked at Charlie's knee. He pulled up a small stool and sat down to examine it more closely. Gently he felt the bruised area. "Doesn't feel like anything is broken," he said more to himself than to Charlie. After a few more touches and a few more unintelligible grunts, Brother James pushed away from Charlie.

"Looks like it's just a bad bruise is all," he said. "I would recommend you staying off it as much as possible. It will just have to heal itself. There's not much we can do. Go ahead and get dressed."

"Thank you, Brother James," Charlie said as he stood up and pulled his pants back on. "Oh, Brother James," Charlie whispered as Brother James started to return to his office.

"Yes? Is there something else?" he asked.

"I was just wondering how Howard is?" Charlie asked.

"He has a mild concussion and some bumps and bruises, but nothing broken," Brother James reported. "I want to keep him here a few more days."

"Has he said anything about what happened?" Charlie inquired hesitantly.

Brother James shook his head. "No," he sighed. "No, I'm afraid not. Seems the bump on his head may have messed up his short-term memory. We should know more in a few days."

Charlie looked across the room at Howard. He wished Howard was awake so they could talk. He was now surer than ever before that Father Mark was the mastermind behind the attacks and that he was definitely after the key. Charlie sighed as he left the infirmary.

WORK CREW

The new building was bigger than Charlie had imagined. Slowly, he walked up to the front doors. The entrance facade was made of smoked-glass panes and looked very modern compared to the Abbey building. Under a portico that stretched out from the roof were three sets of glass double doors. Charlie decided to use the middle door.

The late afternoon light shone down through the domed skylight inside the large foyer. Charlie remembered watching the builders install it just a few months ago. He looked around the empty room. Two walls were made of glass, while the other two, to his right and left, were unpainted drywall. The bare concrete floor was coated in a layer of white chalky dust from when the dry wall ceiling was installed. Large chips of drywall lay on the floor under the electrical outlets. To his right was a set of oak double doors. Charlie resisted the urge to take a peek inside. He was instructed to report to Mister Hertz in the lobby for his work crew assignment and that was where he would wait. He did not want to get into any more trouble.

"So, you are the infamous Charlie MacCready."

Charlie spun around sharply. His heart pounded in his chest and he tried to catch his breath after being startled. He looked across the room at Maxwell Hertz.

"Yes, sir," he answered.

"Well," Maxwell started toward him, using a push broom as a sort of odd-looking walking stick. "I understand I will have your assistance for an hour each day for the next two weeks. Very good," he nodded. "You may begin by sweeping out the lobby. There's a dustpan and garbage can in the utility closet over there." He pointed to the third door on the wall opposite the oak double doors. "When you finish, come and get me. I'll be inside." He motioned with his head toward the clear glass wall behind him.

Charlie watched Maxwell walk through one of the two sets of glass doors into the inside common area. Slowly he walked over to the glass wall and looked inside. The far wall was semi-circular with four oak double doors that Charlie assumed were the doors to the new dorms. A hole in the floor separated the common area from the wide walkway in front of the doors. Charlie caught a glimpse of Mr. Hertz by the stairs leading down into the hole. He quickly turned away and began sweeping the floor.

In no time Charlie finished his chore. He put the broom, dustpan and garbage can away and looked around the foyer. It looked a lot nicer even bigger with the floor clean. Certain it would pass inspection; he went to find Mister Hertz.

Slowly he entered the common area. He walked the center and stood looking around. He was amazed that from his vantage point he could see all around the main floor as well as the rec room below on the basement level. Only the sub-basement with the new classrooms and faculty offices was not visible.

Quietly Charlie searched for every room on the main floor for Mister Hertz making sure he stayed away from the edge of the hole in the floor. With only a makeshift wooden rail, he could easily fall to the concrete floor of the rec room. Charlie was right; the four sets of oak doors were to the new dormitories. He was surprised to see they all appeared to be the same size.

Cautiously he made his way over to the stairs leading down

to the recreation floor. The stairs were open on either side and the rails were not yet installed which made Charlie feel anxious inside.

The recreation floor was surprisingly well-lit by all of the windows on the west wall. Charlie thought that with it being a basement it would be dark. He quickly found the staircase down to the sub-basement. This stairwell was more to his liking, with walls on either side of the stairs. The only thing it lacked was a proper handrail.

When Charlie entered the sub-basement, he found the light not as bright. With classrooms on either side of the hall, the light from the windows was blocked, only the bare lights hanging from the ceiling provided illumination. Charlie searched every classroom but no sign of Mister Hertz. In the last classroom, Charlie walked over to the windows and looked out. The view was of the forest on the west side of the hill only a few yards away from the back of the building. Charlie could see that the sky was growing dim as the sun was starting to set. He quickly resumed his search.

"Ah, you found me, good," Maxwell said when Charlie walked into the janitor's room.

"This place is a lot bigger than I thought," Charlie admitted almost awestruck.

Maxwell smiled. "Yes, it is. And we still have a lot of work to do inside before it's ready for you boys this fall. I take it you've finished sweeping the lobby?"

"Yes, sir."

Maxwell looked at his watch. "It appears your hour for today is finished. I'll see you tomorrow. Good night."

"Good night, sir." Charlie said and headed back to his dorm.

Charlie went straight to his cubicle when he reached Saint Nicholas' dorm. Rick and Gus sat in the lounge, comparing blistered hands and complaining about how hard the brothers worked them. Charlie was glad he did not have work crew with them. He could just imagine how awful it would be having to listen to Rick whining and complaining for an hour every day.

Charlie grabbed his pad of stationary and lay down on his bed. He wanted to write his grandmother a letter before dinner. He had so much to tell her. He began by telling her once again someone was stealing his mail. He told her how his plan backfired and about Howard. He explained about his being demoted and having work crew, but he assured her it was not so bad because Mister Hertz was nice. He sealed the envelope just as the dinner bell rang out.

The sound of the small block of wood striking against the head table started a flurry of chatter among the boys. Gus leaned into the table to get closer to Charlie.

"I hear Dougary's back from the hospital and he's already stirring things up in Saint Peter dorm," he said quietly.

Charlie glanced at Dougary. He was busy talking to Austin and Travis.

"I can't wait until Howard gets back," Charlie said wistfully, turning back around.

"Well, I heard he'll be out next Monday," Rick said in his know-it-all manner.

"Where'd you hear that?" Charlie asked.

"I heard it from Brother James himself. I had to scrub the infirmary floors on my hands and knees, no thanks to you." He turned up his nose and looked away angrily.

Charlie ignored him and turned back to Gus. "So, where did you have to work?"

"Me?" Gus thought for a moment. "I was helping the brothers get the cloister garden cleaned up. Today I had to do some weeding and put down bark dust. In addition to blisters I also have slivers." He looked at his pudgy hands and frowned.

"So, where were you assigned?" Rick turned back to Charlie.

"I was assigned to work with Mister Hertz, sweeping out the new building," Charlie admitted.

"Oh my," Gus cringed remembering how upset Maxwell was the night before when Larry was brought to the infirmary.

"He's really not that bad," Charlie assured Gus. "Actually, he's very nice."

"So, how's the new building look inside?" Rick changed the subject.

For the rest of the meal Charlie told them all about the new building. He told them it was supposed to be ready for them to move in by September. "That is, according to Mister Hertz," he added.

As the week went on, Charlie became used to the looks and snickering behind his back over his being removed from the Altar Boys' Club. He did not even mind spending an hour a day in work crew. It meant not having to listen to Rick's constant complaining. Even Gus had stopped complaining and viewed it as a rest for his ears.

When Friday came, both Rick and Gus were excited. It was the last day of their work crew. At lunch Charlie noticed that Gus was acting a bit antsy. He seemed excited about something. After the prayer they sat down. Gus watched the head table, his eyes focused on the wooden block. The second it hit the tabletop, he turned to Charlie.

"Father Mark just told me that I get to spend the weekend with my cousins," he announced. "They're going to pick me up tomorrow morning and take me shopping and out to eat at a real restaurant with waiters and everything."

"Big deal, I get to go home right after P.E." Rick said smugly.

"But what about work crew?" Gus asked, his mouth open in shock.

"Abbot Ambrose gave me a note excusing me," he said, and pulled the piece of paper from his shirt pocket.

"That's not fair," Gus moaned.

Charlie smiled. He was happy for his friends. At least their punishment was over. He still had another week to go, but he did not mind. It gave him time to think and come up with an even better plan for trapping Father Mark. When the time was right, he would let the others in on it.

Classes ended with the final bell. Even though the students were going home for the weekend, they still had homework to do for Monday. By the time Charlie walked into the dorm, Rick was already gone. Gus was still changing his clothes, getting ready for his final hour of work crew. Charlie dropped his books on his bed and headed over to the new building.

"Hi, Mister Hertz," Charlie greeted as he entered the recreation room.

"Hi, Charlie," Maxwell smiled. "How's that leg of yours? Still bothering you?"

"It's actually feeling a lot better today," Charlie answered and rubbed his thigh.

"Noticed you're still limping a bit. What does Brother James say about that?"

"Oh, he doesn't say much. Just that it'll take time, is all," Charlie said, a bit uncomfortable with the questioning. "So, what are we doing today?"

Maxwell turned around and looked out the windows at the forest behind the new building. "Today we're going to be working outside. There is some scrap wood and some other trash that needs to be hauled away. The brothers have a place in the clearing just on the other side of the trees there." He pointed at the woods. Charlie squinted and tried to see where Maxwell was indicating, but he could only see trees. "Don't worry, I'll show you," he assured Charlie.

The two walked out the back door. The ground behind the new building was very uneven making it hard for Charlie to follow Mister Hertz. He grabbed an old two by four and steadied himself.

"That's it," Maxwell nodded when he noticed Charlie picking up the scrap. "All of this stuff needs to go. Be careful," some of it may have a few nails stuck in them. I wouldn't want you to get hurt. Pick up as much as you can carry. I need to run and get something I forgot. I'll be right back."

Charlie watched Mister Hertz disappear around the side of the building. He looked around at the scrap wood and noticed that it seemed to be confined to the small area just outside the recreation door. "This won't take any time at all," he said to himself and started to gather the wood into a single pile.

"Good idea," Mister Hertz said when he returned carrying a heavy rope.

"I figured it would save some time if I piled all the wood in one place first."

"Smart boy," Maxwell nodded. "Why don't you grab an armful and I'll show you where it needs to go."

Charlie picked up an armful of some of the smaller pieces and then joined Mister Hertz. The two started through the forest.

"It's not too far," Maxwell assured Charlie. "You ever been in these woods?"

"No sir," Charlie admitted. He had only been on the east side of the hilltop. The west side has been off limits since the construction began.

"Well, stay close, we wouldn't want you to get lost," Mister Hertz warned.

Every few yards, he would turn around to assure Charlie it was not much further. But Charlie was beginning to wonder since the forest was becoming darker the further they walked and the wood was getting heavier and heavier in his arms.

"Here we are," Mister Hertz suddenly stopped and turned around to face Charlie.

"But this isn't the clearing," Charlie said, looking around at the thick dark forest.

"This isn't the clearing," Maxwell mocked in a whiny voice. "What a foolish little boy you are!" he hissed.

Charlie dropped the wood and stumbled backward, away from this man who had suddenly become a stranger to him. "I-I don't understand," he said suddenly afraid.

"So, tell me," Maxwell said, while he slowly walked toward Charlie. "Having any more nightmares? Seeing any more shadows in the dark?" He gave a slight laugh.

Charlie felt the color drain from his face. He stumbled as he backed away from Mister Hertz. "H-h-how did you know about that?"

"Gee, I wonder?" Maxwell continued to mock him. "Does this look familiar?" He pulled his black knit hat down over his face and looked at Charlie through the eye holes. He hunched over reaching out his hands, his long thin fingers curled, toward him.

Suddenly Charlie realized Mister Hertz' coveralls and boots were black. In the growing darkness of the forest he seemed like a mere shadow but not just any shadow, *the* shadow.

"It was you?" Charlie gasped.

"Guess you aren't as dumb as I thought!"

"Then my grandma," Charlie thought out loud. "She meant that you were the one and not Father Mark!" He continued to back away.

"Your grandma?" Maxwell stopped and thought for a moment. "Oh, I remember her, how is the dear? I hope well. Now, hand over that key!"

Charlie's back hit against something solid. His hands felt the rough bark on either side of him.

"What key?"

"Don't play games with me, boy!" Maxwell drew closer. "I know all about the key your grandmother gave you, and I want it."

"Why? What's it to?" Charlie stalled, while he felt for something he could use to protect himself.

Maxwell stopped. "You don't know? She didn't tell you? Oh this is rich!" He leaned his head back and let out the most wickedly evil laugh Charlie had ever heard.

Frantically Charlie groped around the ground at the base of the tree. His hands felt closing around leaves and twigs until he felt a fallen limb, the thickness and length of a baseball bat. His stood back up and he pulled it free from the undergrowth.

As Maxwell tilted his head back to look at Charlie again, Charlie swung the branch at Maxwell's head. It hit hard but the old rotted wood broke into pieces. Maxwell fell to the ground groaning in pain.

For a split second Charlie stood stunned that he had actually hurt someone. As Maxwell stirred to get up, Charlie took off in a limping run through the dark woods. His bruised knee sent lightning bolts of pain up and down his leg with every step, but he kept running.

Suddenly he heard someone call his name. He stopped and turned around, cocking his head to listen.

"Charlie!" The voice called again. Charlie spun around.

"Charlie!" It came from behind him.

"Charlie!" No, from the side.

Charlie stopped, his head becoming dizzy and confused. He shook his head and took off running again, not sure if he was heading away from or back to Mister Hertz.

The voices grew louder, then fainter. Charlie stopped to catch his breath.

A twig snapped behind him. Charlie spun around again and strained to see in the darkness. The warmth of adrenaline rushed through him when he saw a shadow move behind a tree only ten feet from him. He held his breath and took a step back.

He froze as a hand closed around over his mouth and an arm wrapped around his waist, pinning his arms to his sides. Charlie pulled and twisted against the grasp but it only tightened around him.

"Charlie? Charlie?" the voice gently whispered into his ear. Charlie felt its hot breath against his neck.

"No! Let me go!" he screamed and twisted.

"Stop it, Charlie. You're safe. We've been searching for you."

Charlie stopped struggling. The voice was not Mister Hertz. The arms released him and he turned around. He wrapped his arms around the old monk.

"Father!" he cried.

"There, there, now," Father Ichabod squirmed in Charlie's tight hug. "We'd best be getting back to the Abbey. Father Abbot will want to see you right away."

Charlie released his pottery teacher and followed him out of the woods. He kept looking over his shoulder for Mister Hertz, and wondered why Father Ichabod did not seem worried.

As they cleared the woods, the flashing lights on the police car caught Charlie's attention. He looked at the squad car just as one of the officers handcuffed Mister Hertz. The officer put him in the back seat and closed the door. A feeling of relief filled Charlie and he hurried to catch up to Father Ichabod.

Abbot Ambrose, Father Mark, Brother Simon, and Howard huddled together in the light of the new building's portico.

"Father Abbot, I found him!" Father Ichabod announced.

"Charlie!" Howard yelled and ran to his best friend. The two hugged each other when they met. Together they walked back to the light.

"I'm so glad you're okay," Howard said happily.

"But, I don't understand." Charlie looked at them. "How did you know?"

"When Master Miller couldn't find you or Mister Hertz in the new building, he came to me," Brother Simon explained. "He was worried and when he told me it was Mister Hertz who had attacked him—"

"We immediately called the Brothers to start searching for you," Abbot Ambrose interrupted. "We found the pile of scrap wood behind the building and followed the trail you left into the forest."

"Yeah," Howard laughed. "Good thing you kept dropping stuff."

"But what about Larry?" Charlie asked.

"It turns out he was helping his father all along," Abbot Ambrose said. "The police have taken him into custody and I'm sure he will not be returning here this time."

"They were after my key, you know," Charlie told them.

"Well, I sure hope you didn't hand it over to them," Father Ichabod said indignantly.

Charlie glanced at Abbot Ambrose. Abbott Ambrose just smiled and leaned closer to Charlie's ear. "He's talking about your key to the pottery studio. Not everyone needs to know the whole truth." He smiled and stood back up.

"Oh," Charlie smiled relieved. "No. I didn't. There was no way I would part with it, Father."

"Thank goodness," Father Ichabod sighed. "I'd hate to have to change the lock on the door and have a whole set of new keys made. Do you know how much that would cost, and with funds already tight? The thought gives me chills." He shivered. "But I always knew I could trust you, Master MacCready." He smiled, patting Charlie on the back. "Well, I need to be going. Good night, now."

"Good night, Father," Charlie called after him. "Thank you."

The bells in the tower rang out.

"Mark, let the brothers know we have found Master MacCready," Abbot Ambrose instructed. "We best be going. Don't want to be late for dinner."

ABSOLUTION

The sun shone brightly in the sky, but there was still a chill in the air as Howard and Charlie walked across the front lawn. Howard had not said a word about Charlie's red surplice and Charlie did not mention the masking tape holding Howard's glasses together.

"It's a good thing I ran into Brother Simon the other night," Howard explained. "When I came out of the new building, he was right there. Actually, I think he was checking up on you too."

"So what, he's not ol' B. S. anymore?" Charlie asked, realizing Howard just called their prefect by his name.

"Okay, you were right," Howard conceded. "He's not such a bad guy after all. You know, when I told him I couldn't find you, he was really worried. I've never seen him run before, but he hiked up his robes and ran back to the Abbey building to get help," Howard gave a little laugh as he remembered.

"Pssst, Charlie," Austin called to him from behind a tree.

Charlie turned around. "What?"

"I'm really glad you're okay," Austin said and smiled. "I knew you'd be."

"Don't talk to him, Charlie. After all, he's one of *them*."

Howard glared at Austin.

"I'm sorry you were hurt, Howard. I never thought you'd be caught in the middle," Austin apologized.

Charlie closed his eyes for a moment as he tried to sort out the thoughts in his head. He opened his eyes and looked at Austin. "So, was what happened supposed to be what you tried to warn me about?"

"Yes," Austin nodded.

"You mean you knew what was going on all along!" Howard nearly yelled as he became filled with anger.

Austin took a step back. "I didn't know every detail. I just overheard Larry talking to someone on the telephone. He mentioned your name, Charlie, and something about a key and that he'd get it even if he had to take it off your cold dead body."

"Why didn't you just go to the Abbot about this?" Howard demanded. "You could've prevented all of this. You let them hurt Sister Margaret and Dale."

"Not to mention your own friend Dougary," Charlie added.

"I'm sorry. I had no idea anyone else would get hurt," Austin apologized.

"You do realize we could go to the Abbot now and tell him you knew who was behind this all along?" Charlie said.

A worried look came over Austin. "You could." He nodded. "But I hope you won't. I mean, I'll be through with my probation in two years. Please, I'm begging you not to."

Charlie looked at Howard. A fiendish thought caused Howard's mouth to curl in a wicked smile. He whispered into Charlie's ear. Charlie smiled and looked at Austin.

"Okay, but you owe us both," Charlie said. "And we intend on collecting."

Austin looked worried. He nodded then turned around and left before Dougary or Travis caught him talking to the enemy. Charlie and Howard continued on their way to the new building.

"So, I'm waiting," Charlie sang. He stopped and folded his arms over his chest. Howard turned around.

"For what?" He recoiled.

"Ah, for an apology?" Charlie answered.

"You mean about Austin's warning?" Howard frowned. "You've got to be joking."

Charlie did not answer. He just kept staring at Howard, letting him squirm.

"Okay, fine!" Howard gave in. "I'm sorry I gave you such a bad time."

Charlie smiled and laughed. "Come on, let's go—"

"I'm waiting," Howard mimicked Charlie, folding his arms over his chest.

"For anything in particular?" Charlie asked, confused.

"For my apology."

"For what?"

"Well, actually, it's for Father Mark's apology," he said. "I admitted I was wrong about Brother Simon. The least you could do is admit you were wrong about Father Mark. Besides, I told you Father Mark wasn't your shadow guy."

"True," Charlie sighed. He remembered.

"So, you need to come clean with Father Mark and tell him." Howard insisted.

"Tell him?" Charlie pulled back.

"Yes, tell him," Howard said firmly. "Everything."

Charlie looked at Howard while he thought about what he would say. "Okay," he relented.

After lunch, while Howard looked on from a distance, Charlie asked Father Mark if he could have a word with him. Father Mark suggested they meet in Saint Nicholas dorm in twenty minutes. Howard cleared the other guys out of the dorm and sat with Charlie in the lounge. As the clock above the door ticked past twenty minutes and approached an hour, Charlie started to feel nervous.

"Do you think he'll be mad?" he asked Howard.

"He's a nice guy, remember?" Howard answered. "So, relax."

Just then the door opened and Father Mark walked into the dorm. His robes rustled as he drew nearer. Charlie and Howard jumped to their feet.

"I'm sorry I'm late, boys," he apologized.

"It's okay." Charlie smiled nervously. "Please, sit down."

Father Mark sat down on the sofa. Howard dropped down into one of the chairs and left Charlie standing alone.

"I guess I owe you an apology," Charlie began timidly.

"An apology? What on earth for?" Father Mark smiled a bit confused.

"I'm not sure if you noticed but I wasn't very nice to you when you first came here," Charlie explained. "You see, last year my grandmother told me about a man who went with my uncle to see her. I thought you were that guy."

Father Mark listened silently and nodded. Occasionally he glanced at Howard and smiled.

Charlie explained how they had secretly taken pictures of him and sent them to his grandmother. And how she had identified the guy in the last picture they took. But they misunderstood and assumed she meant him, but actually it was Mister Hertz.

Charlie also admitted that he had intentionally avoided him for months and mistakenly accused him of being the shadow.

"I just wanted to tell you that I'm sorry," Charlie concluded.

Father Mark nodded. "I see," he said. "Well, before I can give you absolution, I need to give you your penance." He turned to Howard. "Do you still have your camera?"

Charlie looked at Howard and bit his lip.

"Actually, it was Rick's camera," Charlie admitted. "We borrowed it."

"I see." Father Mark nodded with a smile. "Well, do you think he would mind if you borrowed it again?"

"Nah," Howard shook his head. He jumped up. "I'll go get it."

Charlie watched nervously as Howard dashed over to Rick's cubicle and pulled open his nightstand drawer. He reached in and took out the camera but then stopped. He appeared to be looking at something in the drawer. He glanced over his shoulder and saw Charlie watching him. Quickly he shut the drawer and returned with the camera.

"Good." Father Mark nodded. "Now, Master MacCready, have a seat right here next to me." Charlie obeyed. Father Mark put his arm around Charlie's shoulders. "As your penance, I want Master Miller to take another picture but this time of us. You can write a letter to your grandmother and send the photograph with it. Explain to her that I'm not the bad guy," he smiled. "Whenever you are ready, Master Miller."

Howard smiled and put the camera to his eye. "Say cheese!" he said. Click. Flash. Whirl. The camera spit out a white card. Howard caught it and fanned the air with it. He looked at it and then handed it to Father Mark.

"Very good," Father Mark commended. "Nice balance. You should take the photography class this summer."

"I've been trying," Howard answered under his breath.

"Now, Master MacCready, after you send this photo to your grandmother you will be absolved. Agreed?"

"Yes." Charlie nodded and took the picture.

"I'm afraid I must be going." Father Mark stood up. "But I'm glad we had this chance to clear the air."

"Me too," Charlie agreed. "See you at dinner."

They watched Father Mark leave the dorm. Charlie waited until the doors closed then turned toward Howard.

"What were you looking at in Rick's nightstand drawer?" he asked. His smiled faded, replaced by a look of curiosity.

"You'd better see for yourself. Come on," Howard replied, and headed back over to Rick's cubicle. He opened the drawer, then sat down on the edge of Rick's bed to give Charlie room to see what was hidden away.

As Charlie peered into the drawer, his eyes widened. With lightning speed, he grabbed the bundle of letters, all addressed to him in his grandmother's handwriting.

"I don't believe it," Charlie breathed. "It was Rick all along?"

"What're you two doing in my cubicle?" Rick shouted when he saw the two of them.

Charlie turned around, letters in hand. His eyes burned with anger as his temper flared.

Rick saw the letters and his face became pale. His mouth dropped open but he didn't speak.

"So, you're the one who has been stealing my mail!" Charlie said through clenched teeth. "Some friend you are."

"You know, Rick." Howard stood up. "Stealing people's mail is illegal. You could get into some serious trouble if Charlie were to tell Father Mark and the police. You could even end up cellmates with Larry in juvie."

"I didn't steal it," Rick snapped.

"Well, what do you call it then?" Charlie asked.

"Ah, I was just holding it for you."

"You liar! I am so angry I could just hit you!" Charlie shook as he struggled to control himself.

"That goes double for me!" Howard added and stood up behind Charlie.

Rick took a step back.

"You knew how much these letters meant to me. You even helped us with a trap. I can't believe you would stoop so low. I have a good mind to tell Brother Simon about this," Charlie said, seething. "See what he thinks I should do."

"No! Don't!" Rick panicked. "I'm sorry. It started as a joke but then it sort of got out of hand and I didn't know how to stop. I won't do it again. I promise."

"I don't believe you," Howard snarled. "He didn't sound convincing enough to me, what do you think Charlie?"

"No, he didn't," Charlie answered, still wanting to get even.

"I'll make it up to you," Rick offered. His eyes darted back and forth between Howard and Charlie. "I'll do anything you want."

"Really?" Howard smiled fiendishly.

"What's this have to do with you?" Rick snapped at him.

"This is between me and Charlie."

"That's where you're wrong!" Charlie said coldly. "You have to buy his silence too. Otherwise he could go to Brother Simon, or worse, Father Mark."

"Yeah, I wonder what he would say?" Howard sighed, thoroughly enjoying seeing Rick squirm.

"Okay, fine!" Rick conceded. "What do you want?"

"I don't know, I'll have to think about it," Charlie said.

"What about you, Howard? What do you want?" The words seemed to stick in Rick's throat.

"I'll get back to you, too," he answered and started to leave with Charlie. "Oh, by the way, thanks for the use of your camera." He handed it to Rick.

"What?" Rick gasped and glared at Howard.

The cold days of winter had passed, and life at Saint Michael's returned to normal. Charlie walked beside Abbot Ambrose along the narrow path in the cloistered garden. There were still many questions that lingered unanswered in his mind about Larry and his father.

"What I don't understand," Charlie said to his great-uncle. "Why would they hurt Sister Margaret Mary?"

"I wondered that myself," Abbot Ambrose admitted. "But as it is, Master Hertz has no loyalty whatsoever. When the police began questioning him, he ratted out his father. He explained how, over the course of last year, he and his father had secretly dug out the new tunnel. They threw the dirt into the barnyard thinking that no one would notice, and I hate to admit it, they were right, we did not. Then he admitted that he had borrowed your white surplice from the laundry—an idea he also borrowed from Master Duggan, you recall—and went to meet with his father by the pig barns to discuss their plans. They did not anticipate that Sister Margaret would be walking home at that same moment. She had overheard their conversation about how they intended to get your key and threatened to turn them both in. That's when Mister Hertz struck her."

"How awful," Charlie said. "But what about Dougary? Why would they beat him up?"

"Master Duggan found out that Master Hertz had stolen his key to the pottery studio. They exchanged words and then blows. Only, like his father, Master Hertz grabbed a piece of wood and continued to beat Master Duggan until he was unconscious."

Charlie shook his head in disbelief. He pulled the chain out from under his robes and looked at the tarnished brass key.

"All over this stupid key," Charlie muttered. "Why won't anyone tell me what it is for?" he asked, and looked at his great uncle.

Abbot Ambrose smiled. "To everything under the heavens there is a time and season, Charlie," he said thoughtfully. "You will learn soon enough. But until then, you have to trust and be patient. Right now is neither the time nor the season for you to know."

Charlie sighed as he looked around the garden, at the budding cherry blossom trees and freshly tended flowerbeds that waited for the warmth of spring to push forth their magnificent blooms. He tried to hide his disappointment once again at not being told the purpose of the key, while they continued to walk slowly.

"There is other reason I wanted to speak with you today," Abbot Ambrose continued. "It's about your suspension from the Altar Boys' Club."

Charlie looked at his red surplice and then back at the Abbot.

"I think it is time to reinstate you, wouldn't you agree?" Abbot Ambrose smiled.

"Yes!" Charlie said enthusiastically.

Abbot Ambrose gave a slight chuckle. "You will find your white surplices on your bed when you get back to your dormitory."

"Thank you," Charlie said, and started to rush off but stopped. "I'm sorry. Is that all? May I go?"

Abbot Ambrose chuckled softly. "Yes, son, run along and try to stay out of trouble."

"I will." Charlie nodded. "Thank you so much."

Charlie rushed back to Saint Nicholas dorm in record time. Howard, Gus, and Dale stood at the foot of his bed, waiting to congratulate him and welcome him back to the Altar Boys' Club. Charlie quickly changed and stuffed his red surplices down the laundry chute.

GOOD BYE

With spring came the sun and warmer weather. The senior class was especially excited as it also meant graduation day for them. However, for Charlie and Howard, it meant losing a friend. After they completed the last of their final exams, Charlie, Howard, Dale and Gus met on the front steps.

Still on the outs with Charlie and Howard, but fearing he was missing out on something exciting, Rick tagged along behind the others as they walked across the front lawn.

"So, when are your cousins going to pick you up?" Charlie asked Gus.

"They said they'd be here before dinner." Gus nodded.

"So they are really adopting you," Howard sighed. "I'm sorry I gave you such a bad time about it. I really am happy for you, Gus."

"M-ma-me to," Dale stammered.

Gus smiled, even though his eyes welled with tears. "Thanks, Howard, guys. You know, I'm really going to miss you guys."

"This place isn't going to be the same without you." Charlie forced a smile.

"Sure it will," Gus said coyly. His cheeks blushed at all of the attention.

"I don't believe this," Rick finally spoke up. "The year you finally get to be in the Altar Boys' Club, you get adopted."

"I know," Gus smiled. "Strange, huh?"

"Well, what am I supposed to do next year for Halloween?" Rick asked.

"You could always go as Benedict Arnold," Howard said snidely and glared at him. "Or better yet, just come as your back-stabbing self."

Rick opened his mouth but did not respond to Howard.

"Howard—" Charlie said quietly. This was not the time to be picking on Rick. This was their last few moments with Gus.

"Well, I guess I should get back to the dorm and bring my things down. I want to be ready when my cousins arrive," Gus said.

"We'll help you," Charlie offered.

"No," Gus insisted. "I'd rather do it alone. I hate goodbyes."

"So do I," Howard said, and slugged Gus in the shoulder softly. "Take care of yourself and don't forget us."

"D-da-don't f-f-forget to write," Dale added.

"I won't," Gus assured them, and then ran back to the Abbey building so they would not see him cry.

The sound of a car pulling into the parking lot caught everyone's attention. Charlie watched the black van slow to a stop outside the garage. He watched as Father Vicar stepped out from behind the steering wheel. The passenger door opened and a nervous young teenaged boy stepped out. He took his two matching suitcases from the back of the van. Father Vicar had already started across the front lawn. The boy struggled with his suitcases while he tried to catch up.

Charlie could not help but remember his first day at Saint Michael's when he made that same walk. He was so scared. It seemed so long ago and yet, just like yesterday.

ABOUT THE AUTHOR

James M. McCracken spent much of his teenage years away from his family in a seminary boarding school. It was there that his love of writing began. It is his experiences while at the boarding school that serve as the inspiration for the Charlie MacCready series.

James M. McCracken currently resides in Central Oregon. He is a longtime member of the writing group Becoming Fiction and the Northwest Independent Writers Association.

www.ingramcontent.com/pod-product-compliance
Lightning Source LLC
LaVergne TN
LVHW022002060526
838200LV00003B/58